THE TROUBLE WITH ERNIE
&
OTHER STORIES

With best wishes
Bob Wild

THE TROUBLE WITH ERNIE
&
OTHER STORIES

Bob Wild

PENNILESS PRESS PUBLICATIONS

Published January 2019

Also by Bob Wild

The Dogs of War and other Autobiographical Stories (PPP)

Death of a Seagull and other Poems (PPP)

The Elongated Octopus: Poems for Children

Some of the stories in this collection first appeared in Issues of "The Crazy Oik" published by Ken Clay

© Bob Wild

The author asserts his moral right to be identified as the author of the work.

All rights reserved. No part of this publication may be reproduced, stored in a retrieval system or transmitted in any form or by any means, electronic, mechanical, photocopying, recording or otherwise, without the prior permission of the publishers

ISBN 978-0-244-75239-2

Cover : *Self-portrait – John Bratby*

CONTENTS

THE TROUBLE WITH ERNIE	7
THE FIDDLERS ON THE ROOF	18
GIVE AND TAKE	39
SHOPPING THIEVES	51
ON THE BUSES	74
TERRY THE PRINTER'S DEVIL	79
THE PERFECT TREBLE	87
THE CONFESSION	99
PERJURY	110
THE GOOD LITTLE GOERS	116
ALWAYS HAVE AN ANSWER	128
THE O.U. ADDICT	137
KILLING TIME	144
THE SAGA OF DANNY & ANGIE & BENNY	154
TAPPING INTO MONEY	176
MISS AITKEN	188
BLACKIE	212
MOVING	230

Acknowledgement

I would like to express my warm thanks to Ken Clay for his many helpful comments, suggestions and encouragement and for his tireless efforts with the production of this book.

Disclaimer

Some of the stories in this collection are loosely based on autobiographical incidents; they are the product of memory and imagination and in some cases gossip and scandal overheard, but they are fiction, not fact. If by chance readers know or knew people with similar names they should not make moral inferences about them on the basis of these stories.

Don't be absurd he said to me
I think that folk should let me be
I'm really quite as good as you
Despite the fact my hair is blue.

We don't all have to be the same
And really, I am not to blame
I come from elsewhere, can't you see?
You'll have to just get used to me.

THE TROUBLE WITH ERNIE

When Shakespeare wrote: "some are born great, some achieve greatness and some have greatness thrust upon them . . ." he certainly didn't have Ernie in mind. Had he known about Ernie he would have substituted 'trouble' for 'greatness' and then gone on to say "so let it be with Ernie". Ernie was trouble from the word go. He must have precociously decided in the womb to go for trouble 'three in a row': birth, childhood, manhood. He just couldn't wait to get out and cause trouble. Perhaps had he known how many there were waiting to thrust it upon him or help him achieve it he would not have been quite so hasty.

His mother's pregnancy was a surprise and on a bleak January day Ernie popped out prematurely, unwanted, into an unprepared, impoverished family in the midst of the 1930 economic depression. Three weeks early, he was small, under-weight and slightly yellow. The birth left him with a Ben Turpin squint in one eye and, as it turned out, he grew along what today would be called the autistic spectrum. The birth left his mother with post-natal depression. She temporarily rejected the squawking new-born child which allowed Ernie's newly widowed, paternal grandmother, in whose house Ernie's unemployed parents were living, to take Ernie to her bosom, so to speak. And, if certain Viennese Psychologists are to be believed, may account for later speculation about Ernie's repressed, unrequited, sexuality. Ernie's grandmother was the archetypal mother-in-law. She treated her son's wife not as a mother but as an inferior domestic assistant: insisted on the name Ernest in memory of her late Communist husband Ernest who, ironically, had died prematurely. Ernie's mother, in a gloom of depression and revolutionary pique, deserted her own Communist husband, child, and lodging, and ran away to Buxton. She was located some three months later, brought back and reunited with Ernie, who by this time had bonded with his doting grandmother. Needless to say his father disliked him and his mother, to compensate for the guilt of her desertion, indulged and protected him. All of which did his character a world of troublesome good!

During childhood Ernie managed to simultaneously attract and achieve a disproportionate amount of trouble on account of the squint in his weak eye, which was lazy and required him to wear glasses with a black patch over the lens of the good eye. In the infants and junior school he couldn't see the blackboard so he was always talking, playing pranks, and putting his hand up to go to the toilet. He spent a lot of time standing in the corner or behind the coat-stand because he was such a nuisance. He couldn't do anything practical such as tying his shoe laces or even cleaning his mossy green teeth, so he was regarded as either perverse or stupid. Neither could he manage real writing but fortunately he was an omnivorous reader with an exceptionally retentive memory so he got by in the classroom with only a moderate number of canings.

In the playground though, he was bullied, hit, bit and harried. Amalgamated Press brought out a children's comic called "*The Knockout*": the cartoonist Hugh McNeil did comic-strips featuring 'Deed a Day Danny' and a ridiculous character called 'Our Ernie' who Ernie found himself required to emulate. He was nick-named with the unflattering sobriquet: 'specky-four-eyes'. His glasses were frequently cracked or broken which caused endless financial worry to his impoverished parents. More often than not one of the lenses had sticking plaster over the crack. As he grew older the black patch provoked pirate jokes and quips about wooden legs and parrots to which he replied with imaginative ripostes, puns and, later, aggressive retaliation. He was invariably outnumbered and ended up with cuts, bruises and torn clothes which got him into more trouble at home where, in his absence, he was always referred to as 'that one', never by his name. "What's that one been up to today?" his father would ask as soon as he came in through the door, spoiling for a row with his wife or his mother over Ernie's latest misdeed. There was invariably some trouble to report.

Ernie resented the attention given to his two younger brothers. He managed to turn their games into opportunities to inflict spiteful injuries on them. Once, when sitting on the low garden wall with his four-year old brother on his knee, he deliberately opened his legs and let him slip down between them: little Morris caught his head on the edge of the wall. Stitches were required. Another time, playing cowboys and Indians, he threw a log of wood at Morris, hitting him on the forehead: again stitches were required. This caused yet another row between his mother and father as to how the money could be found to pay the doctor's bill. Ernie was about to get a good hiding but his Grandmother saved him, saying she would pay the bill. The doctor gave Morris a Jack-in-a-box for being a brave boy and not crying while being stitched up. The first time it was used Ernie deliberately tripped and stamped on it.

If the trouble brewing seemed likely to be severe, like when a boot he'd thrown at his brothers hit the kitchen window and smashed it, Ernie would keep away from the house, go to the cinema and ask someone to take him in to see an adult film unsuitable for unaccompanied children: usually a horror film. He would watch the whole programme twice round and afterwards go to his Grandmother's flat some four miles away to seek asylum by staying over-night. On several occasions his frantic mother would have the police out searching for him.

Ernie, though in many ways gifted and potentially academic, still couldn't write by the end of primary school and was not entered for the eleven plus. In consequence he was consigned to the dustbin of academe in the remedial class of the local secondary school. It was wartime: many elderly teachers had been brought out of retirement: often their teaching skills were poor. Ernie was a problem they simply put to one side so Ernie joined the Library and took his library books to school. He was happy to read: the teachers were happy to let him do so and eventually, despite not being able to write, he was well informed and transferred to the 'B' stream for his final year. However, sports, P.T. and the rough and tumble of the playground were a misery to him and he suffered endless ragging and bullying in the school-yard breaks. He spent weekends and holidays with his grandmother who gave him delusions of self importance and further alienated him from his mother. The constant predictions of his father: "he'll never work that one," voiced throughout Ernie's childhood, often within Ernie's hearing, looked like coming true.

Fortunately for Ernie his grandmother got knocked down by a motorcyclist and was left with a lame leg but also a small amount of compensation. When Ernie left school at fourteen she used the money to send him to a private commercial college in Manchester. They identified his writing problem, gave him sheets of paper with lines and arrows on and sample letters for him to repetitively copy. When he could reproduce letters he was instructed to join them up in pairs and eventually create words and 'hey presto' he could write. He was also introduced to Spanish, French and Italian and was set up with pen-friends abroad. He made remarkable progress but had to leave before School Cert, when the compensation money ran out.

*

School was one thing, work quite another. Fortunately, jobs were plentiful during post war reconstruction and economic expansion. Ernie got and lost numerous low grade clerical jobs in insurance companies through boredom, inefficient filing, secret desk-drawer reading, distracting co-workers with gossip and disappearing to the toilets. He clocked up enormous phone bills for his employers by spending hours chatting with pen-friends abroad. He did rather better at "The Odd-Fellows Friendly Society", probably felt more at home, but like home, it was far from friendly.

Surveillance was constant and oppressive. The senior manager was a bully and bullying went on down the pecking order: even the ordinary clerks harassed and made a scapegoat of the office junior and office junior was the position Ernie filled. If Ernie slacked or day-dreamed his sarcastic manager, in his imperious, biting way, would make some remark such as: "Gone on strike Wilde: a wild cat strike is it? Be careful, it doesn't turn into a lock-out." He meant it. Most of the staff kept their heads down, in fear for their jobs. With such a boss, Ernie, being Ernie, was inevitably at risk.

Ernie's first job of the day was to deal with the post: stamp it in and put it in the correct pile. It was boring work and Ernie would go into reveries. He was quite imaginative and not without a sense of humour. He creatively made up advertisements for two Insurance companies he'd invented in his mind: "Insurance from Womb to Tomb" for one, and more salaciously, "Insurance, from Erection to Resurrection" for the other.

The stories in Ernie's head were often funny and used ridiculously inflated language. One, about an encounter with a customer even made Ernie laugh out loud:

"At the counter was a lady of great girth whose personage was crowned by a large hat which resembled a three-tiered wedding cake. Flowing down from the wedding cake were frills and flounces. She was like a galleon in full sail afore a freshening wind. As I approached the counter the ship in full sail spoke in a deep booming, refined voice which echoed round the office. 'Young man, my name is Victoria Plum. Have you a policy in my name?' I doubled up and collapsed with laughter. I had no control over the rippling sound that came out of my throat. I roared with laughter. I cried with laughter until tears ran freely down my cheeks. Mr. Jones came out of his cubicle, astonished".

Ernie's creative day-dream was interrupted by his own Manager shouting at him: "What are you laughing at? Bring those files to my desk and tell me exactly where you are up to. I'd like to know just how much work you've done this week".

The other clerks kept their heads down thankful it wasn't them he'd picked on. Ernie did as he was told: picked up his files, walked to the Manager's desk and put them down. He felt annoyed, humiliated and threatened.

"I want you to show me where you are up to and exactly how much you have done since Monday," the Manager demanded. Ernie felt he would like to hit him and hit him hard. He stood stock still whilst the Manager inspected the files.

Ernie was not listening to the Manager's irritatingly critical tirade. Involuntarily his body rocked forwards and backwards as though he was about to start running. His mind sprinted away on an aggressive flight of fancy whilst his feet remained rooted to the floor. He clenched his fists and breathed in short, shallow gasps as his mind created yet another imaginative fantasy.

"Ernie saw himself moving round to the back of the Manager's chair intent on garrotting him with a cheese wire. He held the handles on the ends of the wire one in each hand and quickly crossed hands to make a loop and flung it over the Manager's head. He pulled both hands outwards and felt the wire cut into the flesh

round the manager's throat. He could hear strange gurgling and spluttering noises coming from the Manager's mouth: he could hear his twitching legs kicking his feet like drum beats against the front panel of the desk. He released his hands and let the Manager's head fall with a thump on the desk, squashing his ugly nose: gushes of blood splashed over the files".

"Well? I'm waiting. What have you got to say?"

Ernie stopped rocking and came back to earth. He picked up the files he had just put down and crashed them violently onto the Manager's head. The Manager leapt to his feet: his face livid and contorted with disbelief. The whole office watched silently: nobody moved. Ernie turned and looking neither to right nor to left walked out of the office, down the stairs and into the street.

It was bitterly cold outside and he had not thought to get his coat. Without a doubt he would lose his job. He could not stay in the street without a coat. He walked quickly through the city and went into one of the big stores. Two hours later he decided to go back to the office. All was quiet: the clerks looked at him queerly with a mixture of respect, admiration and pity. One of them said in a low voice: "The Branch Manager wants to see you".

*

Having exhausted the insurance job market Ernie took his troubles and a bogus Reference, acquired from a pen-friend who was doing well in the Italian Ministry of Agriculture, to the Local Authority, getting a job first in the Education department, where he didn't last long, and then in the Housing department where he lasted far too long. He was by this time fluent in French, Spanish and Italian and had a good knowledge of other languages too.

He took a group from the Town Hall holiday club to Paris, acting as their courier. He managed to leave a bag containing all their passports on the Metro. He was not popular that day! Fortunately the bag was handed in and, after a couple of day's anxiety, retrieved. Ernie's group managed to miss the boat back to England. They had to wait four hours for the next one, all because Ernie, despite some objections, had asked the coach driver to make a detour to facilitate one of the women going to a roadside furniture shop *'Du Berceau au Tombeau'*, to buy a cheap wooden coffin for her mother's eventual funeral.

Some of the younger travellers took the opportunity to buy more than the duty free allowance of cheaply priced booze at a supermarket next door. They stowed the booze in the coffin only to have it confiscated when Customs opened the coffin thinking they were going to find a dead body. They were much relieved to find it full of contraband booze rather than a stowaway or someone's dead grandmother.

*

Within a few years of starting work in local government Ernie acquired, at night school, a Diploma in Public Administration and a London external degree in Economics but remained a menial clerk. On paper he was better qualified than the Town Clerk but personality and behavioural problems precluded promotion. One day he 'blotted his copybook' well and good.

Ernie was identified by the Personnel Director, a humourless friend of the new Labour Lord Mayor's, as the person who had mocked the Mayor during his inaugural speech to the Council and Town Hall staff. The mayor, referring to that great Gothic Revival, the Town Hall Building, which was indeed an architectural gem, as "that magnificent manifestation of munificence" had prompted Ernie to shout out aloud "more alliterate than illiterate." The chorus of laughter from the assembled staff and Tory Councillors caused the new Mayor a great deal of embarrassment.

As a consequence of 'having his card marked' Ernie remained in a Catch 22 situation: highly qualified but stuck as a menial clerk, resentful and bored.

The longer Ernie waited for promotion the more he acted in a manner which prevented him from getting it. He increased his free personal telephone calls, his desk-drawer reading and his gossiping, adding long loo breaks to his subversive activities. As years went by the un-promotable Ernie was tolerated as a character by most of his co-workers who found him an interesting odd ball. Management couldn't easily sack him: they'd been vindictive and had turned a blind eye for so long to Ernie's resentful incompetence it would have been awkward for them to get rid of him. They did get rid of him eventually though.

The Manager of the Housing Department retired. A new Manager was appointed from 'outside'. Everyone had been expecting the Under-Manager to get the job as was customary: others were expecting to move up a rung on the short, seldom used ladder of promotion. Ernie had hoped for an extra increment or excrement as he malapropally put it. Everyone was disappointed, morale dropped. The new Manager's brief was to tighten things up, cut costs and get rid of 'dead wood'. Everyone felt vulnerable, Ernie especially so.

The new Manager's first step in the war of attrition was to stupidly do away with the fifteen minute tea break, morning and afternoon: resentment rose. Ernie suggested to his co-workers that they club together, buy a kettle and make a rota for bringing tea bags, coffee and milk.

There was a cleaner's cubby hole with an electric power point in the toilets. Each morning and afternoon the subversive staff went in three groups of three relays for a brew and a break. The disgruntled passed-over Assistant Manager, who worked beside staff inside the office, turned a blind eye.

The used tea bags were deposited in the waste-bin attached to the wall in the washroom. Towards the end of each day, Ernie slipped into the washroom and collected the tea bags from the waste bin and put them in a plastic bag he brought to work for the purpose. He'd heard they were a good fertiliser and, being the parsimonious person he was, thought they would save him money.

Not being a gardener he didn't realise it was the contents, not the bags them-selves that were fertilizer. He cleared an overgrown patch of garden, salvaged some weeds he mistakenly thought were plants, and planted the tea bags in neat rows alongside them. The tea-bags didn't do much good to the garden but they certainly helped to grow Ernie's reputation as a tight-fist: rumour had it he was reusing the bags at home to make tea.

THE TROUBLE WITH ERNIE

*

Each day, morning and afternoon, the new Manager stood behind a screen, out of sight of the street entrance, fob watch in hand, checking who came late and who went home early: Ernie of course did both. He was called into the Manager's office.

"You came late yesterday morning and left early in the afternoon. What do you think you are playing at?" Ernie felt his years of pent up frustration and resentment welling up but for once managed to control himself. The Manager stared him in the face, waiting. "Yes, you're quite right, I did come late and I did go home early".

"That is not an explanation, why did you come late and go early?" Ernie stared back at the manager: "Because I didn't want to be late twice in one day" Ernie said, keeping a straight face.

The Manager's angry face went livid. "How dare you speak to me in that tone of voice. I've had reports that you frequently loiter in the toilets: why would anyone want to do a queer thing like that?"

Ernie blanched at what he took to be a deliberate aspersion. "What damned business is it of yours!" he shouted, and almost tearful, Ernie slammed the door as he left the room.

The following day Ernie found a letter on his desk summoning him to see the Personnel Director.

*

Ernie pressed the button on the Personnel Director's door. A green light flashed: the signal to enter. Well, this is it he thought. He knew he was about to be dismissed from the sinking feeling in the pit of his stomach, a feeling which he knew only too well.

The Personnel Director's room was large and over powering, the ceiling high and the walls oak panelled. The P.D., a small man, sat behind a huge oak desk in a Captain's chair that was much too big for him. It was a good eight yards from door to desk. Ernie thought it ridiculous that such a small, insignificant man should sit so far away behind such an excessively large desk. He knew it was deliberately designed to intimidate interviewees.

The P.D. did not look up but continued reading the document before him, occasionally writing something in the margin. To preserve his calm Ernie looked round the room at the bookcases with their bound leather volumes of employment law thinking surely it doesn't take so many books to sack people. He noticed, with some surprise a small table with a plaster bust of Handel standing on it. The P.D. at last looked up and saw Ernie, not looking at him in fearful anticipation, but staring at the bust of Handel. To the Director's annoyance Ernie continued staring at the bust.

"Do you know that fellow Hallé?" the Director said, sarcastically. Ernie continued staring at the bust.. "Yes I do but that's not Hallé".

The Personnel Director gave a short contemptuous laugh. "Of course it's Hallé. He lived in Manchester and founded an orchestra". Ernie continued looking at the bust: "Yes, the Hallé, Orchestra, but that's not Hallé, it's a bust of Handel: George Frideric Handel the Baroque composer. Handel came from Halle - Ernie's tongue lingered languorously over the German pronunciation - the birth place of Handel. He offended the Elector of Hanover so he came to England to the court of Queen Anne. Then George of Hanover became King George 1st of England and Handel was in trouble again".

"Like you."

"No not like me, like you. It's a bust of Handel".

Ernie was right, of course but it didn't do him any good. The P.D. was clearly rattled. "I'm sure you are wrong. The bust was here when I took up the post from the previous Personnel Director. Given Hallé's connection with Manchester it *must* be a bust of Hallé."

Ernie lit the match that finally burned his boats: "The only *must* about it is that he must have been as ill-informed as you are."

The Personnel Director was furious. "Anyway, all this is immaterial. One thing I do know for certain is that we can't have people like you coming late, going early, gossiping for half the day and being rude to Management. I'm afraid we are going to have to let you go. You can either take voluntary redundancy or face dismissal. Think it over and let me know which you prefer by the end of the week".

"Thank you very much for giving me the choice Mr er, er, Hobson isn't it, or will you tell me I've got that wrong as well?"

*

Ernie's colleagues having heard the account of his dismissal bought him a bust of Handel as a leaving present. The local authority gave him a large water jug with the City of Manchester coat of arms engraved on it. Ernie had been expecting £50 but to cut costs the local authority had instituted the water jug instead. Ernie managed to drop it on the way home.

THE FIDDLERS ON THE ROOF

It was raining. Ernie stood in the garden of his former council house, as motionless as a grey heron waiting for fish: his gaze fixed on the leaking roof. The garden round him, if you could call it a garden, was over-grown and rubbish-strewn. A casual passer-by, glancing in, might have thought Ernie was something rejected from bonfire night, or perhaps a scarecrow: there certainly were no birds about. It was nearly mid-day. Ernie was still in the old flannelette pyjamas bought ten years ago for his birthday by his now deceased mother. The too-short, too-tight, well worn, buttonless raincoat, over his pyjamas was tied round with string. The charity shop boots he'd struggled into had no laces. The dark, stained, Deer-stalker hat on his head of thin, grey, once sand-coloured hair, was pulled down over his forehead to just above his glasses. Two days of stubble, left until his shaving cuts healed, grew on his chin. The rain came on heavier. He was not a happy Ernie.

Ernie's council house was in a block of four. It was an end one next to a cul-de-sac. It had an extra large side-garden in addition to a front and back. With the exception of 'problem families', most people maintained their properties: kept them pointed and painted and not in garish colours: their gardens tidy. The concrete forecourts, neglected gardens and tawdry appearance of 'buy-to-rent' ex-council houses hadn't hit the Estate yet: it was a bit far north of Manchester for students. But Ernie's neglected property *was* exceptionally disreputable and attracting hostile gossip and increasingly troublesome attention from vandals. "Oh dear! Oh dear! Oh dear! What am I going to do, what am I going to do!" he endlessly repeated to himself.

Though not yet run-down, the Estate was not what it used to be. The original tenants had died or moved out. New-comers had moved in. Ernie hardly knew anybody to speak to these days. A 'difficult to house' family had been planted by the Council in the house on the opposite corner. Ernie was constantly plagued, taunted and verbally abused by a group of rowdy, unemployed teenagers. They congregated on the street corner outside the house. He was constantly rowing with them over their football coming into his garden. They were noisy and abusive at night, drinking and drug-using under the street lamp. Pools of car side-window glass glistened like scattered diamonds in the shadows beyond the lamp. Ernie had not found the police helpful. He'd reported the stolen gate and the bricks that they had thrown at his windows. They advised that he should keep a record of the incidents. What use was that!

Life was increasingly depressing Ernie. He was depressed by retirement, depressed by old age and depressed by change. He was, he knew, a totally impractical person. The house, the garden, the aggravation . . . were making him anxious, distracted, ill. He had always been a whinger but whingeing had now become a neurotic habit: he hankered for a golden past. He phoned friends with: "Oh I do wish I could go back to work. Do you think they would have me back at the Housing Department?" This was a man approaching 80 in an age of public sector cuts! He would not be consoled or count his blessings. His friends felt sorry for him but were fed up with his constant moaning.

Ernie had been a vulnerable person from birth and had what today would have been diagnosed as a 'syndrome', like Aspergers or OCD or something like that. Spending money would have solved some of his troubles but although he had savings, he was constitutionally incapable of spending money. Childhood family poverty, a low paid local authority clerical job, well below the qualifications he had auto-didactically acquired since leaving school at fourteen, fear of unemployment and over the years neurotic anxiety had made him frugal to the point of miserliness. Since retiring he lived in a state of personal and environmental neglect. His incessant phone calls and moaning mantra: "Oh! I do wish I could go back to work!" had lost him many of his friends. His once well tended garden was a squalid mess. The grass was long: weeds had invaded the borders. The crazy paving was overgrown. The privet hedge which almost surrounded the garden was hopelessly out of hand: too tall and too woody to be clipped. The fence beyond the privets had gaps in the broken palings wide enough to let stray dogs through. Drinks cans, beer bottles and plastic bags, thrown over the hedge, had spilled and scattered rubbish.

Ernie's parents had been the first tenants in the house, built in the early 30's. His father, an unemployed labourer and casual gardener, had laid out a formal garden like that of a French Chateau. The borders had been full of night-scented stocks, which attracted Golden and Silver Y moths, and antirrhinums that attracted bees. The centre beds were a riot of roses and in the late summer and early autumn dahlias and gladioli made a colourful display. As a child Ernie used to catch the bees. He would put a jam jar over the flower head and clamp the lid on, snapping the stem and catching the flower along with the bee. His father boxed his ears repeatedly for this offence but Ernie was addicted to the frighteningly amplified buzzing made by the bees. His mother had kept the garden going when his father died. When his mother died Ernie had tried, but failed, to keep it up.

As the garden became overgrown Ernie had difficulty distinguishing weeds from flowers. He dug up weeds and replanted them in straight rows until a neighbour told him what they were. To save money on fertilizer he took a small shovel and bag and collected horse manure for the roses from the riding tracks in the local park. He was thrown off a bus once because of the smell emanating from his Tesco's plastic bags. He even got himself in trouble at work collecting tea bags from the Town Hall which he scattered about as 'fertilizer'. If you dug down half a spit into the borders you would find layers of newspapers, copies of the *Financial Times* and the *Guardian*, wads of which he had buried believing they would compost on their own. "Digging up the past" his brother said when he unearthed dozens of old *Guardians* when he once came to help tidy up the garden.

Ernie's mother would have been appalled to see the garden now. His mother had lived on the Estate long enough to have rights to the house. She bought it with a deposit reluctantly loaned her by Ernie, in the 80's when Maggie Thatcher sold off public utilities and encouraged Councils to sell off houses to make the great British public members of a Capitalist, property-owning democracy, and, she hoped, Tory voters. "Selling the family silver" Harold McMillan disparagingly called it.

Not long after the sell-off, and much to the chagrin of the buyers, the Council renovated and upgraded the remaining rented houses. Years later, after his mother died, Ernie paid off the mortgage and inherited a valuable, though unimproved property.

Looking at the state of the house now, as he stood in the garden, in the rain, made Ernie even more miserable. The cracked pantry window had a hole where a stone had hit it. The upstairs landing window had two small, round holes with star shaped cracks emanating from them where air gun pellets had struck. The frames were rotting and in need of replacement. Despite the considerable rise in the value of the house Ernie hated the responsibility of maintaining it. He hated spending the money but he needed a roof over his head and the roof leaked. There were slates missing and the chimney stack did not look at all right.

As Ernie looked at the chimney he remembered a scene from childhood.

His father couldn't afford a chimney sweep. He borrowed a ladder and a flue-brush kit and climbed up the slope of the roof to the chimney. There were four chimney pots. He put the brush down one: twiddled it around and covered next door's newly decorated front room with soot. Mrs. France, the next door neighbour, dashed out of her house screaming, holding her soot-covered child in the air, and looking as black as a thunder storm.

The rain came on harder. The gutter dripped water: it bounced off the cracked paved path below and hit the house wall. The pointing was perished. The water seeped between the bricks into the plaster and had peeled the wallpaper off the hallway inside. Something had to be done but what, by whom, and what would it cost? Ernie just couldn't face it!

As he turned to go in, out of the rain, Ernie noticed a white van had mounted the pavement and parked outside the house. Two doors slammed shut and a pair of youngish workmen wearing steel toe-capped boots, scruffy blue jeans, faded T-shirts revealing tattooed forearms and woolly knitted hats, walked up the path towards him.

"Are you the owner of this house 'ere?" The younger of the two men said, in a surprisingly broad Lancashire accent.

Startled, Ernie took a step back: "Yes, I am. What is it you want?"

"We were just passing and thought that there 'edge needs cutting. We could do it for you - real cheap".

Ernie agreed about the cutting but instinctively said he couldn't afford it, then added: "how much would you charge for doing it?"

"It 'ud be about £100 quid to do that, big job that", the older one said, nodding his head towards the hedge.

"Oh I can't afford that much: I'd have to think about it".

Ernie didn't much like the look of the pair but the Lancashire accent had softened his attitude. "You've got a good, strong Lancashire accent: where do you come from?"

"Clitheroe" the older of the two replied, concealing the fact that they actually came from Darwen. "There's not much work up there so we thought we'd look for some down 'ere".

"I know Clitheroe quite well. I once met the Queen on the railway station at Clitheroe. She has an estate in the Trough of Boland you know. She was walking up and down the platform with a headscarf on and I said hello to her".

Ernie was an inveterate name dropper with an obsessive need to bask in the glory of casual encounters with celebrities. Given half a chance he would tell you how he met Toscanini in the toilets at La Scala in Milan or Gore Vidal, walking his Afghan hound up a hill in Ravello or how Kathleen Ferrier came and sat next to him in the interval of a Recital at the Free Trade Hall. He could regale you with tales of meetings, real or imaginary - one never knew - with strings of other members of the glitterati he'd fortuitously met.

The older man looked impressed. The younger man, clearly the brighter of the two, said: "I once had my hair cut by Alan Shearer's barber".

Ernie didn't know what to make of this: he knew nothing about football and not much more about other people's jokes, but words triggered puns and Ernie often punned without realising he was doing so. His conscious puns were often tortuously contrived - "it was the soda scon that made her so disconsolate" or even worse, clichéd - "people who make puns should be punished" or so feeble nobody took any notice, but Ernie would tiresomely repeat them despite the groans.

"Who's Alan Shearer? He's not an Australian is he?" Ernie asked, hoping for at least a grin.

The older man tried to change the topic in asking "What were you doing standing in the garden in the rain?" but once Ernie started punning it was difficult to stop him. "I was hoping to grow sage: perhaps I will if I get some thyme". Ernie said with a hint of triumph in his voice.

"Oh ay! Well I think we'd best be off." The older man said.

As they left, the younger man said: "You'd be wise to think about getting the hedge cut: we'll call back sometime tomorrow".

As they walked to the van the younger man said: "We've got a rum 'un here mate, but he shouldn't be too difficult".

Early the following day the white van came again. Ernie was in bed. The door bell went. He ignored it but he couldn't ignore the persistent rapping with the door knocker and the loud flapping sound of the letter-box cover. He looked out of the bedroom window through a gap in the curtain and saw the white van with a set of ladders strapped to the roof-rack. He went downstairs in his pyjamas.

In the hope that the two men would go away he shouted. "I can't open the door. I've lost my key: it was in my pocket but I can't find it. You'll have to come back some other time".

The two men ignored this. They shouted through the letter box:

"We've come to see if you've thought about the hedge".

"I haven't decided yet. I'm not dressed. You'll have to come back later".

"What's this on the wall: it's a key safe isn't it? What's the combination?"

Despite realising he was being stupid Ernie shouted out the code number and they opened the door.

"I haven't decided about the hedge. I'm not dressed."

"We'll come in an' wait" the younger one said, and without waiting for Ernie to agree he pushed against the door and the two of them squeezed past Ernie into the hallway".

Ernie didn't like this, he felt intimidated: they were both big, well built men. "You'd better wait in the front room while I get dressed. Switch the light on and draw back the curtains. See if you can find somewhere to sit. I'm in a bit of a mess at the moment".

As they tried to get down the hallway, towards the kitchen to access the front room door, the older man said: "By heck Mister, it's worse than the garden, you need a bloody 'sat-nav.' to get through here".

The hall floor was strewn with shoals of junk mail and free newspapers lying on top of the several layers of dusty carpets loosely lain over the original fitted carpet. The passage was cluttered with battered furniture: a rickety telephone table, a large oak hallstand festooned with old suits, overcoats, macs, umbrellas, two grubby duffle coats, a Deerstalker and several cloth caps. Two broken Hoovers trailed leads. Boxes of books, several odd shoes, a pair of galoshes and a couple of fallen walking sticks added to the hazards.

The two men went into the front room and switched on the light. It was just as squalid as the hallway. The threadbare dusty carpet had bits of food trodden into it. A lopsided piano that had lost a couple of casters stood with its back against the wall. The keyboard lid was open and despite the film of dust, the name Bechstein, inset in gold letters, could be seen above it. The white keys were well on their way to being black for want of a clean. There were sheets of music and a variety of ornaments and knick-knacks on top of the piano and a pile of music on the piano stool. The younger of the two men, struck a few notes as he passed. The sound was tinny. "He must have a terribly bad ear. It needs a damned good cleaning and tuning", he said to his mate.

Two pieces from an old, bulbous, fawn, moquette three-piece-suite took up a disproportionate amount of space in the room: the grubby looking sagging settee, held a scatter of books and dictionaries, an easy chair had a stack of three cushions on it to make it easier to get up from. A couple of low glass-topped tables held more books, a large portable radio and a pile of CD's. In front of the chair was a tall tea-trolley on wheels. The lower shelf on the trolley held open books and magazines together with a jumble of envelopes and sheets of writing.. The top level held a plate with a half-eaten meal of spaghetti, with tomato sauce congealed to its surface. A polystyrene container with fish-batter and a few left over chips inside it stood on top of a thick, open book. A low table with a television set with video cassette and DVD player was squeezed in between the piano and a tall book-case fitted into the recess to the left of the fireplace. The bookcase shelves were crammed with books, box files and cardboard shoe boxes filled with hundreds of CD's and DVD's obsessively collected because, they were free, from W. H. Smith's and various Charity shops.

"The place is a bloody tip" the older man said as he drew the curtain to let in more light. In doing so he knocked over a vase of dead flowers and spilled stagnant water onto the windowsill which held half a dozen or so plant pots containing the remains of what had once been Cyclamen. The younger man cleared the books off the settee. He looked at the titles and flicked open the pages: Don Quixote in Spanish, Pere Goriot in French, Trollope, Michener and Henry James in English.

"Bloody 'ell we've got a right odd ball 'ere", he said to his mate.

In low voices they discussed strategy. They had no intention of cutting the hedge. The plan was to talk Ernie into having the hedge done, persuade him to put money up front and then scarper without doing the job. They had done this kind of thing before and Ernie seemed like an easy touch. They would tell him that to do the hedge they would have to hire a chain saw and an electric power hedge trimmer. They could save him the cost of hiring a skip by taking the cuttings to the tip in their van. They would need £100 up front for a deposit, returnable to Ernie when they returned the tools. They would emphasise that as they needed work and because he was a pensioner, they were offering to do the job at half what they would normally charge. But first they needed to find out if Ernie kept money in the house and if not they would offer to take him to a cash point or a bank. Before they could finalise their plan they heard Ernie coming down the stairs.

When Ernie came into the room he was still not dressed: he'd put an old, well off-white, dressing gown over his pyjamas and secured it with a worn leather belt from his trousers. In his haste to get down to see what the two men were up to he'd put odd shoes on his feet. The two men were sitting side by side apparently looking at the large print of Van Gogh's 'Sunflowers' on the wall above the hearth. The gas fire in the hearth had a Gas Board official notice attached saying: "DO NOT USE THIS APPLIANCE". They looked at Ernie and exchanged glances. Ernie perched himself on top of the cushions on the easy chair.

Before they could say anything Ernie said: "I've thought about it. I don't want the hedge doing, it's not a priority. I've got to get the gutters and the roof done first, there's water dripping into the back bedroom. There are slates missing and the chimney stack looks as if it needs pointing. I need to get new window frames before I do anything with the garden, they're all rotten"

"The Council 'll do that won't they?" the older man said.

"No, they won't. They don't own the house: it's my house".

The two men exchanged more glances. "Well, it's your lucky day. We are actually builders and roofers. We only do gardening jobs when we've no building work on. Do you want us to have a look at the roof: we've got ladders with us?"

"Make us a cup of tea we'll get the ladders and have a look at the roof for you: two sugars in Rick's and one sugar in mine".

The tea was almost cold when they got back but they didn't complain.

"Sit down. You are not going to like this. All the guttering is corroded and leaking. It must be the original: these days it's all plastic. It'll all need replacing. The roof's in a bad way. There are a lot of cracked slates and about a dozen missing. I'm surprised you haven't been hit by one. There must be water dripping in somewhere. The roof timbers will almost certainly need replacing: it's a big job. You might even have to move out for a time. There's worse to come: the chimney stack could collapse any minute: it's not safe. If it comes down and hits somebody it could kill them. You'd be liable. You'll have to get that done right away".

"If you leave it you won't need a builder, you'll need a bloody undertaker!" the younger man joked.

Ernie had been expecting bad news but this was worse than he'd expected.

"I don't think the Insurance will be happy to cough up much on this one: you've left it too long. You have got insurance haven't you?"

"No I haven't. I used to have but I've let it lapse these last few years".

"Well, it could cost an arm and a leg. How are you going to pay for it?"

Ernie's mother had missed out on the Council renovations but since her death he had slowly built up his own renovation fund. He wanted the pantry and coal house converted into a small kitchen as had been done to the council-owned houses on the estate. An eccentric friend who, despite, or perhaps because of, his working class oikiness, dabbled in shares and financial speculation, had advised Ernie to put money into as many Building Societies as possible so as to benefit from the share-out when they de-mutualised. He'd also told Ernie to buy shares when public utilities were denationalised. Ernie, as usual, went over the top and with his savings put £110 in 21 different Building Societies then bought shares in Gas, Water, Electricity, and later, Premium Bonds. By the time the public utilities had been sold off and a dozen or so Societies had de-mutualised he had amassed a sum of nearly £9,000. Ernie gloated, but the house deteriorated: he could never bring himself to spend any of it!

Somewhat slowly and nervously Ernie asked: "How much will it cost? I do have a small amount put by for the roof, but how much?"

"We'll have to have a look in the loft and bedroom ceilings to see what needs to be done. Where's the loft access?"

"It's on the landing upstairs. I've got some steps in the pantry if you want them".

The loft was, for the most part, dry. There were one or two shafts of light where slates were missing or had slipped but the timbers were sound enough. The younger man, knowing Ernie couldn't climb the ladder, shouted down: "Come up and have a look: all the wood's got wet rot, the timbers are in a terrible state: I'm amazed it's not collapsed. There are so many holes in the roof I'm surprised you haven't got bloody bats nesting up here".

When the men tried to get into the bedrooms they found one stacked almost to the ceiling with beds, mattresses and furniture, the other locked. Ernie went downstairs to find the key. When they opened the door they discovered it too was full of furniture and junk: on the floor was a bed-mattress made up with sheets and a duvet. A radio and alarm clock and an open book, face down, was on the floor beside it. Miscellaneous sideboards, bed-side tables, old TV sets, radios, tea chests, pots and pans and other household items filled the rest of the room. From the picture rail, surrounding the room, hung dozens of shirts, jackets and suits. The younger man looked at Ernie and quipped:

"Bloody 'ell you're not related to Steptoe and Son are you?"

"Oh that's all Javad's stuff. . . . he's a friend of mine . . . He . . . oh never mind, it's a long story.

Javad worked for a furnished lettings firm. He had stayed with Ernie occasionally in the past. Some two years previously he had asked Ernie to let him store some furniture in his bedroom for a week or so. Ernie, unwisely, let him do so. Javad promptly disappeared after having filled *two* rooms with furniture and personal belongings. Javad had mental problems. Ernie thought he might be in a hospital or even in prison but really had no idea where Javad was.

Ernie became visibly distressed as he was reminded of Javad and how he had invaded his house. He normally blocked him from his mind.

"Wherre do you sleep then?" the older man asked.

"I have to sleep in the Box Room".

The Box Room was just big enough to accommodate a single bed, a small bedside table and a wardrobe. The floor was littered with shoes and discarded clothes. The bed had mainly old coats for bedding. There was a damp patch on the ceiling and some of the wallpaper was peeling off.

The men left the steps on the landing and went downstairs into the front room with Ernie.

"Its bad news about the roof, I'm afraid it's beyond repair! You need a new roof," the older man said. "Oh no! Oh no! No! How much would that cost? Are you sure? Oh no!"

"Well we'll have to work it out when we've checked the cost of the tiles, the wood and the guttering measured up. Hm . . . well . . . rough guesstimate . . .

with the cost of the labour it could be in the region of seven or eight thousand.

Ernie went silent, pale and thoughtful.

"I can't possibly afford that much. I've got to get the windows done!".

"Well, leave it with us. We'll go to our supplier or perhaps B&Q this afternoon and price things up: we'll get the best price so don't fret about it. We'll come back tomorrow morning. But don't go getting any other quotes at this stage. There's a lot of cowboy builders about and even more dodgy roofers. You have to be careful. We might be able to get the price down a bit. See you in the morning".

Ernie, still in his dressing gown and odd shoes, walked down the path with the two men and watched the white van drive away. He was not happy: he was not at all sure he could trust these two. Seven or eight thousand seemed an enormous amount of money, and the windows too, he kept reminding himself. As he walked back he stopped in the garden and looked up at the roof. There were certainly some slates missing and a lot more were cracked and askew. The chimney stack certainly didn't look safe and many of the ridge tiles had lost their pointing and slipped out of alignment. He needed impartial advice but he didn't know where to get it. The only person he could think of was his younger brother and they were not on the best of terms: he hadn't seen him for almost a year. "I'll give my brother a ring", he said out loud to himself. But then he remembered his phone wasn't working. He'd reported it to British Telecom and they'd told him the fault was inside the house and he would have to pay £90. He had put off asking them to deal with it. He would have to use the public phone at the end of the street: he shuddered. The phone box reeked of urine and stale cigarette smoke.

That evening Ernie phoned his brother. After they had exchanged the usual 'how are you', etc. Ernie told his brother about the roof, the builders and the quote.

"With the state you've let the house get into seven to eight thousand doesn't seem all that bad for a complete new roof and chimney stack. Tell them you would want the side wall pointing and double glazed windows for that price and see what they say. But you *must* get another quote!"

"How will I know if they are proper builders?" Ernie asked.

He didn't know if his brother was being facetious when he said:

"If they look like builders, talk like builders, build walls using a trowel and a plumb line and have two bags of sand and one of cement then they're probably builders" but he was reassured when his brother said "Seriously though, does their van have the name of a builder on the side with a telephone number and email address? If they have a battered, dirty, white van with no firm's name on the side and a roof rack with only one set of ladders and they offer a cheap job for cash in hand then they're most likely a not very smart pair of cowboys".

Ernie's brother guessed the latter description fitted the bill but he also knew that despite his warning, if the men offered a cheap deal, his brother would accept it. Ernie was so naive and gullible, and so miserly he would fall for anything, however implausible, if he thought it would save him money. If someone wanted to rob him and needed to get into his house they only had to offer him some kind of a bargain and he'd be crazy enough to let them in. He just sighed. He'd given up on Ernie and bargains long ago.

When the two men arrived the following morning Ernie let them in.

They sat in the front room where they'd sat the day before. The older man put his hand up his T-shirt and pulled out a few sheets of paper with B&Q headings. "We've checked the prices of everything that we'd need for the roof and it comes to £5,900".

"But what about the windows?!"

"Well, if you want the windows done, UPVC and double glazing, that's another three - three and a half thou."

After a pause Ernie said: "Oh dear, it sounds an awful lot of money to me. I'm only a pensioner you know. I don't think I could afford that much. I've got to get the kitchen done sometime and the side wall needs pointing, it's letting damp in".

"We could probably throw in the pointing on the side wall for you as well. £9,400 should cover the lot. It's a lot cheaper than you'd get from anyone else: your windows would cost you at least £4,500", the younger man interjected.

The older man said: "Well, I suppose we could get the price down if you paid cash in hand. We wouldn't have to pay tax on our wages and you'd save on the VAT,: everybody would be happy, win - win!" He winked at the younger man on Ernie's blind side. "What do you think Rick. Do you think we should stick our necks out to save him some money seeing as he's a pensioner?" Rick said "Aye go-on then, but he'd have to keep bloody quiet about it".

"Let's say £8,000 for the lot then. How does that sound?"

"Well that sounds a lot better than £9,400, but I need to get another quotation. I'll have to think about it. I've got to go to the foot clinic in Prestwich. I'm just going to shoe off to make a cup of tea before I go. I'll make one for you, to boot, while I'm about it".

Though not entirely happy about the VAT fiddle Ernie was clearly cheered up at the prospect of a bargain! The two men exchanged groans. Ernie went into the kitchen to put the kettle on and retrieve yesterday's mugs from the pile of unwashed pots in the sink.

"Don't let the bugger off the hook. If he gets another quote he'll know we're conning him: put 'the bloody frighteners on him'", the younger man urged.

Ernie came back with the tea, caught his foot on one of the many boxes on the floor, and slopped half a cupful of scalding tea into the lap of the younger man. "You clumsy bugger you've scalded my balls off!" he shouted as he leapt up, plucking at his crotch. Ernie pulled out a dirty handkerchief and thrust it towards the man's genitals.

When the older man ceased laughing he said: "Well, look Ernie, we've spent a lot of time on this job already. Any other firm would have charged you at least a hundred quid for a survey and a quote. We've got to fix the chimney now we know that it's dangerous: we'd be held as liable as you would be if it fell on someone. If we don't do it we'll have to report it to the police. They'd probably fine you and send someone else to do it. You could be in for a very hefty bill".

Ernie began rocking backwards and forwards. "Oh no, oh no, don't get the police involved: what am I going to do!"

"Don't worry about it, we'll get the ladder off the van and some tools, then I'll run you down to Prestwich to the clinic, I'll wait while you have your feet done. Rick can make a start on the chimney".

With the thought of the police, a hefty bill and having spilt tea on one of them, Ernie felt he had no option other than to accept this proposal and let them do the chimney.

While Ernie was having his feet attended to he had time to reflect on what his brother had said over the phone. On the way back home he said to the driver: "Why haven't you got your firm's name on the side of the van?"

"We have: but we had a bump in it last week. It's in for repair: this is one we've borrowed".

Despite hearing this Ernie was still uneasy. He felt he was being pressured to let them do *all* the work. He resolved to tell them he wanted to get another quote for the roof and the windows.

Rick, the younger man, came down from the roof when they got back .Ernie told the pair of them he was going to get at least one other quote for the roof and windows.

Rick shouted: "You can't bloody well do that on us after all we've done for you!" He looked menacingly at Ernie, got up and went back to the roof.

The older man said: "Do as you like Ernie but I don't think another firm would be too happy about taking work off builders already on a job. There's an unwritten rule that you don't take work off another firm already on a job. They won't refuse to quote: they'd just quote you an astronomical price knowing that you will turn it down. You won't get a better deal than we've offered you I can promise you that!"

Ernie said nothing. He didn't know what to do. They were big men: they might turn nasty if he refused to give them the job. If he let them do only the chimney he was sure they would up the price for it. He'd been a fool not to find out just how much fixing the chimney would cost. Reflecting again on what his brother had said persuaded him that perhaps the £8,000 for the whole job was not excessive. He could always refuse to pay if the work wasn't satisfactory. "Oh all right then, you can do *all* the work, but make sure you do a good job".

The younger man, who had only been gone a few minutes, returned from the roof and told Ernie that he had made the chimney safe for now but that it would have to come down and be rebuilt when the roof was replaced.

"He says he's happy for us to do the roof, Rick," the older man told his mate, and turning to Ernie said: "You're happy with that aren't you Ernie: £8,000 for the roof, the windows and the side wall?"

Ernie was not happy but didn't say so. Usually he fretted for weeks over spending even the smallest amount of money but deciding to spend thousands didn't seem real, all he felt was a sense of relief: it was as though the roof had been lifted from his head rather than from the house. Relief morphed into elation now the deal was done but he came down with a bump when the younger man said:

"We'll need half the money in cash up front to buy the materials and the other half when we've finished the job".

"I'll have to give you a cheque later," Ernie said.

"We need cash now, for the materials. A cheque can be traced. It would make the VAT deal too risky."

"I would have to give the Bank advanced notice to withdraw cash" Ernie told them.

"Well give them a ring and tell them you're coming to withdraw £4,000" the younger man said.

"I can't, the phone's not working."

The older man went into the hallway and picked up the phone. There was no dialling tone. He traced the wire back to the wall socket. It was not plugged in: someone must have caught their foot in the wire. He reinserted it, picked up the phone, it worked perfectly.

"I've fixed the phone for you Ernie"

"Oh thank you very much. It would have cost me £90 if I'd got Telecom to do it."

"There you are Ernie: we've saved you ninety quid already!"

Ernie began to feel better about the two men.

Ernie's account was with RBS in the centre of Manchester. He phoned and left a message to say that he would be calling in person the following day to withdraw £4,000 in cash.

The two men left saying they would pick him up about ten in the morning and take him to the Bank. "We'll drop you back home and go on to B&Q to buy the materials and have them delivered".

Ernie got very little sleep that night. Everything had happened so quickly. His mind was racing. Four thousand pounds: an enormous amount of money. There was no name on the van. Why did they say they were gardeners and then say they were builders? "Oh dear, oh dear, what have I done!" Ernie said, over and over to himself, as he gnawed away at his knuckle and what was left of his finger nails.

Early the following day the two men arrived. Ernie was in his pyjamas. He answered the door feigning illness, clutching his stomach and groaning, unconvincingly.

"I can't go to the Bank. I've been up all night with the runs. I need to stay near a toilet". "Don't give us that shit, you've over-slept", the younger one said.

"If you're really ill we'll go down to the Chemist's and get you some Imodium: that'll put you right in a jiffy. We'll wait till you're better. You've no need to worry about the runs: we've got a chemical toilet can in the van. If you're caught short you can use that. Make us a brew."

Ernie knew he was rumbled. He went into the kitchen and put the kettle on. When they'd drunk their tea the older man said:

"Get dressed Ernie while we get the ladder off the roof-rack. We'll take some gear up to the roof.

Ernie managed to shave without cutting himself for once. He came down stairs sporting a badly knotted tie and dressed in a blue serge charity shop suit which didn't quite fit. His trousers were a good two inches short. The jacket's remaining centre button was straining to join its long lost brothers. Ernie had somehow managed to get the collar of the jacket folded in. It was tucked somewhere down his back. Other than that he looked tolerably presentable. In the hallway he reluctantly shrugged himself into a bulky, dated, maroon, dinner-stained duffle coat. Donning his Deer-stalker Ernie shuffled his way down the path to the van. He was dreading all this. The two men grinned and exchanged glances as they struggled to heave Ernie up on to the bench seat in the cab of the van.

The van didn't start at the first attempt but Ernie's hopes were dashed when the engine came to life at the second go. To take his mind off money Ernie gave a commentary on the changes the route had seen over the years, pointing out where the Cinema used to be and the vacant site of the infant's school he'd attended.

Manchester was snarled up with traffic as usual. There was "No Parking" outside the bank and none in the nearby side streets. The men had no option but to park conspicuously on a double yellow line opposite the bank. The older man handed Ernie a plain white plastic bag saying: "Be as quick as you can, we don't want to get a parking ticket". The younger man went with Ernie as far as the door. Ernie dragged his feet reluctantly into the bank.

Ernie knew the Bank staff well and the Bank staff knew Ernie, only too well. Until recently Ernie had for many years used his bus pass to go, daily, to Manchester. On arrival he would head straight for the Bank. The waiting area had toilets, easy chairs, free copies *of The Financial Times* and a gratis coffee machine. Ernie spent hours there in winter, saving on home heating. The staff tolerated him as a character. Ernie had a substantial savings account and was never overdrawn. Despite looking like a down-and-out they knew Ernie was well educated. He had a good speaking voice. He entertained the clerks with quirky facts and stories when they were on their tea break.

Ernie joined the shortest counter queue. By the time it was his turn he was dithery and visibly distraught at the thought of parting with all that money. He told the counter assistant that he'd phoned and left a recorded message that he would be coming in to withdraw £4,000 in cash. The assistant looked astonished. He knew Ernie as a parsimonious skin flint and felt he could ask him outright why he wanted to withdraw such a large amount, and in cash.

"It's normal for people pay by cheque for things that cost a lot" he said.

"Yes I know it is but they want cash in hand for doing the job." Ernie almost shouted.

"What job's that then? It must be some job if it costs £4,000."

"It's for roof-work on my house and they had to have it today: the builders are outside, waiting for the money".

"Have they done the work?", the assistant asked.

"No they haven't. I'm not happy about it but they insisted they have to have some money first to buy the materials: they'll be furious if I don't get it. They said they couldn't do the job if I didn't get money today. It's a terrible lot of money ... but it's very reasonable for all the work involved. Oh dear! ... Oh dear! . . ."

Ernie was getting more and more agitated. The clerk could see that further questions would tip Ernie into a tantrum.

"It sounds a bit dodgy to me. Wait in the reception lounge: I'll just have a quick word with the Manager".

When he had heard Ernie's story the Bank Manager said: "It sounds very suspicious to me; they shouldn't be asking for that sort of money before they've done any work and certainly not cash. I think it might be as well to get the police to check them out".

Ernie became even more distressed thinking that the men would tell the police he had a dangerous chimney and that he'd agreed to them not paying VAT. He had visions of himself being charged with Tax Evasion along with them.

"Oh dear no, I don't want the police involved!"

"Don't worry about it. There *are* con men about I'm afraid. Police Headquarters is just round the corner:. I know the Police Inspector who deals with this type of thing: it's happened before. Calm down and get yourself a coffee while I get in touch with him".

Ernie was too preoccupied to bother with coffee. He sat on the edge of a chair fidgeting and imagining himself sharing a prison cell with the two builders.

As his police car drove up to the Bank the Inspector saw a white van pull off the double yellow lines opposite and drive away before he could get its number. "Damn it, I bet that's them" he said to his Sergeant.

It didn't take long for the Inspector to recognise Ernie was a vulnerable person and the victim of some kind of scam: literally and figuratively taken for a ride.

"They'll almost certainly know they've been rumbled: get him into the car as quick as you can. I'll contact Bury" he said to the Sergeant.

"We'll drive you back to the house Ernest: from what you've told me there's a good chance they've gone back there to collect their gear."

The Inspector switched on the blue flashing lights and the siren. In the back Ernie clicked his seat belt into place then held tight to the upper strap handle above the door as the car made its way through the parting city traffic and sped along the arterial road towards Ernie's house. Familiar places came and went: StrangewaysPprison, 'The Half Way House' pub, the Jewish Synagogue, Heaton Park, all flashed by at an alarming rate. Ernie was too terrified to enjoy his moment of fame. He closed his eyes, he was sure they were going to hit the cars that miraculously pulled over to let the wailing police vehicle have a clear run as it sped through numerous red traffic lights. Ernie was hoping against hope that the roofers would have been and gone by the time they arrived at his house but by the speed the police were travelling there was a good chance they would be there first. Ernie couldn't bear the thought of a confrontation and them revealing that he had agreed to the VAT scam.

The Inspector switched off the blue flashing lights and the siren before they turned off the main road into where Ernie's house was located. The white van was on the pavement outside the house. One of the two men was on the roof: the other coming down the ladder. The Inspector parked the police car behind the van. Ironically it was concealed by the high, uncut, privet hedge. The Sergeant got out and concealed himself at the side of the gate. The Inspector radioed a check on the van's registration number and told Ernie to stay in the car. As the Inspector got out, to join the Sergeant, a Black Maria from Bury drew up behind the police car. Four officers jumped out and on the Inspector's instruction deployed themselves round the perimeter of the garden.

The radio check indicated that the van had been stolen in the town of Darwen and that the vehicle was neither taxed nor insured.

The two men offered no resistance when the Inspector approached them but refused to give their names and addresses. The Inspector cautioned them and told them they were being arrested on suspicion of stealing a vehicle, driving it whilst it was neither taxed nor insured, and on suspicion of attempting to commit a fraud. The two men obviously knew the ropes: they each said "no comment." They were promptly hand-cuffed, bundled into the police van and taken into Custody.

After the police van had left the Inspector helped Ernie out of the car "We'll send a team round later to take the White Van away and we will need a statement from you but we'll leave that until tomorrow. I'll send an officer round in the morning. Go inside and make yourself a cup of tea. Nothing to worry about now."

A couple of Ernie's inquisitive neighbours from the small group that had gathered to watch all the excitement were only too willing to help Ernie into the house and make him a cup of tea. It wasn't everyday that so many police descended on the Estate and they were eager to know what it was all about.

The following day two policemen came to Ernie's house and took a full statement of events. It took the best part of the day. Ernie's account was detailed and accurate, for the most part, but he made no mention of the VAT fiddle. He had convinced himself that it was he, not the two men, who had suggested the scam and it took the edge off his the sense of importance at being victim and chief witness in an investigation. If the police got to know of his complicity he might end up in the dock with them.

A few days after the police visit there was a knock on Ernie's front door. He was convinced it was the police come to arrest him. Reluctantly he opened the door. An official looking man with a clip board said: "Good morning, I'm from the Trading Standards Office: I've come on the instruction of the police Inspector in charge of the case against the bogus roofers they arrested at this property. Do you mind if I carry out an inspection of the work they did and the work they said needed doing".

Ernie was so relieved that, despite being in his pyjamas and having resolved never to let anyone he didn't know into the house ever again, he almost hugged the official and invited him in.

After inspecting the roof outside and inside through the loft, the Trading Standards officer told Ernie the roof needed a number of slates replacing and that the pointing of the chimney stack the two men said they'd done, needed redoing. It was pointed on the two more visible sides but it was a very amateurish job. He said the roof was basically sound and needed only repair work though all the gutters would need to be replaced.

He told Ernie that as the Report had been requested by the police it would be sent to them but that Ernie would receive a copy in due course. When Ernie asked how much it would cost to get done the work needed he said: "I'm not in a position to say". When Ernie pressed him he said: "I'm not supposed to give an opinion but unofficially, at a rough guess, the roof work and guttering shouldn't cost much more than £1,000 and you should be able to get the windows done for about £3,000".

A week later the police phoned Ernie to say that a copy of the Report was in the post and that they had asked Victim Support to contact him and the Trading Standards people to supply him with a list of reputable, registered building firms from which he could choose one to get the work done.

Weeks went by. Ernie had been expecting to go to Court to give evidence in the case but both the men admitted the charge of stealing a vehicle and of attempting to commit fraud by false pretences: they asked for two similar offences to be taken into account when sentencing took place, so Ernie was not required to attend court. He was greatly relieved about that. It had been making him ill that it might come out in Court that he had colluded with the men in the VAT fraud. He'd been having nightmares about it since their arrest. Every night it was the same dream: he'd been put in a cell with them and they were torturing him and beating him up!

Two months later the two men, who turned out to be gardeners, never builders, were sentenced to over three years each.

Ernie, as usual, bought a *Prestwich and Whitefield Guide:* the front page headline was:

Conmen Jailed for Three Years
Bogus pair tried to get £4,000 from 79 year old pensioner.

The newspaper report named the bogus men from Darwen as Richard Loveridge, aged 23, jailed for 3yrs 1 month and William Loveridge, aged 34, jailed for 3 years 8 months.

Detective Inspector Collins of the C.I.D. was reported as saying: "I hope these sentences serve as a warning to other criminals who think they can prey on the more defenceless members of the community. I want to thank the staff of the RBS for their quick thinking in contacting the police".

Ultimately, as it turned out, the two bogus builders had done Ernie a very big favour: Victim Support arranged for his hedge to be cut by volunteers, his roof to be repaired free of charge and double glazed windows fitted. With the help of the police they got Ernie funding from various charitable organisations. All Ernie had to pay for was the price of the actual windows and a bit of pointing on the side wall of the house.

At the luncheon club for pensioners, where Ernie regularly enjoyed a free lunch, he regaled the diners with his tale of the 'fiddlers on the roof' and how he didn't need to put money in a Hedge Fund any more.

Ernie's brother commented: "Jammy bugger: I bet he's planning to stand in the garden again, in his pyjamas, motionless, like a grey heron, hoping to catch a bogus Interior Designer or a couple of fiddling kitchen fitters. Perhaps he's not *that* crazy after all!"

GIVE AND TAKE

Today was Ernie's 85th birthday. He woke early feeling miserable. He hated growing old: false teeth, bad feet, falling over, forgetting things. He hated retirement: social isolation, loss of purpose, loss of pay. Most of all he hated spending money. True, spending money couldn't do much about age but it could have alleviated the worst of his miseries: got him out of the house to concerts, plays, the cinema: all the things he would have liked to do, but just couldn't bring himself to spend the money on. He was pathologically incapable of spending on anything other than the bare necessities of life - and only then if he could get a bargain.

He pulled up the overcoat he'd put over the blankets during the night, tucked it under his chin and tried to get back to sleep. But his mind was racing, grieving over the loss of a five pound note he'd absent-mindedly lost in a charity shop the previous day. After much tossing and turning and many weary sighs he managed to drop off again.

The previous day, despite his crippling feet and the threat of rain, Ernie walked, with the aid of his stick, the half mile from the council estate where he lived, to the charity shops on the busy main street. He needed a new jacket and shoes. His old one was threadbare and his shoes were falling apart. He could well afford new shoes; he'd plenty of money. As an impoverished child he'd saved in a money box and in a post office savings book. Later when working at the Town Hall he'd saved from his meagre salary in Building Societies and in Premium Bonds but he just couldn't bring himself to spend any of it. He kidded himself that by getting clothes from charity shops he was doing what many good people did: supporting worthy causes, helping the poor and needy, recycling resources: "Saving the planet!"

It had of course occurred to him, in more reflective moments, that buying second-hand clothes might be putting people in the Far-East out of a job or be joining the ranks of the self-serving, middle-class bargain hunters, depriving the poor of the best of the cheap clothes on display. Ernie had often argued the case against charity shops, and charity in general, whilst eating his regular mid-week free lunch at the Friends' Meeting House, or Fiends' Eating House as he liked to call it, pontificating that: "Charity, the much-loved salve to the conscience of the upper class, is an anti-social, degrading palliative, a confidence trick perpetrated by the rich on the poor". He could quote statistics proving it was poor people, not rich ones, who gave more of their income to charity. "Haven't you noticed in charity shops you see lots of kids' toys ordinary people have donated but you don't see many bags of golf clubs, yachts or Mercedes the rich have chipped-in!"

Despite knowing all the arguments Ernie's obsessive reluctance to spend money and the buzz of a bargain overrode any ideological qualms he might have felt. He just couldn't resist a charity shop.

The soles of Ernie's shoes flip flopped open showing rows of nails like crocodile's teeth chattering away as he walked to the shops. He was spoilt for choice. He passed by Oxfam with its display of Anthony Powell, Jane Austen and Dickens - leather bound books with gold embossing. Outside the Co-op he was confronted by a small, overweight, ethnic-looking woman with a dark-haired, large-eyed child in a sparse cotton dress. The woman had on a black dress, down to the tops of her shoes, a dark green woollen fleece and a headscarf. Ernie had seen her many times. "Big Issue" she said, "No thank you" and he walked on towards Cancer Research with its mannequins clad in stylish dresses. He bypassed Mind - too up-market. He looked into Barnardo's and The Children's Society, crammed between Santander and Barclays Bank, couldn't see any men's shoes so he continued on past a couple of Takeaways and an Estate Agent to arrive at Animal Rescue. A man who he took to be a Romanian gypsy was walking up and down the pavement playing a piano accordion. A well dressed woman coming out held the door open for him. He didn't notice the dog on a lead. He looked the woman in the face and thanked her as he squeezed passed. Unfortunately his stick slipped off the step and Ernie tripped over the dog, narrowly missing a collision.

The shop had a claustrophobic feel about it. It was laid out well enough but there were too many racks. They stood, shrouded in dresses and coats, like a herd of woolly animals, each bearing its burden of women's top coats, men's-jackets, assorted trousers and jeans: no fur coats or leather jackets in here though. The wheels of the racks squeaked and bleated like a flock of sheep as Ernie pushed his way through the maze of aisles. The side walls had shelves displaying bric-a-brac: rows of ladies' high-heel shoes, a collection of handbags, pottery, jugs, teapots, flower vases, glass-ware, picture frames and other old fashioned curios. Ernie glanced at the pottery hoping that one day he would find a 'Clarice Cliff' or some other collectible. Fat chance! The staff had first pickings and charity shops now had professional managers. As he passed the three or so yards of floor to ceiling bookshelves he stopped to check a J. K. Rowling in the vain hope is would have a signature. He'd heard a first, signed edition of a Harry Potter had been found and sold on eBay for £10,000. No such luck.

A box on the floor next to a glass-fronted display cabinet was crammed with shellac 78s. He wished they wouldn't put them on the floor: it was difficult to bend down these days. He scavenged through the boxes, flipping through records, CDs and DVDs with the speed of a bank clerk counting a stack of bank notes - always hoping to come across some early classic; a Caruso, Schipa, Beniamino Gigli, or a Nellie Melba. Over the years he'd amassed a considerable collection of early opera gems performed by renowned singers: Dame Clara Butt, Norena, and virtuoso instrumentalists: Richter, Horowitz, Menuhin and others. Vinyls were coming back in fashion. Ernie thought the 50p he sometimes had to pay was a good investment. But shoes and a jacket were today's quest so he mustn't dawdle. He made straight for the men's shoes. They were on a high shelf he couldn't reach so he went to the counter.

A large, African looking lady, exotically dressed, sat behind the till, brightening up the otherwise drab interior. A blonde, slattern, teenage girl was listlessly tidying the racks. He stopped in front of the counter:

"I'm looking for shoes but I can't reach them". Before the lady had a chance to respond he added: "That's a very nice dress you have on. Which part of Africa do you come from?"

"Chorlton" she said, in a refined voice which took him aback.

"Oh you don't sound like a native of Manchester. I thought you must come from Africa." And digging the hole deeper he turned to the teenager saying: "Where do you come from: are you a native from round here?"

"What's it to do with you? Mind yer own business" she said, in an almost indecipherable Glaswegian accent," confirming a view Ernie had that the Scots were only happy when fighting.

"Now don't be rude Aileen. Help the gentleman find some shoes please".

As she turned to do so Ernie took a good look at the girl's ashen face and the dark pouches beneath her eyes. He concluded she was probably a drug addict on probation, perhaps doing community service.

The girl handed down several pairs, brought Ernie a chair and left the shop, fumbling in her pocket for a crumpled pack of cigarettes. He tried on several: they were either too large, too small, too narrow. He put his own back on and went to the counter to ask had they any more in the back room. The black lady was busy bagging a dress for a customer. Without permission Ernie went into the back room to nosey. On the floor, between a rack of spare coat hangers, he found a couple of boxes awaiting price labels. One of the boxes was marked "nearly new". He sat on a chair and rummaged in it, found a pair of size nine brogues and tried them on. They fitted perfectly. He put his old shoes in the box, kept the brogues on and went back into the shop to search for a jacket on the men's clothes rack.

He had no qualms about wearing second hand clothes. In childhood he was used to wearing "hand me downs" from the children of the rich Jewish families whose houses his mother cleaned and where she lit the fires on the Sabbath. The fact that clothes in many charity shops came from the wardrobes of the deceased didn't worry him. He jokingly quipped to his free-lunch friends: "I've spent most of my working life waiting for dead men's shoes so it's a great pleasure to finally wear them!"

The charity-shop jackets he'd had over the years had given him endless material for his imagination, probably derived from his early reading of Gogol and Dostoyevsky's story *The Overcoat*. He imagined his newly acquired jacket on an avatar of his invisible self orating at a political meeting, the jacket waving its arms about maniacally like Adolph Hitler or on the corpulent body of the vainglorious Mussolini. Or sitting in a restaurant, or at the pictures, with its arm round the girlfriend he'd never had. He imagined the holiday trips the jackets had made in the pre-war days to Vienna, Warsaw, Prague or Berlin, which had the added advantage of saving him the cost of paying the air fare to those places.

Most of the jackets at Animal Rescue were from two or three-piece suits with trousers to match: they were not what he wanted. Ernie was stuck in the Harris Tweed era and wanted a jacket as near as possible to the one he was wearing but without moth holes, frayed cuffs or the scuffed leather elbow patches. A voice behind him said:

"Can I help you love?" It was the Manageress. She picked up the jackets he'd let fall on the floor and put them back on their hangers. He didn't recognise her, the staff in charity shops changed from day to day like the weather.

"No thank you, I can manage. I'm just looking".

"What is it you are looking for?"

"I was looking for a Harris Tweed jacket like the one I have on."

"Well you're about 60 years too early if you want a jacket as well worn as that one. I've seen better coats on the sick animals we're trying to help" she said, only half in jest. "Come into the clearing room at the back; you're in luck, some new jackets have just come in from a Receiver. They're from a bankrupt clothes factory shop. There might be one that would suit you".

"Oh I can't afford a new one. I'm a pensioner you know".

"Don't worry about that. I can see you haven't much money and we like to help people as well as animals!" Little did she know Ernie had almost enough to buy the shop, never mind a jacket "I'll get Aileen to help you try one or two on".

Ernie wasn't too pleased about having Aileen's help. She reeked of cigarette smoke but he let her help him out of his coat. He soon found a jacket which fitted him. It wasn't Harris Tweed but it was thick and warm. "Beggars can sometimes be choosers" he said to Aileen but it was lost on her. "I'll keep it on he said to the Manageress, as she came back to see how things were going.

"I'll leave you mine in exchange: it's good quality material you know, you might be able to get something for it". Aileen burst out laughing.

"I don't think so. Put it in the bin over there Aileen, the re-cycling van's due to collect in half an hour".

"Will 50p be alright if I leave you my old one?"

"Don't be silly, just take the jacket, but don't go telling folk you got it for nothing or we'll be in trouble".

"Oh that's very good of you: thank you, thank you!" he said. "And thank you too for your help Aileen".

On his way to the door, in his new jacket and nearly new brown, brogue shoes, the elated Ernie stopped to also thank the black lady from Chorlton.

Outside the shop he turned and looked at his reflection in the window. "This calls for a celebration", he said out aloud, congratulating himself on the money he had saved: musing that the jacket would have cost him perhaps £100 if he'd bought it in a menswear shop - and the brogues, well goodness knows. He assumed the Manageress purposely made no mention of him paying for the shoes. Ernie positively glowed. He went to the Co-op cafe, opposite to treat himself to a pot of tea instead of his usual cup.

The ethnic lady with the small child again thrust a *Big Issue* at him. Ernie again said "No thank you" but felt embarrassed for some reason and avoided giving her his eye. After a few steps he slowed, rummaged in his pocket for some loose change, then went back and dropped 30p into the child's hand. His buoyant mood immediately became enhanced by a frisson of virtuous self regard. "Difficult concept Charity", he said to himself.

As he sat down with his pot of tea he noticed the girl from Animal Rescue come through the cafe and into the main shopping area of the Co-op. A few minutes later she left holding what looked like a bottle of wine. He wondered how she could afford it. Hand in the till? he thought, fleetingly.

He liked to linger in the Co-op café. It was warm and saved him having the heater on at home. He thought about the effect his new jacket and shoes would create at the 'Fiend's' Eating House' where his reputation as a skinflint was well known. They'd wonder where he'd got the money from. He knew one or two suspected he'd more money than he let on. They pulled his leg about it. When he turned up in a charity shop suit on one occasion, after going to a funeral, someone quipped: "Is your brother on nights?" He frequently put his fork into half a sausage or a potato someone had left on their plate saying: "Waste not, want not." He'd even refused to chip in for a birthday present for their regular waitress saying: "I don't believe in birthdays: it should be the mother who gets the present, not the child". "Mean bugger, I bet his mother never got one" someone mumbled, instead of the hearty laugh Ernie was hoping for.

After two cups of tea and having read both the free newspapers he was about to leave the cafe but noticed an assistant clearing a table. He asked for a jug of hot water and managed to squeeze a third cup from the teapot before going to the till to pay.

The lady at the till knew Ernie; she was a neighbour living two doors down from him. If her Manager wasn't around she often didn't charge him.

"How are you Ernie?"

"Oh I'm not so bad but I do wish I could go back to work!"

"You wouldn't say that if you had to stand here all day: my feet are killing me and my varicose veins are playing me up. You're looking very smart today: is that a new coat you've got on? I haven't seen you in that before".

"Yes I've only just got it; bought it from the charity shop across the road".

He didn't want her to ask what he had paid for it so he quickly added: "How much do I owe you?"

"The usual was it: cup of tea?"

"No, I had a pot today". He started fumbling in his trouser pocket for the £1.50. He put one or two small coins on the counter and resumed rummaging. "Oh dear, I don't think I've got enough change" he said, as he fished out his comb and keys and put them on the counter.

"Well just give me a pound then".

He added another two 5p pieces. "I don't think I've got a pound. Oh just a minute, I'm sure I put a five pound note in my inside pocket".

He unbuttoned the coat. No five pound note. Panic, "Where is it?" He plunged his hand deeper into the pocket, shouting: "It must be there! Oh where is it? Where is it, it's not there! I put it in before I left: It must, it must be there!" Then he suddenly realised he had the charity shop jacket on. It was his old jacket he'd put the five pound note in. "Oh no. No!" he shouted, as he beat his forehead repeatedly with his tightly clenched fist. "It's in the one I gave to Animal Rescue!"

He was working himself up into a state of monumental histrionic distress.

"Well don't make such a fuss about it Ernie. It'll still be there if you left it in the pocket."

"No, it won't. It won't, it won't be there!"

"Don't be so daft Ernie: it'll be there. Just go over and ask them. Don't bother about the tea." "Oh what am I going to do? It won't be there!"

"Just go and ask them!"

The traffic was bad. It was nearly closing time. He stood on the kerb waving his walking stick. In exasperation he started to cross, venturing into the road despite the oncoming traffic. A car skidded and almost hit him. The driver wound down the window.

"Bloody idiot, d'you want to get killed!" Ernie took no notice and continued as fast as he could to the charity shop. The Manageress was outside locking the last of the shutters.

"Don't close, don't close, I've left five pound in my jacket, five pound in my old jacket!" he shouted. The Manageress waited for him to get to her.

"I'm very sorry love. The rag-bin bag was collected just after you left the shop. It'll have been sold on by now: they use the rags for paper-making."

"Oh what am I going to do? My five pound was in the pocket: it's a lot of money!"

"Well I'm very sorry love but there's nothing we can do. There's no way I can get your jacket back."

"Are you not insured for that kind of thing?"

"No we are not!" the Manageress said, emphatically. In despair

Ernie conjured up Aileen in the Co-op and the bottle of wine.

"You could ask Aileen did she find a five pound note in the pocket."

"No, she would have told me if she'd found it" the Manageress said. She was beginning to lose patience with Ernie and let it show in the tone of her voice.

"Well, I saw her at the Co-op buying a bottle of wine."

"Yes. I gave her money and I sent her out to get some wine: we're having a drink. It's my birthday. OK? I really don't know what all this fuss is about - it's only a fiver you've lost and I'm very sorry! But think what it would have cost if we'd charged you for the jacket: to say nothing about the shoes that somehow escaped our attention". With that she locked the shutter and went back into the shop leaving Ernie on the pavement, fretting.

The Manageress stood for a second or two in the shop, reclaiming her professional calm before going into the back room where one of the volunteers was pouring drinks.

"Hey girls, just listen to this! You're not going to believe this!"

By the time Ernie reached home he was desperate for a pee after all that tea. He hopped about as he fumbled ruefully in his new jacket pocket for the key which luckily he had remembered to transfer from his old jacket. He let himself in, went for a pee, then switched on a bar of his electric fire and flopped into a chair. After two minutes silence he got up, turned off the electric fire and went to bed, fretting and miserable.

Early next morning the telephone rang. He let it ring. When it stopped he turned over and went back to sleep. A couple of hours later it rang again. He didn't pick up but looked at his watch. He knew it would be his brother phoning to see if he was O.K and to wish him a happy birthday. He was so miserable he didn't want to talk to him. Despite having slept he still couldn't get the loss of the fiver from his mind. He knew if he told his brother he was feeling miserable or said he wished he could go back to work he'd only be told he needed counselling. He went downstairs into the kitchen to put the kettle on. On the table was the library book he'd finished but forgotten to take with him the day before. "Damn it, it'll be overdue now. I'll have to tell them again that I've been ill." He took his mug of tea upstairs to drink while he washed and shaved and dressed.

As he was going downstairs again he heard someone fiddling with the door. He'd put the key back in the lock on the inside instead of on the hook a neighbour had screwed into the door jamb. He opened the door and let his brother in.

"For Christ's sake Ernie, I'm sick of having to tell you to put the bloody key on the hook after you let yourself in!" How many times do I have to tell you? It's no use my having a key if I can't get in. And why didn't you answer the phone? I've been phoning you all morning. I thought you'd dropped dead or had a fall or something. I've had to come round specially. You're a bloody nuisance!"

"Don't tell me off. I've had a terrible night".

His brother didn't take him up on this. He knew only too well if he said: "Why what's the matter?" he'd have to listen yet again to Ernie moaning about being lonely and wanting to go back to work. It was, after all, his birthday.

"That's a very smart coat you've got on. Have you come into money? Had a win on the Premium Bonds?"

"Don't talk to me about money. I've had a disaster" and Ernie launched into the events of the day before; telling his brother at great length, and much whingeing, how he had left the fiver in his old jacket. His brother listened patiently but getting more and more annoyed as the tale unfolded.

"For Christ's sake Ernie, what *are* you going on about? Those shoes would have cost you at the very least forty quid, and that jacket a damned sight more. Stop moaning over a measly fiver you miserable bugger. What's the point of having money if you never spend it: buy a telly with a decent sized screen, or a radio that works, for a change, instead of moaning on about a piffling lost fiver? I'm not telling you to change your kitchen or to get a new sofa every couple of years. Just get a set of teeth and a decent hearing aid, something to improve your life, for god's sake. I'm fed up with seeing you munching away on your bloody gums, like a tortoise, and having to shout and repeat everything two or three times. You've all that money and you're living in worse poverty than when we were kids. And I'm sick to death of hearing excuses - saving for a rainy day! It's pissing down now Ernie! You're wet through! You need a fucking umbrella right now, you mad bastard!"

His brother was on a rant. Ernie had heard it all before and he could see he wasn't getting much sympathy over his lost fiver.

"Please stop lecturing me: I can do what I like, it's my money!" and to change the subject he said "What's in that parcel?"

"It's your present: have you forgotten? It's your birthday today? It's that book I said I'd get you." Ernie unwrapped the book:

"Oh it's that one" he said dismissively. "I've already read it. I got it from the library. It's there on the table as a matter of fact".

"Oh for god's sake: I told you I was getting it for you. Why didn't you tell me you were getting it from the library? I bought it especially for you, you're the bloody giddy limit!"

"I forgot. They'll change it for something else. Maybe you can take the library book back for me on your way home: it's not far out of your way and it'll save my legs?" Ernie failed to mention that the library book was overdue and his brother would be asked to pay the fine.

His brother was not pleased about being asked to detour through the village. "You're a pain in arse you are Ernie, it's difficult parking." After again telling him not to leave the key in the door and to answer the phone in a morning when he rang, he rewrapped the unwanted present, picked up the library book and left Ernie to his misery.

The librarian was engrossed in conversation with a borrower. After a minute or so he interrupted, saying: "I'll just leave this: I'm returning it for my brother."

"It's O.K. we were only gossiping". She flipped open the library book. A five pound note fell out. Ernie's brother laughed out loud. The librarian looked puzzled.

"Sorry . . . that brother of mine: he's had a sleepless night over that fiver - thought he'd lost it!"

"Well, the book's overdue, there's a fine to pay".

"The crafty old devil!"

"Have you got change or shall I take it out of this five pound note?" the Librarian asked.

"Umm . . . take it out of the fiver. A bit of give and take wouldn't do him any harm: might even do him a bit of good!

Instead of going back to the car Ernie's brother went down the street to the shops with the present. He'd bought the book some time ago in a bookshop elsewhere. He no longer had the receipt and didn't want the bother of taking it back. He decided to go to Animal Rescue and donate it. A piano accordionist up the street was playing a cheerful tune: he hummed along with it. An ethnic lady in a dark green woollen fleece and a headscarf was selling *Big Issue*: he stopped, bought a copy with money from the fiver and crossed the road to the charity shop. The black lady at the till un-wrapped the book:

"Oh it's brand new, thank you so very much!" she said, giving him a big smile.

Ernie's brother put what was left of the fiver into the collecting box on the counter.

SHOPPING THIEVES

When Eddie left school in 1949, aged almost sixteen he'd no idea what job he wanted to do. His mam was keen for him to get a job: any kind of a job. She wanted to have some regular money coming in. His dad was out of work again, having left his job with the Council where he worked as a bin-man and road mender. She had part-time work doing school dinners and did a bit of house-cleaning but there were hire-purchase payments to be met on the three-piece-suite she'd bought 'on the never-never'.

"Don't be lying in bed all day Eddie: you must get up. Go to the Career's Office and see what jobs they've got. I don't want you getting in with that gang of thieving shop lifters that hang about smoking and drinking half the night under the lamp across the road. If you get a conviction you'll never ever get a job! Go and see if he'll take you back at the Grocer's."

The Grocer's was the last thing on earth Eddie wanted. He'd worked in the local Grocer's shop after school and in the holidays throughout the whole of his school days: running errands, delivering orders, sitting hidden behind the counter like a watch-dog looking out for people pinching things; customers slipping a tin of peas or a small brown loaf into a shopping bag. It was boring and the pay was poor. He didn't want any more of that!

A neighbour told his dad that Lewis's, a large Department store in Manchester, was taking on staff. So on Monday morning Eddie, fed up with his mam nagging him, told her he was giving the Careers Office a miss and going to Lewis's to see if he could get a temporary job while he decided what kind of work he wanted to do.

"Good: while you are there you can get me a small suitcase with a bit of that money your Grandma sent. I need one to put my things in when I go to stay over with her next weekend".

Eddie knew the store quite well: he'd been there many times over the years, though not recently. The doorman told him to go to the fourth floor and ask for Personnel. As the escalator slowly approached the fourth floor Eddie had a Proustian Madeleine moment. His mind flashed back to Shude Hill and visits to Lewis's Pet's Corner.

When Eddie was at Secondary school he used to play wag on a Wednesday afternoons instead of football. He used his season rail ticket to go home but stayed on the train and went to Victoria station in Manchester to meet his friend Twissy who went to Art School there. They would go to Tib Street or Shude Hill where, on the pavement, housed in cages and cardboard boxes, or between the roadside rickety bookstalls beyond the tiny Poets' Corner pub, you could buy different coloured mice or rabbits, white rats, guinea pigs, tortoises, pigeons, jars of goldfish and even snakes. Myth had it that the budgies and cockatoo's from Tib Street were trained to fly back to the shop if they escaped when you let them fly around in the house.

If it was raining, the two friends would go to Lewis's Store to ride up and down on the escalators for fun and, if lucky enough not to be chased out by the Store Detective, visit the Pet's Corner on the fourth floor where there was a glass-walled area with cages of exotic animals and birds inside. The cages were too small and the monkeys lethargic: they spent most of their time scratching themselves and examining each other's fur. Occasionally, out of the frustration at being so confined, one would leap into the air and swing itself round and round the cage a dozen or so times in a noisy, neurotic frenzy. There was a coypu, an American woodchuck, a porcupine and two white rats. There were two or three caged Mynah birds which made high pitched whistling screams. Chained to a perch, was a colourful Macaw, with scaly claws, that refused to learn any of the rude words they tried to teach it.

Eddie stepped off the escalator and looked around. No sign of the Pet's Corner: the fourth floor was devoted entirely to dining-room furniture, settees and beds. The glass-walled area had been converted into the Personnel Office. He knocked on the door and getting no response turned the door-knob and went in a step or two. A formidable looking middle-age lady with short, bob-curled steel grey hair, like capstan lathe-turnings, stopped tapping her typewriter and looked over the top of the black horn-rimmed specs perched on the end of her nose. "Have you an appointment?" "No, I've just come to ask if you have any temporary jobs." She looked back down at her typing saying: "The Personnel Manager isn't in until 10.0 o'clock today and you need an appointment: but it's no use seeing him, we only take Temps on for Christmas and the January Sales." Undaunted Eddie said: "I've had experience of working in a shop: he might give me a temporary job if I speak to him personally. Can I make an appointment?" She still didn't look up. "No, I'm afraid you can't, there's no point: you'd be wasting everybody's time. Try not to bang the door when you close it." Eddie could understand why miserable Miss Keyboard might say that.

Eddie wasn't too bothered that he hadn't got a job in the Store. Store work didn't really appeal to him: too much like the Grocer's. He took the lift down to the Basement. His mam had seen the suitcase she wanted last time she was in the store but she hadn't bought it. She'd described it and given him the correct money so it was easy to spot. Eddie picked up the suitcase and handed over the money. The salesman put it to one side and immediately started tut-tutting and drumming his fingers on the counter.

"All the cash-carrier flasks are down below at the moment, Sir, but one should be up in a minute or two if you would like to wait for a receipt."

Eddie didn't want to wait "Well, I'm in a bit of a hurry" he said.

"That's alright Sir, you needn't wait. I'll put this piece of tape on the handle so that Security knows you've paid for the item and he tied the tape on the suitcase in a flamboyant bow.

Eddie went back to the lifts and pressed the button. He stepped aside when it came, to let a woman with a pram and her two four or five year olds get in the lift. He stood next to them as it filled up. One of the two boys jumped up and down as the lift rose: the other one began drumming annoyingly on the case dangling from Eddie's hand. "Stop that. Leave that case alone. And stop that jumping up and down or I'll smack the pair of you".

"It's O.K. they're not doing any harm" Eddie said. Eddie let them get out of the lift and followed them to the main exit.

As Eddie stepped outside he felt a hand on his shoulder. A voice said: "Would you mind returning to the Store Sir". It was the Doorman and by his side a Store Detective, The Doorman said

"Sorry to trouble you Sir: just a routine check. Did you purchase that case from the Store? "

"Yes, I did" Eddie said.

"Would you mind showing me your receipt?"

"I haven't got one. The Salesman told me I didn't need one. I was in a hurry. He put a tape on to show I'd paid for it." To Eddie's dismay he saw that the tape wasn't there. "The tape must have come off: one of the kids in the lift must have pulled it off".

"Yes Sir, we've heard that one before" he said, as he guided Eddie into a small side room. "Just wait in here. The police will be along shortly".

The Store Detective said to the doorman "Don't call the police until I've checked with the staff on Leather Goods" and he hurried off down the stairs to the Basement.

Eddie was in a panic but he quickly calmed down. It was only a few minutes since he'd bought the case: he'd paid for it: The Salesman was bound to recognise him but Eddie started to worry again as the minutes ticked by. "What a fucking disaster: if those bastards gang up and say I nicked it I'll never get a job!"

Eddie had a vague feeling that he'd been in the room before. There was a rocking horse near the window: it must be to keep the kids quiet while their mums are being questioned for nicking things he mused. As he stared at the rocking horse Father Christmas came to mind.

Eddie went into a reverie: he hadn't started school so it must have been before the war. He would have been four, getting on for five. His mother had left his two brothers at home with his grandmother and taken him on a tram to Manchester to see Father Christmas. He was standing in a queue. There were lots of mothers and crowds of children. They shuffled slowly towards Father Christmas's Grotto, down a narrow corridor shrouded with tinsel and illuminated with Christmas tree lights. There was a Rocking Horse at the entrance with a paper hat on its head and a notice round its neck saying "Buy a raffle ticket here". He wanted his mam to buy one but she wouldn't. "Raffles are a waste of money: nobody ever wins." He'd thrown a bit of a tantrum and started crying.

They reached an artificial patch of snow with a huge sledge with long, curved runners, standing on it. The sledge was piled high with sacks of parcels and presents. Six stuffed reindeer were harnessed to the sledge. Father Christmas sat in the sledge: a massively square looking figure dressed in a floppy red gown with white edging. On his head was what looked like a 'wee-willy-winky's red night-cap. It had a white bob dangling from the snood which rested on the back of the floppy red gown: white curls fringed Father Christmas's forehead. His enormous fluffy white beard left only two red blobs of cheek and two beady brown eyes visible. There was no mouth until he spoke. Eddie remembered being extremely frightened: he clung to his mother's leg.

"Don't be silly Eddie: tell Father Christmas what you want him to bring you". Eddie wanted to ask how he would manage to get down their little chimney and what the reindeer had for their Christmas dinner but he didn't say anything. "You want a train don't you?" his mother said. "No, I want a Rocking Horse." Eddie remembered. Eddie heard a gruff voice say: "I'll see what I can do on Christmas Day."

A finger and thumb emerged from Father Christmas's sleeve and pinched his cheek and shook it before Eddie could pull away. He remembered he'd let out a scream and tried to run away but one of the fairies, wearing a white tutu and red top and holding a wand with a star on the end, grabbed him and took him back to his mother. "Some of them get over excited, don't they" she said, as she gave his mother his present from Father Christmas: a few sweets and a Christmas cracker.

He didn't get a Rocking Horse that Christmas so he stopped believing in Father Christmas after that.

Eddie came 'back to earth', still staring at the rocking horse and saying to himself, "But why was my mam in this room, or one very much like it?"

It was a good twenty minutes before the Store Detective returned, accompanied by a Salesman who looked at Eddie before saying "Yes that's him. He left before I could give him his receipt".

Eddie was greatly relieved but puzzled. The Salesman looked very similar to the one who sold him the case but there was something different about him. Eddie wasn't going to argue about that though.

There was a brief conversation between the Salesman, the Detective and the Doorman. The Doorman turned to Eddie and said "I'm very sorry we had to detain you Sir but there was no security tape on your purchase so we were obliged to check it out". The Detective interjected, "Fortunately the Staff found your receipted Bill. It came up from Accounts after you had left. He handed the receipt to Eddie. "You are free to go now Sir," the Doorman said.

Eddie couldn't understand why it had taken so long to sort out if they had the receipt all along. The "Bastards must have just wanted to keep me stewing" he told his dad.

Eddie's mam was more disappointed than Eddie that he hadn't got a job. "You shouldn't have mentioned temporary, you don't know how long it will be before you get something better. Ring up and ask for an appointment for a full-time job, the woman was only the typist. You didn't give her your name. Put your suit on and a different tie, she won't recognise you. If she does, tell her you've changed your mind". Eddie didn't like the idea, especially after the suitcase incident. He didn't do immediately what his mam said but after a week of job rejections here and there, he rang up and got an appointment.

To his relief, Miss Keyboard didn't recognise him when he turned up at the Store the following week for his Interview with the Personnel Manager,

After some hesitation Eddie smoothed down his hair, knocked on the door and went into the Interview Room..

The Personnel Manager was clearly an ex-R.A.F. type. His blue pin-stripe suit well cut, his tight-knot tie, R.A.F. His impressive moustache, unlike the close clipped style of an ex-army officer, was bushy and curled upwards, either side. His voice more 'wizzard-prang'. He invited Eddie to 'take a perch'. Miss Keyboard took down Eddie's name, age and address. Flying Officer Kite looked approvingly at Eddie's school leaving certificate. Eddie was asked to "Tell me about yourself."

When Eddie said he'd worked in a grocer's shop as an errand boy and later served behind the counter this seemed to clinch matters. "Righty-oh, I can offer you a job as a probationary salesman. If you make a good show, keep on the straight and narrow and get along with the rest of the crew, in three months time, I'll recommend we make your appointment substantive. The Store opens at nine a.m. to customers and closes at six p.m. but your working hours are eight thirty a.m. to six fifteen p.m. with a fiteen minute break morning and afternoon and one hour for lunch, Monday to Saturday, with a half-day off on Wednesday afternoon when the store closes at one p.m. The pay as a junior trainee salesman is twent-five shillings, paid at the end of the week."

Eddie thought "Bloody Hell! The pay's as bad as the bloody Grocery and the hours longer, and then there are the fares!" But he'd had enough of the Grocer's so he'd no option but to accept.

"You can start next Monday. There'll be an induction talk by Sales and Security after which you will be assigned to a Department. Ta-Ta-for now. See you Monday, then".

Monday came. Eddie's mam had him up bright and early. He clocked in at eight thirty a.m. and went directly to the Personnel Office as instructed. He joined two other trainees on a conducted tour of the Store and Staff Canteen prior to induction talks by the Sales Manager and the Security Officer.

The Sales Manager, a short, self-important, pot bellied man in a dark suit with a waistcoat displaying a heavy gold watch-chain, spoke first, in a surprisingly loud authoritarian voice:

"You must address customers as Sir or Madam, and address staff as Mr or Miss, no Mrs. The Store does not employ married women. There are one or two war widows but you must address them as Miss not Mrs.

Eddie wanted to say "What's wrong with married women working?" His mam was married and she worked. Many married women on the Estate worked, they had to work, their husbands were out of a job. During the war most of them had worked. He didn't say anything: he hadn't the confidence.

"The Account's Department is in the sub-basement below the Basement. A Bill is made out for each sale and placed in a cash container flask. The flask is sent by either overhead wire or by suction tube to the Accounts Department: the staff will show you what to do. The receipted Bill and change if required, is despatched back to the Department to be handed to the customer with a "*thank you* Sir or Madam. If the Counting House is busy and the customer has to wait you must say how *very* sorry you are for keeping them waiting."

The Security Officer took over. He introduced himself and said in a loud and solemn voice "I have to tell you that these days there's a considerable amount of thieving in shops so I want to tell you what to look out for. Before I do I want to introduce the two Doormen who man the Staff entrance and three of the squad of Store Detectives.."

Eddie recognised one of The Detectives as the bloke who used to chase Twissy and him off the escalators and boot them out of the Pet's Corner for taunting the monkeys and perverting the parrot. He didn't recognise Eddie, or if he did he didn't let on, but Eddie caught him staring at him from time to time with a frown on his face and his eyes narrowed.

From what the Security Officer said you would have thought most of the customers were thieves. Perhaps most of them would be if they got half a chance to nick something, mused Eddie.

"When you're not serving a customer you must patrol your sales area. Watch out for people pilfering, people picking up and putting down goods, looking furtive, suddenly making off without buying. Watch unaccompanied school kids particularly: they think nicking things is a game".

Eddie knew all about that. His mind flipped back to his school days: the times he and his pals had competed to see who could nick the most toffees from the Sweets Counter in Woolworths or swipe an apple from one of the boxes outside the Greengrocer's shop. And then there was Mrs. Garner in the Grocery where he used to work, slipping tins of fruit and bars of soap into her carrier bag.

"Look-out for anyone wearing a baggy rain-coat, especially on a dry day: it'll probably have pockets inside the lining".

"Women thieves often work in twos or threes to give each other cover. They walk about with several items pretending to show them to their friends. They talk about the clothes: skirts, jumpers, underwear: hold them up whilst looking in mirrors. Before they return items to where they got them one item at least will have been passed on to a friend who secretes it in her bag. The friend then goes off to the toilets where she cuts off the price tag, puts the jumper or whatever, on under her own and leaves the Store as innocent as the day she was born: Cheeky eh!"

"The more audacious lone thieves wear slacks or trousers with elastic waist bands. They tuck things down the front of their trousers, or in their knickers, or low down behind the middle of their backs where we're not allowed to touch should we frisk them".

"Experienced thieves can spot a store detective a mile off but they get blasé if they think there are none about. A common trick is to tuck stolen items under their armpits, inside their coats, gripping them so as to leave their hands free. Then they pick up some cheap item, which they pay for at the till, and then leave the Store amongst all the other customers".

"I can't stress strongly enough that staff must keep a sharp eye out for thieves and point out suspicious customers to the floor Detective: so get to know the Store Detectives!"

"When you sell something, be sure it's wrapped in the Store's brown paper or put inside one of the Store's bags. If it's a large, unwrapped item, for example a suitcase, you must tie a distinctive piece of coloured tape on to it to signal to the Store Detective and the Doorman that it's been paid for". Eddie didn't say he already knew about that.

"Are there any questions?"

No one asked any.

After he'd gone one of the two trainees said to Eddie "Bloody Hell, you'd think we were joining the fucking police force. The other one said: "Yeah, a couple of women in our street got done for shop-lifting. They were down on their uppers, husbands unemployed.

They got done for pinching food. If I saw someone pinching food I think I'd look the other way".

Eddie was surprised to hear them talking like that: he'd wrongly written them off as a couple of 'nowt a pounds'. He'd recently joined the Labour League of Youth and then the Socialist Outlook Trotskyite group. He sold *The Socialist Worker:* they might be up for buying the paper, he thought.

"Me too" said Eddie. "Every time you buy something the fucking Capitalists are stealing off *you*. Store Detectives and 'the fuzz' are paid to stop you pinching it back: that's the way the system works!"

Eddie was allocated to the Basement: 'Travel and Leather Goods' of all places. The Sales Manager took him to be introduced to the Salesmen. On his way down to the Department Eddie wondered why there had been no mention of theft by staff, but thinking about it, why would the Security Officer want to tell you how staff might go about pinching things?

There were three seedy looking Salesmen, deep in conversation in Travel and Leather Goods. They didn't notice the Sales Manager and Eddie arrive. The Manager coughed. The three men turned and lined up in a row as though on parade. Eddie could hardly keep his face straight when the Sales Manager announced their names. "Mr. Black, Mr. Brown and Mr. Grey", he said, but he didn't indicate which was which. "The bastard's having me on" Eddie thought but he wasn't.

Although Eddie held out his hand, none of the three made a move to shake it so he raised it and scratched his head to hide his embarrassment. "These gentlemen will take you under their wing and tell you what's what" he said, and left without having told them Eddie's name. Eddie was tempted to say: "I'm Mr.Green, as in novice", but held back. He couldn't bring himself to say Mister, despite what he'd been told about colleagues using formal modes of address when speaking to each other, or tell them his surname. "Just call me Eddie" he said.

With the Sales Manager out of sight the three men gathered round and said their names as they shook his hand. Easy to remember

Eddie thought: how wrong he was! Eddie didn't clock that Mr Black had brown hair, Mr. Grey had black hair and Mr Brown had grey hair. Their suits were very similar: Demob suits: off the peg, badly fitting, single breasted, without turn-ups and made of poor quality cloth: herringbone pattern, brown, grey, black but not matching name nor hair colour.

A bloke from another Department who knew them told Eddie later, "They come from Salford." Salford was notorious for smog, pollution and bronchitis with the lowest life expectancy in the country. "When conscripted into the army in the early 1940's none of them passed 'A1' but the army needed men: so the three of them ended up as clerks in the Royal Army Pay Corps. They became mates, watched each other's backs and stuck together after the war".

Eddie tried to avoid gaffes by not using names: when he did he never managed to get them right. They were each about the same height. They had the same smoker's grey-faced unhealthy complexion. Each had a thin Clark Gable moustache on the upper lip. All three had weak eyes and wore identical round, steel-rimed N.H.S. glasses which helped their eyesight but made the three of them look similarly Japanese.

Through working together during the war and now in the Store, they'd copied each other's speech patterns and talked with similar, quiet, Mancunian voices, each out of the side of his mouth. They used dated catch phrases from the radio: 'I don't mind if I do' and the more current 'I thought, right monkey' when telling each other how they'd got one up on an awkward customer.

They had a repertoire of similar physical mannerisms such as dragging a hand over face to change smile to misery and for some unfathomable reason, which Eddie never got to the bottom of, they called each other Uncle.

They had the irritating habit of crunching knuckles together and cracking their finger joints. After Eddie got used to their hackneyed clichés and mannerisms he found the three of them even more boring than their nondescript names and colourless appearances. They had no conversation other than cricket and football, read only newspapers, never books. Not one of them showed the slightest interest in Eddie or anyone else as far as he could make out. None of them recognized him from the suitcase incident and though he knew one of them must have been involved, they were so alike he couldn't be sure which and he certainly wasn't going to ask them. Eddie made his dad laugh out loud when he got home the first day and said "If a kangaroo or a giraffe had turned up as a trainee they probably wouldn't have taken any notice of it or even thought to ask it a question!"

The Basement was open-plan and housed the customer's Café which took up approximately a quarter of the space. The rest of the floor was the Travel and The Leather Goods Department, Menswear, Electrical Goods and Kitchenware. Leather Goods departmental space backed onto the Customer's Café area. The front of Leather Goods displayed a variety of cabin trunks and a tiered display of travel cases ranging from posh Antler Brand leather sets with name labels, to cheaper 'His and Hers' matching sets of cases in a variety of muted colours. Behind and above these items different sized, single travel cases and on the sides of the Departmental area were tiered displays of suitcases, attaché-cases, briefcases and a range of varied quality school satchels and miscellaneous leather goods: comb cases, wallets, wash-bags, leather belts and ladies' leather handbags. At the side of the Sales Counter there was a tall open cupboard housing the tube for despatching and receiving the Counting-House flasks. Behind the counter and the tube was a small, private, encapsulated space with a single folding chair and a cupboard for staff to put personal belongings. In slack periods during the week the three Salesmen took it in turns to slip in there to take the weight off their feet.

The Basement was over-heated and airless: cosy and warm if you were there for a coffee but stuffy, enervating and soporific if you had to work there all day. There was a Juke Box in the café area playing pop music, above the clatter of crockery and the crying and shrieks of children: loud, clear and annoying. The same records repeatedly played in sequence throughout the day. Once round it was tolerable, but torture to listen to all day, every day: the same daft tunes with even dafter lyrics round and round. By the end of the first week they were indelibly etched in Eddie's own personalised, interior Juke Box. He couldn't get the bloody things out of his head: "Put another Nickel in, in the Nickleodeon", "Now is the Hour" with Gracie Fields; and Alan Breeze, of "The Billy Cotton Band

Show," fame singing: "Sparrow in the Tree Top". The first time Edward Lisbona, a Jewish singer with Portuguese antecedents, sang: "It's my mother's birthday today" Eddie's mind went back to childhood. The Lisbona family lived in Prestwich: close to a cluster of Portuguese Jewish families living in the Sedgely Park area. Eddie's mam used to work for some of them.

Eddie tried to engage one of the Clones: "My mam used to house-clean for Edward Lisbona's mother and light her and other Jewish peoples' fires on Saturday mornings in winter. She used to take me with her before I started school. I played in the garden while she worked. Edward Lisbona was also known as Eddie 'Piano' Miller. He's played and sang with Glen Miller and Duke Ellington!"

Eddie got absolutely no reaction to what he thought was highly interesting information. "He just glazed over like a zombie. I suppose I must bore them as much as they bore me," he told his mam when he got home that night.

Eddie never felt he belonged in Leather Goods despite being initiated into their ritualistic routines. Every morning the Clones arrived at work, each with a different newspaper, *The Daily Express*, the *Daily Mail*, and the *Daily Telegraph*. They took it in turns to disappear to the staff toilets on the top floor where they could read each other's papers and have a fag. They read the same news over again in each other's paper just to add to their boring day. Why they did this was a mystery to Eddie.

"I suppose it makes a change from the infuriating music and the mind-numbing tedium of watching the clock tick round to six o'clock in the basement" Eddie told his dad. "None of them want to borrow my *Daily Worker* or buy the *Socialist Outlook* I try to sell them. They're so shit-scared of Management they wouldn't be seen even with the *Daily Mirror*. But as I only read my one newspaper and didn't want to read their rubbish in the toilets of all places, they let me extend the morning and afternoon tea breaks from the official fifteen minutes to half an hour. How about that!"

One morning, prowling round the perimeter of Leather Goods, observing shoppers: pretending to be on the look-out for thieves but in reality relieving his boredom by creating imaginative biographies for customers, Eddie recognised a couple of lads. They were members of the street-lamp gang on the estate where he lived. They were leaving Menswear and heading towards the Gents toilets. Eddie spotted them again when returning from his tea break. They were strolling nonchalantly towards the exit, their open-neck shirts replaced by new ones and sporting flashy ties. One of them, the short one, who looked like a movie gangster, was now wearing a Trilby hat. His trousers were hoisted high to show off his yellow socks. Yellow socks and Trilby hats were currently all the rage with teenagers.

There was no doubt in Eddie's mind the two of them had nicked the shirts and ties they were now wearing but there was no way he was going to shop them: he was too scared of the consequences. He been at school with them and he knew what they were like. They were not mates of his. They were out of work, in a gang and they knew where he lived. There'd be windows smashed, he'd be beaten up. "No, sorry, it's a blind eye to this one" he said to himself. Apart from this sighting Eddie never did spot a customer stealing anything.

On Saturdays, when there were a lot more customers the routine newspaper reading was suspended and the breaks curtailed. The Counting House below ground was frequently inundated with cash container-flasks. Customers were often kept waiting for receipts and change. If only small change was due some customers didn't bother to wait for it. On some occasions, when all the cash-flasks were in use and customers had the correct money, the Clones attached a paid-for tape to the purchase and the customers went happily on their way without a receipt like he had done once.

On Eddie's first Saturday he noticed that sometimes, when a customer had left, the Clones would put the Bill and money on one side, presumably to be sent down in a slack period. When later he asked should he put the Bill and money in a flask and send it down one of the Clones said: "No leave it for now". Eddie asked again in the next slack period. Mr. Black or perhaps it was Mr. Brown, sidled over to him, took his arm and guided him into the secluded area behind the desk and said through the side of his mouth:

"How much a week are they paying you trainees these days, if you don't mind me asking?"

"Not much, they pay me twenty-five bob, but I'll get a review in three months, if I'm still here".

"Bloody hell, it must cost you more than that in bus fares and dinners!"

"Not quite but there's not a lot left after I've paid my expenses" Eddie said.

"That's bloody terrible: the mean buggers! You know, some Stores pay more than that, *and* give trainees free meals and travel expenses. I'll have a word with the Uncles and see if we can help you out a bit". Eddie didn't cotton on immediately. There were customers to serve.

In the next slack period Mr. Clone sidled over again. "I've had a word with the Uncles and we think you ought to be paid more, in point of fact we think we should all be paid more, and expenses for fares and travelling time, but there's no chance they'll do that".

"Can't you get the Union on to it?" Eddie said.

"Union, there's no Union here".

"Oh" Eddie said, "can't we organise one?"

He laughed. "You'd get the sack immediately if you mentioned Union to Management. You'd never get anyone to join anyway: it's every man for himself here."

"When we get the right money we sometimes keep it back to redress matters. Everyone does it: the supervisors know it goes on. They turn a blind eye. They like to think it gives them power over us. They've always got a reason if they want to sack you. So if we did help you out you mustn't mention it to anybody: what do you think?"

Eddie was a bit perplexed by this proposition and didn't at the time fully realise its implications. He looked around furtively for eavesdroppers, lowered his voice and said: "It sounds alright to me: it's very generous of you".

But later, when he reflected on what they were doing, he was less happy about it. He lay awake at night thinking about what would happen if they got caught. A folk song his grandma used to sing to him when he sat on her knee as a child somehow kept coming back to him from the depths of memory. It was as though she was singing it to him as a warning from up there on the astral plain that he knew in his rational moments didn't exist:

"Johnny used to grind the coffee mill
Mix the sugar with the sand
After his work was done
Drinks all round he'd stand
But he grinds a different mill just now
Breaks a lot of stone
All through the poor boy mixing
His master's money with his own".

Eddie convinced himself they were bound to get caught out when stocktaking was done. When he asked the Clone about this he said: "We're only taking what they should be paying us and we don't overdo it: the cost of losses is built into prices, and anyway, we do the ordering and stocktaking ourselves: the system's chaotic, there's no way they could prove anything". "Yes", Eddie thought "'stock taking' is precisely what they *are* doing and I wish I wasn't part of it".

Eddie knew they were all being exploited. He'd had the nature of Capitalism dinned in his ears from his dad's 'soap box' since childhood and had first-hand experience of exploitation in the bakehouse of the Grocer's and Confectioner's shop but despite this he'd been brainwashed so thoroughly by convention he couldn't separate stealing from stealing to put right an injustice. Eddie imagined himself in Court, charged with theft. "We were simply redressing the ills of Capitalism me lud." He'd be laughed out of Court, imprisoned, sacked. With a criminal record he'd never get another job let alone get in to the printing industry which he'd recently decided to try for.

The more he thought about it the more worried he became. He lay in bed thinking about what the *Socialist Outlook* group that he met up with on Sunday mornings in the Thatched House pub, would say if he ended up in jail for theft.

He'd listened to Harry Rattner, the Salford Jeweller and Jim Allen, the Socialist writer, denouncing the type of individualist actions the three Clones were up to as futile left-infantilism. He knew he ought to radicalise them into Unionising: get the whole staff to act collectively for better pay and conditions. But he also knew he had as much chance of getting Messrs Black, Brown and Grey to turn Red as persuading 'the three bears' to stop eating porridge. Then he thought, perhaps if they did get caught and were out of work they might start to think and develop class consciousness so he wasn't going to shop them, it would be 'class betrayal'. But by taking the money he'd be shunned by his Socialist friends for giving the mainstream Labour Party another excuse to accuse a Socialist Worker supporter of being a Trotskyite 'entryist' betraying the collective struggle by encouraging individual criminal subversion!

Towards closing time Eddie saw one of the Store Detectives walking towards the Leather Goods Department in a purposeful way. It was the one who used to chase him and Twissy. He nearly shat himself: "he's remembered me, the bastard's coming to get me!"

Eddie immediately left the counter and slipped round the side of the stock stack and peeped from behind a pile of cases. The Dick said something to one of the Clones. Eddie heard them laugh and go into the closet behind the counter. He could hear them talking but he couldn't make out what they were saying. He looked again and saw one of the other two Clones put a white envelope on the corner of the sales counter. As the Dick and the Clone emerged from the closet Eddie saw the Detective scoop up the envelope and slip it into his pocket.

"Bloody hell: that's why they aren't bothered. That time when I got stopped they must have made out a new Bill, and got a receipt to 'cover up'. Well bugger me: the Dicks are in on it too!"

*

Personnel had a policy of shifting trainees around the Store and one Monday morning, to his relief, Eddie found himself on the ground floor, alongside three young Salesgirls, selling bulbs for autumn planting. The girls introduced themselves. The first one said "Hello, I'm June." Eddie thought: "Oh for Christ sake no! Don't let the other two be April and May!" "And this is Penny." He resisted the temptation to say 'for my thoughts'. But his propensity for punning overcame him when the third one said "And I'm Monica". "Ha Ha Monica" Eddie said. Monica feigned a laugh and said "Very funny, but I've had that one played on me before." Nice one Monica, Eddie thought. "I'm relieved I don't have to call you something like: Tulip, Lily or Hyacinth". Monica groaned, the other two girls giggled. Eddie was even more relieved. They had honesty written on their faces: there'd be no fiddling here.

The atmosphere on the ground floor was a big improvement on the Basement. Despite the 'double-door-trap', separating the outside world from inside. It was nowhere near as stuffy as the Basement: a breath of fresh air came in with the customers. The windows on the frontage of the Store let in daylight and you knew what the weather was like outside despite tall buildings blocking out the sun.

The bulb section had advertising stands round it featuring tulip fields in Holland, typically English bluebell woods, banks of primroses and roadsides fringed with daffodils. In slack moments Eddie took in the smell and feel of the bulbs. He even imagined, when he shut his eyes, he was in the woods and fields depicted on the Stands.

The three girls were a welcome change from the three shades of misery lurking in the Basement below. They were not especially beautiful girls, like those on the Cosmetics counter, but pretty enough and one of them, you would have said, was quite good looking. They wore the Store's uniform grey skirts but their jumpers were their own: bright reds, blues and yellow primaries, a welcome change from the sombre clothes of the Clones. They smelt of perfume instead of tobacco and despite the tedious work and poor pay they were cheerful enough. They'd no need to constantly disappear to the lavatory for a pee and a fag, or to read a newspaper to relieve the boredom. They spent slack times gossiping, whilst Eddie entertained himself eavesdropping on their conversations.

Their talk went endlessly on about boyfriends, clothes, scent smells, jewellery, lipstick colours, pop songs and the sexual exploits and infidelities of their friends in other Departments. Eddie had been reading Alexander Pope in the lunch hour: Pope was spot on when he wrote ". . . with every word a reputation dies". Eddie thought to himself, "Christ, I mustn't tell them anything about me, it would be all over the Store in ten minutes. But by the end of the first day he'd been quizzed by one or another of them so much that between them they knew as much about him as he knew about himself, and probably a bit more.

After Eddie'd been on Bulbs a day or two the Juke Box music going round in his head, stopped: the fuse must have blown. The boredom persisted but was not as relentless. He was still tired out as ever when six o'clock slowly came round. He still went to sleep on the bus home. Often he ended up at the terminus and sometimes even went to sleep on the way back: he was like a tennis ball going back and forth over the net at Wimbledon. But the fear of being caught with his hand in the metaphorical till and labelled a thief receded and he started to have a good night's sleep.

They were quite busy on Bulbs throughout the week but when Saturday came life was hectic. They were all so busy punching their fists into brown paper bags and counting out bulbs: putting tulips, snowdrops, anemones, daffodils and hyacinths into separate bags, billing, despatching cash down the tube, giving change and politely bidding goodbye to Sir or Madam, they hardly had time to go for a pee or a quick swig of tea. Things slackened off just before closing time.

Two of the girls were chatting and giggling and discussing what they were up to at the weekend, the other one had disappeared, presumably to the loo. They were at the end of the counter but Eddie as usual was eavesdropping.

The chat was mainly about where they should go dancing at the weekend: Mecca or Bellevue, and what they should wear. Eddie learned that both of them had boyfriends doing National Service.

"I'm going to write him a 'dear John' letter. He won't like it but I've gone off him. I'm going to tell him I've met someone else and I can't wait 18 months till he gets back from Burma".

"I don't blame you: I'd do the same if Jack got an overseas posting".

"Shirley in Perfume and Jewellery, you know, the one that gives us the scent sample-bottles she nicks, was stupid to get married: she's only nineteen. Hey don't tell anyone she's married: she'd get the sack if they find out. Her bloke's signed up for three years. She's desperate to get 'a bit on the side' but all the lads are in the army. I told her we'd look out for someone."

The conversation shifted from 'boyfriend talk' to work.

"It was bloody murder this afternoon. I'm whacked out. I haven't even had a cup of tea since lunch time. I've never known it so busy. I don't know where they all get their money from. They must have damned sight better jobs than we've got".

"No, I don't know how I'd manage if . . . you know . . . Christ, she's a long time, I hope to God everything's O.K."

There had been delays to the return of cash-container flasks from the Cashier's Department. Eddie had left a couple of correct money Bills and the money, on the shelf near his place on the counter. When things quietened down he flasked them up and sent them down the tube to the Counting House. He noticed that one of the girls, who'd again begun talking and giggling, was clocking what he was doing but she didn't make any comment and she turned her attention to the returning Salesgirl.

"We were frightened you'd got lost or something Penny".

" No, I was on the way back and I thought we ought to get 'you know who' on board so I went back to re-do the 'you know what'." and she slipped something into each of their hands.

As Eddie was about to leave to go home June sidled up to him and slipped a few silver coins into his hand saying "that's your share: we keep a bit back for meals and bus fares. Don't let on to anybody. See you on Monday. I'll introduce you to Shirley. She works in Perfume and Jewellery. She's a friend of mine and she said she's dying to meet you" and off she toddled.

Eddie stood, gob-smacked, staring at his hand, thinking to himself: "Well bugger me: this lot are at it too, but Shirley, what's Shirley got to do with it?" Then it dawned on him, the crafty blighters were offering him Shirley to keep his mouth shut!

Eddie was looking forward to meeting Shirley despite the fact he now knew she was married and 'lifting' perfume, the odd piece of jewellery and who knows what else. But if Shirley was that upmarket, classy looking, curvaceous brunette he'd been eyeing up in the canteen he couldn't see her being interested in a sixteen year old inexperienced oik like himself. As it turned out he didn't ever get to find out, or to meet her in the flesh.

Eddie dozed off on the bus on the way home and fantasized about having a torrid encounter with Shirley and he dreamed about her in bed over the weekend but he never actually got to meet her. She was away on holiday the following week, spending her pickings no doubt.

At home a letter had arrived for him to go for an interview at a printing firm. Eddie took a morning off, sick. The firm offered an apprenticeship and wanted him to start the following week. Eddie jumped at the chance.

The Store was not happy about Eddie leaving but after a bit of arguing waived his notice. As Eddie shook hands in farewell with the three girls in Gardening he put an envelope, with the money they'd given him over the couple of weeks he'd been with them, in the hand of the last one saying: "a leaving present for the three of you" and before they could say anything he was on the escalator and away.

*

A couple of years later Eddie was called up to do National Service. He needed to buy a small travel case to carry personal belongings in so he went to the Store to buy one. He was curious to see if anyone he knew was still there. He purposely walked past Perfume and Jewellery but there was no sign of anyone resembling the Shirley he had kept in my mind's eye. Gardening had been relocated to the first floor and Ladies' Accessories had expanded into its space. He went up on the escalator hoping to see the three girls he used to work with but there was no sign of them. He thought "Perhaps they've been caught nicking money and sacked, jailed, or maybe got married and been forced to leave or perhaps just got pissed off and left for better pay and prospects elsewhere. Who knows?

He took the lift down to the basement. The Café had gone but Leather Goods was still there. Eddie was a bit surprised to see two of the three Clones, hands behind backs, heads bent forward, separately pacing feebly round the perimeter like neurotic zoological animals. They were both in the same suits as when he'd last seen them but with now 'fashionable' leather patches on the elbows concealing wear and tear. He found the case he was looking for and took it to the counter. He didn't let on to the Clones that he used to work with them: neither showed a flicker of recognition.

Eddie had planned in advance to have plenty of change and to give the correct money to Mr. Black/Brown/Grey to see if they were still on the fiddle.

Eddie bought the case, picked it up and without waiting for a receipt walked quickly off towards the lifts. As he did so he passed the third Clone returning from his break. Eddie wanted to have a closer look at him and at see what was going on so he turned and walked back as though to take the escalator. The returnee, Mr. Grey Brown Black took a newspaper from inside his jacket, swopped it with the Clone who had just served him who, in turn, tucked it into his jacket without exchanging a word. Eddie saw the Clone who had served him scoop the money he'd just paid for the case off the counter and into his pocket and make his way, ahead of Eddie, towards the escalator. As Eddie overtook him he glanced at Eddie and Eddie thought he saw his expression change to a flicker of perplexed half-recognition. Eddie kept walking but stopped at the foot of the escalator to let the Clone again overtake him. As he stepped onto it Eddie said in the Clone's ear, for devilment: "Have a *very* good lunch" and without glancing back Eddie quickly headed for the lift and up to the ground floor.

As Eddie made his way towards the Store exit he mused about the Clones being 'still at it': *plus ca change plus c'est la meme chose* he thought to himself.

The moment Eddie stepped outside a hand gripped his shoulder and a voice said: "I'm sorry to trouble you Sir: just a routine check. Did you purchase that case from the Store?"

Yes, I did".

"Would you mind showing me your receipt?"

"I didn't wait for one."

"Oh shit!" he said out loud, as he realised he hadn't got a tape on the case!"

The doorman escorted Eddie into the side room where the Rocking Horse stood.

"Would you please wait in here: the police will be along shortly".

ON THE BUSES

There was a big queue when I got to the bus that first Monday morning, but a quick calculation relieved any anxiety about my getting a seat downstairs. They were mostly men, smokers who'd be going upstairs. It was my first day on this route. With a bit of luck it would get me to Manchester for a connection to Salford in time to clock in at 8.0 a.m.

I was in good spirits. I'd recently married and moved into a cramped self contained flat, the top half of a 1930's 'semi'. Our old gaff was on a busy, well served route convenient for getting to Salford where I worked at the Palatine Press as a Compositor. The flat was on the edge of a housing estate six miles from Salford served by an infrequent bus. I could afford the increase in bus fare but we'd be struggling a bit with the rent. This was the 1950s. The chance of a proper self contained flat for newly-weds far outweighed having to penny pinch to pay the rent.

I was unaware of the territorial seating arrangement of the regulars and I was equally unaware of the traffic delays on the new route. I stood in the aisle of a badly sprung spine-jarring bus for the whole forty minute journey. Young males will know what a priapic-inducing experience it is to be standing with ones genitalia in close proximity to a female face on a juddering, stopping and starting, slow moving bus.

I got a seat and then gave it up to a bloke in a suit who wasn't much older than me. He claimed it was his seat and that he always sat next to Miss Somebody. Bloody cheek! By the time I'd got up and looked around all the other lower deck seats had been taken or were being reserved. I saw no sympathetic looks, only a sense of hostility on the faces of the other passengers. I had no option other than to stand or go upstairs.

There were seats on the upper deck but within a few seconds the dense fug of smoke up there was making me choke. It made me wish my dad's gas-mask shoulder bag, in which I used to carry my lunch-time butties, still had a gas-mask in it. After a few bars of the bronchial coughing coffin-chorus, I went back downstairs to stand in the smokeless but stale-smelling air of the lower deck, hoping for a seat later. No chance, they were all going to the terminus in town, same as me.

The bus arrived late: I missed the connection to Salford and was quarter-houred.

Second day: I got to the bus stop early. Bugger me, despite being early all the seats inside were again taken. What's going on? Exactly the same people sat in exactly the same seats as before, grim faced and menacing like a collection of cloned Spanish bulls eyeing up a matador invading their corrida. I stood again with my genitalia in the same proximity to the same blonde sexy 'Jane of the Daily Mirror' look-alike for the full forty minute journey. I had a newspaper with me but it was impossible to read it whilst holding on to the dangling strap and arching my chest forward and my bum back to avoid poking sexy 'Jane' in the ear. I spent the journey musing about the lives and work of my fellow passengers.

Apart from a few unmarried office girls, they were all men, a bunch of look-alike, Liberal or Tory young old fogies. All dressed in Co-op or Burton's ready-made, off the peg, blue pinstripe or plain dark grey suits with white shirts and sober, tight-knotted ties. All aping their bosses, aspirant and ready for work in the quiet, competitive jungle of the back scratching, arse licking, white collar world. All bound for Manchester's Victoria bus station and on to the Bank, the Town Hall, The Refuge, or the Co-op Insurance Office to be chained to a desk for eight and a half hours and having to put their hands up when they wanted to go to the lav. "Yes Mr. Peabody, I'll be back in a jiffy" The young 'unmarried' office girls, probably working in Banks or Insurance offices, looked subdued: cowed by their underpaid subservience to a bullying boss. Doubtless they were living in fear of losing their job and returning to poverty and domestic drudgery, if their 'guilty-secret' marriage was discovered: the pre-war 'no married women' rule still operated. Then there were the shop girls and male floor walkers, working at Lewis's, Afflecks or Kendals, who would be given Wednesday afternoon off in exchange for working all day Saturday, with no extra pay. Bored out of their minds, occasionally dreaming of a Sale that would make them Commission or a Christmas bonus, they would be spending the day urging on the clock to 6.0 p.m.

The bus was again delayed by traffic: quarter-houred again!

Day three: determined not to stand, I got to the bus stop so early I was first in the queue. I was dressed as usual in my army surplus battle dress tunic and an open neck shirt advertising my working class status. Like my dad I was a bit of an upside downer, wanting to beat 'them' rather than join them. I'd been in the Labour League of Youth before National Service and I was still a Labour Party member but a Marxist of sorts and sympathetic to the Trotskyite International Socialists. I was first on the bus.

I walked slowly along the lower deck aisle to the front seat I'd been pressured to relinquish on Day One. As I did so, I put a copy of the *Socialist Outlook* on every pair of seats. Miss Somebody was close behind me and I let her sit near the window but refused to budge when Mr. R. Sole came to claim his place. Rather than stand he quickly sat on a seat a couple of rows behind, creating a domino effect and disrupting more and more passengers as they arrived to claim their usual seats. Chaos resulted as they played a variation of 'musical chairs' with each other, feigning politeness but refusing to pass the parcel. As more and more passengers arrived and seating options diminished, arguments broke out between those fearful of not getting a seat and prepared to take any vacant one and those already seated and wanting to save the seat beside them for their usual neighbour. Rows broke out, eventually voices raised, even scuffles occurred as people were forced into giving up a saved seat. The rumpus only ended when the bus conductor turned up and sorted matters out saying: "There are no reserved seats! Sit down where you are, it's first come first served". Grudgingly they all obeyed. Instead of their familiar conversation they had the *Socialist Outlook*.

Each day, after that, the Clones arrived earlier and earlier so as to get their favoured seat. It took two weeks and two more issues of the *Socialist Outlook* before things got sorted out. Mr. R. Sole, who was often late, finally capitulated and surrendered the charms of Miss Somebody to me, and committed slow suicide by going upstairs to choke in the smoke.

Despite my little victory over R. Sole, the bus journey to work was still a problem. There was no earlier bus and the 7.0 a.m. was frequently late because of traffic snarl-ups on the approach road to

Manchester. I could just about cope with the increased fare but the expense of time docked for being late for work was damaging our finances. I thought of moving back to where we used to live. By the end of the third week it was obvious something would have to change. But then I found a solution.

The Palatine Press where I worked was in James Street in the heart of the slums of Salford. I could jump off the bus at the lights on the corner of Chapel Street, run down Blackfriars Street, and catch a number 12 to work, rather than spend six or seven minutes getting in and out of the terminus. I'd been late and quarter-houred twice already in Week Three. The bus was late yet again. I couldn't afford more pay loss so I jumped off and ran down Blackfriars Street and round to Bridge Street. As I ran I saw a number 12 leaving but in my haste I tripped on a raised paving stone. I fell arse over tit on the wet flags. I tried to save myself but my shoe-sole ripped back. Oh Shit! I shouted as I went down hard on my hands and my right knee. The gas mask bag flipped over my head and clouted one of my outstretched hands. The bottle of milk had smashed but I didn't register this at the time. I was outside the Telephone Exchange and telephone girls going in to work shrieked and scattered. One girl bent to see if I was alright but I was up before she could say anything. As I limped to the bus stop I wiped my swollen hands down my coat to get rid of the blood seeping through the mud stains. The milk was dripping down my back. I could hear my shoe sole clip clopping like a lame horse. My knee hurt and my leg felt cold and began to sting. Just then another number 12 came round the corner and I speeded up behind three other 'last minuters' running for the bus.

I managed to grab the hand-rail with my right hand and got a foothold on the platform with my right foot which left me unstable. The bus jerked into motion and rapidly accelerated. It swung me back and round against the back-side of the bus but I hung on to the rail and righted myself. The inside of the bus was full and the aisle and platform packed. The bus didn't stop at the first two stops on Chapel Street but someone rang the bell for James Street.

Two late women who worked in the Bindery won the race to the Palatine and beat me to the clock. As I put my card in the minute hand clicked off three minutes past 8.0 a.m. and clicked on to four minutes past with a ping. After all that turmoil I was quarter-houred again!

I didn't go in to work immediately: I was buggered if I'd go in to work the ten minutes for nothing. I sat on the steps reflecting.

I concluded I was living too far from work and that the 7.0 o'clock bus was no good for someone like me, someone who had to clock in at 8 o'clock. It was all very well for the 8.30 a.m. office and shop workers who didn't have to race in to beat the clock but not for the clock-governed likes of me. There was nothing I could do about it this side of The Revolution. It was no use fantasising about worker solidarity and about organising that bunch of falsely class conscious creeps on the bus for a better service. It would take at least two years exposure to the *Socialist Outlook* to shift the politics of that bunch of crypto-fascist fogies and they'd only had a couple of editions. I imagined *them* on strike, the headlines: "Sit in on Bus! Intruders Out! Preserve our Seats!" I was going crazy! All the anxiety of the journey, all that scrimping and penny pinching! Right that's it. Foolish move – We're moving back! "I'll be quids in!" I shouted to no one in particular. We'd swopped two spacious rooms with shared facilities for a pokey little flat, which we couldn't really afford, to get a kitchen in which you couldn't swing a mouse round never mind a cat. I'd lost pay and I'd lost hours a week of my free time to nerve jangling travel. I was getting aggravation at home for us being stuck with a lousy bus service miles from shops and family and friends. What had I gained? One up on Mr. R. Sole and a lesson on the sociology of bus travel. Big Deal!

The following week I was back on the convenient old bus route – Phew, what a relief! I'd moved back, with my long-suffering wife, to the two rooms we'd had before: they'd been redecorated by the landlord and carpeted in red - just my colour! But bugger me, the bastard had put the rent up.

TERRY THE PRINTER'S DEVIL

When Terry, the new apprentice, joined us at The Palatine Press or Pantomime Press as we called it, he didn't know his arse from his elbow. He was, as usual, the butt of ribbing and practical jokes: the standard workshop stuff: "go and ask Stores for a Long Stand" only to be kept waiting for half an hour. He didn't complain at this kind of 'leg pull' but got close to it when we played 'tossing the quoin' on him.

Quoins were wooden wedges used to lock up type into steel-frame chases. Tossing the quoin was a favourite traditional trick. You bent your head back and tossed a quoin off your forehead into a funnel stuffed down the front of your pants. We demonstrated and Terry agreed to have a go. When Terry's head was tipped back Alf Owens poured a jug of cold water into the funnel. Terry shrieked and swore, ripped the funnel out of his pants and flung it after Alf as Alf scarpered down the Comp Room. Loud whoops, cheers and clanging rang out as the Comps banged their mallets against their metal galleys. Terry looked pretty 'pissed off' as he stood in the spreading puddle round his feet but he didn't complain. Surprisingly he revealed a hitherto unsuspected vocabulary of sexual and scatological obscenities that would certainly have made the vicar blush. He'd passed the test but we hadn't realised what a quick learner he was. Within a couple of weeks he was getting his own back.

Terry quickly learned and played all the typical apprentice's pranks such as changing font labels on type cases so that the Comps would incorporate wrong fonts into texts. He was caught swapping boxes of p's with q's in type cases and turning lines of type upside down in type forms going to press for proofing, but he soon became more innovative and ambitious.

Terry got to work early one morning and filled a number of cardboard boxes with the confetti-like paper perforations from the spools produced by the Monotype keyboard machine. He balanced them on the cisterns in the toilet cabins.and attached strings from the chains to the boxes so that the contents would tip over unwary chain pullers. Unfortunately for Terry his first and last victim of this prank was the Deputy Overseer, Joe Butterworth, who habitually went to lav to read his newspaper after he'd doled out the Comps their work. He pulled the rigged chain and came storming out looking like a newly wed shouting: "Where is he? I'll kill the bloody little devil!"

Terry went into hiding in the space between the type-cases mounted on the composing frames. The Comps kept their chuckling heads down. After a day or two in the 'dog house' Terry resumed his tricks.

Terry hid behind the partition wall of the type-casting machine-room. As soon as George Malone wound the metal pot home and started the Caster, Terry scraped a piece of metal along a Galley to make it squeak in time with the rhythm of the machine: eek eek eek eek eek. George grabbed his oil can and went through the routine of oiling the moving parts. Terry waited a few minutes and then started the squeaks again. This routine went on for most of a morning. Eventually George stopped the Caster and began to strip down the cam shaft. Even Joe Butterworth had a laugh about it.

*

The bell rang for the ten o'clock tea break. Terry went to collect the tray of tea and toast. I collected two folding tables from the store-room and put eight tubular steel chairs round them. Terry distributed the *Daily Mail*, the *Mirror* and the *Daily Herald* and the packets of fags he'd been out to the corner shop to buy. Dave Canavan had been working as usual on the daily Bet on the Nags. He was in a grumpy mood: he couldn't decide which horse to go for and it was needling him. It was the wrong day to play a joke on Dave but an almost ready-made prank had suggested itself to Terry whilst he'd been reading the newspapers in the 'bogs'. He couldn't wait to tell me. It was a winner. I agreed to help.

Terry had spotted a report in the *Daily Mirror* about a couple of women working at Gallagher's cigarette factory being convicted for stealing cigarettes. They'd been caught stuffing cig packets with toilet paper instead of cigarettes and selling the cigs loose in the local pubs.

As he sent each of the women down for three months the Judge pontificated about it being an utterly foolish thing they had done as the packets of Senior Service and Players Navy Cut cigarettes were encased in a cellophane wrapper with a sealed red tag for opening the packet. The cellophane was intact when the packets of cigarettes were sold by retailers. It was obvious the cigarettes had been removed by someone who worked at the factory, namely the two women, before the packets were sealed.

Dave Canavan smoked Player's Navy Cut: everyone else smoked cheaper Woodbines, Tenners or Weights. Dave ordered a packet of Players every day so he was the obvious target. Before Terry delivered the cigs that day the two of us met up in the 'bogs'. Terry took the cigs out of Dave's packet and I stuffed the box with toilet paper. We replaced the cellophane and glued it back. Good job, well done. The packet looked perfect. Terry put the doctored packet of cigs on the table in Dave's place.

Dave sat down, took his false teeth out, wrapped them in his handkerchief and popped them into the top pocket of his dust-coat. He picked up a piece of toast and began munching it on his gums like a tortoise eating a lettuce leaf. I picked up the *Daily Mirror* and opened it at the page with the account of the theft at Gallagher's. "Ha ha! Just listen to this!"

I read out the account of the missing cigs and the conviction of the two women. Dave grabbed the newspaper and read the account for himself. "Bloody hell, he exclaimed! I thought you were having me on!" Alf said: "No, it's straight up Dave. That Judge: what a stupid fucker! He should have praised them for their ingenuity"

Someone came up with the golden oldie: "Have a cigarette Judge: no thanks I've got a scar (cigar) on my knee". George Malone followed with: "You should never offer a woman a cigarette Judge: you might get a packet in return". Alf capped it with: "If you put it in her hand Judge she'll say I don't smoke Woodbines".

Dave put his teeth back in, picked up his packet of cigs, pulled the red tag, and stripped off the cellophane. I was watching carefully hoping the bearded sailor in his uniform on the front of the packet would keep his face straight and not wink at me and Terry. Dave pushed up the contents of the packet with his thumb and tore off the silver foil. No cigs. He immediately knew he'd been set up but he was in no mood for joking.

"You bastards!" he shouted as he pushed his chair back from the table: "You fucking bastards! That's it, The Bets off!"

Everyone was pissing themselves laughing.

"The fucking little devil: he should be 'Chapelled'!" Dave shouted, pointing at Terry.

"Come on Dave, you've got to admit it's the best yet" Joe Butterworth said.

"Bloody best yet my arse: I've had enough of it! You two think you're so bloody clever! You can do the bloody Bet on your own" he said, looking daggers at me and Terry. He got up and went into his aisle with his newspaper, back turned, to sit on an inverted scrap metal drum, He'd never done that before: he really had taken the hump this time.

Dave didn't speak to anyone all day. He didn't join us at the next tea break or mention the Bet. He'd had sulks before but this was serious. We were into the flat racing season again. The coming Wednesday was the first in June, Epsom Derby Day, the middle leg of the three Classics that make up the Triple Crown along with the 2,000 Guineas and the St Leger. Dave had done well in the Derby last year with Dave Dick on ESB and we'd been hoping for a repeat winner from *our* Dave this year too. Alf offered a few suggestions for the Bet and others chipped in but most of the lads didn't want to swap horses, so to speak, from Dave's to Alf s choice. Though they'd had a laugh at the cigs prank they were more than a bit 'pissed off' with me and Terry at the outcome. Something had to be done and done quickly or Wednesday's Bet would, as someone said, be spread like horse muck all over the field.

The following day Terry took me to one side and suggested another prank, one that would get Dave some attention and sympathy and bring him back to the table. It was an absolutely crazy idea! Terry proposed making a 'bomb' and putting it inside the drum Dave had taken to sitting on. It would only be a small bomb and it wouldn't be dangerous. It would make a lot of noise and it would get Dave back to the table.

Terry's crazy idea was to put a tin with a burning night-light inside it into a larger tin filled with gas obtained from the tap in the Store Room and plant the two tins inside Dave's drum. The 'bomb' would be arranged so that when the air was all burnt from inside the smaller tin the gas would enter from the larger tin and explode with a loud boom. It was an utterly dotty idea. I was sceptical as to whether or not it would work and fearful that if it did work it would be very dangerous. Terry assured me he had experimented and perfected a similar device at home: it would work and wasn't dangerous. I said "Oh yes, but supposing he has a weak heart! Just forget it you daft bugger! Go and say you're sorry, for God's sake!" Terry wouldn't be dissuaded. I said: "If you do that Terry you're on your own" thinking that would deter him.

Just before the tea break the following day Alf Owens asked Dave to help lift a heavy Chase onto the Stone. I spotted Terry quickly nipping into Dave's aisle while Dave was absent. He substituted Dave's tin drum for another one, presumably with a bomb in it. The bell went and Dave took his tea and toast and retired to the drum.

All the lads took their tea and sat down round the table as usual. We'd only been seated a minute or so when a loud boom exploded from Dave's aisle. Dave's head and shoulders appeared above his frame as he leapt into the air in fright. It put the frighteners on me too: I thought he'd been injured but the explosion had only been a small one. The boom had been amplified by the hollow drum. Someone said: "Is that Dave farting?" Everyone leapt to their feet and ran into Dave's aisle to see what had caused the explosion. Terry disappeared to the lavatory. Dave was a bit shaken but otherwise unharmed and had no idea what had caused the bang until the drum was examined and the burnt out night-light found. "It'll be that bugger Terry" someone said. A mug of tea was brought for Dave to replace the one spilt in the explosion and he sat down at the table to join in the chorus of condemnation of Terry.

When Terry returned he denied he'd planted the bomb and refused to give an explanation. Later, when confronted by the Father of the Chapel who said he would be formally 'Chapelled' if he didn't own up and apologize to Dave: he admitted responsibility, apologised, and accepted his punishment. He was off the Bet for a week and would have to have his tea break on his own.

*

Despite his professed contrition Terry spent his time thinking up yet more pranks to get up to when things quietened down. He decided to switch his activities to the Bindery.

A dozen or so women and girls worked in the Bindery, which was two floors below the Comp room, under the beady eyes of Jessie Downs, or Dressy Down as the women called their frumpy-dumpy forelady.

For the planned escapade Terry needed mice. There were plenty about: the whole of the upper floor, where the Comp Room was situated, was infested with them. They lived in the cotton-fluff-filled cavity between the floor of the Comp Room and the ceiling of the Machine Room. They often appeared in the open but the problem was catching the little blighters.

 One day when work was slack and the machines were shut down for cleaning, Terry disappeared behind the 'diss' galley racks at the far end of the shop floor. He had with him a box to sit on, a biscuit tin, a wooden reglet and a ball of string. He tied the end of the string to the reglet, propped the tin up with It. He scattered some shredded cheese and some cake crumbs under the tin and in front of it and sat down to wait, with the patience of a cat, for the mice to appear. It wasn't long before he'd caught a couple which he transferred to his dust-coat pocket. He trapped shut the pocket with his hand and went downstairs to the Bindery with a bogus request for a back copy of one of the numerous knitting magazines the Palatine Press produced. Jessie Downs went into the Storeroom to get one. I followed Terry down and stood at the Bindery door so as not to miss the performance.

Terry leaned against the table where a dozen or so of the table-hands were inserting leaflets into magazines and packing them into boxes. There were piles of *'Knitwear'*, *' Stitchcraft'*, *'Tatting Yarns'*, *'Quick and Clever Feltcraft'* and other publications stacked on top of the table and on the floor behind the stools the girls were sitting on.

Terry released the mice from his pocket. The mice ran down the table, in and out of the piles of magazines and then jumped off, one on either side. There were shrieks and screams as the women leapt to get out of the way of the mice. Stools fell over, piles of magazines were knocked down and scattered over the floor. Leaflets cascaded off the table. Someone knocked over a glue pot in the panic to escape. Jessie Downs came running back from the store-room to see what the commotion was about. "Mice! Mice!" the girls screamed! Jessie shouted: "Don't be ridiculous you daft buggers! You've seen a mouse before haven't you? Get those magazines picked up and get back to your work".

Terry didn't wait for the magazine. He scarpered quickly back upstairs to the Comp Room. Jessie chased upstairs after him. She burst into the office to complain to the foreman, Tom Tyrer. She was 'spitting feathers' as they say. She wanted Terry sacked. Terry of course denied he'd taken the mice to the Bindery, claiming the whole place was over-run with mice. George Malone, the Father of the Chapel at the time, persuaded Tyrer to give Terry one more chance, saying the Chapel would discipline him when it next met. The lads in the Comp Room thought the whole thing a bit of a hoot and when the Chapel met the matter was deliberately forgotten about. Terry resumed his activities in the Comp room.

*

Had Terry known that his next victim, Frank Hogan, a five feet one inch tall 1st World War 'Bantam', had fought in the trenches, survived gas attacks, and won the Military Cross for taking out a German machine-gun post by running across no man's land under enemy fire with a hand grenade, he might have chosen a different wheeze. But he didn't.

Frank was an elderly, reclusive type of chap, nearing retirement. He would never discuss with anyone his war-time experiences, nor anything else for that matter, though he did come to the table for his tea break. His one pleasure in life, so it seemed, was his Meerschaum pipe. Frank kept a tin of wonderful, brandy and treacle-smelling, St. Bruno tobacco in his drawer. Everyone liked the smell of it and Terry realised that to substitute horse manure would be unlikely to work: he would have to think of something else.

Frank had a regular routine. Prior to the ten o'clock tea break he would charge his pipe with tobacco to smoke after his tea and toast. He would remove a couple of strands of 'baccy' from the tin, cut it up, shred it between his finger and thumb and tamp it down into the bowl of his pipe. He would then put the pipe on his work frame and go for a Jimmy Riddle before the bell went.

While he was gone Terry nipped round to Frank's frame, removed the top layer of tobacco and concealed in the bowl of the pipe a couple of Bengal match-heads saved from bonfire night.

Frank returned, joined the group at the table, drank his tea and ate his toast. He struck a match. Terry hid his face behind a newspaper. Frank had trouble lighting up. He tried again, tapping his forefinger into the bowl like a bird eating bread crumbs and re-presented the match. This time the tobacco ignited. Frank pursed his lips round the pipe stem and gave a few quick, intermittent sucks. Terry looked over the top of his newspaper. Puffs of smoke rose from Frank's pipe. Suddenly two fizzing pops went off, not very loud but loud enough to turn all heads to look at Frank. It was a spectacular sight.

Shreds of burning tobacco were erupting like a mini volcano from the pipe and two clouds of smoke, one red the other green, rose and mingled as Frank, in shock and shaking, flung his pipe into the air and dived under the table shouting "Gas lads, Gas!" When Dave and Joe bent to pull him out they found him curled into a ball with his hands over his face gasping for air, shouting: "I can't find my mask. My mask! I can't breathe!" Frank was off work for three days, recovering. Terry really had gone over the top this time!

*

At the Chapel meeting Terry was asked what the hell he was playing at and told it was about time he grew up. He was fined half a week's wage and given a final warning by the F.O.C and told that in future he would not be supported if Management took action against him.

Terry seemed appropriately contrite when he apologised to Frank but got little sympathy when he complained that he was bored and only given menial jobs to do rather than proper training. This was true but the wrong moment to bring it up. In response he was told that he would find out what a boring job really looked like. He was set the task of re-labelling all the type cases in the Composing room. He was to set a short sample line to show the appearance of the type in the case and print beneath it the size and name of the font.

It took Terry over a week of constant mind-numbing work to set the type and print the labels. But when Joe Butterworth saw the result he was so furious he smashed a mallet through a Type Forme in anger and gave Terry a mighty kick up the backside. Every case had an identical sample line: 'The devil makes work for idle hands'.

You had to admire Terry's spirit!

THE PERFECT TREBLE

It was Dave Canavan's big day: Saturday, 24th March 1956, Grand National day. The idea was that at three o'clock, after work at The Palatine Press, Dave and the rest of us would meet up with Joe Kemp, or Guy Mitchell as he preferred to be called, at 'The Horse and Jockey' where he lodged, to watch the race. Joe didn't do overtime on Saturdays. He did a bit of bar work in the pub on a Friday night and a slot impersonating Guy Mitchell songs such as: "I don't know why I'm singing the Blues," for pints and to help pay his lodging. He never got out of bed before eleven o'clock on a Saturday morning. He'd have been no use in the Composing Room anyway, shivering and shaking with the D.Ts: he'd have 'pied' more type than he set. Guy had squared it with the landlord to let us join the after hours drinkers to watch the National on the pub's new TV. The set was small, old and second hand. It had a magnifying-glass cover to make the picture bigger: it was grainy but watchable.

Dave was busy working on the Bet by the time I clocked at six minutes past eight: late and quarter-houred! The Saturday morning overtime had been fixed by Joe Butterworth and the foreman: time and a half till twelve o'clock noon and double time until three o'clock finish. Dave, with the racing papers fully spread, wasn't even pretending to be working on the job on his galley. Joe was watching Dave with his 'blind eye'.

Though deputy foreman of the Comp room at the Palatine Press or Pantomime Press as we Comps called it, Joe was not your typical boss's nark. If anything he ran with the Hares rather than the Hounds. He'd been on the shop floor before he'd inherited dead man's shoes. He kept in with the lads. He took his tea-break with us, played Cribbage and went to the Bellevue Dogs with George Malone and Wally Rowley. He knew all about the betting Syndicate; he'd always been in on it, but he had to keep his nose clean now he was Deputy. He couldn't openly approve of Dave's 'homework' on the bet but he turned a blind eye to it. He didn't much like my nipping out to the Bookies with Bets for the Syndicate either but he didn't stop me. Joe colluded on occasions with the foreman, Tom Tyrer, who we all knew *was* a boss's man, but Tyrer was salaried and didn't come in on a Saturday. He left the Saturday overtime supervision to Joe and Joe knew it was in his interest to play ball with us, especially on Grand National day. We could 'drop him in it' in all sorts of ways if he didn't. He'd kept a 'rush job' back to make sure the overtime materialised.

In the racing season Dave spent the first hour of each day reading the various racing pages from the newspapers passed to him by the lads as they came in to work. He kept the papers out of sight in the open top drawer of his work-frame. He read the tipsters, studied form, consulted his record books and prepared the Bet. If Dave took longer than an hour we kept an eye open to tip him the wink in case Tyrer came out of his cabin to have a sniff round to see what we were up to. At ten o'clock tea break Dave would give us a run-down on the racing 'form', and tell us the odds on the horses he'd picked for the Syndicate Bet. He'd give comment and advice for personal Bets. The Syndicate Bets were complex, never straight to wins or each way Bets; they were always accumulators, cross Bets or Bets such as fifteen tanner doubles to make them worth winning with the small stakes we contributed.

Most days Dave's selections were accepted on the nod. He could get ratty if his proposals were challenged and like many gamblers he was superstitious. If someone made a joke such as: "I've heard Snotty Nose is running well Dave" or when Paul Lucius said: "Do you think Green Vomit's going to come up today Dave?" Dave would stub out his cig and shout: "Shut up you fuckers! Don't you know you'll stiffen the Bet! You'd stiffen a bloody soft collar you lot would - bugger off!"

Dave's feuds with tipsters and trainers were notorious. He was having a personal vendetta with two in particular: Peter Cazalet, the Queen Mother's trainer and the famous Captain Elsey. Some time back a Cazalet trained horse had pipped one of Dave's selections at the post in a photo finish. Dave lost the twenty quid staked-up on the last horse of an 'Accumulator' Bet. Ever afterwards, when up against one of Cazalet's nags, he talked as though he was personally going to ride the horse he'd backed saying: "I'll get that bleeder Cazalet today, just you see if I don't!"

National day was 'The Big One': the Bet was serious stuff. Dave announced we should go for a treble - two short-odds Bets on earlier races at Aintree: the winnings to go on E.S.B. in the National. First: Prince Stephen in the 11.30 a.m.: winnings on to Caledonian the Second in the 2.15 p.m.: then all each way on E.S.B. which was not well fancied by the Tipsters, and not one of the top favourites, but the odds were pretty good and worth the risk. Despite this advice Dave's choice didn't go down as well as expected with the Syndicate.

The National, posed a multitude of problems - a left hand Course, many runners, high hedges and a water jump, the notorious Becher's Brook. Every syndicate member had a 'dead cert' horse, jockey or trainer up his sleeve to challenge Dave's selection. It was anybody's race but they'd all read their papers. Alf Owen had been boning up on past form with the aid of a secret book of sporting facts he kept locked up in his top drawer: "Joe Mercer's ridden 63 winners - go on form: what's better than that?" Andy Hill said: "Go for Henry Wragg or Joe McGrath". Joe Butterworth fancied Devon Loch, the Queen Mother's horse: "It's one of the front runners in the betting: Dick Francis is riding it; he'd never take a dud horse". Alf agreed, spouting that Devon Loch had won two races this year and was third in the Cheltenham Gold Cup last year. Beasley got a mention, despite the fact that he wasn't even riding. George Malone chipped in with Must. We must have Must: a must is a Must! John Goodman didn't help, saying he wanted Early Mist because his glasses had steamed up on the way to work.

Dave was getting very cross. I tried to cool things down by re-stating the blindingly obvious: "It's anybody's race, the jumps are too high. 'The Chair' will bring some down and the water jump will sink a few hopes. With twenty-nine runners in the field there'll be falls and loose horses all over the place: half of them won't finish. What's the point in arguing!" Joe Butterworth looked at his watch. Dave banged his fist on the table: "This is bloody ridiculous. I've had enough of this! We're going on E.S.B. for a treble and that's final!" He stood up and gave Joe Butterworth a malevolent look for daring to mention the trainer Cazalet and Devon Loch. Joe said: "O.K. lads, back to what you're paid for".

I wrote down the bet, collected the money, hopped on my bike and headed off for Billy Brady's on Chapel Street. Salford council was clearing the slums to build new high-rise flats. They were demolishing row after row of soot-blackened terraced houses leaving only the pubs standing on the corners of the un-peopled rubble-strewn streets to guide me. Two weeks earlier, when I'd gone to Brady's, the streets were crowded with women gossiping outside the numerous small shops. Dogs were fighting and barking, raggedly dressed kids were playing skipping and hop-scotch. The place had hardly changed since the nineteenth century when desperately poor women borrowed dead babies from one another to trick insurance companies or to get money out of a funeral club to pay for burying a bogus dead child that was actually round the corner boarding with a relative for a week or two. Today I had difficulty knowing where I was. It took an age to negotiate a route through the debris to Chapel Street and on past the Catholic Cathedral and Bexley Square towards the Flat-iron Market where Billy Brady had his betting shop.

Billy Brady's legitimate shop fronted onto Chapel Street and was for wealthy people with registered accounts and betting over the phone. Casual street-betting for the ordinary punter was illegal but took place nonetheless. Everyone knew this but not everyone knew where to go to do it. I did, of course. There was a narrow road either side of the small block of shops with the road behind forming three sides of an oblong. Two scruffy looking men in flat caps and mufflers stood one on each corner, feigning idleness but looking out for the police. The shops had small backyards separated by tall, seven feet high walls. Unlike the others, Billy Brady's yard, where the betting went on, had a makeshift roof of corrugated iron.

The look-out man on the corner didn't recognise me. He stopped me to ask if I was after Billy Brady. He told me to leave my bike with him and to go on foot. "It's jam-packed in there today and there might be Coppers about. It would be just like the bastards to do a raid on National day". For security reasons Brady's yard had an unmarked, plain, black wooden door with no fittings. It had no knocker, no lock, no key-hole, no spy-hole. The paint was worn off to form a pale patch in the centre about two thirds up. I knocked hard three times, the signal, on the bare patch and a third scruffy scout, a dead ringer for the other two, let me in.

A brick wall stood immediately in front of me. To enter the yard you had to squeeze through one of the narrow gaps either side. As I entered I could hear the rapid voice of a radio racing commentator describing a race. "They're neck and neck as they head up the straight towards the finish but Speedy Boy is gaining ground. Can he do it! He might have left it too late. No, he's overtaken Fit-start and Lightening Rod has lost ground. As they cross the finishing line it's Speedy Boy from Fit-start with Lightening Rod in third place followed by Dunmore, The Witch of the North and Always First, predictably, coming in last!"

I elbowed my way through the sour-smelling pack of bodies: the heads for the most part invisible in the mist of tobacco smoke which hung a couple of feet from the ceiling like a giant cobweb. If my dad, a Communist sympathiser, had been with me he'd have thought the French revolution was being re-enacted, there were so many headless people about. No women, just a crowd of men jostling each other to get near the rough brick walls, papered with racing pages torn from the day's newspapers. Each eager punter wielding a short, stubby pencil and a square of paper, pushing and shoving to squeeze their way to the narrow wooden shelf fixed to the wall below the papers to write down their Bets. Then more squeezing, more elbowing, to get to the open sash window in the back of the shop wall to place the bets.

Billy Brady's cashier in the window was a comical contrast to the drab punters and the flat-capped look-out men outside. He was hatless, balding, with tufts of red hair around his crown. He was wearing a large green eyeshade supported by a broad black strap. His white long- sleeved shirt had broad red armbands round the biceps. Over the shirt, a yellow felt waistcoat; beneath his chin an enormous red-spotted bow tie. He'd have looked more at home in a circus ring. I handed the clown the slip and, trying to suppress a laugh, paid over the money for the Bet. "I saw you", he almost sang. "It's my Grand National outfit. I always dress up for the National: it makes the losers happy." "Yes", I said, but thinking I don't think so.

It was 11.20 a.m. by the time I'd placed the Bet. Prince Stephen was running in the 11.30 a.m. I might as well stay, I thought, despite the smoke. I liked to listen to the quick clipped voices of the commentators, the mumbled curses and the despairing 'oh no's!' of the disappointed losers. The expressions on their faces as they tore up their betting slips were quite moving. Some punters were smiling, including me. Prince Stephen won: he'd been front runner all the way. I left the droning commentator and the smoking punters to it and slipped out of the door into the quiet of the empty street, collected my bike from the man on the corner and headed back for the Pantomime Press.

"You've been a bloody long time" Joe complained when I got back. "I thought you'd want me to stop on for the eleven thirty - not good news Joe" I said. And practicing the alliterative vernacular skills I'd learnt on National Service (Ha Ha!) to wind him up, I said: "The fucking fucker fell at first fucking fence." They were all listening. "Are you having us on?" Dave asked. "Straight up Dave, they had the wireless on. I heard it." "Well that's really fucked it. What do we do now?" said Andy, looking as though he was about to weep. Dave frowned, thought for a second or two and said: "We'll have to have another whip round and go for a straight win on E.S.B. Leave it till lunch-time." I left it till lunch time to tell them the truth that Prince Stephen had won. Dave was incandescent. "You've stiffened the Bet, good and bloody proper this time, you bastard! It'll be

E.S.B. that falls now, just you wait and see!"

At 2.30 p.m. I was back at Brady's to find out how Caledonian the Second had done. Our luck was in. Caledonian also won. It was all up to E.S.B.: the mood back at the Pantomime was jubilant. At 3.0 o'clock we couldn't get to "The Horse and Jockey' quick enough.

*

When we got to "The Horse and Jockey" Joe Kemp, alias Guy Mitchell, was not pulling pints, he was pulling birds in the back room. He was on his feet on a little platform giving full voice to a hand-held mike, singing another Guy Mitchell favourite: 'What am I doing in Kansas City when you're in New Orleans?'

George Shawcross went to the door, out of sight, and sang along, mimicking him: "What are you doing in the small back room when we're in need of pints?" When Guy took no notice he shouted: "Come on Joe, get 'em in!"

First pints didn't touch the sides. You would have thought we were a bunch of thirsty fire-fighters just back from the Manchester blitz rather than a Chapel of Comps who'd been sat on their arses all morning. By the time we'd got the Telly tuned-in some of the lads were on their third pint

The commentator grandiloquently informed us the race had been inaugurated in1839. The weather at Aintree was fine for the 117th Grand National. The race was open to Steeplechasers over seven years old. (E.S.B. was a ten year old). The left hand track over a distance of four miles and three furlongs and one hundred and ten yards might be too much for some. Recent rain would make the going on the soft side which could prove taxing for the older Steeplechasers.

Dave said E.S.B. didn't mind a soft turf and age wouldn't be a problem but Must might be. Must was the favourite and Early Mist, a previous winner, was also well fancied as was Devon Loch, one of the two horses in the race owned by the Queen Mother, with Dick Francis on its back.

E.S.B. was not among the top favourites but all ears pricked up when E.S.B. was paraded. Shushes reverberated round the pub when the commentator said the dark bay gelding had been bred by Sheila Burke in

County Kildare and trained in Britain by Fred Rimell. It was owned by Mrs. Lenard Carver who, we were told, was fortunate to have it ridden by jockey Dave Dick. There was a great deal of laughter at that. Someone shouted: "Hey Dave you've a good dick: better get over to Aintree two six or you'll miss being top jockey for that long jump you've been pining after". Dave was not amused.

"Shut the fuck up, the lot of you! How many times do I have to tell you! You'll stiffen the bloody Bet!" As they came under starters orders the odds on E.S.B. had lengthened to 100/7.

The start was delayed, adding to the tension. A couple of horses were reluctant to go to the tape. With a bit of pushing and pulling from a couple of grooms they lined up and were off to a clean start.

The front pack was very bunched up for the first fence and the two most fancied horses, Must, the favourite, and Early Mist, a previous winner, both fell leaving the Queen mother's M'as tu vu in the lead after the first jump and Eagle Lodge in fourth place. Devon Loch was going well in the mid field, with the front bunch still battling it out for an early lead. E.S.B. was there but wasn't getting a mention. Alf, always a Job's comforter was convinced E.S.B. was one of the fallers. When E.S.B. did get a mention the excitement increased. Dave was crouched in front of the Telly, bobbing up and down like a jockey, with a double fist-full of imaginary reins in front of him: occasionally releasing a hand to slap his backside with an imaginary whip to 'gee' himself up. Everyone was shouting: "Keep your fucking arse down Dave we can't see a bloody thing back here!"

After the first circuit E.S.B. was still there but loose horses were making trouble for the survivors. Devon Loch was making good progress when a horse fell in front of him. He managed to swerve and miss it. E.S.B. made it over 'The Chair' and cleared the water jump and was going strong, up there with the leaders. There were still more than twenty of the twenty-nine starters in the race and Royal Tan and Eagle Lodge were well up along with Devon Loch and E.S.B. Irritatingly the T V camera kept switching to the Queen Mother in the Royal Box. She was all pearl ear-rings, big hat and binoculars. A fox fur was wrapped round her fulsome bust which was bursting with pride in her well placed horse. The camera panned back. They were all still there towards the end of the last circuit.

The tension in the pub increased as they approached the last jump. They were all over and turning for the long run in to the straight. The 'go ons' and 'come ons' for E.S.B. got ever more excited. Dave Canavan was slapping the arse off the seat of his pants as E.S.B. battled it out with Royal Tan, Gentle Moya, Eagle Lodge and Devon Loch but hopes of a win faded. Dick Francis pulled away, half a length ahead of Eagle Lodge, pushing ahead inch by inch. Eagle Lodge was beginning to tire. E.S.B. took up the challenge as Eagle Lodge dropped behind but there was still plenty of power in Devon Loch: he was pulling away rapidly. There was no doubt in any of our minds that none of the others could possibly catch him he was so far ahead. "There can only be one winner," the commentator shouted in a breathlessly excited voice "and that's going to be Devon Loch. He's fifty yards from home. He has so much power in his stride. He's romping home!"

The TV camera briefly panned to the Stand and the jubilant Queen Mother. Men in the Stand were throwing their hats in the air to congratulate Devon Loch, Dick Francis and the Queen Mother. We in the pub were totally pissed off. Dave had given up riding and was standing up giving his backside a rest. Then, to everyone's utter amazement, disaster struck Devon Loch. He had at least a five length lead over E.S.B. when suddenly, in his dash for the winning post, with the back legs taking his weight and his front legs at full stretch he half jumped up into the air. Devon Loch's back legs skidded away from him and he 'belly-flopped' onto the turf. For a brief moment he looked exactly like one of those paintings by Stubbs which artists did before photography revealed how horses actually gallop. He was only down a second, his legs splayed fore and aft like a rocking horse, and then up on his feet again with Dick Francis cajoling him to carry on. But it was hopeless. E.S.B. streaked past to win by ten lengths, the best race of his career, with Gentle Moya ridden by George Milburn a close second followed by 'Royal Tan' and Eagle Lodge fourth.

After the proverbial pin had dropped, in the shocked second's silence in the pub, a great 'Y...ee... eesss!' roared out. Everyone was on his feet, jumping and dancing and hugging each other. Dave just stood there, in front of the Telly, totally dumbstruck. Alf, more composed than the rest of us, slipped away unobtrusively to the Gents with his book of racing records tucked out of sight in the pocket of his coat.

In the TV interviews after the race a great deal of concern was expressed for Devon Loch, but when checked in the stable later was found to be unharmed. Dick Francis walked off the track in tears, totally dejected and inconsolable. The Queen Mother was clearly disappointed but in a later interview she quite stoically said of the incident: "Oh that's racing!" E.S.B.'s jockey, Dave Dick, said, when asked to comment on his unexpected win: "Devon Loch had me stone cold. I was terribly lucky to win".

Celebratory pints were drunk all round but the 'Kitty' ran out well before five o'clock when Brady's would start to pay out on the National. We got the landlord to let us have drinks 'on the slate' on the strength of the win.

At five o'clock I went yet again to Brady's. I was expecting a big queue but it was only back as far as the yard door. Clearly most of the punters had been on the favourite , Must and the well fancied Early Mist and Devon Loch. The winnings were £21 which was a tidy sum considering a journeyman Compositor's weekly wage was £8.3s.6d.

After the landlord had been paid, the slate wiped clean and the regulars treated, the remainder went straight into the 'Kitty'. No one had gone home after the race and they were all too boozed up to bother about wives and fear of consequences. Guy Mitchell was singing his heart out to the 'birds' in the back room. The rest of the lads were all engrossed in theories as to what made Devon Loch do a 'belly-flop' when the race was all but won.

Dave, the daft bugger, accused us of putting the mockers on it: "It was you bloody lot making all that flaming row. You frightened the bloody horse to death". He'd conveniently forgotten that when he'd previously accused me of stiffening the Bet he'd predicted E.S.B. would be a faller. George Malone thought there must have been a wet patch of grass that made Devon Loch's back legs slide away. Joe Butterworth thought the shadow of the fence made the horse think there was another fence to jump and it spooked him.

*

Alf who prided himself on 'knowing' these things came back from nearly half an hour in the toilet said: "It's happened before." Dave was incredulous: "I don't believe it. I've been betting on the 'gee-gees' for nearly forty years. I would have heard about that."

"Anyone want to Bet?" Alf challenged. Despite the booze and betting fatigue and Dave's incredulity there was some interest. Alf had convinced everyone over the years that he had a phenomenal memory for sporting events. He did know quite a lot of amazing facts but Terry, the junior apprentice and me, had got to know his strategy. Alf would secretly consult his hidden book of sporting facts and then pose a question at tea-break time to get everybody going, even get them to lay Bets. He had clearly just been to the bogs to mug up the topic. "Well go on, tell us then Alf", George Malone urged.

Alf took a swig from his pint and happily began: "Devon Loch's was not the first time a horse had seemed to jump some form of ghost fence on the final run in of the National" It was clear to Terry and me that Alf was reciting instead of simply telling us in his own words. He saw us exchange looks, realised his mistake and quickly switched to his normal mode of speech. He took another swig of beer and continued: "Well, in 1901 a jockey called Arthur Nightingale was way out in front on the home straight and bound to win but his horse Grudon tried to jump a fence that wasn't there. The horse managed to recover and get going again. He was so far in front that he'd enough time to carry on and win".

"Bloody hell Alf, that's amazing! How the fuck do you remember that?", Fred Dolman marvelled.

What Fred didn't know, but Alf probably suspected, was that Terry and me were on to Alf. A couple of weeks previously Alf broke his glasses and had to go home for another pair - he couldn't work without them. He'd left the key to his drawer in his dust coat. Terry took the key, nipped down to Chapel Street and had a duplicate cut. We now had access to Alf's secret source of information. Each morning before Alf came in to work we would mug up on nuggets of sporting intelligence: things to trip him up with at tea-break time. An even better time to trip him up had just arrived! I nodded slyly to Terry.

"Well Fred, Alf might have a good memory but have you ever tried Bob?" Terry said, looking towards me. I waited a couple of seconds, trying to look bored. Before Fred could get a question in I said: "Well go on then Terry, ask me a question. "Which horse won the National in 1949, Bob?" Terry asked. Without hesitation I said: "Russian Hero". Alf looked from me to Terry and said: "Is this some kind of joke? Every fucker knows that'. He got somewhat unsteadily to his feet saying. "I'm going for a piss: You can be thinking about who Russian Hero's jockey was while I'm gone and then put your fucking money where your mouth is. We'll see whether our Bob's got a better memory than me."

"The bugger's gone to look at his book. We're in luck, lads," I said. What Alf didn't know was I knew everything there was to know about Russian Hero. Russian Hero was the first horse I'd ever bet on. My dad worshipped Stalin and revered everything Russian. His favourite phrase was: "Uncle Joe will sort it out." He'd even tried to learn Russian and had me named

Boris. When Russian Hero ran in the National the whole family was on it. "Hah!" laughed Dave. "That must have been a bit of a bloody handicap." "Shut the fuck up Dave, this is serious, I'm trying to tell everyone the facts before Alf gets back!," and to get one up on Dave I added: "You'll stiffen the bloody Bet you will Dave". It was the 110th Grand National and Russian Hero won at 66/1. He made £13,000 for the owner, £33 for my dad and 33 shillings each for my mam, our Arthur, our Ernie and me. He was ridden by Leo McMorrow, trained by George Owen and owned by Fernie Williamson. I'd forgotten the details so it

was the first thing I'd memorised from Alf's book when Terry and I got the key to his drawer.

"Whatever you do, when he gets back, don't make excessive bets or he'll smell a rat".

Alf returned carrying a tray of wobbling pints. "Right now: you can put your money where your mouth is. I've had enough of you lot taking the piss. You can either put up or fucking shut up. You can go for a Single on the Jockey, a Double on the Jockey and trainer or a Triple on those two and the owner: any takers on Russian Hero - for pints?" "Why not for money Alf"? Terry asked. "I'm not bloody Billy Brady: it's for pints," Alf repeated.

Dave Canavan, keen to be first in for the scam said: "I'll start the betting: you know me Alf, it's my lucky day: I'll go for a Treble." Alf accepted the Bet but lost a little colour. Terry went for a Double, adding that he wasn't sure he was up to drinking much more today. George Malone played safe and went for a Single as did Guy Mitchell who was now so pissed he wasn't sure he could correctly remember who was trainer and who the owner. Alf was looking more and more edgy. When I opted for a Triple he went livid. Joe Butterworth couldn't keep his face straight. Alf jumped up out of his chair, shouting "What the fuck's going on here! He grabbed Terry by the shirt front and said: "You little bastard. You've been in my bloody drawer haven't you? I'll fucking kill you! The landlord pulled Alf off Terry and plonked him back into his chair, saying: "All right lads, it's ten o'clock, you'd better drink up". Alf slumped forward in his chair, his head on the table. He was totally pissed and totally pissed off too. He half stood up to leave but keeled over onto the floor. As Dave tried to pick him up a book fell out of Alf s inside pocket. Dave picked it up and read out the title: "Sporting Facts: Pockets full of knowledge. All you need to know about racing."

As we left the pub Dave put his arm round my shoulder and said: "Bloody hell Bob: we gave the bookies a bloody good thrashing today didn't we: a perfect treble, thanks to good old E.S.B.! And *by god,* we've given Guy Mitchell Kemp *really* something to sing about.. Not only did we win the National: I got that bugger Cazalet, good and proper, and that poor old fucker Alf into the bargain! We're on a roll Bob! I'll get that bleeder Elsey on Monday: just you wait and see".

"Cazalet, Brady, Elsey, the three of them. That really *would* be a perfect bloody treble!"

THE CONFESSION

"Why don't you admit it lad. Come clean. Get it off your chest. You'll feel better for it if you do and you'll save us all a lot of trouble. Shall I read it to you again, eh? All you have to do is to sign it. Just put your name at the bottom and we can all go home: you want that don't you Billy? Of course you do: it's been nearly two days now. They'll be missing you. They'll be wondering where you've got to.

What, you as well? Yes of course you as well: all of us. We can all go home if you sign it.

No, no, no, of course I'm not just *saying* that. Just put your name at the bottom in your usual handwriting and we can all go home and get some sleep. I can't say fairer than that now can I?

It'll be damned noisy down there again tonight what with those drunks making a fuss and those coons shouting for a 'Brief'. You won't get much sleep down there. It'll be absolute bedlam. Sergeant Beattie's on to-night. He won't stand any messing. He'll be down there sorting someone out. He won't stop to find out who it was. It'll be a headlock, a night staff in the goolies: the old one two!

I'll tell you what Billy: I'll read what you've said again, shall I? Shall I read what I've written and then you can sign it and we can all go home. Right":

'The following statement by me, William Jones, aged nineteen, apprentice printers' Caster attendant, concerning the fire at Jackson's four-story converted cotton mill in Jamieson Street, Salford, Lancs., on the morning of Monday, 15th December, 1954, is true and correct and freely given.

On Monday, 15th December, 1954, I Billy Jones was late for work. I'd overslept. The weather was cold, cloudy, dull and misty: the sky, clamped down over the streets like a dustbin lid was threatening to drizzle rain: the smoke from the chimneys of the early morning coal fires billowing up from close packed terrace houses quickly turning into smog. Not a day for going to work on a bike but I'd no option.

The early bus would be gone by the time I got to the stop.

The road down to Salford, when I eventually got there, was gummed up with cars, buses and lorries. I weaved in and out, taking risks, in an attempt to make up time. Half way to Salford the threatened rain arrived. I stopped under a railway bridge to put on the yellow oilskin cape I kept in my saddle bag. The fucking thing wasn't there: those bloody Comp Room apprentices must have taken it out when they were larking about with my bike the other day - filling the saddle bag with heavy type-metal ingots and fixing static cut-out circular sheets of cardboard over the spokes of my bike's back wheel with 'Dr. Crock: Cut-Rate Operations' printed on the cardboard. I'd parked my bike in the dark ground floor paper store. When I'd gone for my bike I hadn't noticed what they'd done. I was half way home before I realised it was me people had been laughing at.

The rain was coming on heavy but I'd no option but to ride on. The sets along Chapel Street leading into Salford needed re-laying and tarring. The bumps turned my new Armstrong Sports bike into a juddering bone shaker. Buses and lorries overtook me, splashing the puddles of water accumulating in the gutters all over my trouser legs.

I was peddling hard and going at speed when there was a sudden violent jolt. I shot over the handlebars and put out my hands to try to save myself and clouted the pavement with them, spraining my left wrist and taking the skin off the palm of my right hand. The knees of my trouser legs were covered with smelly brown slime. There must have been dog shit on the pavement where I landed. Fortunately the duffle-bag with my lunch and my newspaper in it had flipped over from my back and my head landed on that instead of a flagstone. Anyway, I was in a right mess. The bike's front wheel had gone down between the bars of a grid and got stuck.

I prised the badly buckled wheel from between the bars of the grid, cursing the Council for installing grids with bars parallel to the road instead of cross- or angled-bars. I had to carry the bike the couple of hundred yards to work. It was six minutes past eight when I got there, so I was 'half-houred'. I managed to get to the toilets without anyone seeing the mess I was in. I bathed my hands and used toilet paper to wipe some of the dog shit from my trousers. All my sandwiches were sodden with milk from the smashed small milk bottle inside my duffle-bag. I chucked them in the waste bin with the broken glass. I was really pissed off I can tell you.

I went up to the Caster-room: there was nobody about. I lit the gas poker and stuck it into the waste paper sack . . .'

"But I didn't say that! I said 'I was so pissed off I just locked myself in a cubicle to stay in the toilets 'till it got to half past eight".

"No, don't interrupt Billy, let me finish!"

'I lit the gas poker and stuck it into the waste paper sack hanging on the partition wall and went back to the toilets to hide and bathe my hands again.'

"But I didn't say that!"

"Don't interrupt!"

'I heard a commotion but I kept myself hidden. After a short while I came out of the toilets. The stairwell was full of smoke and the fire bell was ringing. Everybody was pushing and shoving through the rubber swing doors and shouting that there was a fire. The smoke was choking. I could hear a crackling sound but I couldn't see anything. There were people from the other floors everywhere. I was very scared. I got shoved down the stairs in the crush.

I don't know what made me do it: I was so pissed off it just came over me'.

"But I didn't do it. I didn't say that!"

"Billy, Billy, we know that Billy. We know you said you didn't do it: we just want a statement for the record at this stage, any kind of statement so we can all go home. You can always alter it later if you're not happy with it. We've got statements from the other apprentices and we can match them up later to establish what started the fire".

"I just want to go home! I'm tired! I can't stand it! If I sign it can I go home?"

"Of course you can Billy, of course you can".

"Right constable he's signed it. Take him below and lock him up. He'll appear on Thursday".

"But you said . . ."

"Take him down below Constable Turnbull and don't stand any lip from him. You know what to do if he gives any trouble".

"But you said . . ."

"Get him downstairs."

"You rotten bastard, you said I could go home if I signed it . . . . You fucking bastards! Let me go home!"

*

"We have listened very carefully to what you have said in Court to-day Mr. Jones and I'm afraid that both my colleagues on the Bench and myself have no option but to conclude that your original statement is what happened and that you have altered your story here to-day in order to evade the consequences of your actions. Indeed, it would appear that not only are you a pathological liar you are a very dangerous young man.

You do not deny that it is your signature on the statement read out in Court yet what you have concocted here this morning is quite at odds with what you recited to Chief Inspector Hardman on Tuesday and corroborated by the account of events, leading to the fire, by your work colleagues. We have asked ourselves is it likely that you would have put your name to something which was untrue and we cannot but conclude that it is not.

You have made allegations of the gravest kind against an officer of the highest reputation and integrity: a man who has devoted almost twenty-four years of his life to protecting the public from the likes of you and we find that disgraceful. Furthermore, you have displayed not the slightest contrition for what you have done, and we find that unpardonable.

A building worth almost a quarter of a million pounds has been gutted. A young woman in the prime of her life died a terrible death in the most appalling inferno. Seven other young women were badly burned in their attempts to escape and two firemen had to be taken to hospital suffering from the effects of smoke and fumes: it is unlikely that one of those two brave men will ever be fit to take up his duties again. The public has a right to be protected from the likes of you and you deserve to be severely punished. It is not enough that you will have the death of that young woman and those scarred bodies on your conscience for the remainder of your life. We do not have sufficient powers to deal with a case of this gravity in this Court. Accordingly, you will be taken to a remand centre until you can be dealt with in a place where they have.

Do you have anything to say?"

"No. What's the use of me saying anything?"

*

"Hey. Robinson, did you hear what Billy got?"

"No, what happened?"

"He was up at the Crown yesterday. Seven years"

"Seven years! You're bloody joking".

"Straight up".

"Bloody hell, I don't believe it. Seven years for something he didn't do. Christ that's terrible! We'll have to tell 'em. We can't let him do seven years".

"Don't be so bloody daft Robinson. If we tell 'em it'll be us doing seven years instead of him, you daft bugger!"

"Us! What do you mean us? It was an accident. They can't do anything to us if it was an accident".

"'Can't do anything to us. You try telling those buggers that, and see if they can't!"

"Christ, what a mess I wish I'd never listened to you: I wish we'd told them straight away what happened".

"Well we didn't so get a bloody grip of yourself or we'll all be in the shit".

"What does Pete say?"

"He says we've got to stick together and keep quiet - all of us".

"But we can't let him do seven years. It was bloody stupid to try to blame it on Billy, we should have just said we didn't know how it started."

"Well we didn't so that's that . . . . Listen Robinson, you pillock, you'd better get a grip of yourself or we'll *really* be in the shit without a shovel".

"But we can't let him do seven years. I can't sleep for thinking about it. We'll have to tell them".

"Don't be so fucking stupid".

"But I keep waking up at night. It wouldn't be so bad if that Mavis Lowe hadn't been burnt to bloody death. Why the fuck did he have to go and say he'd done it! We must be fucking mad: we should have told them the truth at the beginning. I thought they'd just have a chat with him and he'd deny it and they'd leave it at that. I never thought he'd sign a bloody confession".

"Well he did, so don't be so bloody daft. And don't go blabbing about it or you know what'll happen. Leave it for now, there's someone coming."

*

"Just go straight across the yard Mr Robinson and through the door on the left: the one with the blue light above it. If there's no one there ring the bell on the desk. The sergeant will attend to you".

"I hope you realise the implication of what you've just told me laddie. I wouldn't be in your shoes if you're not telling the truth this time round. Why the hell didn't you come and tell us all this sooner for God's sake. How could you say you thought *he'd* done it when you knew damned well he hadn't? The Chief will hit the bloody roof when he hears this, I can tell you. It wouldn't be so bad if it hadn't gone to Court but it's all over and done with: there'll be hell to pay. Still, I'll have to take it down now that you're here. Let's start at the beginning. Robinson isn't it? Gordon Robinson: yes? Now then, take your time, speak slowly and the whole truth."

"We were messing about in the Caster room, me Terry, Alfie and Pete. We all go in there each morning to make a brew before the foreman gets in. We have a gas ring and some hose we fit to the metal-pot feed pipe. Pete had been cleaning off a type-forme with Benzine and Alfie said they'd been doing Benzine at the Tech. Alfie said that Benzine was inflammable. Terry said it wasn't and Pete bet him two bob it was. We'll soon see I said. I tipped the tin: Benzine funnelled out onto the floor. I struck a match down the thigh of my dust-coat and lit the gas poker and held it to the edge of the slowly spreading pool. There was a loud phut and a blue glow, like a gas stove light, hovered above the Benzine stain. 'There you are Pete', I said, 'inflammable'. Just then Alfie came galumphing across the room in his size tens. He caught his foot on a loose floorboard that Billy had been asked time and again to put a screw in. He fell 'arse over tit' and kicked a petrol can over. The cap flew off and the petrol went glugging across the floor. The whole bloody lot went up with a whoosh! 'Christ' you've bloody done it now I shouted!' I was in a right panic. Alfie was up in a flash: 'Get the fire extinguisher, quick. For Christ's sake-get the fire extinguisher' he shouted.

Pete and Alfie ran into the office, lifted the big cone-shaped red canister off its stand and dragged it into the Caster room. Alfie hit the knob on the top as it said on the side but nothing happened. 'It's a bloody dud. Nothing works in this fucking place!' he said.

'Get that sheet of stuff in the corner and try to smother the flames', I shouted.

It turned out to be a sheet of highly inflammable acetate from a firm upstairs where they did some kind of Government aircraft work. Alfie threw it on the flames. All the petrol shot out round the sides, caught fire and spread the flames even further. The waste paper sack on the wall caught fire sending flames up to the ceiling. The acetate flared up again and I could see that most of floor itself was well alight. Years of accumulated cotton fluff in the cavity under the floorboards must have been set on fire. I remember saying: 'Bloody Hell, let's ring the fire alarm!'

Two plastic foam chairs in the corner caught fire; the smoke was choking. We ran upstairs to tell the Bindery girls to get out but they'd heard the bell and were already tumbling and clattering down the stairs. Mavis must have gone in the hoist. I remember seeing Billy Jones coming out of the bogs carrying his duffle-bag. The pair of us were just swept along in the crush. Billy was next to me when we were flirted out of the downstairs door in the panic. The place was full of smoke. I don't know how it managed to spread so quickly.

By the time we got into the yard and looked up there were flames coming out of the third floor windows. In a couple of minutes there was smoke coming from the fourth floor and shortly afterwards flames from those windows as well. It must have gone up the partition from the sack somehow and set fire to the aircraft fabrics they were making up there. The windows started exploding and part of a frame crashed into the yard in a shower of sparks.

Just as the first fire-engine turned through the yard gates and rattled over the cobbles there was one hell of an explosion from inside the building and shatters of glass came showering down. It must have been the gas pipe to the melting pot There were several more loud bangs and then one all mighty crack followed by a rumble like thunder: 'Jesus fucking Christ all the floors have collapsed!' I heard someone say. It was terrifying.

They got the first fire-engine into position and fixed a long, slack, snake of hose to the hydrant just outside the yard gate. The automatic ladder zoomed upwards. I remember thinking how small the bloke on the end looked. He was gripping the hose under his right arm and holding on with his left hand. I could see water travelling up the hose like someone slowly blowing up a kid's rip rap. Just as the water spluttered out of the nozzle a second fire-engine skidded round the corner into the yard. It went straight over the hose and the coupling came apart. The hose went berserk, snaking about and spraying water over everyone. By the time they'd got it fixed again it was too late to save the building.

I'll never forget looking up at the flaming mill: it was like on the films. Flames like blowtorches coming from the fourth floor windows and a red glow behind all the window holes on the other floors. Smoke was billowing from the top of the building and sparks were showering down.

The police arrived. There were about a dozen flashing electric blue lights. They cleared everybody out of the yard and across the street. I was scared to death. I just couldn't believe what was happening. I picked my way to the front, grabbed hold of Alfie, Pete and Terry. I said: 'Christ, we're in trouble! What are we going to say?' I can remember the conversation very clearly.

Terry said: 'Don't panic, for fuck's sake. Say we had nothing to do with it. Say you don't know how it started if anybody asks you. If

THE CONFESSION

we stick to the same story they'll never find out. O.K. Just say we were in the Composing room and the first thing we knew the fire bell was going'.

Alfie said, 'No, let's say Billy Jones was in the Caster room'.

I said: 'Don't be a prick, you can't say that, he'd tell 'em he was nowhere near the place. Just say nothing'.

Pete said: 'Well it was his bloody room where it started and he's always pissing about with that gas poker and forgetting to turn it off. They're bound to ask him if he had anything to do with it. He'll say it was us if I know him'.

I said: 'How can he say it was us, he was only just coming in. I saw him coming out of the bogs with his duffle-bag as we went down the stairs'.

'Well, anyway, we'll stick together and say we don't know how it started, otherwise we're in the shit: they'll send us to bloody prison, or Borstal or something', Terry said.

In the end Pete said: 'Just say we were at the bottom end of the Comp. Room larking about and the first we knew the fire bell went and we could see smoke and flames coming from the Caster room'.

*

When we heard Billy had confessed and been arrested we were more than gob smacked I can tell you.

'How the fuck have they managed to get him to confess?' Pete said to Terry. They neither of them knew that to cover myself I'd told the Copper who had interviewed me after the fire that I'd seen Billy in the Caster room before the fire broke out. I didn't want the police thinking we'd been involved. When I heard he'd signed a confession I was so scared I was actually sick. I couldn't have admitted it was our fault even if I'd wanted to, Sergeant!

But when I heard Billy had been sent down for seven years I just couldn't believe it. I went round to Terry's house and told him we had better own up. He said I was bloody crazy: so did Alfie.

I'd not been able to sleep. I kept having nightmares; seeing Mavis Lowe all charred and black in the hoist in a huddle, trying to get out. I kept thinking how I would feel if I was put inside for something I hadn't done. Anyway, the more I thought about the fire and the consequences the more sick I felt so I told the others I was going to own up. They said I was fucking crazy and they'd give me a going over if I didn't keep quiet.

I wish I hadn't said I'd seen Billy in that Caster room Sergeant. I still can't believe it happened. It was all under control one minute and all out of control the next. They can't do anything to us if it was an accident, can they? Well they can't, can they, Sergeant?"

*

Later that year Billy was in the pub having a quiet pint with a mate to celebrate his release from prison. His mate said:

"So how do you feel about it now that you're out Billy?"

"How would *you* bloody feel if you'd spent nearly nine months of your one and only life inside for something you hadn't done?"

"You'll get compensation".

"Compensation: don't be a prick! I don't want bloody compensation. I want my life back. There's no compensation that'll pay for what I've been through. How would you like to wake up each day knowing you'd got seven years for something you hadn't done? Those bastards won't have to suffer what I suffered".

"What did they eventually get then?"

"Borstal: twelve months Borstal. I'd have given 'em twelve fucking years, the bastards! All they had to do was say it was an accident in the first place and that would have been the end of it. All they'd have got was a bollocking, but no, they had to blame me, the rotten bastards! Still, that fucking Chief Inspector Hardman got what was coming to him for altering my bloody statement and conning me to sign it".

"What did he get then?"

"Too bloody little, really: dismissed from the force and twelve months inside. The bloody Judge was soft on him. Even after saying it was 'a crime of the utmost gravity for a policeman to fabricate a statement to get a conviction, and of all people a Chief Inspector who must have known that what he was doing was a criminal offence'. They only gave him twelve months. And I bet the bastard doesn't have to do it in 'Strangeways' like I had to. They give bent Coppers a nice little number in a cushy library in an open prison somewhere out in the countryside. They ought to stick the fuckers in 'Strangeways', with some of the nut-cases that gave me a going over, and let those bloody Fascist screws loose on 'em: see how they'd like that!"

"You're being a bit bitter aren't you Billy?"

"Bitter! Yes I am bitter. I'll drink to that. Another bitter please love".

PERJURY

The after-echoes of the slammed cell door reverberated with a deafening Clang! Bang! Clang!, through the body and brain of 22689083 making him visibly wince and disturbing his concentration as he lay on his hard wooden bunk under his grey prison blanket, reading.

"Jesus Christ! If it's not the new bloke in the bunk above belching and farting it's the bloody Screws, shouting and bawling and banging us up" he said to himself.

He found it difficult to concentrate on the dog-eared Bond novel he'd got that morning from the prison library. There was no chair in the cell and he hated reading in bed. He forced himself to go on but his mind kept wandering, brooding on his two year sentence. Twenty-one he'd be when he got out. Twenty fucking one! He'd have no job and no prospect of getting one. All the best girls would be gone and those left wouldn't give him a second look.

As 007 got into another tight spot the story quickened. 22689083 breathed short, shallow breaths, sucking in the fetid air through his clenched teeth to avoid the body odours of the new bloke above and the whiff of urine that lingered long after the evening slop-out.

"Bloody Screws! Noisy bastards! And for Christ's sake stop interrupting me with your fucking questions will you!" he shouted at the bunk above.

An hour later the light went out without warning. It was like going blind. There was a sudden rush of blood to his head as the after-image of the sharp printed page faded slowly away and darkness closed in.

"You bastards! You fucking lousy bastards!" he shouted, hardly moving his teeth: "Just as I was in the middle of a sentence."

The bloke above laughed out loud at the ironic, unintended pun, interrupting him yet again, but this time 22689083 saw no point in objecting.

"I'm in for three months for non-payment of maintenance. How long are you doing?" the voice of the new bloke asked.

"Two years if you must know" 22689083 said.

"Bloody hell?: two years! How come you're doing two years?"

"Perjury."

"Perjury: what the fuck's perjury?"

"It's telling a few porkies, you know porky pies, lies . . . in Court, to keep your mates out of trouble."

"And you got two years for that! Two bloody years! I don't believe it; are you having me on?"

"Are *you* calling me a fucking liar too?"

"No, but every bugger lies in Court: it's the name of the game. The Coppers lie; Prosecutors lie; defendants lie; Briefs lie; witnesses lie; even Judges lie when it suits them. It's written in gold fucking letters three feet high over the Court's front porch: "Here lies fucking justice". And bloody politicians . . . they're doing it all the time: being economical with the truth they call it. You can't get two years for telling a few fucking lies: it's bloody ridiculous!"

"Well I did! I got two bleeding years mate. I'm not lying here rotting away for the fun of it".

"Jesus Christ on a bike, it must have been a bloody whopper. Did they make you a licentiate?"

"Stuff it shithead: it's not a fucking joking matter."

"Come on then . . . tell us what happened".

"Go to fucking sleep".

"Come on tell me. I'd like to know".

"I don't want to talk about it: I'm too pissed off".

"*Come on*. I need to know what you're in for. I need to know I'm not banged up with a bloody murderer or a fucking paedophile or something".

22689083 sighed wearily. ". . . Oh all right then, if you must know"

"We'd been to Bury Palais hadn't we, to the Stones concert, me and my mates, Billy, Pete and Alan. It was terrific. We met some birds in the queue and got to chatting 'em up. Two of 'em were good looking but the other two were a bit grotty: they were all scrubbers really. One of 'em, the nice looking one with the brown hair kept giving me the come on. Her ugly fat mate had her eye on Billy, you could tell.

We said we'd see 'em in the 'Drover's Arms' after the gig. We never thought they'd turn up but they were already in there when we arrived. They were a bit giggly and we couldn't manage to split 'em up for a bit of kiss and cuddle. I wanted to go for the train but Billy seemed to be getting somewhere with this fat little Angie so we decided to leave it and go home on the all-night bus.

Anyway, one of them had to be in early so we decided to walk home with 'em. It wasn't far and they lived quite near each other. We got to this bird's house - the one that had to be in early - and found her mother was on a night-shift at the mill. I don't think her old feller lived with them. She had a young sister, which was why she had to be in early. Well, we went in and started canoodling with 'em. Billy, the crafty sod, slips into the back room with this fat little Angie. There was a right bloody noise going on: she kept squealing and giggling and shouting 'Ooh, lovely, ooh-arr, arrha! Go on do it'. We all thought they were winding us up - having us on.

On the way home Billy told us he'd scored but we didn't believe him. Anyway we'd arranged to see the four of 'em at Squiffers the next Saturday but something cropped up and we didn't go. So that was the end of that: or so we all thought.

A month or two later Billy came round to our house and said he wanted to see me. He'd got a letter from that Angie, the one he said he'd had it away with that night we'd been to the Stones' concert, saying she was preggers and that *he* was the father. She must have got his address somehow. He was in a right fucking state. I nearly pissed myself laughing: she was a right scrubber. Anyway, he said he'd put a 'nodder' on that night so he couldn't see how he could have got her pregnant. He said if she followed it up and anyone asked it would be better if we said he was in the room with us all the time we were there that night. He'd been to see Pete and Alan: they'd both agreed. I thought no more about it but a few weeks later Pete, Alan and me each got a letter to appear in Court as witnesses for the defence. We all thought it was a bit of a laugh . . . going to Court.

So we go along don't we and say that Billy was with us all the time and that he couldn't possibly have 'done the business' without us knowing.

"Jesus Christ on a bike! You didn't get two years just for that did you?"

"Hang on, hang on a minute, I'm coming to that.

Angie was looking daggers at us across the courtroom. Then she turns on the waterworks. It was a good try but obviously a put on. She was as hard as pre-stressed ready-mix that one, a right scrubber, even worse than I remember, all done-up in a pretty, flowered dress and pale stockings to make her look young and vulnerable. Her white face looked like it had been paint-sprayed on. Fat as a prize pig she was even though she'd had the kid months before. I don't know who was worse though, her or her mother. If you'd have put the mother in white socks and plimsolls with a ribbon in her hair they'd have had the pair of 'em in an Institution in no time.

Things went our way. The magistrate gave Angie a right bollocking: said that she was 'not only promiscuous but a pathological liar and had concocted a wicked accusation for base pecuniary motives', whatever that meant, 'regardless of the consequences for the accused'. He threw the case out.

We all went off to the boozer afterwards to celebrate. Poor bloody Billy spilled his pint all over the place: shaking like a bloody tree in a gale."

"Well how come you got two years then?"

"Don't be so fucking impatient. I'm telling you aren't I.

Well, we all thought that was the end of that but it wasn't. Billy, the cunt, starts going off his head, doesn't he? Not that we noticed at first. He couldn't sleep for thinking it might, after all, be his kid and he ought to look after it. The silly berk had worked himself up into a right bloody state. He told us later he used to wake up in the night wet with sweat and his mind racing. He never said anything at the time. We did notice he'd lost weight though: thin as a bloody rake he was. We all thought he'd been training to get fit for the start of the football season. Anyway, one night he really flips it. Gets up in the middle of the night and goes to the fucking police station. Doesn't say a bleeding 'dickey bird' to us: just goes to the fucking Coppers and confesses. Tells 'em he thinks he's the father of

Angie's fucking kid.

Next thing we know we're all up at the Crown Court, this time on a charge - Perjury. My dad did his bleeding nut. Billy's old feller got a solicitor to represent us: fat lot of bloody good he was. Said the Judge would take a very serious view of the matter and that we had better confess, plead guilty, throw ourselves on the mercy of the Court. I thought he meant we'd just get a bollocking.

So we went to Court. The place was packed out: half our bleeding council estate in the gallery, nosy sods, and five or six reporters in the Press Box. It was just like on the Telly: there were blokes in curly wigs poncing up and down clutching their lapels and shuffling piles of paper about. It was all 'me lud' this and 'me learned friend' that: a right fucking carry on. I didn't understand a bloody word of what they were on about.

Then this bastard, Justice Knibbs or something, starts up with all this shit about the foundation of justice depending on people telling the truth on oath, came on real heavy. I've got a transcript in my locker that our bloke sent us after we'd been sent down. I've read it so many times I nearly know it off by heart". I can still hear him".

22689083 put on a plummy voice: 'What disturbs me most about this case is not so much that the accused should have put the young lady in question through the ordeal of humiliation in Court, wicked though that may be, but that they blatantly conspired to pervert the course of justice by telling lies on oath. Nay, by telling premeditated lies on oath!'

'Our solicitor tried to say it was just a thoughtless prank of innocent adolescents who'd imbibed a code of honour - I think that's what he said - that friends should stick together and help each other out. But the Judge wasn't having any of it. He just griped on about the state of Society and the corruption of present day youth and all that fucking shite. I still thought he was just going to give us a bollocking but I started to get a bit worried when he said:

Again 22689083 put on a plummy voice: 'Such conduct strikes at the very bedrock of British justice. If we who spend our lives daily seeking the truth in the Courts of Law cannot believe evidence sworn on God's Holy Bible what are we to believe? I would be gravely erring in my duty if I failed to punish most severely those who pervert the course of Justice and conspire to flout the truth for their own evil ends. The exemplary sentences I intend to pass should be seen not only as a punishment for the accused, deserving of it as they are, but as a deterrent to all those yet to come before this Court who might mistakenly believe they can conspire to pervert the course of justice and get away without suffering the consequences of their misdeeds'.

'When he said he was giving Billy three years I went weak at the bloody knees. I couldn't believe what I was hearing. Billy collapsed: he freaked right out. They had to carry him down to the cells like a sack of spuds. His old lady was screaming blue murder: shouting 'No! No! I won't let them!' It was terrible.

Anyway, when he came to me, Pete and Alan he gave us two years a piece, the bastard. Said we were lucky to get off so lightly.

The crazy thing was that by the time Billy went to the Coppers this Angie had married a bloke who'd been having it off with her regularly and who *was* the father. She'd had a row with him when she told him she was expecting. He'd wanted her to get rid of it but she wouldn't, she wanted to have a child. She'd known all along - well before the Stones concert - that Billy was not the father; she was already pregnant. She must have thought she could stick it on Billy and get maintenance in case her bloke wouldn't marry her.

Billy didn't know any of this, of course, when he freaked out and went to the Coppers. It was ironic: she was the one doing the fucking lying. If Billy had admitted in Court, first time round that he'd had it off with her he'd have been paying maintenance for the rest of his bleeding natural- for someone else's kid! But that was too fucking subtle for the Judge: all he was concerned about was bloody Justice.

So that's what Perjury is - lying. Lying here for two fucking years for helping a mate out of something he hadn't done and all because some bloody stupid Judge didn't know what justice was when it was staring him in the bloody face".

"Christ you must be fucking choked!"

"Choked, Choked! Go to fucking sleep will yer".

THE GOOD LITTLE GOERS

I had begun to wonder if I was some kind of conjurer with a magic word hidden in my vocabulary that made Penny disappear. Or maybe I was some kind of computer with a virus in its speech mode which produced a magic word. We'd be having a drink in a pub, Penny and me, or be out for a meal at a restaurant and I would produce the word, like abracadabra, and the whole evening would suddenly disappear off the screen. I never discovered what the word was but it must be a fairly common one. Something associated with eating or drinking because it usually happened in pubs or restaurants. If I said the word, (or perhaps forgot to say the word - there's a thought!), Penny would simply vanish. If I'd used the word I only had to focus on the menu for a second or turn to catch the waiter's eye or rummage under the table for a dropped fork and she'd be gone. No cryptic message on the seat like "You bastard!" or "Stuff you!" like Maggie, Sandra or Sue would have left, or even screamed. Just gone. You could do as many spell checks or memory checks as you liked; let people search your top-hat or even saw the space in half to prove it but she would have disappeared. Vanished from the box where she'd been the moment before. Exited by some feat of legerdemain: the word's perfect: taken her mouse home. Of course you kidded yourself she had gone to the loo. By the time it dawned she'd done a runner it was too late.

Penny was not on her own though: Angie, Mary, Claire and a string of others had been and gone before her. Heard the word and run on ahead you might say.

Now you may be one of those nine hundred and ninety-nine in a thousand who don't use the word and don't have disappearing women at their table in restaurants but I'm the other one. I've seen you all enjoying yourselves: attentive with the chair, pensive with the menu, a bit formal but chatty over starters, seriously conversational with the main course, animated over the pudding, mellow and relaxed over the coffee and liqueurs, like on the telly, and discreet with *l'addition s'il vous plait*. If there's just the two of you, and it's somebody you fancy, you're chatting her up, touching her hand, plenty of mouth and lots of eye contact - straight from one of those interpersonal relations books, Michael Argyle or some-such - until the flattery works its magic and she becomes dreamy and relaxed, doe-eyed and pliant. People at the next table nudging each other saying "I bet he's on a promise".

Well, as I say, I'm the other one: the one with the word. The one with the woman with the tense white face; or the one with the woman sitting grim-lipped and silent; or blowing her nose and quietly crying into her handkerchief, seeking attention: a malicious form of public exhibitionism.

Or the one with that woman, rabbiting on, you can hear three tables away.

"Twenty-eight: twenty-eight women, it's disgusting! Where did she get that number from?"

"Had I known before-hand I'd never have had anything to do with you! You don't have normal emotions. You don't! You give absolutely nothing back! Fiona has my sympathy!" Fiona was the woman I used to live with.

"You just won't let anyone get close to you! And you're always undermining me!"

When she has finished her rosary of complaints I say,

"Look, I thought we had just come out for a quiet meal. I don't remember volunteering for a course of psychoanalysis and you can spare me the aversion therapy. If I had known you were Sigmund Freud in drag I'd have chosen a woman to eat out with". I could be nasty when I was riled.

She spits out expletives through her tense tight lips and the born again Christian at the next table gets up and has a word with the manager. Before I can say "shut your tits" I'm asked to leave for using bad language!

More often than not though Bill Giles is having a night off, there's no forecast, Penny or whoever just simply does a runner and I'm left sitting there with the growing realization that I must have said the word and she is not coming back. She'd have kept her coat on saying it was cold, or draughty, or it might be stolen, and taken her handbag with her to the loo. It was that which made me think it might be predestined or is the word premeditated? But whatever it was the word worked and it seemed to work with most other women too.

There was that time with Angie in 'The Crown' at Whitley Green. The main meal was finished and she went to the loo between courses and didn't come back. I must have used the word. She took her coat, discreetly, and I sensed she was up for a runner. I went almost directly after her and posted outside the ladies' but she'd already gone. Never been in! I asked someone to check and double check. I searched the pub, ran out to the car park, nowhere! I went back, apologized, paid the bill and drove off to see if she was on the road home. Not a sign! I drove a good two of the five miles back to her place before turning round and going back to the pub. I re-searched the place so carefully I could have got a PhD on pub interiors, or played hide and seek for England. I asked the staff had anyone been asking for anyone so many times they looked at me as if I was some kind of escapee myself.

I was trusted with a key to Angie's house in those days but when I got there the door was locked on the inside. I kept my finger on the bell so long even I was worried about the neighbours. When her daughter opened it to say "my mam says she's not in" I rushed upstairs and found her in bed.

"How dare you come into my house after what you said!"

"What I said!", I said. "What have I said?"

"You know what you said!" It was the nearest I came to learning the word.

"Get out! Get out! Get out or I'll call the police!" she screamed. How the devil had she got home, I thought?

"Where did you put the broomstick!" I shouted back up the stairs. "And don't forget to feed the cat!" I could never resist gelding my own jokes.

More recently, though, I've adopted the strategy of making sure I have something vital to her left behind when the woman I'm with goes to the loo in case I have unwittingly said the word. Even so, it's no guarantee. I won't bore you with Jackie disappearing for two days on Ios, or Greta in Turkey for example, who felt she just had to get away on her own on a boat to an island for the day without having previously mentioned her Garbo syndrome. But last Easter, coming back from France with Mary, I had her overnight bag and her duty frees. We were in the lounge. I was reading. The boat was docking in 15 minutes. I leant to one side to rearrange my things in the small travel bag we were sharing. I said something trivial into the bag about the tedium of the journey but it must have had the word in it. When I looked up she'd vanished.

I went immediately to the door and I thought I recognised her leg going into the loo. I wasn't too concerned. Ten minutes went by. People gathered up their belongings. My anxiety grew. The lounge emptied. She did not come back.

I asked a woman coming out of "C" deck toilet would she mind going back to see if there was anyone ill in there and to shout the name Mary. She said all the stalls were empty. As I looked through the door I saw there was another exit on the far side. Christ! I thought, the donkey's done a runner. In a panic, thinking she would get off the boat and I'd be left anguishing all the way back to Manchester on my own, racking my brains for the word, I ran to the information desk and asked them to make an announcement.

"Will Mrs. Mary Walker please report to the information desk on B deck" boomed out over the Tannoy.

"That'll scupper her" I thought, but she didn't come. I went to the desk again. "I think she must have gone overboard" I said, with as much flippancy as I could muster. They announced again "Will Mrs. Walker please report to the nearest member of the ship's crew or come immediately to the information desk on B deck".

I was in the process of explaining about "the word" and where I had last seen her when she strolls nonchalantly up saying she had decided to have a shower and was going to join me on the car deck when the call came. But I knew damned well she'd taken her passport: she wouldn't admit it.

"What was it I said?", I said, but she said if I didn't know she wouldn't say.

"I could have been left at the docks all night, thinking about it", I said, "biting my lips off."

About a month ago I was in 'The Gay Dog' with Penny. Lovely time, quiet chat, all was well in the metaphorical garden. She had duckling I remember and I had the rack of lamb. The home made bread pudding was superb. Her strawberry meringue looked good.

When the coffee came I said I fancied a Scotch. Now whether I had used the word or she had heard a woman with a Scottish accent somewhere in the pub or not I don't know, or whether she thought I was being cryptic about a Scottish O.U. professor from Pennicuick called Halfpenny who had fancied her at a Summer School and whom she was "toutchy aboot". She had not spoken to me for a week when I said I'd do porridge for him if he ever came round. I am at a loss to guess, but when I got back from the bar she'd gone.

It was raining a fine drizzle outside (I think she'd call it a Scot missed) and the visibility was not good. I collected the car and drove down the road as far as I thought she could have run. No sign. I drove back and noticed a phone box on a corner. It was out of order. I look to see if she's hiding nearby. In a state of desperate rage I turn and drive back towards home which, incidentally, is a mere twenty-one miles from the Gay Dog, and catch her in the headlights dodging into a hedgerow.

"I'm walking home!" she shouts and stamps her foot in the grass. This is a forty-year-old woman.

"Tell me what it was I said," I shout back. I grabbed hold of her arm saying "Don't be so bloody stupid, it's raining cats and. . .!". She hits me full in the face with her free hand and pulls away weeping hysterically, shouting "Don't you come near me!"

A miserable looking dog with a huge man suddenly materialises out of the rain: another conjuring trick. In embarrassment I say "Excuse me. Can I ask you to be a witness? This lady is with me in the car but she wants to walk home in the rain without a coat. If anything happens to her I want it known I did not desert her in the middle of Cheshire, in the wet, in the dark, on a dangerous lonely road without a coat." (I could hear her telling her friends). "If she gets attacked and killed or run over I want people to know that!" He looks at me as though I'm Woody Allen or some kind of maniac. I realise he's the landlord of the pub but he hurries on with his even more miserable looking dog.

I remonstrate with her to get into the car but she won't.

"Penny!" I say, "I can't take any more of this! It's making me ill! What did I say for Christ's sake!?" She sets off to walk.

I drive along behind her at three miles an hour shouting through the window

"Why don't you just tell me what I said and let me take you to a phone booth, for God's sake!"

Then I remember a lay-by near by so I drive past her, park and walk back, barring her way. She runs past me and I grab at her arm but she struggles free as a car is passing. It stops and the door half opens on the driver's side. I feel embarrassed, but not Penny, she runs up to it and exchanges a few words, jumps in and the car speeds off.

"Christ!" I think "What is she doing! Does she know him? It could be anybody! The Chelford rapist! the Romiley ripper!" I roar off after her. Round two bends and out onto a straight stretch. Two red lights in the distance. I increase speed. The bastard's clearly trying to lose me. We are on the outskirts of a town now and approaching a complex of roundabouts. He circuits them three times trying to interpose cars and speeds off towards the town centre. Who is this crazy fucker?

He stops in front of the Town Hall and lets Penny out. She slams the door and runs down a steep cobbled side street. I pull up as he drives off. It's a no parking area. I leave the engine running and stand with one foot out of the car screaming down the street "Penny! What in the name of fuck did I say?!" She continues running. I park the car on the pavement with the hazard lights flashing and run after her but she's disappeared. I'm no wiser.

When I get back to the car a police van is pulled up close behind it and a Copper is booking me.

"Penny for your thoughts?" he says.

"I wish I had one!" I said.

When he's finished writing he looks up and says

"Would you like to follow me to the station for a breath test?"

"You mean I have a choice!"

In the police station I'm annoyed to see Penny standing at the desk holding a telephone and talking quite affably to the woman desk-sergeant. So much for that liberal anti-police attitude of her's I think as I walk up and interrupt saying:

"Look Penny, this is ridiculous. Just tell me what I said".

"Is this the person?" the desk-sergeant asks, looking at Penny.

"Yes" she says.

"You hypocritical. . .!"

"I've had a complaint from Mrs. Pincher here that you are harassing her. I'd like you to leave".

"I'd love to but your colleague here with the breathalyser might not be too happy about that".

"I have to caution you Sir, that if the test is positive you will be arrested".

I take a deep breath.

Fortunately the reading is just below the thin red line. I go over to Penny and say in my Laurel and Hardy voice, "Another fine mess you've gotten me into . . . .".

"If you don't leave the station immediately you will be arrested", the desk-sergeant says.

"I'm only trying to see that she gets home safely!"

"Will you please leave".

As I turned to go I said with all the gravitas I could muster,

"I will, but watch she doesn't do a runner. She's got form this one and she'd outstrip you Bow Street cripples any day of the week".

*

I stand in the rain on the drive wondering if she will come home or go to her sister's. I can't believe so much 'aggro' can turn on such an unspeakable word.

A taxi drives up and stops opposite. She sits inside talking to the driver. They both get out. He's a short man, fat and forty, with a bald head and barrel chest and wearing a luminous blue pullover. He looks like a moulting budgerigar but he's chirpy enough and they chatter away as they cross the road.

I start to say "Can I have my things please and I'll go" when he flits between Penny and me and puts his fist under my nose.

"If you give this lady any trouble mate I'll floor you!"

"Just try it", I say, "But remember the old punch line. Nothing succeeds like a beakless budgie!"

The remark's lost on him, and I must confess it was nearly lost on me, but the diversion is long enough for Penny to insert her key and let herself in.

"I want my things" I shout and rap the door knocker.

The taxi drives off and I ring the door bell repeatedly. I am just about to go to the car to press the horn when a police car draws up. Christ! Has she called them or was it one of her neighbours?

I decide the best strategy is to lead with the cheek.

"I don't know who called you but I think I had better explain what's going on here".

"I think you had better go home and leave the lady alone!"

"But I need my things and I need to know what I said that's upset her. It's infuriating: I feel like Franz Kafka!"

"I think you had better go", he said again.

Before I could say anything to the Copper, Penny opens the door in response to his ring.

"Can I have my things please and I'll go", I say. "And by the way what . . ."

"They're in a black plastic bin liner in the garage. I've unlocked the door. Take them. I never want to see you again!"

"That's a bit heartless isn't it?"

"Heartless! You haven't got a heart: you've got a swinging brick!"

"Did I hear that correctly!"

The policeman went inside.

I put the black plastic sack in the car intending to go, but anger got the better of me and I thought sod it!

I went back to the door and rang the bell again. If she wouldn't tell me what I'd said I'd mix things for her.

Earlier in the week she had asked me would I mind giving her brother a hand upending her trailer tent and hooking it onto the wall when he returned it. There was a stout hook fixed high on the inside garage wall and a rope attached for hauling it up and securing it.

The policeman answered my ring.

He said: "If you don't leave immediately you'll be arrested for causing a breach of the peace."

"You mean a lull in the war don't you . . . O.K. I'm going but I want your number first. She threatened to commit suicide this afternoon. Look in the garage you'll see she's got a rope attached to a hook in there. I suggest you contact her mother." She'll not like that, I thought. "She's in no state to be left alone". The policeman frowned. "Just give me your number so I know who I've left her with in case anything happens". He shows me his left shoulder.

"Right", I said, "I'm going. She's your responsibility. But if she does anything stupid I wouldn't fancy your chances of becoming Chief Constable!"

*

A couple of weeks later Penny phoned me and said she wanted to talk. I put the phone down but relented and called her back. We agreed to meet.

The meal at 'The Crown' went tolerably well, at least to begin with. I went meticulously through the standard pleasantries from my: "How to succeed with women" check list:

"Penny you're looking (well/fit/better/beautiful/particularly attractive) to-night".

I chose particularly attractive.

"Penny you've grown your hair/had your hair (Perm any one of the following, cut/dyed/styled/straightened/shortened) since I last saw you".

I chose styled to be on the safe side.

"Penny you've got my favourite dress/frock/coat/jumper/top/hat/stockings/bra/panties (on or off) on tonight".

I chose jumper.

I said at one point, "How very perceptive you are!" You could hear her purr.

I even managed to do quite well in the obligatory examination I was required to sit whenever we met for a coffee - the elevenses-plus. The test required me to remember precisely where I had told her, over the phone, I had been and with whom in the intervening days since we last met.

Unfortunately 'you can't teach an elephant to play the piano with its toes', as they say, and I made one or two giraffes, I mean gaffes.

"But I thought you said you went out with John on . . ."

"Oh yes: how silly of me!"

"You don't have to lie to me you know. I'm not checking up on you".

Oh No? I thought.

I turned the conversation to our fiasco at 'The Gay Dog' hoping I would get some clue about the magic word. It was a mistake. She quickly went into earache mode. The 'runner' had cost her a pretty penny and she was not pleased. The taxi fare had been £11 but the driver had no change and she had ended up giving him three fivers.

In return for the extravagant tip he must have thought he was doing her a favour by radioing his office to send the police round.

She couldn't understand why the policeman had thought her suicidal though.

"I was certainly murderous but definitely not suicidal!" she said. "It wasn't you who told him there was a rope hanging in the garage was it?"

"Rope: me! Of course not" I said.

"My brother was not pleased to be got out of bed at two in the morning but the police wouldn't leave until someone came to look after me. I could kill that taxi driver!" she said.

Penny had got it into her head that on this occasion we should go Dutch so ao be on an equal footing.

"Don't think there is any sex on offer to-night because there isn't: you think if you pay for my meal you've bought my body don't you. Well I'm paying for my own meal and keeping my body to myself tonight!"

"That's a very mean minded Thatcherite thought", I said. "A woman could make herself into a whore thinking like that. Has it never occurred to you that someone might want you for your own sake, or may even be doing it though they don't feel like it so as not to disappoint you, or just doing it because its enjoyable. But seeing that you've put the thought in my head I'll tell you what: why don't you pay for both our meals from now on and I'll let you have my body.

If you want it, my body will be round at my place" and I disappeared to the Gent's.

I was surprised to see her still sitting there when I got back. I thought I had set the scene up for a women's marathon but it was Quiz Night and she couldn't resist a Quiz. She liked the word-games and the Quiz gave her the opportunity to display her apparently limitless knowledge of popular culture.

She had been lacing up her trainers, so to speak, when they had come round with the Quiz Sheets and she'd taken them off again.

I called our team 'The Good Little Goers'.

"Very funny!" she said.

We came last which made us eligible for the booby prize. She pushed me towards Mike, the Quiz Master.

"Right" Mike boomed out "For a pint now, one question on a subject of your own choice. Do you want music?"

"He can't face it" Penny shouts.

"Do you want Art?"

"He hasn't got one!"shouts Penny.

"Do you want sport?"

'Yeah, I'll try sport", I said in my best Australian.

"Right, for a pint then: name as many Runners as you can, in one minute beginning . . . . NOW"

"Owen, Wooderson, Brasher, Chataway, Christie, Modahl, Daley, Shergar, Red Rum, April, May, June, Scarlet, Angie, Susan, Claire, Joyce, Janice, Janet, Sarah, Anne, Fiona, Mandy, Marian, Frances, Cindy, Lydia. . ."

"Twenty-seven, Time's nearly up!"

I looked to where Penny had been sitting. and shouted. "Penny!"

The Mike shouted: "Twenty-eight! One pint! Going, going, gone for a Penny! Well done!"

*

When I got home I phoned her:

"One final Quiz question Penny. What exactly was that magic word that made you all disappear?"

"It was not *a magic word*" she said. "It was YOU!"

But then I thought, she would say that wouldn't she.

ALWAYS HAVE AN ANSWER

If I'd known beforehand Joe'd been a Copper I'd have switched pubs: gone to 'The Royal Oak' instead of 'The Albert'. I was glad I didn't. I'd never liked Coppers, you just couldn't trust them. Even as a kid I'd never liked them. They came to school to tell you how to cross the road. Then they'd pick you out for pinching coal or throwing stones or writing rude words on shop windows. The only Coppers I liked as a kid were those you got for taking jam jars back to the shop, or those the Gas Man left after emptying the meter. My dad used to say: "Coppers would nick their own grandmother given half a chance". But Joe wouldn't: Joe was different. I hadn't realised he'd been a Copper until after I'd got to like him. It just goes to show: you think you can spot 'em . . . .

Joe didn't do well in the Coppers: sidelined to Manchester airport for insubordination - the usual dumping ground. They just couldn't handle him. Too much of a character; and being a piss-head didn't help: they took their time getting rid of him but they managed it eventually. A Mafia choice - health grounds: leave whilst you're fit or we fit you up to leave. Good pension though. He helps his dad run a drinking club now, in Coventry of all places. I miss him. He used to tell us stories about his time in the Coppers: he comes back to 'The Albert' on a bender now and again: when he's had a win on the "GeeGees". Generous chap. Buys everyone a pint. Life and soul of the party: imitates Monty Python and Blackadder sketches - very funny. But he has his weakness: talks louder and louder as the evening wears on, then, after fifteen pints, glazes over and goes quiet.

Despite having been a Copper Joe fits in perfectly with the group of trainee alcoholics who frequent our local. A lively, shifting, motley crew comprised at any one time six or seven people revolving round Berthe an intelligent, witty, and larger than life, sixteen stone, crossword addict, journalist invariably shrouded in a voluminous black dress the size and shape of a carelessly pitched, wind-blown Bedouin tent and Danny her partner, a diminutive, thoughtful, creative, amusing ex-deputy headmaster, who could pass for Picasso: permanent fixtures who use 'The Albert' as an extension of their living room.

One Monday evening - a quiet night at 'The Albert' - I was on my own in the Snug. Out of nowhere Joe appeared, pint in hand.

"Ah it's Bob!" he roared, "Mind if I join you?"

He'd been in since lunch time and between trips to the Bookie's downed probably ten or more pints, which accounted for the slippage on his volume control. He would have sat down anyway so there was no point in trying to dissuade him.

"Good to see you Joe!"

"Just a quick word before I go to the Quiz in the back room."

Amongst his many talents Joe was a Quiz freak possessed of a ragbag of useless information such as the name of the fourth American president, the height of Everest, the distance of the moon from the sun or how many people *The Guinness Book of Records* said you could fit into a phone box. The kind of clutter Quiz freaks study into the early hours of the morning to impress their less well-informed friends. But he could tell a good story.

As Joe flopped onto the bench beside me the air squeezed out from the foam furnishing. "Excuse me!" he shouted, which made the tall blonde, just entering the pub, swivel on her high heels and look in our direction. I held her eye for a second. She lowered her gaze, and walked towards the bar.

"Give over Bob!" Joe shouted. Then in a lower, more conversational voice said. "You can't go chasing after classy stuff like that. It would be like a dog chasing after a car. What would you do if you caught it?"

"There's no answer to that, Joe", I said.

"Oh Oh! Always have an answer Bob. I learnt that in the Bobbies". Joe looked at me across the top of his pint, tilted it and ate down half the content of the glass in four great mouthfuls. As he came up for air he said: "That blonde, she reminds me of a woman I once knew. It was when I was on night duty in Withington I used to collect the 'rent' from the pubs: donations to the Police Benevolent Fund. The Sergeant and the Inspector weren't in on it but they'd been in the ranks. They knew what went on. They didn't like us getting free pints. We had to be careful. There was a lot of after hours drinking in those days. One night after the briefing parade one of my mates in CID asked me to do him a favour: phone a woman who lived in Ladybarn, the beat next to mine, and arrange to interview her informally. 'Try and find out what she knows about a burglary at the shop below her flat', he said. Apparently she had phoned in to say she might be able to shed some light on the matter but she didn't want to get officially involved.

I phoned early next day but got no reply: later her answer machine. If that's her voice on the recorded message, I thought, she's seriously sexy. When she finally picked up the voice sounded sleepy not sexy. 'Did you phone earlier', she asked. 'I work evenings and sleep late'. 'I know the problem', I said. We arranged to meet in a pub in Heaton Moor which was on her way to work. 'How will I know you?' I said. 'Oh you'll easily recognise me. There aren't many six feet one inch blondes about. Not wearing mink coats'. I thought she was having me on but it was straight up. She worked as a croupier in a Stockport casino. Rich boyfriend. Nowt doing there, I thought. But I didn't get chance to find out. Well, not for some time that is. There was a suspicious death in Withington and I got stuck guarding the perimeter tape. I passed the assignation with the blonde back to my mate in CID. He got someone else to go and I forgot all about it.

A month or so later I was in 'The Grapes' in Stockport. I was off for a couple of nights and catching up on my mates. I was on a stool facing the bar. Dave, my oppo, was facing outwards, leaning back on his elbows like you do. We were quietly disagreeing as to whether or not Sergeant Kiljoy was a real bastard or just a nasty bastard when I noticed Dave straighten up. 'Bloody hell Joe, get an eyeful of that!', he said, through the side of his mouth. I looked in the mirror and saw a couple of strikingly well dressed women in their late twenties. One was exceptionally tall, good looking, and Nordically blonde. I thought: that must be the Ladybarn blonde, but I didn't let on. I racked my brain for her name, but it wouldn't come. 'Fucking hell Joe', Dave said. 'Just look at those threepenny bits 'Totally unsupported!' I said. 'They stand up a bloody sight better than what you've just been arguing: unless it's a trick of perspective'. He could be funny could Dave. The blonde went straight to the loo while the other woman went to the end of the bar and ordered drinks. I said: 'I think I'll chat 'em up Dave'. 'No bloody chance. Premier league those two. *You'd* never make the second division. And I don't mean her cleavage'. 'I'm just going to powder my nose', I said. 'You watch this!' I stopped beside the one ordering the drinks. I'd learnt a thing or two from a spell in plain clothes. 'I hope you don't mind me intruding. I think I know your friend but I can't recall her name'. She looked up at me with a half-frightened, quizzical expression. 'Who, Jean?' 'Yes, I know it's Jean, I mean her surname'. 'Cleaveley', she said. Is she having me on, I thought, as I carried on into the Gents.

By the time I came out the blonde had rejoined her friend and the two were sitting in the window seat. I could see in the mirror they were watching me. Dave said to me: 'Fucking hell Joe what did you say to her?' 'Oh, I just asked her for a fuck. You know, the usual question' 'Oh yeah. What did she say: you wouldn't be able to afford it or join the queue?' Later, the friend went to the loo and Dave followed, to weigh up her arse. The blonde, Jean, walked over to the bar and ordered more gin and Martini. After picking up the drinks she half turned towards me. 'I know you', I said. 'Try something original, I've heard that one before' she said, but she put the drinks back on the bar. A good sign, I thought. 'How about: if those buns aren't for sale they shouldn't be on display'. She picked up the drinks again and turned to walk away. 'Piss off', I thought I heard her say, but then I caught her trying to hide a smile. 'I'm not saying I've met you, but I have spoken to you. We were supposed to meet in 'The Anvil' in Heaton Moor for a chat about a burglary', I said. She turned back and put the drinks down again. 'Oh are you that policeman? I'm terribly sorry. I couldn't make it. I tried to get through on the CID number but no one answered and I didn't have yours. Oh! I really am sorry'. She seemed genuinely embarrassed but I didn't let on it wasn't me she'd stood up. 'Well not to worry: it got sorted', I said.

Dave came back and I introduced him: 'Why don't you join us?' Jean said, when her friend came back. We had a bubbly half hour with the two women but they had to go to work. Dave didn't get anywhere with the friend. I was getting the come on from the blonde all the time. She said she liked big men and uniforms: 'Especially Copper's helmets'. I told her I was on nights in Withington next week, not far from her flat in Ladybarn. I wasn't too surprised when she suggested I pop in for a nightcap: she gave me her phone number and told me to give her a ring after twelve-thirty on Monday. When they'd gone Dave said to me: 'You jammy bugger, Joe! You jammy bugger!'

Monday had been a bad day. I'd been on Holts at 'The Griffin' all day Sunday. I woke up with a blinder. Bloody brass band playing inside my skull. Four o'clock it was. I'd lost most of the day and I got rid of another hour getting used to the daylight. I bucked up a bit after a pint at 'The Crown' but I couldn't have more than one, Kiljoy's nose was like a bloody ferret's and I was on duty later. I called at a Chippy on the way back. I'd had nothing to eat since Sunday lunch-time. I ate the chips out of the paper. I'd had a bad day: anyway, I got to the Station by ten o'clock, in time for the briefing parade. Kiljoy gave us some car numbers to watch out for. He mentioned a few trouble spots: premises to check and stressed the importance of keeping the two-way radio on. Then he gave us his usual homily on the importance of meeting punctually at the rendezvous points. Before dismissal he puts his face into mine and said. 'Is that alcohol I can smell McAdam?' I said, 'Yes Sarge, I'm afraid it is - my new aftershave'. 'Don't try taking the Mickey out of me McAdam'. 'No Sarge. I was simply stating a fact'. 'You always have an answer don't you McAdam. I don't have to remind you that it's a serious disciplinary matter to drink whilst on duty. And that goes for the lot of you. Parade, dismiss'. 'That bastard's out to get you Joe', Dave said, as we left the Station. 'Tell me about it', I said.

The early part of the Beat took me over towards Didsbury and Chorlton: I'd be nowhere near Ladybarn until about two a.m. I was to meet Kiljoy in Withington, at the corner of Firs Avenue and Barlow Moor Road, at two fifteen. If something cropped up he would contact me by radio. This posed a problem. I wanted to visit Jean shortly after midnight. The problem was not meeting up with Kiljoy nor skipping part of the Beat, but how to get from the Chorlton side of Withington over to Ladybarn without using up precious shagging time. Clearly, I would need a car and I hadn't got one. A taxi was out: too conspicuous. Besides, taxi drivers are curious; they ask questions. They'd remember a Cop in uniform. I needed to cover my back.

"Time to 'call in a favour' Bob".

I phoned Pete in the Panda on his mobile. After a bit of umming and arrhing he agreed to meet me at twelve fifteen. and run me over to Ladybarn. If anything came up and he couldn't make it I would have to cancel with Jean. Fortunately nothing did and Jean answered the phone promptly. My lucky night, I said to myself.

I had no trouble finding Jean's flat. I pressed the buzzer three times as arranged: two short and one long. I was about to press again when a voice through the speaker said 'Come on up Joe'. She sounded nervous rather than sexy. Understandable, I thought. After all we had only met the once. By the time I reached the top of the stairs I was gasping like a mountaineer with an attack of altitude sickness. I remember thinking I must cut down on the booze, or do a lot more horizontal jogging: a difficult choice. Jean was framed in the doorway, silhouetted by the subdued lighting. She was holding a cocktail glass, affecting an Art Deco stance. I thought: she has class this girl. Certainly not the Bimbo Dave said she was. If there's no inner soul in a woman she's just a Bimbo. And even then, if she's young enough soul might develop and she may grow interesting. In an older woman, I'll grant you, if she hasn't got it she can only deteriorate.

She gave me a 'mmwa' on the cheek, then looked searchingly into my eyes before leading me into the sitting room. 'Let me get you a glass of bubbly, Joe', she said. I could have murdered a pint but Kiljoy was on duty. 'Just a small one', I said. She pouted her lips in mock disappointment. She handed me the glass and said: 'I won't be a minute. I'll just slip into something more comfortable.' It gave me time to relax and look round the apartment. It was expensively furnished in a very elegant neo-Art Deco style. I thought: she's either on the game or spreading her legs for a very rich sugar daddy this one. The settee and chairs had a square 1930s' look about them but were upholstered in a fashionable, modern silver-grey, striped silk material. There were four or five Tiffany lights dotted about the room. I tapped one with my finger: definitely not plastic. Her mink coat had been thrown carelessly onto the back of a chair. At the side of the fireplace was an elegant chrome vase with four or five tall Bird of Paradise blooms. The green pointed beaks and spiky orange crests looked slightly menacing. I thought they were artificial but they were not. There were a couple of very good Pre-Raphaelite reproductions of long-haired women, on the hearth wall. On a side wall was a picture which looked original. Two women, one head cradled against the neck and chest of the other. Expressive eyes and red lips. One wore a green cloche-shaped headscarf, the other had chestnut hair. The lines of the faces were sharp. I read the name of the artist: Tamara de Lempicka. I smelt Jean's perfume as she came into the room. 'You like Art Deco do you Joe?' 'Art Deco? Oh yeah, I love Art Deco: Bloody good group'. She smiled and fingered the lapel of my tunic again.

She was dressed in a silk kimono and looked available as she descended onto the settee and draped her arm languidly over the back. She curled her legs up and raised her glass. I perched rather awkwardly on a chair next to the Birds of Paradise. She seemed relaxed but untouchable. We chatted about this and that. I was thinking: there'll be no nooky to night if we don't do something about this soon. Suddenly she got up and said: 'Well I'm going to bed Joe: you can let yourself out when you've finished your drink', and with that she disappeared into the bedroom. But she left the door half open. Was that on purpose? I sat for two or three minutes puzzling what to do. I decided my only hope was to go into the bedroom, thank her for the drink, and give her a good night kiss. I would slip my hand between the sheets and if she had nothing on take that as signal. I downed the dregs of champagne and put the plan into operation. I thought she was asleep but I was wrong. As soon as my hand went between the sheets she grabbed it and before I knew what was happening she'd handcuffed it to a ring on the side of the bed. 'I've got you now policeman haven't I? Let's have a look at that truncheon and that helmet of yours' she said, as she unzipped my trousers.

When I woke from my post-coital doze I didn't know where the hell I was. I lay for a few seconds until I remembered. Bloody hell, I thought, I'm supposed to be on fucking night duty!

I fumbled for the light but my hand wouldn't reach. By the time I got my other hand from under Jean's leg and switched on the light I was wide awake and panicking. I looked at my watch: five past bloody two. 'Christ! I shouted, I'm in the shit!' Jean fumbled for the key and mumbled: 'You're a big boy. You'll be all right'. I bloody near jumped down the stairs to let myself out 'Oh no!' I shouted. While I had been in the flat there must have been a huge downpour. Everywhere was sopping wet. There were enormous puddles stretching across the road, flooding over the pavement. Just my fucking luck! Then the radio came on. 'Where the Devil are you McAdam? It's two-fifteen!' I had to think quickly.

"Remember Bob, always have an answer".

'I was just wondering the same thing about you Sarge' I said. 'What do you mean?' he said. 'Well, I'm here waiting for you at the corner of Furze Road Sarge'. 'No you're not McAdam, I'm on the corner of Firs Road and if I stand here much longer they'll be shedding their bloody cones'. 'There must be some mistake Sarge, I'm at the corner of Furze Road. 'Well I'm standing by the road sign McAdam. F.I.R.S. Road' 'Oh dear, I said, that explains it. I thought I was to meet you at the corner of F.U.R.Z.E. Road'. 'Furze Road! Furze Road! Where the blazes is Furze Road?' He sounded apoplectic. 'It's on the edge of Ladybarn'. 'Ladybarn! What the bloody hell are you doing in Ladybarn! Get your arse over here immediately McAdam it's due for a kicking'. "Right Sarge", I said, and switched him off.

"Sex seemed to have sharpened my wits, Bob, in proportion to it having blunted my pencil".

'As I hurried along Barlow Moor Road I thought: that bastard Kiljoy will notice I'm dry and suspect I've been in the pub. If he starts sniffing my breath I'm done for. I dabbed on some aftershave from the bottle I always carry with me and popped a couple of peppermints into my mouth. Then I stopped at the first tree I came to and gave it a good shake. Unfortunately it hadn't many leaves so I had to spend time looking for an evergreen. I eventually found a *Leylandii* hedge and rolled myself along it. I overdid it a bit but that was all to the good. 'Took your time getting here, didn't you McAdam' 'Yes Sarge', I said:

"It's always best to agree, Bob"

'I saw a couple of parked cars that hadn't been there earlier so I thought I would just check them out while I was passing. You never know what might turn up Sarge. You never know your luck' 'You didn't pop in to see a lady friend or nip into a pub then, while it was raining, did you Joe?' Christ, I thought, the bastard knows! 'No Sergeant, I did not'. He put his face near to mine. Then he noticed I was sopping wet. 'You're all wet McAdam.' 'Yes Sarge'. 'Been Swimming?' 'No Sergeant', I said. It was then that I noticed he was completely dry. Got you, you bastard, I thought. 'You ought to have sheltered', he said. 'Oh no Sarge, I wanted to get round the beat in time to meet you at two fifteen'. Then I added: 'I see you kept nice and dry Sarge'. Before he had time to collect his thoughts he said: 'I took shelter in 'The Dog and Partridge'. Then he realised what he'd said. 'Well, *you* occasionally nip into a pub when it's raining, don't you Joe?'

'Oh no Sarge', I said, and I stuck my face into his and sniffed. 'I never go into pubs while I'm on duty. It's a very serious offence'. The Sergeant tried to stare me out. 'You've always got an answer haven't you McAdam? Always got an answer' 'Yes Sergeant I said, but I'm not sure I'll need one in future'. Just then an aeroplane flew overhead towards Manchester airport. The Sergeant looked up into the dark night sky. As he turned away he said: 'you may well be right there McAdam. You may very well be right'."

THE O.U. ADDICT

Not many O.U. tutors get to kill a student and I'm not absolutely sure that I did. But I'll leave you to judge. It happened 35 years ago. The student was called Alf.

In those days, back in the 70s, students who missed the D101 Social Science T.V. programme could watch it on video before the class. The topic was immigration. We watched harrowing scenes of population exchange at the partition of India; British troops evicting European Jews attempting to illegally enter Palestine from Cyprus and scenes at the London docks of West Indians disembarking from the Empire Windrush. I turned off the telly and followed my students up the stairs.

Admin gave us a different room each week. It was small, square and drab. All the chairs were occupied, except mine and one other, but there was someone sitting on a stool, shrouded in smoke in the far corner. Between the puffs I saw a figure through a bluish haze, like a chrysalis wriggling in a translucent cocoon. Magically a hairy grey goblin with bushy sideburns emerged through the fug.

"Hello. Are you Dunn?" I asked.

"No, Merssah" a slurred voice said.

"Mercy?"

"Not Mercy, Merssah."

"Not Dunn?"

"No, Merssah"

"Right. Alfred Mercer," I said.

"Not Alfred, Alf. Alf Merssah".

He sat there puffing his pipe; contained in his own private space.

"Come up to the table and join us" I said, but he didn't budge: just chuffed out a couple more puffs.

Despite the halo of smoke I couldn't help being struck by his natty, maroon and white, spotted bow-tie. It seemed to leap out and grin, carnival-like, with a cheeky kind of confidence. He stopped puffing. The smoke cleared a little. A small man with a brewer's goitre materialised. Below the bow-tie an off-white shirt gave way to a felt waistcoat, mainly mustard coloured. His 'where were you in fifty-two' blue-grey bird's-eye suit, darkened with age and mapped with dinner stains, looked much too small. He sat with his legs crossed: his 'flared' trousers hoisted far enough for his suspenders to show: they supported what had once been yellow socks. He looked like one of those blokes harking back to 'the time of their lives" who remain forever Teds, Mods, Rockers or these days aging pony-tailed Hippies. Alf pre-dated them all: he was more late '1940's milk-bar, 'Mocking-bird Hill' man.

"Well, come up to the table and join us" I said again.

Eventually he came and sat between Rachel Cohen and Myrtle Wood. They edged away as if to give him room but their aversion escaped me at the time. Later I noticed an odour of diabetic sweetness and dried blood.

"What did you make of the Race Relations Unit?" I asked, to take the focus off Alf and to get things going.

Neil Coffey, a black trainee nurse on Alf's left went first with a closely reasoned support of Peach's analysis linking immigration to job vacancies: citing the TV programme and his own family's response to Enoch Powell's 1948 invitation to West Indians to come to Britain to work in the N.H.S. Nancy chipped in with some more general 'push' and 'pull' factors ranging from war and famine to religious persecution and the London Transport ads to recruit for the Underground. Rachel, who liked history, got going on the Jewish Diaspora in her upper middle class accent. I prompted with a question or two and gave them a handout with statistics showing the favourable net contribution to the economy that immigrants make, no matter what the Daily Mail says.

Alf was fumbling with his trouser pocket and rolling back and forth on his chair. One hand was resting on the table. I saw the lower joints had 'LOVE' tattooed on them: there was presumably 'HATE' on his other hand. His face was flaking, like after sunburn. Blood seeped from the corner of his nose. I was about to ask if he felt all right but he pre-empted me by taking out a bloodstained handkerchief. Burying his face in it he blew, producing a sound like the ships in Salford docks. It was like the last trump. From anyone else it would have raised a laugh but no one spoke.

Joyce broke the spell with a question about police discrimination. She was generating a lot of nodding, white middle-class condemnation of the SUS Law when a slurred slow voice said:

"One of my daughters was raped by three niggers".

Neil Coffey stared blankly at his pen. Nancy Mountjoy scrabbled for her dropped notes. Don Kolakowski fished in his briefcase. Three or four others rummaged through purses and handbags. Alf followed up with:

"Bastards! I hate the fuckers. Spiked her drink in a club. Only 18 year old she was. Took her to a flat one of 'em had rented. Said she asked them for money. Said they'd paid her five quid each. I'd send the bloody lot of them back to where they came from I'd cut their . . . ".

"O.K. Alf, you've made your point", I interjected. "I can understand Alf feeling outraged about the . . . err . . . alleged rape of his daughter but bearing in mind that rapes are also carried out by members of all ethnic groups, as sociologists we have to be cautious. When is a rape not a rape? Who decides? Then there's the problem of 'all' and 'some'. Is it wise to generalise about the moral character of all black or foreign people from the behaviour of a few, or from unverified, selected, anecdotal incidents such as Alf has provided".

Despite my remarks and an explanation that biologists might focus on genes or male testosterone levels, psychologists on behaviour, and sociologists on issues such as social rules and cultural norms, the discussion got heated. Accusations of 'racism', and 'all men are rapists' were exchanged. Someone shouted 'Mr. Mercer is a Nazi'. Alf countered saying they had maps in Africa with Paradise printed where England should have been.

"It's getting late" I said "We'll carry on next week, after you've had time to reflect on the points raised more analytically. I want you to write this down . . . " and I framed something about questioning 'facts'; problems with Weberian notions of typification and stereotyping; the dangers of 'all and some' and of not deconstructing stereotypes when interacting with individuals.

Alf hung back while I tidied the chairs. I walked down to the bar with him. The corridor lights were out and I lost him on the stairs. He was bad on his pins. I waited and let him overtake me. I could hear the voices of the others ahead of us down below in the darkness.

"Did you see all those coloured pills he kept taking from those boxes?" . . . "Like a kid eating Smarties.". . . "What about that silver box with that white powder he kept sniffing up his nose". "Yeah! That wasn't snuff you know." . . . "I didn't mind that so much but he turned and sneezed it all over me!. . . ." "I'm sure that sweet, sickly smell on his clothes was bugs. I've smelt it before. .Does the Open University have to be so open . . . they should never have let him enrol."

The crowd in the bar was mostly those tall-story telling public school Businessman of the Year types: if you know the breed you know the dog. The name's Nigel, sleek hair, well down on the ears, a lank lock managing to hang affectedly over the forehead, but never unruly. A dark-blue, dateless, pin-striped-suit; a tiny, tight knot in the 'old boy's tie'. Well fed, a slightly over-weight thirty-five year old: the stereotype down to a 'T'.

The O.U. students stood out like bandaged thumbs; Alf in particular. I hadn't fully realised how unsteady he was; and no more than five feet two in his darned yellow socks. He had a glide in one eye; the other seemed oddly brown, not blue. His long, narrow head swung away like a lodestone to focus on my drink, pulling his head round to look meaningfully at the pint in my raised right hand. I bought him a pint. I needed to know more about him: 'to match my teaching support to his unique learning style' as advised by the O.U.

Alfred Mercer had no formal educational qualifications but had completed a foundation course at a Polytechnic. He was a chronically sick, unemployed, divorced, ex steel-erector of no fixed abode. He had three daughters but no income. I wanted to know why he was doing the Course and whether or not he needed help with the fees. I asked why he hadn't replied to the letters I had sent him.

"My daughter's address: never got them."

"Well, I'm glad you finally made it. Have you been ill?"

"Yes but it's all iatric" he said, slurring his words like a drunk. I was surprised he knew the word for 'caused by the quacks'. After a pause he said: "But you're a doctor, you'll know all about that sort of thing." I should have stopped him then, told him I was not a medic, but I let him go on.

"That sort of thing . . . .? " I said, waiting, trying the old trick psychology, but he was better than me at that game. He sucked on his pipe making deep, wet gurgling sounds, like a schoolboy sucking milk dregs through his straw. There was a good five second pause. I waited expecting smoke but no smoke appeared.

"Yeah, you're a doctor, you'll know all about that sort of thing" he slurred, his pipe wagging in agreement. I marvelled at the way pipe smokers did it: two great lung-shaped cancerous clouds of fleecy, choking smoke puffed into my face through a hole in the top corner of his mouth. I expected a genie to appear.

"I'm a Doctor of Philosophy, not a medic" I croaked, as he disappeared again. He couldn't hear me for the coughing. "Let me get you another and we'll go in there where we can talk" I said.

"No I mustn't have another, I'm supposed to be 'off the sauce' really because of my condition and the pills" he said, holding his trembling pint pot tight with both hands. I bought him another saying: "A couple of pints won't kill you Alf." I thought a couple of pints would loosen him up and get him talking.

"Well you're the doctor" he said again.

"Are you having any trouble with the Course?"

He took a long pull on his pint.

"Trouble. . . Trouble", he said, all slurry and slow. "Don't talk to me about trouble: my father died last week and I had to fix the funeral. I had one of my bad do's on Tuesday. They're trying to get me off the needle and on to pills. I blacked out and fell down the bloody stairs, that's why I'm limping. I cracked a couple of ribs: they're strapped up and I can't breathe properly. I moved in with my daughter but I couldn't stand it: kids got on my nerves: always rowing and fighting, especially Elvis, the black one, he's a right little bugger. So with all that going on how the hell can the Course be a trouble to me?"

"Umm, I see your point."

"Anyway, I'm not at Wythenshawe now, I'm back in Gorton. My son's been collecting the Course Units for me: came over tonight and brought me on the back of his Norton. Daft bugger forgot to bring them though. I'm only doing the O.U. 'cos I can't see me going back to scaffolding. I've always been a reader. I thought I might be a Social Worker. My kind of experience: bringing up kids, being on the dole, divorce, drugs, twelve months inside and a spell on probation would be good training for a job like that. It'd be a doddle for me: don't you think?"

"Umm, I'm not so sure about that Alf. Let's see how you go on. Want a fag?"

"Never use them these days: prefer my pipe", he said. I put the cigarette in his top pocket saying:

"One cig. won't kill you Alf, have it for later"

"You're the doctor", he said, again. I went to the bar to get a couple more pints to keep him talking. We were both pretty slewed by the time they closed the bar.

It was Thursday again. I was sitting in my room wasting my time with the *"Evening News"* before going to the Business School for the next O.U. tutorial. I was only half reading what I saw, my mind switching between a report of urban riots and Joyce's essay: musing whether or not Nancy would get Summer School support. I thought about the tutorial, reminding myself of the pitfalls of typification, racial stereotyping, labelling and the 'halo effect' when my eye alighted on a headline: "Addict Died in Fire." I read: 'He was a registered drug addict and on the previous evening had been out drinking, against the advice of his doctor. The combination of drugs and alcohol would have. . .' About half way through the piece the name suddenly started to mean something. No! It couldn't be! I read the item again more carefully:

Addict Died in Fire

The careless disposal of a cigarette may have caused a fire in which a forty-seven year old man died. A Manchester inquest was told that Mr. Alfred Mercer was found dead in the burning bedroom of his home in Cloth Street, Gorton, early one morning. He was a registered drug addict and on the previous evening he had been out drinking against the advice of his doctor. Dr. Godfrey Garrett said the combination of drugs and alcohol would have put Mr. Mercer into a deep sleep. Death was due to the inhalation of smoke fumes. Fire Station Officer David Slingsby said the blaze was probably caused by a discarded cigarette.

Verdict : 'Accidental Death'.

I stared blankly at the newspaper in a state of shock. . . Alfred Mercer. I'd bought him pints, given him a . . . Then I heard a voice, quite distinctly say: "I'm not supposed to drink you know" and my voice: "A cig. won't kill you." Alf, having the last word: "Well you're the doctor: you'll know all about that sort of thing".

KILLING TIME

"It's the last fucking Monday I'm standing here in the bleeding cold. If he doesn't come tonight you can stuff this fucking job and the fifty quid with it. I could be down the pub, nice and warm with the lads".

"O.K! O.K! Not so loud. It's not exactly my favourite fucking pastime either".

It was the third Monday the two of them had waited together, behind the hedge, in the damp entry at the side of the garage. They'd been there for nearly an hour now, waiting. It was a strictly "no talking" job and both men were cold and bored.

The younger of the two said "What's this fucking job all about anyway? You've still not told me! I hate doing someone over when I don't know why".

"Don't ask fucking questions: you're getting paid aren't you. I don't like it any more than you do".

After a couple of minutes silence he relented.

"If you must know, it's a grudge job for Eddy's mother. Eddy's doing time for a Stately Home job the pair of us did two years ago. I owe her one. But for Christ sake keep your mouth shut".

"Bloody Hell!" The younger man said: "If I'd known it was for her I wouldn't have touched this job with a bleeding bargepole: she's a mad fucker that one! You know what: I bet it was her the druggies were talking about outside the pub last night while I was having a fag. They were on about some batty woman who'd paid them for doing a job round here: cutting the steering wheels off cars. One of the cars belonged to her "ex" who'd moved out on her. She didn't want to be a suspect so she'd had them do some others to make it look like crazy random vandalism".

"One of 'em said a couple of months ago she'd had a red paint job done on all the furniture, carpets, books, pictures, bedding and clothes in the poor fucker's house so he'd have to move back in with her. I'm sure it was round here. I'd bet any money you like it was her they were on about. This'll be her next fucking move!"

"Shut the fuck up will you. It's none of your business. He'll be here any minute now!"

The fog off the playing-field by the railway and the black, murky, moonless November night made them almost invisible, even to each other. The darkness suited their purpose but the lack of diversion, now the beer was gone, was getting on the nerves of both of them. Their two mates, hidden in the lane, further down, would be just as pissed off.

The older, stocky man, in his fifties, pulled down the chin of his Balaclava. He tilted the can of Boddington's to drain the last few difficult drops but most of what was left missed his mouth and dribbled down the front of his half-open duffel-coat. "Shit!" he said, "who the fuck designed these bloody cans!" He wiped his coat with his sleeve and stood in silence as footsteps came and went in the lane where, on the other side of the tall wooden gate, their two mates were concealed. It was just a passer-by.

"Make sure you put those empties in your coat pockets and get behind the wall: he should be here any minute. And keep fucking quiet!" He too was cold and beginning to think that, yet again, 'the mark' would not be coming. He hoped those two 'idle bastards' hidden in the lane hadn't got themselves so pissed they would make a balls of it. They were nutters those two: two unreliable nutters!

Beyond the lane, across the playing field, a maintenance engine laboured slowly along the nearby railway track. The drilling racket made by the diesel engine rickered deafeningly on and on through the fog. Intermittent clangs, bangs, clunks and clanks rang echoingly out. Distant voices came and went. A detonator exploded with a loud boom! The two men jumped, the younger one letting out an involuntary "Uaah!" Before the older man could finish "Be quiet will you!", the first bang was followed quickly by a second, equally startling bang. Shortly afterwards the London Express screamed endlessly by. "So much for quiet", he thought. "How could anyone live near a bleeding railway?"

The Diesel Engine gradually moved down the line out of earshot and the silent fog closed in again.

"My God: This waiting's boring!" he said yet again to himself. He wished he'd known beforehand what he had just heard from the younger man about the car job and the red paint. Despite the debt he would not have got involved. She was a vindictive cow and he'd suspected her motives from the start but she'd insisted that he organise this and that he went along to keep an eye on things. But why, when he asked, would she not tell him that 'the mark' was her "ex" and why no mention of what he'd done to her? Why that steely, vacant, psychopathic tight-lipped look? All she would say was: "Nobody does what he's done and gets away with it: you don't need to know so don't keep asking". He realised now she was vindictively crazy and why she'd told him to say to the mark: "That's for fucking my daughter" when she didn't even have a daughter. The crafty cow was covering her back again to avoid being a suspect if the police checked her out.

Time dragged on: he felt in his bones he was getting too old for this game. True he did owe her one and he had to keep her on side. She had not been happy for Eddy to take the rap for that Stately Home job. She could have shopped him, and still could, but she hadn't blabbed. Later she'd let him store a roomful of antiques in her cellar at short notice: no questions asked. He'd been tipped off by a police insider but it was a close thing. She'd saved him from an almost certain five year stretch. He definitely did owe her one and he couldn't refuse when she'd asked him to set this one up. But she must have known beating up her "ex" was not really in his line.

A brief one-note whistle from the two accomplices in the lane beyond the entry interrupted his thoughts. He heard a car engine throbbing. The cold was forgotten. Adrenalin pumped. He came alive. It was the old feeling: the excitement of danger he'd known since his youth.

The car crunched the pebbles in front of the garage. A car door clicked, footsteps, a metallic clang as the garage door handle turned and withdrew the bolt bar. A rumbling sound: the up-and-over corrugated door ran along its tracks to clank and judder against the stops. A door slammed. The car drove, surprisingly quietly, into the garage. He could smell the whiff of the exhaust caught in the fog. The back of his head tightened. He held his breath and strained to listen.

The car door slammed again in the silence of the garage. He heard the footsteps of the two lads in the lane crunching gravel. "The stupid bastards: he'll hear them!" The light clicked off and the side door to the garage slowly opened. He could see a figure darkly framed in the doorway, standing, silent, listening. "Christ!, he's on to them!"

He pushed forward through the hedge and grabbed the lapels of 'the mark's' coat, thinking as he did so: "Why the fuck didn't Eddy's mother say the bloke was taller than me! How can I head-butt a big bastard like this? Jesus! I hope the cunt's not wearing glasses?"

"What the devil's going on?" came a desperate shout.

He pushed forward, harder, trying to force the bloke into the garage but he was too strong. He would have to change tactics. He jerked the struggling figure towards himself, stepping back towards the hedge, trying to turn him: as he did so he saw a stick swish down towards the back of 'the mark's' head. There was a loud crack. "Christ! Not so hard" he thought, you'll bloody kill him!

Two more hefty swipes hit the back of his head. "Help! Help me!", the victim shouted, with surprising volume.

"That's for fucking my daughter!" he said, in a gruff disguised voice, as she had told him to.

Another whack! And another!

"Jesus Christ! he's overdoing it! I wish to fuck the bastard would stop shouting Help me!"

There was a loud thump at the end of the entry and a soft rush of air as the tall, side entry door fell with what he remembered later as a surprisingly soft thud. "Thank Christ!, they're here!", he thought. He let go his grip and the new arrivals went to work.

"Help me! Help me!", the figure on the ground sobbed "Help me!"

He heard the crack of the final blow to the head and the whack of a stick across 'the mark's' knee as they had planned.

"That's for fucking my daughter!", he said again, remembering later, with some consternation, that this time he had forgotten to disguise his voice.

The figure on the ground half-rose, struggled into the hedge and collapsed, mumbling something about the wrong person, and lay still.

"Bloody Hell! I hope to Christ they've not done him in. The silly bastards were hitting him far too hard. Glancing blows to the side and outwards I told them. And round sticks, walking sticks, not fucking great pieces of one and a quarter! Jesus! I wish I'd never got into this one. . . ." At least they'd kept their mouths shut, though, and left the messaging to him.

He was out of the entry and into the lane now, running. There was no sign of the others. He paused to listen. "Oh! Jesus Christ! No!" he said, as he suddenly realised they must have gone the wrong way. "This way!" he shouted as he ran, "This way!"

His voice dispersed into the fog a few feet in front of him. He was running into his own sound trap: it baffled out any answering shouts yet amplified his own voice and increased his chances of getting caught. But there was only silence when he stopped shouting. "Where the fucking hell can they have they got to?" he said out loud. "Why the hell does everything have to go wrong these days! Jesus Christ! Why the fuck can't a simple, straight-forward job just be fucking simple and straight fucking forward for once!"

There was a taste of blood in his mouth and his chest ached. He was out of breath. "Bloody cigs!" He slowed to a walk. "Christ! I could do with a fag right now! I'm shaking like a bleeding belly dancer!" He suddenly remembered the second time he had given the message he'd forgotten to disguise his voice: "What if the fucker had recognised it?" He had only met him once at Eddy's birthday party and that was two years ago. "He might do though! . . .. but then again he might be dead . . . Dead! Jesus Christ! I hope to God he's not dead! . . . . Why the fuck did they have to hit him so bloody hard, the fucking animals! Oh please: please God! Don't let him be fucking dead!"

The fog diffused a pale yellow halo of light as he passed the street lamp near the end of the lane. He kept to the shadows and instinctively wiped his face with his hand to avoid recognition as he passed a dog walker.

When he got to the car he found they were already in it.

"How the fuck did you three get here?", he said.

"Never mind that, the fucking thing won't start, will it!"

"Give me the key you dumb fucker!"

He stopped the car a few minutes later in a lay-by a mile or so down the road, took out his mobile and tapped in her number.

She answered immediately. "Job done" he said.

She rang off.

*

The blows had stopped: he slowly regained consciousness. "Help me!", "Help me!" he shouted as he managed at last to raise himself and struggle through the gap in the tangled privet hedge into next door's garden. He felt his legs weaken again, as though at each step they were sinking further into a soft swamp, but he refused to let himself faint. The feeling passed: he could see a light.

"I'm not going to let them kill me", he said to himself, keeping close to the wall, back bent, holding the damaged hand close to his side. Skip-limping, groaning with pain, blood from his bleeding knee running hot and wet down the inside of his trouser leg; the wound on his head beginning to throb, blood running into his eyes and on down his face. "If only I'd kept my glasses on I might have seen them. What was that he'd said? That's for fucking my daughter!" He knew the voice: where had he heard it?

Christ!, I must make it to the window. "Help me! Help me!"

*

Well what was that, then?" his neighbour, Julia said, laying down the book on Creative Gardening she had been looking at and inclining her head to listen.

"What was what?" her husband barely bothered to reply; his face fixed firmly on the TV screen.

"I thought I heard someone shouting."

"Oh stop fussing will you! I'm trying to watch the Snooker" her husband said.

"No, listen Graham, There was someone shouting "Help me!" I heard it distinctly".

"Oh it's probably kids playing about in the back lane. You know what they're like round here".

"No, no, be quiet. There *is* someone shouting: I heard it again, distinctly: "Help me!"

"Well, if you're so concerned, go and have a look!"

"No, *you* go. You know I don't like the dark. I . . . there it is again! You *must* have heard that! Go and see what's happening, please

Graham".

"Oh! you're a damned nuisance. It's the final!"

"Graham!"

"Oh alright: if I must".

As he went into the hall to put his coat on there was a loud bang against the lounge window.

"My God! What the hell's going on!", he said.

He hurried towards the door but his wife managed to catch hold of his arm.

"Graham! Graham!" she shouted, as he tried pull loose. "Don't go out there! For God's sake! Don't go out there. Go round the front!"

There was a feeble beating at the back door and the sound of sobbing. She could hear a weak voice saying: "Help me!".

Someone was shouting in the back lane.

*

A crumpled figure lay in a foetal ball at the foot of the back-door steps. Despite the shock she remembered later that he looked serenely still. As she turned him over by his shoulder she recognised their next door neighbour. The blood from his spongy soaked coat oozed out between her fingers and onto the back of her hand.

"What's happened? Are you alright? Good God! Oh no!"

She held his wobbling head, fragile in her half cupped hands, and stared with the same wide-eyed look of horror and disbelief a bad fortune teller feigns about a terrible future. But there was no feigning: she was shocked and stunned and fearful he was dead. His thinning hair had matted to reveal a gaping wound exposing the cracked shell of broken bone. His crossed arms, cradled on his chest, loosely held each other. She saw that the third finger of his right hand was misshapen and curled down to point, unnaturally, at the palm of his hand.

Graham reappeared through the mist saying: "I can't see anyone in the lane", then: "Oh my god, who's that?"

"Get an ambulance! Phone the police!" Julia said, desperately.

As they half carried him into the house his right leg dragged along the ground, uselessly. The kitchen chair slid backwards as they attempted to sit his limp body down. They laid him on the floor, gently. Gently she held his head in her hands. (Later, his blood would glue her fingers together).

*

As he phased in and out of consciousness he heard his own thick, strange voice, slurring the words. "Where am I, where am I?" The light dimmed: he was back at the bottom of the garden, in the entry, next to the side-door to the garage, hands gripping his lapels, beery breath full on his face. A squat, stocky figure pushing, pushing, pushing . . . . He tried pushing back, somehow sensing that if they got him into the garage he would be dead.

He heard a voice faintly say: "Just try to lay still: the ambulance will be here soon".

The rushes of that slow motion film one's resident cameraman takes of life-threatening events were being shown. He watched with curiosity: one surprising frame at a time. At 'take two' there was a crack on the back of his head. Lights flashed. He was falling. Christ! he thought again, I must not let them get me into the garage.

He pushed forward again and fell. "If they break my glasses . . ." He clawed at his face and pushed his glasses into the privet hedge. Another blow to his head! His hand went back to shield his skull. Crack! He felt his finger break. His hand went numb. He clasped it with the other trying to pull the finger straight, thinking: Bloody hell! They really mean this!

Another blow: from someone emerging round the corner of the garage. Help me!" "Help me!" he heard himself shout.

The tall wooden door to the entry was kicked down. (They must have sawn off the padlock and unscrewed the hinges earlier). It fell with a surprisingly soft thud. There were two more of them. He felt the whack, but not the pain, as the stick cracked across his knee. A voice he thought he knew said again: "That's for fucking my daughter!"

"The wrong person!" he mumbled, feebly, "You've got the wrong person".

He tried to struggle through the hedge but was beaten.

There was silence. . . . He lapsed in and out of consciousness. . . . He could hear them distantly shouting to each other. . . . Faint voices receding into blankness in his mind. . . .

He was somehow standing outside himself now, listening to his own voice shouting: "Help me! Help me!"

He managed to kneel on all fours and raise himself. Hugging his arm and holding his head, he crouched, stumbled, and skip-limped slowly across the garden, through the outer hedge, along the wall and into the light shouting: "Help me! Help me!".

If only I could get to the window, he thought.

"Help me! Help me!", he shouted again, thumping the glass.

The light dazzled his eyes. "The light, the light!" he heard himself say. "I'm going to be sick".

He could feel wet hands around his head. They seemed to be holding it together.

He said weakly: "What have I done . . . . Why me? Surely even she wouldn't do this to me!"

He knew it was self-pity but what else was there to say? "Why *did* it happen to him?"

As the tunnel darkened he vaguely remembered where he had heard the voice that had said to him "That's for fu . . ." but the picture dimmed. The spot of light on his interior screen faded. Blood seeped out of his ears.

*

It was ten minutes or so after Graham had put the phone down before the police arrived: two fresh faced boys, almost, and a young woman constable. And a further five minutes for the ambulance.

The paramedic prised the lid off his sticky, blood-sealed eye. The police helped with the stretcher.

"Just stay lying down. . . You'll be alright . . . . Keep still now. Can you see my hand. No? Just try to move your toes for me . . . . O.K. Try to sleep now".

"I could do with a sleep", he thought. "Christ! . . . I could do with a sleep".

*

Julia, his neighbour, sat for the rest of the night, silent, in the white waiting room, upright, on a hardback chair: her hands held each other in a gesture that was almost prayer.

The door opened with a doctor in a clean white coat, a stethoscope hanging from his chest. He looked at her with level gaze but was unable to sustain it. He lowered his eyes and said nothing.

She knew from his demeanour.

"I'm sorry", he said at last. "I'm very, very sorry. He did manage to mumble the name of his attacker which we'll pass on to the police . . . but really . . . there was really very little we could do".

THE SAGA
OF DANNY AND ANGIE AND BENNY

Saturday morning I got a phone call from Trish. She'd heard I wanted some decorating doing and might be able to help. She knew a bloke who was down on his uppers and in need of work. I'm a bit wary of getting work done through a friend: if things go wrong it's embarrassing. I ummed and arred and said I was thinking of doing it myself but she insisted he was getting desperate. She wanted to help him so I allowed myself to be persuaded: "he's done a college course in decorating and he's good and cheap too, he's called Danny" she said.

Cheap is a word I associate with nasty but in this case, expensive, feckless and incompetent were just as good. I was paying Danny by the day at a rate less than anyone else was paying in Manchester but I could have papered a small housing estate in the time it took him to do a room: it was ridiculous, as well as embarrassing. It cost me a small fortune and for a job I could have done myself. I didn't feel I could sack him for fear of upsetting Trish - she might never speak to me again.

For a start, Danny's concept of a day was not the usual eight hours, nine till five, but more like three and a half. On a good day he would stick up a couple of strips, sign on for the dole, meet a few mates for a pint, and I suspect, liaise with some woman or other - perhaps a regular mistress when she wasn't busy with a client, given that he lived in the red light district of Moss Side - before coming back to clear up.

Though into his middle years Danny was a good looker and despite his age, almost pretty in a feminine sort of way. Above average height, athletic build, fair wavy hair, large blue eyes with eyelashes models would have envied, and he certainly had the "blarney". His speech and accent had become anglicised but he still retained quite a few quaint Irish expressions, "bejaysus". Women found him attractive despite his rough hands.

I was lucky if he managed to apply a couple of strips per session and most days he wasted more paper than he put on. I bought the wallpaper myself but gave him some money for lining paper and told him to get good quality. I suspect he bought cheap stuff and spent the change in the pub because when it dried it came up in air bubbles. I made him strip it off and gave him money for another lot.

For some curious reason known only to himself and the leprechauns he felt he had to do the wall above the picture rail not with small vertical pieces but horizontally round the room with one continuous piece. I won't go into how he pasted and folded the roll into a manageable pack. To stick it up he arranged a series of ladders, chairs and tables so he could hop from one to another as the strip went on and on like a snake. There was paste on some of the tables and inevitably he slipped 'arse over tit' and laid himself up for three days with a bad back out of which he conned Social Services for the rest of his "bad back: not able to work" life. I was only saved from a massive insurance claim by the fact that he shouldn't have been working whilst signing on.

Then there was the paste. He could never get it right: too little or too much water. One way or another it was never just right. I remember one occasion when the paste was as rock solid as cement. The wooden spoon he used for stirring was standing upright like a phallic totem in the centre of the bucket. "Bejaysus", he said, reverting to his best Irish brogue. "Yer could walk yer donkey across it".

The chimney-breast required three short pieces above the mantelpiece and one long piece either side. Painstaking calculations took place, - "this is what they taught me at college" - , pencil lines were drawn on the chimney-breast, measurements drawn on the wallpaper, pieces cut, rejected, more pieces cut. Any other decorator would have simply started with one long piece at the side and worked across the breast above the fireplace matching up the pattern and making sure the pieces abutted and finally put the second long side piece on. Not Danny. He put the two long pieces either side on first then found that the short pieces above the fireplace wouldn't fit and the pattern didn't match up. He'd wasted a whole roll of paper before he took my advice to forget measurements and start with a long side piece.

When the chimney breast was eventually done I thought all would be well: half a day ought to see the back of him. I couldn't have been more wrong. It was two more weeks before the job was completed. On what should have been his last morning he burnt his hand and couldn't work: he was lucky he didn't electrocute himself. He'd brought with him an electric kettle. God only knows why because I'd been making brews for him for weeks. It was one of those tall plastic jobs with an exposed coiled element inside at the base. He was about to put water in it when for some reason he wondered whether or not he had already switched it on so he made his hand into a fist and plunged it down onto the element to feel if it was hot. I heard the scream from the kitchen and found him hopping round the room with his hand gripped between his thighs. I had to rush off in the car with him to A&E. We waited five hours: another day gone!

To my surprise it was Trish who came round a week later for his money. She told me Danny wouldn't be finishing the job. He'd decided he didn't like decorating and was giving it up. I gave her the money and said, "Thanks for everything. I hope he gets better", but the irony was lost on Trish. She was in a hurry and had no time to talk. After all that hassle and a lighter wallet I had to finish the job myself. As you can imagine I was pretty pissed off. I never wanted to see Danny again but I had the dubious pleasure of his company a short time later at a dinner party to which he had not been invited.

*

It was one of those 'groupy' middle class do's academics and their self-righteous armchair socialist acolytes stage, to put the world to rights without getting off their backsides; slag off absent friends and rubbish the reputations of colleagues. I'd arrived late and didn't have chance to speak to Trish about Danny before the meal. Danny arrived at nine, shortly after the starters had finished, to pick up Trish. She was expecting him at eleven, or so she said, and here he was at nine. If she had colluded to get Danny a freeby meal, which is what I heard being whispered behind a cupped hand into an eager female's ear, Trish must have been a star RADA pupil: the embarrassment she displayed was remarkably convincing. Danny's explanation, that his watch must be gaining and his offer to go and come back, was much less so.

Naturally the hostess, who never missed an opportunity to get the low-down on her colleagues' private lives, and the private parts of some of them, might I add, said he must join us for the rest of the meal. A chair was brought and Danny was invited by one of the more ribald piss-head male academics to squeeze between the thighs of two of his more militant feminist colleagues who promptly rose to the bait and threatened to leave: "We've not come here to listen to your fucking sexism!" When the expostulations got to the: "all men are bastards and rapists" phase, Danny, who had up to this point remained silent, said he wouldn't mind being a woman. It was a remark which everyone took to be an effort to diffuse a situation he felt responsible for having caused. Little did any of us know, least of all Trish, what lay behind this seemingly innocuous remark.

More courses and more Rioja and Macon Lugny. The topic changed in the direction of Danny and what he did for a living. He revealed that he'd not had much schooling: the priests had done things to him and no he didn't wish to elaborate. His father had kept him at home to help on the farm but he'd done all sorts of jobs since leaving Ireland in his teens: from being a Beater on the grouse moors of stately homes in Scotland to odd jobs gardening and tarmacadaming drives but more recently he'd been on a painting and decorating course as a condition of receiving job seekers allowance. "You could have fooled me" I said, *sotto voce*. He was between jobs at present and though on Social Security he was doing evening gigs in the local pubs with an Irish Folk Band. He played the Accordion and the Tin Whistle and had met Trish through the band. This was news to everyone.

Trish was an academic linguist and though it was known that she was a talented artist and a pianist from a musical family she had kept quiet about playing the flute in pubs with an Irish folk band. She had kept even quieter about Danny. She was divorced and lived with her teenage daughter in a terraced house on the fringe of a rundown inner city area near the University, that much was known, but it came as a surprise to learn that she and Danny were, in the clichéd phrase Danny used "an item". Trish looked much embarrassed. She had clearly not wanted that information to come out at this time and in these circumstances. It was early days in their relationship and there were aspects of Danny's past and his current behaviour that she needed to verify and reflect upon.

Fortunately someone at the far end of the table who had not been following the deconstruction of Danny's biography asked the hostess had she found her lost car keys. The answer was "no, damn and blast it" but she feared she must have thrown them into the very large wheelie bin outside the flats when she threw a bag of rubbish in the bin earlier in the evening. The bin was circular, nearly six feet high and had only a small amount of rubbish in it and she couldn't see how she could get the keys out. All ears pricked up at this: fists were applied to foreheads: Rodin poses were taken up. Lots of solutions were offered by the four or five PhD's sitting round the table. All were racking their not inconsiderable brains, offering competing solutions, ranging from a garden cane fishing rod with a magnet dangling from the end of a piece of string as its hook, to a stepladder up which the Management Scientist, by then pissed as a squirrel, proposed to hold on to the feet of the upside down English Lit. hostess, suitably changed into her swim suit whilst she rooted through the rubbish at the bottom of the bin. "Not a pretty sight", slurred the academic piss artist, setting off the feminists again. Meanwhile the Economist was waving his arms about like a crazy octopus shouting: on the one hand this: on the other hand that, and there must be a formula.

While all this was going on Danny got up, left the table and went out of the room. They were still at it when he returned, grin on face, with the keys dangling from his hand. "Jesus Christ on a donkey!" one wag shouted out. "How the fuck did you get those!" the others cried in chorus.

"I just put me foot at the bottom of the bin and pulled it over," said Danny. " Bejaysus", I'm covered in shite!" While I was pondering, not for the first time in my life, the merits of higher education, Trish said, "Come on Danny, it's eleven o'clock, time to be going".

*

People move on. Time flies by. I'd been out of the country for a year on a sabbatical and I'd stayed on for a further year at my own expense. I'd let the house while I was away. It was in a mess and the kitchen needed redecorating which turned my mind to thoughts of Danny and Trish. I hadn't seen or heard of either for at least a couple of years. I'd split up from my partner before going abroad and lost touch with the old crowd who were mostly her colleagues and friends. I was bound to encounter one or the other of them sooner or later and sure enough within a few days I did so.

I was entering a small Italian restaurant I used to frequent in the old days. As I opened the door Trish walked out. After the "long time no see" silly business I asked after Danny. "Oh that finished ages ago", she said, "I've bought a flat near where you live and I've got a new bloke. He lives in London but he's selling his half of the family house to his "ex" and coming to live up here. I'm hoping to buy a house with him jointly in the catchment area of a good school I want to get my daughter into". So much for Socialism I thought: not quite Dianne Abbot but well on that way. "I am surprised", I said. "I really thought you and Danny were, to use his eloquent phrase, 'a solid item' Trish". "I thought so too, but I found out he was having affairs with not one but with a couple of women and a neighbour told me he was having kinky cross-dressing blokes round whilst I was at work. He denied it all of course. Said they were musicians from the Band round for rehearsals, but that's not the half of it".

Trish went on to tell me that one of the women he was having an affair with was a black lady from Moss side. She came home one night and found him wearing her clothes, dolled up in high heels and make-up. She had him beaten-up and kicked him out. "Poor fucker: that was a bit drastic", "Yes: but you're not going to believe this," said Trish.

"One of his friends, who I always thought was gay but turned out to be a transvestite, told me Danny went to a Catholic priest for advice about a sex change and got very short shrift. He told Danny - if I can remember it correctly - something like: "the hand of the Almighty reaching down into the mire wouldn't be able to raise you up, even to the depths of degradation, if you ever countenance having a sex change".

"It didn't deter him: he's been having counselling and he's hoping to have a sex change any time now: says he's always felt he was a woman trapped in a man's body".

"Fucking Hell Trish! he must be out of his tiny mind: he's in his mid fifties! He's no money. He won't get that on the NHS". "He will you know: you don't know Danny". "Has he told them he's been married a couple of times and has grown up children?" "I don't know whether or not he has, but for the record he's actually been married three times and he's got eight or maybe nine children: I made enquiries", Trish said.

We must have spent a good ten minutes discussing the ins and outs of Danny's sex life, marvelling at the ingenuity of his deceitfulness. Though she didn't elaborate, Trish didn't seem surprised he was thinking of a sex change; she should have known, she had lived with him for nearly two years. "Well, I've every sympathy with someone with physiological or genuine psychological problems or gender role difficulties but even after what you've said I'd be hard pressed to count him amongst them. On the other hand it's a pretty drastic, irreversible step to take, even for a con artist like Danny. We'll have to wait and see Trish: I'll believe it when I see it: proof of the pudding . . . and, dare I say it, watch that space!"

Sometime later I was given by a friend a cutting from the *Evening News*. It was an item about an unnamed local person awaiting a gender reassignment operation, dressed in women's clothing and carrying a small pet poodle in his arms, being ejected forcibly from a couple of local pubs owned by a well known local brewery. The brewery had to pay £3,500 for discrimination and hurt feelings in refusing the complainant access to both the Ladies' and Gents' toilets.

*

When I did finally meet up with Danny (call me Angie, now) a couple of months later, he quite proudly told me it had been a good little earner, milking the pubs.

I bumped into Danny again, in Tesco's car park, where he was admiring his new blue Ford car, stroking it: "Twelve years old 'bejaysus', only 80,000 miles on the clock!" His big stubby fingers, tipped with nibbled, red-painted nails were making snail trails across the bonnet. No small dog in his arms to-day. Flat shoes, Lisle stockings! Where the fuck do you find those in this day and age? Trench-mac, chiffon scarf, pony-tail, badly smudged lipstick and looking blowsy but with those 'classy' sun glasses, like flat black eyeshades, you can buy for two pounds in The Pound Shop, bound tight round his pale powdered face.

I noticed the dog on the front seat, lying inert in a pile, like a crumpled skein of white wool. "How's Benny the doggy Danny? . . . err Angie". I struggle with this gender realignment business. I can never get it right, even though I know he's going to go ahead with the operation. "Bejaysus I nearly lost him". "Wandered off did he?" "No, I mean lost him". "Oh, lost him!" "Yes lost him. He nearly died; he can't wander off these days. He's almost fourteen; he's got cataracts; he's almost blind. He bumps into things. I have to carry him. He pretends he's taking me out for a walk: pulls my leg when he wants to go.

The other day he took me for a walk down the Mersey. Off he went for a pee, sniffing around in the grass at the edge of the path, enjoying himself, then he let out an almighty scream!".

"Jesus Christ on a bike Danny!, err . . . Angie! What happened?" " He'd found a bumble bee and it stung him right there on the nose. He collapsed on the path! I thought bejasus he'll be after playing dead so he will! I'd taught him loads of tricks and that was his favourite. He can shake hands you know. Sings like an Irish linnet when I play the Tin Whistle for him. Dances up-right on two feet when I'm playing the Accordion. I've bought him a bow tie and a little evening suit: he loves it. We'd have made a small fortune, Benny and me, if I'd got him when he was just a pup. We could have been on TV with a "Dogs Come Dancing Show". He could have sung 'Often Bark for them': they'd have loved it. Anyway, he wasn't 'playing dead'. I just couldn't rouse him, or get him to stand up. Luckily I'd bought a mobile at Tesco's the day before. I dialled 999 and told them me friend Benny had collapsed and would they send an ambulance to get him to A&E double quick. I was just so frantic. I tried palpating him and I gave him mouth to mouth but he wouldn't come round. I even played me Tin Whistle to him. He was still alive 'cos he bit me lip. There was blood all over my coat. It took them 20 minutes to get here - 20 very long minutes!

They rushed from the road with a pile of gear and a police escort shouting: Where is he? Where is he? They were not best pleased when they saw that Benny was a dog. Said I was wasting their time. The Copper took me name and address; told me to take the dog to a Vet. I says to him: Benny's just as important as any person you could name on this earth but they wouldn't have it: the bastards! The medics said I should go to A&E meself, after I'd got the dog sorted out, for a tetanus injection. One of 'em said maybe it was perhaps a rabies injection I needed - fucking cheek! Anyway, I phoned the Vet and he told me to bring him in right away.

Benny was still unconscious when I got there. The Vet said he'd gone into shock and given his age may not come out of it. He gave him an injection and told me to leave him over night. He was very kind. He held Benny in his arms but said if he was no better in the morning he would 'put him down'. I was in a terrible state. I signed the form and went home to have a good cry.

The following morning the Vet rang to say Benny had recovered - me prayers had been answered! I collected him just now and there he is, but he's still very sleepy. Cost me £180 but I didn't mind paying and 'Every cloud has a silver lining': the Vet told me it might be possible to operate on Benny's cataracts when he'd got over the shock of the bee sting. It wouldn't be cheap: getting on for £2,000 including the three night's stay, but what can you do? I'd give me last brass penny for Benny to see me again. But I've only got £1,000. It's money left from the compensation I got from Hyde's brewery. You remember, I told you, they threw me out of two of the pubs I used to go to despite me telling them I was waiting for me gender realignment op. They didn't refuse me money for a pint though, the bastards, but they wouldn't let me go to the Ladies' for a pee. I'd got me women's clothes on so I couldn't have gone into the Gents. I'll have to think of some way of raising the money".

"Why don't you get the *Evening News* on to it?" I suggested.

"Great idea that - thanks for that: I'll think about it" said Danny, err ... Angie.

*

I heard quite a lot about Danny over the next month or two from occasional conversations with mutual acquaintances. I'd been told he'd moved into a flat in a terraced house in a somewhat seedy area quite near to where I lived. Apparently he now dressed exclusively in women's clothing, albeit second hand stuff that did nothing to enhance his appearance. Despite many counselling sessions and deportment training, opinion was that he would never pass as a woman. His gait and stride were very much the same as they had always been and much more suited to clumping over plough-land or treading the turf and bogs of rural Ireland than trying to trip daintily down the urban streets of a city. His voice if anything had deepened with age and become gruff and gravelly from drink - he was reportedly hitting the bottle quite regularly and hard.

The hormone treatment he'd been having prior to the operation had fattened him. The bosom pads he used to wear been replaced by genuine flesh but the treatment had increased and thickened his torso. The extra weight made him look like a corpulent middle age woman. His lengthened hair, now swept back in a pony-tail had turned from fair to grey. His beautiful eye lashes had somehow disappeared. His makeup skills were minimal. All in all he had translated himself from a good looking man to a frumpish looking matron. "You wouldn't recognise him", friends said.

*

Danny's major sex change operation had apparently been successful but despite a couple of extra minor ops. the voice remained as gruff as ever as I discovered when I finally came across her in a local newsagents' where I'd gone as usual, like an addict, for my daily dose of *The Guardian.*

At first I didn't take much notice of the rather tall, full-bodied woman in front of me. My mind was on other things, but the reek of cheap perfume turned my attention. I remember glancing down and thinking those feet in those brown brogue shoes are a bit large for a lady. After being served she turned and I saw a small white poodle dog clutched to her bosom. Full-face I realised it must be Danny.

"Hello Bob", a gruff, gravelly voice croaked as a big horny hand was thrust out to shake mine. I hardly recognised him, no, her - will I ever get the hang of this? It wasn't just that he was now wearing glasses: his hair had lost its colour and his heavily powdered face was flabby, the skin coarsened.

"Ah! you've caught me on a bad day Bob: I'm not usually after looking like this. Hold the dog a minute", he said, thrusting the little poodle into my arms. "I'll show you what I really look like" and he produced from his mac-pocket a postcard size glossy photograph. After taking the beloved dog back he put the photograph into my hand. I saw a person I didn't recognise perched on a tall stool clad in a low-cut sequinned top, displaying a considerable cleft of cleavage. A very short skirt, in fact almost no skirt, facilitated the display of exceptionally long legs, like a chorus girl's, clad in black fishnet stockings, crossed provocatively and entwined in a sexy pose. She looked professionally made-up: manicured, plucked eyebrows, full glossy lips and very long red nails. The blonde wig with curls made her look like a once beautiful but much faded film star.

Apart from the curved false eyelashes, which echoed those of the former Danny as a bloke, there was absolutely no resemblance to the frumpy middle aged person standing in front of me. "Oh! very nice Danny", I spluttered. "Don't call me Danny, I'm Angie now: Angela O'Toole. I've changed me name to what me mother was called". "Oh, O.K. Da. . . err. . . Angie, I'll remember that". She took the photo out of my hand saying she had to be at the doctor's by 8.30 a.m. "I'll catch up with you some other time", she said as she left the shop.

*

I didn't encounter Danny, err. . .Angie, again for some time: it must have been at least a month. I had to see the nurse at the local Group Practice for my annual M.O.T., as they now ridiculously call a 'medical check-up'. I didn't use the ramp but chose the steps. As I climbed them I saw a pair of large feet clumping down. I panned my eyes up from the shoes to the coarse brown stockings and on up to the trench-mac, belted today. It was Angie - 'by Jingo', I've got it right at last! The dog was there on her chest. There was a bulky, grey chiffon scarf concealing Angie's throat. Her face was bespectacled, raddled and blotchy and un-made-up: a far cry from the dishy blonde model of the photograph. "Hello err. . .Angie", I said, thinking: I'm getting there! "How are you?" "Terrible!" "Why what's the matter?" "Women's problems, but I don't want to talk about it. I've got to go to the Chemist's straight away" she said, clutching around the area of her crotch with her free hand. "There's something I want to talk to you about though. Can I phone you later in the day: I'm having trouble with the neighbours", and with that she hobbled away, still clutching her woman's parts.

Later in the day Angie phoned and asked me to phone her back as she was on the pay-phone in the hallway of the house where she lived and hadn't any change. She said she was depressed about her health and having trouble with her bedsit neighbours. The operations to feminise and improve the quality of her voice had not been successful: if anything they had made it worse. When people heard her speak they treated her like she was a man in drag, a transvestite, rather than a *bona fide* woman. Her GP feared she had early signs of throat cancer: she'd always been a heavy whiskey drinker. If that turned out to be the case and she had to go into hospital she was worried what would happen to Benny. "He won't be able to live without me and I'm not sure I'd be able to live without him", she said.

The problem with Angie's neighbours turned out to be that though they didn't mind the music they didn't like her friends, especially her transvestite friends. There was one particular neighbour who liked neither Angie; her music, nor Angie's friends. Angie explained that she often invited pals from the Band round for drinks and rehearsal when the pubs closed. Some of them were transvestites. When they'd 'had a few' they went crazy playing Irish music: the drummer banged away she said: "like a bull in a brothel!"

The neighbour who didn't like Angie - a Protestant woman from Belfast - shouted up the stairs while they were celebrating 'Trans-dressing Day' on the 14th of August : "If you want to play Irish folk music take yer fucking frocks off and fuck off back to Dublin, the lot of you!"

She reported Angie to the Council for noise nuisance so Angie, thinking that was racial discrimination, sent letters in retaliation to her MP, the Race Relations Board and The Equal Opportunity's Commission together with a tape 'of her Protestant obscenities'.

Angie had met the 'prot-woman' on the stairs later and called her a 'fucking kill-joy' and a 'crazy old cow'. In retaliation the woman had cut down all the shrubs Angie had planted in the small square of garden in front of the house to which all the tenants of the six bedsits had access. Angie called the police. They came but said it was a 'domestic' and left it at that. "Totally useless!" Angie said.

Next day the Protestant woman, incensed by the police episode, shouted up the stairs: "Ye're gonna end up fucking dead with a bag over yer head yous are!". Angie claimed that this was a serious threat to murder her and she would be going to the police again. The only thing holding her back was the landlord might think her a troublemaker - "Oh really!" I thought - and turf her out on the street.

I gave Angie the unremarkable but sensible advice that it was unlikely to be a serious threat, that the woman was angry and upset, and that maybe Angie should find another venue for late night Band practice, and that maybe her friends should wear women's clothes behind closed doors when visiting her. "Things will settle down I'm sure", I said. Angie didn't seem happy to let matters rest there, saying: "I'll get back at that fucking 'ejit' old cow somehow".

Angie's other problem was to do with 'fighting the Council', with help from The Citizen's Advice Bureau, for housing benefit. She'd won and they were now paying her £120 per week but as a consequence the Revenue was going to take half her tax credit away. She wanted me to write a supporting statement and to give her a general Reference 'as to me good character' to use if she ever needed one. I reluctantly agreed to write one for her but when she started boasting as to how, since her operation, she'd been enjoying not inconsiderable support from the Benefits System, and saying, jokingly: "I'll be able to move to Didsbury soon." I was, to say the least, somewhat irritated, no, infuriated, by this. I told her she wouldn't get a reference from me.

Instead I gave her a lecture on what I thought about 'Benefits Cheats' who gave the bloody Government Coalition ammunition to dismantle everyone's much needed Social Security status. Actually what I said was: "What the fuck are you doing: trying to get yourself on the front page of *The Daily Mail* in the 'benefit scrounger slot?' You fucking feckless, greedy self indulgent bastard!" We got cut off at this point. I guess she must have realised I was totally unsympathetic to her manipulations and she had put the phone down. She didn't phone back.

I didn't hear from Angie directly but was told she'd been in a convalescent hostel for weeks, as a guest of the Hospital Saturday Fund, recuperating from a throat cancer operation so a little remorsefully I sent her an unfunny 'Get Well' card.

*

I was on a bus using my free bus pass instead of my gas guzzling car, reflecting on the fact that the Coalition want to take the pass off me despite me having always paid my tax and National Insurance contributions - half a million over an average working life so I read somewhere. I drifted into thinking of nothing very much at all and, in the idle moment, picked up one of the free local newspapers littering the bus aisle.

Now I don't usually read the local papers: as a matter of fact I have an aversion to them. They're full of titillating triviality: accounts of petty crime, sensationalised sex or heart wrenching personal predicaments; sob stories about someone's 'little princess' and her 'miracle cure' or the 'Cash Blow' that's ruining the life of another IVF couple.; 'City Councillor's expenses scandal'; 'Footballers accused of gang rape'; 'Big Brother Girl Sharon and X-Factor Star in Three in a Bed Romp': people famous for being famous. The names change but it's the same story every week. Perhaps not quite as sensational as those of the Red Top Nationals, and no page three nude displaying her tits, but running them a close second with their lurid adjectives and graphic descriptions of what should be done with this or that 'sex fiend' or 'cannibalistic monster' who'd accidentally bit someone's ear in a drunken melee.

After my reverie I turned my attention back to the paper I'd picked up. There, staring out at me from the front page, clutching her pathetic opaque-eyed poodle was a picture of Danny, err . . . Angie: damn it I've lapsed back! Bespectacled and sporting a new set of dazzlingly white teeth. Not looking as glamorous as the photo she'd shown me that time in the shop when she looked like a model advertising 'Botox' or 'Cosmetic Improvement' but passably attractive in an 'older-woman' sort of way. The headline, in 72 point bold, black type read: '"heartbreak of Blind Pet Poodle in a Million' and in 18 point type at the side, enclosed in a circle: 'See page three'. She had obviously taken my advice.

I turned to page three: another large headline greeted me: 'Please Help Benny to See' together with another photograph of Angie looking like an advertisement for teeth-whitening. Three ropes of pearls were wrapped round her neck, presumably to hide a scar from her voice operation. The dog was looking a little less pathetic, more appealing - anyone would want to save him. The caption read: 'CASH PLEA ANGELA with her blind pet dog Benny who needs an expensive eye operation to restore his sight'.

From the column of text at the side of the photograph you would have thought that amongst the dog's many attractions and accomplishments he was also a sex therapist and a cancer specialist the way he had 'helped his owner through her tough times': the emotional trauma of the sex change and her throat operation. Readers were treated to an account of how Benny was 'there for her' during those gruelling days after the gender reassignment surgery and a pile of sob stuff about how the dog was her 'rock' when family and friends had disowned her.

'My grandchildren deserted me, every last one of them. Benny is my best friend, my sweetheart, my baby. Benny is all I have', she was attributed to have said.

I couldn't help remembering that Angie, when Danny, had confided in me that "he hadn't the faintest clue how many grandchildren he actually had!"

Amongst the little dog's other qualities I was not surprised to learn that he was also a fitness coach and an essential ingredient in Angie's rehabilitation. Benny takes Angie for 'walkies' down the Mersey day in day out. He was twelve years old when kindly Angie took him in as a stray and she has calculated that this little dog has walked 4,500 miles to help her get over her operation, but now the poor dog can't go for 'walkies' any more: 'It breaks my heart to see him crashing into things all the time. I've put padding round the legs of my chairs and tables at home so he doesn't hurt himself' she told the reporter.

The item ended with the information that Angie needs another £800 to add to the £1,000 savings she has accumulated by sacrificing all life's little pleasures for Benny to have the operation. No mention, I noted, that by continuing to booze in pubs she'd given back to the brewers nearly all of the £3,500 she had claimed from the brewery in compensation for her shameful loss of human rights a while back. No mention of her squandering money buying bottled beer to entertain her dissolute friends from the Band. The righteous Angie will pray for you if 'you can help her give back Benny the quality of life he deserves' in making a donation by phoning the following number * * * * an *Evening News* Special help-line.

Not exactly the Mother Theresa of Manchester, I thought, but not

far removed from that narcissistic, self-promoting, solipsist charlatan - just my opinion.

I couldn't wait to get my hands on the next *Evening News* instalment, headlined on the front page: 'Reader's Gift of Hope for Blind Pet'. There was grinning Angie with the doggy Benny held tightly to her bosom with one hand, the other clutching a sheaf of letters, cards and cheques from the 'big hearted readers of the *Evening News*': 'the great British public,' who had 'pulled all the stops out' and 'despite the recession, dug deep into their pockets' and 'inundated the paper with donations'. I could almost hear the clapping, and the National Anthem playing. I was surprised not to hear that zero hours contract workers had been called in to help clear the office which was 'flooded' with cheques, cards and letters from well-wishers or that little Benny's blindness had not turned round the Economy.

Mrs. Sharron Maudlin of Reddish wrote to tell Angie how the story in the paper had touched the strings of her heart and brought back memories of: 'my darling pets over the years.' Mrs. Olive Overtop of Tarporley wrote with her donation that 'Benny is totally enchanting. He will be so glad to see Angela again'.

I was of course even more surprised that no Vet had 'stepped up to the plate' with the gift of a free operation: it's such a caring profession and I mused over my own latest pet Vet-tale. I'd recently seen on TV just how generous and caring some Vets really are.

Some cunning BBC reporters took a dog, declared perfectly healthy by Vets at The Peoples' Dispensary for Sick Animals, to three different private Vets, telling them the dog had toothache, which it hadn't. Each Vet independently examined the dog. Each said it needed a tooth extracting. One Vet offered to take out 'the tooth causing the trouble' for £70; another wanted £120 for cleaning and taking 'a very bad tooth out' and the third Vet, who was clearly much more interested in the dog's welfare than the other two Vets and didn't want to take any chances said he would 'take out the offending tooth' but the dog would need to stay in his care overnight, and probably a second night. Cost: £320 please.

I thought to myself: 'Danny-Angie' could learn a thing or two from you lot!

The piece concluded by stating that following the appeal Angie had said she wanted to send her sincere thanks and prayers to those who had responded but most of all to 'the magnificent *Evening News* people' to whom she would be forever grateful, a comment which triggered another cynical reverie on my part.

If that much can be raised for a dog just think how much would have been raised from 'the great British public' had Benny been one of those begging derelicts with mental illness or drug problems, or one of those sick, unemployed, or unemployable people. No need to tax 'hard working families' or attack 'Banker's Bonuses' or root out unpaid tax from Tax Havens. Scrap Cameron's 'big society,' just let the newspapers deal with it: that should do the trick.

Imagine the Headlines: 'Readers Gift of Hope for: Drug Addict; Mentally-ill Pensioner; Suicidal Workless Teenager' or: 'Heartbreak of Benefit Scrounger in a Million'. A privatised Water Board would have to be called in by the newspaper to help cope with the floods of tears. The papers could run one of that kind of appeal every week: think of the tax savings it would make! Just ignore those 'whingers' who 'won't get on their bikes' and who keep complaining that they'd paid Tax and National Insurance when working on the understanding that they would get entitlements in 'hard times' and who are always objecting to being called 'scroungers'. They should be made to attend compulsory classes to make them understand that getting 'on your bike' and looking for a job is not about work: it's about the improving exercise.

With the kind of generosity displayed for that little blind dog we could cut those debilitating State benefits to zero and stop all overseas aid as well. No need to 'tax the rich' or 'hard working families' to provide for our 'undeserving poor' As for the billions of people over the seas and far away who 'live' on less than $1 a day and whose wealth those 'do Britain down Johnny Foreigner supporters' say we've plundered over the centuries - just cut all that expensive foreign aid nonsense: set up a couple of newspapers in each poor country and send them a sick dog or two: they'll be quid's in! No probs!

I came back to earth thinking Angie's thanks were an end to the matter. Benny would have his sight restored; Angie would get her beloved sweetheart back; the Vet would be able to have another weekend break in Paris or Amsterdam; the *Evening News* readers would throw street parties where the blokes could eat, drink, have a punch up and vomit while the women had a good cry over Benny.

Angie and Benny would attend the parties when not too busy opening outdoor events for Animal Rescue. Countless photos would be taken by teenagers on their smart phones; the *Evening News* would get lots of headlines and double page photo spreads: sales and profits of the paper would soar through their unbreakable glass-ceiling roof.

*

Imagine my disappointment, three weeks later, when I was congratulating myself on finally having got over my withdrawal symptoms from not reading the *Evening News,* my eye caught another headline on a Newsagent's *Evening News* advertising stand: 'OP HEARTBREAK FOR BLIND BENNY' I thought the dog must have died during the operation so I quickly bought a paper. But no, Benny was still alive, still 'there for Angie'. Still, presumably, taking Angie for 'walkies' down the Mersey and still, presumably, bumping into the padded legs of furniture back in the bedsit. Angie, I learned, was 'reeling' on finding that her blind pet must stay blind. The Vet would have to forego his weekend away; the street parties would have to be cancelled and the *Evening News* would have to search for another 'little princess' who had 'gone to join the Angels': preferably after being hit while playing in the road by a car driven by an illegal immigrant and where the child wouldn't have been but for her 'benefits cheat', single, teenage mother, luxuriating in her brand new council flat. All the more tragic, from the 'hard working families' point of view that yet another scrounging young mum had queue-jumped the Council Housing list by having a baby at fifteen.

Apparently after Angie took Benny to The Animal Medical Centre, as recommended by her Vet, he reluctantly admitted he was out of his depth when it finally came to operating on the cataracts and presumably was 'as sick as a parrot' at having to forego the opportunity to give Benny the 'joy of sight' to say nothing of the £2,000 quid fee. Angie was told by the Veterinary Ophthalmologist the operation could not be done: the dog was too old, the condition too severe and to do with the retinas not the cataracts.

Angie was inconsolable it was reported: 'I'm terribly upset about it. I went home and cried for an hour. I was hoping Benny would be able to see me and the new cap and jacket and the bow-tie and little boots I've bought him as a surprise but the chance has gone now: there's no hope.'

The report concluded by telling readers that Angie will now return the cheques to the *Evening News* Office where staff will destroy them. Anonymously donated cash will be sent to the Pets' Dispensary for Sick Animals fundraising HQ with 'some going to Angie for expenses'. Probably a few consoling bottles of 'hootch' I thought, though that wasn't mentioned. 'Angie will write thank you letters to all those who helped'.

End of story? Not quite. A week later the poor dog died.

*

The phone rang at 6.30 am. It woke me up. I reached out for it and knocked it onto the floor as per usual at that time of day. It was dead when I picked it up but it rang again almost immediately. I knew from the voice it was Angie despite the fact that she didn't announce herself. She was snivelling and weeping and could hardly speak. She managed to get out: "can you come round right away. He's gone - Benny died in the night in my arms. What am I going to do? I can't live without him". "I'll be right over Angie," I said, against a background of noisy, gulping sobs, "as soon as I can."

I found the house with some difficulty. Most of the houses were not numbered and there were gaps in the Terraces where houses had been demolished. The house Angie lived in was un-numbered and a bit of arithmetic was required to get the right one. There were four strips of plastic taped to the wall with names on but no bells and no door knocker. I tried flipping the letter box flap but it made only a feeble sound that lost itself in the hallway. I stood outside and looked up to the attic window where I suspected she lived: "Angie", I yelled but there was no response. I was on the point of rapping on the downstairs windows when I heard the attic sash window being raised. I looked up and saw a key coming down on a string like the thread of a spider. A gruff voice shouted something indecipherable through the two inch space which apparently was all the window would open. I unlocked the door and the key was immediately snatched out of my hand and hoisted back up to the attic.

The hall-way was covered with linoleum. There was no furniture: just a pay phone attached to a wall, and that musty, rank smell that poverty seems to bring to old houses. I climbed the stairs to the final flight which accessed the attic. The banisters of the stairs to the lower levels were well worn but normal looking. The banister to the attic itself took what was left of my breath away. Attached to the banister at about eighteen inch intervals were Snow White's seven dwarfs, each about a foot high. Snow White was at the top, mounted on the wall, waiting to greet them.

Angie stood next to Snow White, waiting to greet me. She was wearing baggy red linen trousers and a turquoise top over which was a slack, whitish string-like cardigan. An enormous pendant made from a horse-brass harness decoration hung on her chest. From her ears hung pendulous earrings with those raindrop shaped pearls dangling down about four or five inches. Her blowsy face with its faded cracked lipstick and flaky white powder was streaked with rivers of mascara running down from her eyes making her look like a badly turned out circus clown.

"Benny's dead," she said flatly. "I've been holding him and praying but last night he went stiff. What am I going to do?" "Where is he?" "He's in a drawer in my room". "A drawer!" I said, incredulously. "Yes, I've lined it with a yard of the finest silk from the Asian shop and laid him inside on a cushion."

The room was even more bizarre than the stairs. Three life-size figures dangled from the ceiling on strings. I thought at first they were bodies and I'd got myself mixed up with Hannibal Lector or his half-brother and sister but the corpses turned out to be puppets Danny had found in a skip somewhere, before his sex change. The facing wall had nailed to it a life-size picture of Jesus Christ which Angie had herself painted. The settee was piled with boxes, papers, books and assorted rubbish. Two tables had dismantled Piano-Accordions laid out on them in ordered patterns, ready for reassembly. Everywhere, including the floor, there was a chaos of dresses, skirts, underwear and shoes. Unwashed pots, with residual meals littered the main table. Two large Piano-Accordions, out of their cases, stood on the floor and an assemblage of Tin Whistles of various sizes littered the sideboard.

"I'm in a bit of a mess at the moment what with my women's problems and looking after Benny," she said. "Where is Benny, exactly?" I asked nervously. "He's in here," she said, pulling open the top drawer of the sideboard. Inside, on a flat cushion was what looked like one of those flaccid still-born dead lambs you sometimes come across in Wales or Cumbria at spring lambing-time. "Christ Angie, you should get him buried quickly: he's very dead and starting to pong!" "No, I can't do that: that's why I phoned you" she said. "You want me to bury him?" "No, no, not that; I can't bear to lose him. I want him stuffed so I can keep him with me: how can I get him stuffed?" "Well it's a bit late in the day but you can try to get it done if you're serious".

'Holy smoke!' I thought. "You'll have to look up a Taxidermist in the Yellow Pages or perhaps the Vet will know of one, but you will have to be quick about it".

"How about taking him to a Vet and having him cremated. Then you could keep his ashes in a beautiful urn". "No, I can't do that to him. I want to feel Benny by my side, hold him in my arms for ever."

She started to weep again and snuffle into her not too clean and very wet tissue again. "I know he meant the world to you Angie but you've got to be realistic. The dog's dead. You could get another loving dog. You must get him buried and get another one", I told her. "No, no, you don't understand: I don't want another dog: I want Benny". She flopped into a chair.

"You must go to the Vet. Let me know how you go on," I said, with as much compassion as I could, and left her to think about it.

*

I didn't hear from Angie for a couple of days so I phoned the house and left a message with one of the tenants, for Angie to phone me: this she did. She told me the Vet said it was far too late to have the dog stuffed and mounted. He'd offered to cremate the remains and put the ashes in a memorial urn for £100 but she had declined the offer. Not because of the money, not at all, but because she couldn't bear think of her 'baby' burnt to a cinder in the incinerator. I didn't argue with her. She had completely anthropomorphised the dog whilst it was alive: she wasn't going to stop now. "Is he still in the drawer? You can't leave him there - you'll get flies and bugs of all kinds round the place: he's been dead almost a week!" I said. "I'll think of something," she replied, and rang off.

I left it a couple of days and phoned again. She said she'd decided to have Benny buried in a proper grave and have a memorial stone inscribed and erected so that she could visit him every day.

"I've had seventy memorial cards printed and I'll be sending them to me friends." Including I presumed, the kind and generous *Evening News* cataract donators.

"I'll send you one" she said, and sure enough she did.

A week later I received a letter with an Irish postmark. Inside was a six by nine inch laminated card, the top half of which showed a photograph of Benny. The inscription below it read:

'My pet poodle Benny, who passed away peacefully in my arms on 24th October 2012 aged 14 years. Angie and Benny loved to walk in the woods: R.I.P. my baby'.

The card was accompanied by a note saying she'd gone back to the old country, to bury the dog where she herself had always wanted to die and where she 'could be forever with her friend Benny'.

She had taken his remains, dressed in his new hat, jacket, bootees and bow tie, with her to Ireland in her luggage.

TAPPING INTO MONEY

Some people are mean with money: they main chance, even when out with friends, choosing the most expensive meal when they know the restaurant bill's to be split. Others are generous, or perhaps approval seekers, they rush to buy you a pint. Some are profligate: "It's only money: you can't take it with you". Joan was not like any of those. Joan was sensible and careful with money, though not ungenerous. She liked to give rather than to receive. She had never been rich but she'd never been poor. Jack's job in Gent's Outfitting had brought in enough money for food and to pay the bills and the rent on their modest flat. It had allowed Joan to stay at home to look after her daughter, entertain friends and to buy moderately generous birthday and Christmas presents. After her daughter started school Joan had taken, on and off, a variety of part-time jobs and occasionally helped out with local charity events: "to get me out of the house" and "keep me in touch with the world".

As Jack aged though, his smoking, betting, and liking for a pint and his 'hail fellow well met' generosity got out of hand to the extent that there was less money for housekeeping and food. Joan, by this time in her early fifties, felt she had no option other than to seek full-time employment again. Not that she minded unduly. The economy was booming: married women had long been able to work full-time outside the home. Experience counted; Joan had secretarial skills, shorthand, fast and accurate typing and she'd worked before marriage in a number of jobs: at a National newspaper, a local Hospital and a large city Church. Her part-time work had kept her up to speed so to speak.

Joan soon got a full-time job: a secretarial post in the Economic History Department at a London University college. It was a job she loved. She now had more money to call her own and independence. She was well known in the wider University community. Though she drank only tonic water, lemon or tomato juice she happily went to the Senior Common Room bar and chatted to whosoever; she would always lend an ear.

Economic History was a small Department and Joan was much valued as an efficient, hard-working Secretary. She acted as a gatekeeper for the two Professors. She listened sympathetically to the troubles of the students and to the gossip and various woes of the Economic Historians to whom she provided solace in the form of small nips of Jack's homemade Sloe Gin which she kept in a bottle in her desk drawer.

Work and independence suited Joan, broadened her horizons, made her realise there was more to life than making jam and embroidery classes but it also made her increasingly dissatisfied with marriage and with Jack. Rows over his drinking became more frequent. Joan moved into a separate room, had a brief affair; even moved out for a few weeks but when her daughter refused to move with her she found she couldn't afford to live on her own. She very much missed her daughter's company so she returned home but thereafter lived a more or less separate life from Jack.

Jack became increasingly apathetic, dissolute, took ill and died from stomach cancer.

Jack's death didn't affect Joan as much as her conscience would have liked. She felt guilty for not realising his drinking was more a symptom than a cause of his cancer. It wasn't that she was indifferent to his suffering; it was more that regrets about the failure of her marriage had left her emotionally inert to the extent of being relatively unaffected by Jack's death, even relieved by it. She had her job, her daughter; she could get on with her life: she had a few years yet before retirement. Her widow's pension and her salary were enough to live on, not in luxury, but in modest comfort.

Unlike some of her colleagues Joan had not been counting the days to retirement: she hadn't given it a thought; put it out of her mind. She still looked good and though not in denial, had been secretive about her age. But she had no option other than to retire when she reached sixty-five and it left her very much poorer.

None of Joan's pre-marriage work was pensionable and she had not worked long enough at the University to get a decent occupational pension: it had never occurred to her that she could have enhanced her pension by making 'opt in' contributory payments from her salary. Her pension was inflation proofed, and she had her widow's pension as well, but there was 'slippage' and she now felt financially insecure and apprehensive. Her daughter had left home for a job in a Northern city so no longer contributed to the household expenses. She could pay the rent but the rising fuel bills caused her increasing anxiety and she began to take frugality seriously.

She sold her aged Morris Minor for scrap and travelled on her bus pass. She switched off the lights to watch TV in the dark. She turned down the heating and wore thick, woolly, knitted jumpers. She cut out several radiators and reduced the time the others were on by staying in bed longer on cold days. She filled a hot water bottle rather than switch on her electric blanket. On very cold days, she switched the central heating off all together: then went out at 9.30 a.m. to travel on her bus pass for over two hours on three different buses to visit Emm, a longstanding friend living in a council flat on the other side of London. But the bus was only marginally warmer than sitting at home with her coat on.

As the years of retirement wore on Joan became more and more concerned about paying her way. She had a little put by from her time at work but the rising cost of living was nibbling it away despite John Major's government being replaced by Blair and New Labour. Joan carefully divided her money and took to saving up to pay Utility bills: squirreling away small sums in tins, boxes and vases about the house before taking it to her Bank. She kept her eyes open for dropped coins near busy bus stops and parking meters and for change left in dispensers at cigarette machines.

The local food shops were going out of business so Tescos was her nearest option but many of their foodstuffs were only reasonably affordable in offers of "three for two" when she could barely afford to buy one. Meals for two looked reasonable at Sainsbury's but she was only one and the price of special offers included wine and she didn't want to drink wine. Everything was so expensive and getting dearer. She was thankful for Charity shops which kept her reasonably well dressed and presentable.

Joan was slumped in her easy chair in front of her gas fire, a shawl round her shoulders. She was on the verge of dozing off. A loud rap on the door made her jump. Though not normally nervous, she felt a frisson of fear. Her scalp tingled, her chest tightened, her pulse throbbed. The cup rattled in the saucer in her hand. Tea spilled into her lap.

"Whoever can that be?"

Since Jack's death and her daughter's departure she had become increasingly nervous: the isolation of retirement hadn't helped either.

"I hope they don't want money" she mouthed as she dabbed her skirt with her handkerchief and put the cup and saucer on the floor. "At this time of night: I'll pretend I'm out!"

The rat-a-tat was repeated and the letterbox flip flapped impatiently.

Joan groaned, bent forward, rubbed her feet and wriggled them into her slippers. "Who's there?" she shouted at the silhouette in the frosted-glass front door.

"Water Board", a man's gruff voice shouted back. "Thames Water Board".

"My god!" She said out loud "Water-board." There'd been something about people being Water-boarded and, oh what was it, illegal rendition, on the Wireless earlier in the evening but she hadn't been listening properly.

It was only just gone 7.00 p.m. but dark now the clocks had gone back, and having dozed off Joan had lost track of time. She had resolved never to open her door after dark ("You hear such tales!"). She kept the chain on, slipped the catch and opened the door a couple of inches.

The man was surprisingly big. His dark woolly hat, pulled down to his eyebrows, gave him a frightening appearance.

"What do you want?" Joan said loudly, in an effort to mask the tremble in her voice.

"Water Board", the man repeated, shifting position and pointing to a photo of himself in a plastic sachet clipped to the top pocket of his black blouson top. "Thames Water Board, love. We're going to shut the water off. There's a mains pipe leak down the road. It'll be off four hours. You'll need to fill your kettle and a few bowls of water. We need to turn your stop-cock off. Can we come in?"

Joan slipped the chain and opened the door. To her surprise she saw there were two of them. Her instinct told her there was something odd about these two: all her fears came flooding back. Their woolly hats and clean shoes didn't look right for Water Board workmen. Joan rubbed her knees, nervously and reluctantly followed the two men into her kitchen.

"Do you know where the stop-cock is, love?"

"I think it's under the sink" Joan said.

One of the men got down on his knees and opened the cupboard beneath the sink. "Just turn the cold water tap full on and keep it running love". After a few grunts and groans and a bit of 'Hmming and Harring' he got up and said to his mate: "No that's not the mains stop tap, it must be in the bathroom. I'll check the bathroom you check the hot water cistern it might be behind there. Keep your hand on the cold tap love and as soon as the water stops give us a shout".

Joan could hear the two men talking loudly to each other but didn't know that neither was in the bathroom. One had gone into the living room and the other into her bedroom. One shouted to Joan "Is it still running love?"

"Yes it is" she shouted back.

The man came back into the kitchen. "I just want to check the tap under the sink again". The cold water tap stopped running. "That seems to be it Fred". He remained under the sink. "Turn it on again Fred," he shouted. The cold tap gushed water.

"Fill your kettle and some bowls with water and then turn the tap off and don't use it after that, love. We just need to pop down the road to tell the team to turn the mains off and to get on with the repairs. We'll be back later".

Joan thought she heard the front door close but a minute or two later she heard a noise. "My god they've not gone!" She quickly turned off the tap. By the time she got into the hallway the two men were at the front door.

"What are you doing?" Joan shouted.

"We were just checking all the radiators were switched off in the rooms. Don't worry love everything seems to be all right. Make sure you fill your kettle. We'll be back later".

"The radiators: what have the radiators to do with it?" Joan said in bewilderment.

Joan bolted the door behind them, put the chain on and lent against the wall, trembling. "My god: that was a near thing! Were they thieves?" But they couldn't have taken anything in the time they had been in the rooms. She checked her handbag was still under the cushion on her chair. Yes her bag was still there and her purse still in it. Nothing had been disturbed in her bedroom. Her jewellery was still in its box in the bottom drawer. "It's a good job I'm careful", she congratulated herself. Despite this she put on her hat and coat and went down the street a short distance. There was no sign of any Water Board activity.

After shilly-shallying as to whether or not to phone the police she decided not to bother, as nothing had been taken. She made herself a cup of tea and calmed herself down in front of the telly. An hour later when she went as she usually did, to phone her daughter she discovered her address book was missing from its place by the phone. "How peculiar: why on earth would anyone want to take that!"

Joan knew she was becoming absent minded and forgetful these days but she was sure she had seen that book near the phone earlier in the evening. But then again she had been equally sure she had put her reading glasses on her bedside table until she found them in the fridge. She went to see if she had perhaps put the address book on her bedside table but it was not there: "they *must* have taken it!"

Joan was sure she could remember some of the addresses and phone numbers of her close friends and relatives but there were many addresses she couldn't recall these days and the address book contained jottings and reminders about birthdays, optician and dental appointments and the complicated names of her prescription tablets.

"Oh dear, I can't live without my address book! I shall have to phone the police after all". She picked up the phone and dialled 999.

The fresh faced uniformed policeman who arrived half an hour later didn't look old enough to have left school but these days most people Joan encountered didn't look old enough to be doing what they were doing. He painstakingly took down Joan's account of the antics of the bogus Water Board men and reassured Joan that they really were thieves.

"You were quite right to phone us. We've had a number of reports of this kind of thing but don't worry, we'll catch them eventually. I'm not sure you'll get your address book back though they'll have probably thrown it away. Let's hope someone finds it and hands it in. It was lucky you spotted what they were up to. Are you quite sure they didn't take anything else?"

"Yes. My handbag was under the cushion where I left it and my purse was still there with some money in it. I've had a good look round and there doesn't seem to be anything else missing".

As he got up to leave the policeman said to Joan "You seem a little bit shaken up. Have you got a neighbour who could stay with you for tonight?"

"Oh I'll be alright. I'll talk about it with my daughter when I phone her".

"I'll see if Victim Support can send someone round in the morning to have a chat with you. Try not to let it worry you and don't ever open the door to anyone you don't know."

As Joan let him out the phone rang. "That will be my daughter wondering why I haven't phoned her". She locked the door and went to answer it.

It was Joan's daughter.

"Mummers! Why didn't you phone at your usual time? I had to go out for a couple of hours. I expected a message on my answer machine when I got back: I was really worried".

"I've been Water-boarded that's why".

"Water-boarded! Whatever do you mean?"

"Burgled: by two men from the Water Board."

Joan gave her daughter a lengthy but somewhat garbled account of the visit from the two bogus Water Board workmen, saying "They only took my address book can you believe!"

"Your address book! I hope they didn't take your debit card as well?"

"No, it's in my purse. I always keep it there. I never use it. As you know I hate those 'holes in the wall' things. I can never remember the PIN number. I go to the Bank to get money with my cheque book. What's wrong with that?"

Oh Mummers! Are you sure it's in your purse? You know you've been forgetting where you've put things: go and have a look".

Joan took her handbag from under the cushion, rummaged through it, found her purse and sifted through the various cards: National Trust, Café Nero, plumber, electrician, an A.A. card from the past but no RBS debit card. Joan searched again.

"It doesn't seem to be here".

"Oh Mummers, they've almost certainly taken it and they've got your PIN number too".

"How could they have my PIN number?"

"Don't you remember, I wrote your PIN number on the front page of your address book where you could easily find it: it said 'My PIN number, RBS * * * *' in big figures. You must go to the Bank first thing in the morning and tell them your card has been stolen and ask them to cancel it for you. Phone the police and tell them you think your RBS card as well as your address book was stolen".

It was getting on for midnight when Joan finally got through to the local police station.

Joan was waiting on the doorstep of the Bank at 10'oclock the following morning when the Bank manager and a clerk arrived to open up. The Manager knew Joan: she'd been a customer for years.

"You're an early bird, couldn't you sleep?" the Manager quipped.

"No I couldn't" and she told him about the two men and the theft of her debit card and asked him to help her cancel it. He brought up Joan's account details on the computer screen. The thieves had used the card and pin yesterday in the late evening at a cash point in an area some miles away: they had drawn out £300 and a further £300 at one minute past midnight.

Joan could hardly breathe: a wave of panic made her feel faint. She held on to the counter. Six hundred pounds: almost all that she had in her account. The Bank manager could see she was in a state of shock and visibly distressed. He brought a chair. "Sit down I'll get my assistant to make you a cup of tea. You reported the theft to the police: it's possible they've already caught them". He didn't think so but felt Joan needed something to cling on to.

When she got home Joan phoned her daughter with the bad news. Her daughter phoned Royal Bank of Scotland. They assured her that the card was cancelled and that no more could be stolen from her mother's account. The whole matter was being referred to the Bank's Fraud Department and that her mother would be hearing from them in due course.

"Don't give up hope Mummers; it's possible they might accept liability or the police might catch the two men if they try that trick again. I'll speak to you tonight".

Joan made herself a cup of tea, switched on her gas fire and tried to remember whether it was today or next week she had to go again to the Memory Clinic: she had written it in her address book but she no longer had her address book. She just couldn't remember: she remembered she hadn't been able to say the alphabet backwards but she'd never in her life had to do that; and why on earth should she be expected to know the Prime Minister. The knock on the door made her jump. She was not going to answer it. A voice shouted through the letter box "Victim Support". "Go away" she shouted back. "I don't need Victim Support".

Joan said out aloud to herself: "Victim Support, Victim Support. I don't want Victim Support! I want my money back. I don't want busy bodies giving me sympathy" and she started going over yet again the events of the night before.

The evening conversation between Joan and her daughter did not go well. Joan neurotically kept recounting the events of the previous evening.

"They won't catch them, they won't. They are too clever those two. I'll never get my money back! It makes me just want to give up. All my savings, all that scrimping and saving: I'm too old. I just want to die! The rent's due on Friday! I haven't enough left to pay it, I'll be evicted!"

"Oh Mummers stop it! You're worrying too much. The Bank are looking into it. You reported it as soon as you could: they'll refund the money. If they don't I'll give it to you! I *do* wish you would stop worrying about it".

"It's all very well for you to say stop worrying. You've not just had all your money stolen".

"Oh stop it mother. It's not the end of the world. I've told you I'll give you the money if you don't get it back: just stop worrying about it. It's only money!"

"Only money! Only money! A lot of sympathy I get from you! I'm going to bed!" and Joan slammed the phone down.

But when Joan got to bed she could not get to sleep.

"I had lurid dreams and my mind kept racing over the robbery" she told her downstairs neighbour the following morning. The two Water Board men had been in the dream but one of them looked a bit like Jack, her former husband. She had been tied up, slapped across the face, her arm twisted up her back until she had revealed her PIN number and the whereabouts of her debit card. All her jewellery had been taken and the contents of the drawers in her bedroom strewn all over the floor.

Over the next few nights the same dream recurred. Joan started to believe the dream was what had actually happened and instead of recovering her normal self she became even more traumatised and increasingly dramatic about her loss of money and the threat of losing her flat. When she phoned her friends and relatives she began to recount the dream instead of the actual event. The increase in sympathy and concern did nothing to reinstate reality.

Joan's niece tried to reassure her saying "Your landlady won't throw you out, she's known you all these years, she's a kind, understanding person". But Joan would not be reassured.

"With all my money gone I won't be able to pay next month's rent: I couldn't bear that. And how can I pay my gas bill and my electricity? They will cut me off!"

Joan's niece was so concerned she phoned her cousin, Joan's daughter to say "I've never known Aunty Joan so agitated; is she alright? She'll make herself ill if she carries on like this. Should I send her something? I don't mean £600 of course, but something?"

The next day Joan's niece sent her a "Thinking of you" card and a cheque for £50 with the message "Hope this will go some way towards paying the rent".

News of Joan's burglary quickly got around and within a day or two she was receiving flowers and "So sorry to hear your news" cards from friends and acquaintances: some of whom she hardly knew or couldn't remember. Joan was pleased: her daughter embarrassed. "You must write and thank everyone but don't keep telling people you can't pay the rent!"

Joan made a list of their names and the amounts given to her but continued to phone round, sometimes the same person twice, forgetting she had phoned earlier and again lamented her loss of the £600.

She phoned her friend Emm to tell her she couldn't face the bus journey to visit her at the moment. She didn't mention that she had set off to see her earlier and absentmindedly got back on to the same bus she had just arrived on and to her surprise found herself back at home. Once again Joan told Emm that she had been robbed of £600 but this time adding "The thieves tied me up and left me when they stole my money. I don't know how I'm going to pay the rent this month or the gas and electric bill. I don't feel well. I can't even remember where I've put things or what day it is. I keep having flash backs. I jump out of my skin at the least noise and run into the bathroom and lock the door if somebody knocks".

Emm was utterly shocked. "They tied you up? Tied you up! I didn't realise they'd tied you up! Oh you poor thing: you must have been absolutely terrified! Oh lord, whatever next!"

A few days later a bulky envelope fell onto Joan's mat. Inside was £200 in £20 pound notes and a note saying "It's all I had in my Post Office Savings Account but what's mine is yours. Cheer up Joan. Emm".

Joan wrote down, Emm £200, but she didn't tell her daughter. She knew her daughter would say it's far too much and tell her to thank Emm but send it back.

By the time Joan got round to phoning yet another friend, still working in the Economic History Department, her account of the robbery had become even more lurid. Besides being tied up, slapped and robbed there were hints of even worse when she told her friend: "I don't want to go into what those two Water Board men did to me". Her friend was shocked and appalled. She told the Senior Common Room Secretary, a very nice lady, who organised a collection for Joan throughout the College.

Joan was remembered with affection in the Department of Economic History for her contribution to the Christmas Parties for children of the staff. Each year they looked forward to her Christmas cakes: two, sometimes three which she adorned with sugar paste holly and mistletoe and plastic robins. The Secretary of the Senior Common Room made an announcement about Joan's misfortune at a *'Beaujolais Nouveau Celebration'* later in the week. The consternation at Joan's news was genuine and two days after the event Joan received a large bouquet of flowers and a cheque for £105. One academic member of the Department's staff, who appreciated Joan's kindness and help with his three children when his wife tragically died of breast cancer sent a note and a cheque for £150 saying: "Joan, I'm so sorry to hear about your brutal robbery. Hope you will accept this small token - can't have British Gas going broke!"

The money total on Joan's list had now grown to just over the £600 she had lost. Joan was delighted: but she continued to ring round, saying she didn't know how she was going to pay her rent.

A few weeks later: Joan received a letter from RBS apologising for the delay in their security response and an assurance that the £600 pounds stolen would be reinstated into her current account. Joan was 'over the moon': "£1,200 she kept shouting! I'm £600 to the good: the 'Water-boarders' are £600 to the good!"

When Joan's daughter heard about this, and learned of Joan's out of character dramatic exaggerations, she realised that her mother was becoming increasingly ill: unhinged by the robbery and in a state of post traumatic shock. She was touched by the generosity of Joan's friends and former colleagues but extremely embarrassed that her mother was quite unnecessarily still 'going round with a begging bowl'. She just didn't know *what* to do. Her mother's behaviour was rapidly becoming more and more bizarre and unpredictable.

Six months later Joan died of dementia.

MISS AITKEN

Miss Aitken had put off going to the doctor's for weeks now hoping the pain, which burnt like an ice cube in her abdomen, deep behind her private parts, would disappear, but it had not. If anything it had got worse. The radium treatment she'd had for bladder warts had clearly been a failure: all that suffering for nothing! She woke up in a wet bed each morning. She'd given up trying to dry the mattress in front of her electric fire after she'd burnt a hole in it. A good thing she had the kettle in her hand at the time. She hated the thought of another spell in hospital. Who would feed her cats? No, she would not go to the doctor's today, perhaps tomorrow, if it was no better. She knew, deep down where the pain was that she *really* would have to go to the doctor's tomorrow. Yes, she would definitely go tomorrow. She would have to keep the cats in though, somehow, they were so hungry, these days, the poor things. And such opportunists!

Whenever Miss Aitken left her flat her three cats contrived to go with her: streaking past her out of the dark, narrow hallway, into the daylight, the moment the door opened. No sooner had she stooped to stop Chloe than Viola would dart between her legs or Blackie would skid on the linoleum and be out behind her spinning back. "Chloe! Viola! Blackie! come back at once! You naughty cats!" she would shout, with what was left of her rich contralto voice. She had been a fine singer in her time but smoking, old age, and now poverty, had rusted her voice away. The cats would twitch a deaf ear and take no notice. They never went far ahead though: they just fanned out in front of her, each alone, each out of reach, a few feet ahead and on down the path, imperiously.

The path was badly paved and poorly drained and if wet from rain the three cats would walk slowly, independently, leaning back slightly, advancing a well-placed foot like dead-marching soldiers escorting a gun carriage; each shaking a paw after each careful step. If the day was dry they would walk on what used to be the lawn, arch their backs, yawn, stop, extend claws and pluck at the patch of matted grass two or three times with each paw in turn.

At the old silver birch, half way to the gate, Blackie would convulsively wiggle his bottom: a shudder would run down his back and up to the tip of his tail and a stream of pungent liquid would declare his territory. Then, their backs arched like bow-saws, all three would walk on with slow dignified steps towards the gate, their tails held high in the air, the tips curling back, beckoning like fingers. Each with the round clenched eye of its pink, brown, and black button-bottom obscenely exposed to Miss Aitken's scandalised view.

"Come back at once: you'll get yourselves killed! And put those tails down!", she would shout, glancing nervously round to see if her neighbours were watching.

Miss Aitken did not get on well with her neighbours. They objected to her playing the piano and she was afraid they would report her to the landlord for still having the cats. If they did it would be the end of the cats and, alas, the end of her too. She had been given a final warning. The cats, however, took never a whisker of notice. They would sit on their haunches whilst Miss Aitken rummaged in her purse for her "Oh, not lost again!" key. Viola would examine the palm of her paw before licking it clean with her bright pink tongue, then apply it gracefully to the back of her head; pulling her ear down over her whiskered cheek to wash it. The other two would be slowly twisting their heads, this way and that, blinking, slit-eyed, at the yellow light of the warming sun.

But when tomorrow came Blackie had gone missing so despite the pain she again put off going to the doctor's.

It was an excuse. Miss Aitken was indeed worried that Blackie had disappeared, but not greatly so, not at first that is. He was an unneutered 'tom' and had gone on the tiles before. He would probably be back in a day or so, minus yet another piece of what remained of his right ear. Those Chinese take-away tales were nonsense, though she was not quite so sure about the fur trade in Eastern Europe. Perhaps she should take him to the vet. But the thought of having him doctored made her wince more than the thought of having her warts removed: it set what were left of her bottom teeth on edge. How could anyone do that to a cat, of all creatures!

Blackie's habits *were* becoming rather dirty, though. He'd recently begun spraying the walls of the flat, and even once or twice the settee, but to have him neutered was, for Miss Aitken, unthinkable. In any case, she did not find the smell unpleasant: it reminded her of the blackcurrant bushes, under the trees, in the apple orchard, in the distant days of her childhood in Cheshire. No, she would not have him neutered. She did, in fact, quite like the smell of a tomcat, and as nobody came to the flat any more, now that her friend Elizabeth had died, what did it matter?. Whatever was she thinking about! No!, she would definitely not have him doctored.

The kit-e-kat tins were quite another thing: she really must get rid of those tins. The smell was becoming unbearable, even though she had almost got used to it: and the flies too. . . . Why could she not bring herself to get rid of those tins and clean the place up? If the neighbours noticed the smell it would be disastrous. And the newspapers, she must get rid of the newspapers: there was hardly space to walk, even in the kitchen She did not want to think about the kitchen. If only she had some energy! By the time she'd got herself out of bed and dressed, and smoked a few cigarettes over a game of Patience, the day seemed to have gone. She hardly had time to do the crossword these days; she prided herself on being able to complete the *Daily Telegraph* crossword. And as for playing the piano: it must be three days since that trouble with the philistine in the flat above after she'd been playing Lutoslowski's Variations on a theme of Paganini. It was, admittedly, two o'clock in the morning but to knock on the ceiling like that . . . . Still, she could not risk another row. It was one of her neighbours, she suspected, who had asked a Social Worker to call, only a month or so ago. She said it was a routine call on the elderly when Miss Aitken asked who had sent her, but Miss Aitken didn't believe her. If she let herself fall into the hands of the Social Services they would have her out of her flat and into a Home, in no time. There would be no question of her keeping the catsthere..

Instead of going to the doctor's Miss Aitken went up the street to call on Jeanette, a recently divorced, kindly, school-teacher who'd befriended her, and for whom Miss Aitken occasionally did 'baby-sitting' of an evening. She wanted to put a proposition which she hoped would solve some of her problems - her rent crisis, feeding her cats, and keeping her out of the hands of 'those damned Social

Workers'.

Her idea was to alter her Will: instead of leaving her belongings and the money from her Death Insurance policy to a 'Cats Shelter', she would leave everything to Jeanette on condition that she took the cats in if she suddenly died, or had to go into a Home or Hospice. Rather than her few remaining valuables being sold off cheap by Social Services, she would let Jeanette buy them for whatever Jeanette thought they were worth, or whatever she could afford. If Jeanette could pay her some money immediately, and perhaps a small sum of money each week, it would, along with her weekly social security money, mean that she could feed herself and the cats and pay the rent. There was a full Coalport dinner service, some very old Willow Pattern plates her mother used to collect, a set of silver serving dishes, two silver cutlery sets and an Ormolu clock which, according to her father, had belonged to her mother's grandmother. She would let Jeanette have her Bechstein grand piano and her rings for a nominal sum on condition she could keep and use them until she died or had to go into Sheltered Accommodation. That way she could be sure that her cats and her other most treasured possessions had gone to a good home, and still have use of her piano!

In reply to Jeanette's questions Miss Aitken told her that she had no near relatives. Her mother had died in childbirth, when Miss Aitken was eight years old, and her father, who had married late, had chosen not to marry again out of grieving respect for his wife's memory. As far as Miss Aitken knew both her parents were only children, though there was a rumour, she remembered, of a sister on her mother's side who had died in a mental hospital, somewhere: Jerricho, near Bury she thought it was. It was possible, but hardly likely, she had married and had children.

Once Miss Aitken got talking about the past it was difficult to stop her. She told Jeanette that after her mother's death, her father, a felt-hat manufacturer, with a factory in Stockport, had arranged for her to be educated privately. At first by a governess, but later as a day girl at a private school in Alderley Edge, near to where they had lived. Miss Aitken was musically talented and had private singing lessons twice a week at the Royal Northern College of Music in Manchester. She was taught the piano by a gifted young man who had studied under Richter in Vienna, but whose concert career was cut off, two days after his debut, by a motor accident in which he lost an arm. Miss Aitken had been secretly in love with him but her father had read her diary and the lessons abruptly stopped.

Miss Aitken was a good linguist: she knew French, German and Italian, but to her bitter regret she had not been allowed to go to University to read French and Music as she had wanted. Her father had thought it "not a proper place for a young woman to be on her own" and that as he had no wife, she should stay at home and look after him in his declining years. "No need to work", he said, "I'll see you are well provided for". So apart from a brief interlude during the war, when she'd been directed into a job as a catering manageress in a British Restaurant, and a short spell in a similar job at a local technical college, she had never worked, nor, as it turned out, had she had to work. By the time her father died of cancer, she was, herself, middle aged, unmarried, and destined to remain so. Her father she'd hated: "for ruining my life", as she was wont to put it, but she had had no option other than to accept what he left her in his Will.

Unfortunately most of Miss Aitken's inheritance was in property: inner city slum property. The rents were difficult to collect and she had received very little compensation from the local authority when those properties were compulsorily purchased, and summarily demolished, "to make way for those abominable post war flats." The little cash that was left her after that "swindling solicitor", as she called him, had "rooked" her, was spent on the highlight of her life, a Caribbean cruise for her and her childhood friend, Elizabeth.

As the years went by Miss Aitken had no option but to sell the family house, and most of the contents, and move into a succession of smaller houses and ultimately flats in a slow, genteel descent into old age and poverty. Now, at seventy-eight, the money had run out before she had.

The initial twenty pounds which Jeanette gave Miss Aitken was rolled up tightly and tucked in a twist in the top of her Lisle stocking and secured by an elastic band. She would buy some prawns for Viola and Chloe and a packet of smoked salmon for Blackie as she had not been able to get him anything for his birthday. She would buy a packet of twenty Kensitas for herself and then call in at the doctor's to make an appointment, if she could summon up the strength to walk that far: walking was not easy, these days, for Miss Aitken.

Miss Aitken was a big woman, even in old age. She must have been at least five feet ten in her prime, though natural shrinkage had now reduced her height somewhat: it had done nothing to reduce her broad back and the huge, though sagging, singer's bosom which now filled out to the waist the capacious brown coat she wore, summer and winter. The coat had a fox fur collar and gave her a 1930's central European look. Her stout, stiff legs were badly varicosed and her elastic stockings showed beneath her thick brown Lisle ones. Her feet were in need of chiropody and the bunions, a legacy from her teenage years, when she squeezed her too big feet into too small shoes, were as big as golf balls. As a consequence, instead of walking, she rocked along from side to side like a foundering ship, sailing a wash of waves, parallel to a shelving shore. Occasionally she would totter off balance like you do when your feet slip on the downhill slope of an icy path. A fall could easily have killed her.

The doctor's surgery was crowded: it was 'baby clinic' day. To get to the waiting room Miss Aitken had to squeeze between two rows of knees, down a corridor of cooeeing mothers cradling what looked like large, ugly, puffy-eyed, pink mice. Each baby was wrapped in an almost identical white loose-knitted shawl. Many of the new babies, she noted, looked too young and fragile to be exposed to the outside air; those with their eyes open had that blank navy blue stare. Some older ones were sitting upright on their mother's knees, held by their two tiny hands. Their wobbly heads followed Miss Aitken in a series of unfocused jerks. Occasionally a baby would burp up a blob of clotted milk and the mothers would pass each other paper handkerchiefs saying, "Orrr, isn't she beautiful!"

The mothers looked to be mere teenagers but even so one or two had two-year-old toddlers pressing themselves shyly between their knees. The more adventurous ones were playing with toys from a large cardboard box; whizzing cars across the waiting room floor. One toddler, scrabbling about under a chair, was teasing the Surgery's tail-twitching, Tabby cat which Miss Aitken bent, with difficulty, to rescue. "Don't pull pussy's tail", she said, with feigned gentleness, whilst giving the mother a look that would have withered a ball-bearing. Though Miss Aitken did not dislike children, she did, without doubt, prefer cats.

The chairs in the waiting room were all occupied, mainly by elderly, ill looking people or over-weight, mid-forty-year-old Pakistani women wearing baggy silk trousers, coloured silk head-scarves and with diamond studs in their nostrils. In the corner was a pale-faced youth wearing Doc Marten boots and camouflage ex-army trousers tucked into his socks. A dirty white sleeveless singlet showed under his brass-studded leather waistcoat which had a reinforced back that reminded Miss Aitken of the sort of thing coal delivery-men used to wear. "I wouldn't like to meet you in the dark", she thought.

The youth's head was shaved in a Mohican cut and tufts of it were coloured bright orange, purple and green. His arms were heavily tattooed with faded looking coloured scroll-designs. An outline heart with an arrow through it proclaimed, in crude lettering, his undying love for "Tracy D". Round his neck a tattooed broken line said, "cut here", and "love" and "hate" were visible on the backs of his finger joints, above the dozen or so outsize silver and gold rings. The paste-diamond stud which adorned his nostril competed with those of the Pakistani ladies. The youth got up to go to the toilet. As he passed Miss Aitken was shocked to notice there were puncture marks, and septic sores, festering on his arm, below the inside crook of his left elbow joint.

Miss Aitken went to the frosted glass screen, marked reception, and pressed the bell. A figure behind the glass was on the telephone but Miss Aitken pressed a second time. The glass parted but by the time it did Miss Aitken had decided not to wait in the queue but to make an appointment for later in the day. No, she did not wish to see Dr. Godfrey, she wanted to see a lady doctor, and yes, it was an urgent matter. Miss Aitken with her upper class manner and superior vocabulary persisted until the almost openly hostile exchange resulted in her getting what she wanted. She gave her name and address in a loud aggrieved voice and said that four o'clock, when the mother and baby clinic was over, would be quite satisfactory, thank you! As she turned to leave she bumped into the tattooed youth who had left his chair and was standing unexpectedly close behind her.

It was not until she arrived home that she discovered that her purse, with her door key in it, was missing from her handbag. "Oh not lost again!" she said, as she transferred a mass of paper handkerchiefs and loose change from one coat pocket to another. Surely, she thought, she couldn't have left it at the fishmonger's. She would have to ask when she went back to the doctor's, later, or it might be in the paper shop where she had bought cigarettes. Fortunately it was lunch time and there were several ten-year-olds from the nearby junior school on their way to the fish and chip shop. It cost her ten pence for one of them to climb in through the the toilet window which she discovered she had left open. So that's how Blackie got out, she thought.

Miss Aitken took a Temazepam and dozed off. She awoke when Viola jumped onto her shoulder and began purring loudly and licking the side of her face. She put her hand up to stroke the cat and as she did so noticed the time. It was twenty to four, barely time to dab a bit of powder on her nose before going to keep her appointment at the doctor's.

With no Blackie to contend with she was able to thwart the attempts of Viola and Chloe to go with her and the time it normally took, stamping her foot and shooing them back down the street, was saved.

Miss Aitken was breathless from hurrying when she got to the Surgery and despite a desperate need to go to the lavatory, to ease the pain and pressure on her bladder, she had to lean against the wall to rest for a minute before going in. "Are you all right love?", the last of the mums said, as she finished tucking her baby into its pushpram and fitted the rain-cover into place. Miss Aitken could barely nod. She was still breathless, and too drained and weary to speak.

She was even more drained and weary when she left the Surgery. After all that prodding and probing down below the pain was worse than when she went in, and she knew now what she had known all along. The doctor had telephoned a Consultant to arrange for her to be admitted to Christie's Cancer Hospital. It would probably be on Tuesday, four days hence. Miss Aitken should call in on Monday and she would confirm the date and time. "Just a check up to be on the safe side", she had said, but Miss Aitken was not so easily fooled. Meanwhile, she would give her some Mogadon tablets, which were a bit stronger than the others, to help her get to sleep, and some tablets to ease the pain which she must take three times a day. She could take an extra one if the pain got very bad but she must be careful with them because they contained Morphine.

To Miss Aitken's great relief her purse had been handed in at the newsagent's. A small boy had seen it in the waste bin when he went to deposit the paper from his ice-lollipop. Miss Aitken said she must have dropped it but she could not understand why anyone would put a perfectly good purse in the rubbish bin. The mystery was soon solved: the purse was empty and her loose change and keys were missing. "Who would do a trick like that, and what use would my door key be to anyone?", she said. As she was too exhausted to walk to the Chemist's shop she decided to leave getting the tablets to the following day when she hoped she would be feeling better. She put the prescription, which she still had clutched in her hand, inside her handbag and willed herself to face the walk home.

Miss Aitken had no sooner turned the corner into the street where she lived than she was knocked sideways, without apology, into the high wall that flanked the inside of the pavement by a passing girl dressed in black leather, punk style clothing, carrying a couple of bulging, black, plastic bin-liners. Behind her was a scurrying youth carrying what looked like a large square box covered by a bin-liner. The youth was hardly visible behind the box but his hair was unmistakeable: 'love' and 'hate' stood out on his knuckles. "Damned cheek!" shouted Miss Aitken, after their disappearing backs. "Care only for themselves these days!", she muttered, as she continued, unsteadily, on her way home.

As Miss Aitken neared her flat Viola and Chloe ran to meet her. The two cats weaved themselves between her legs, meowing and prevented her from walking, their backs arched and their tails held high in the air. They purred a duet as she bent to stroke and talk to them, her hand passing firmly down the back of each cat in turn: each back springing into an arch as her hand passed down the tail and clenched it gently like when a rope passed through it. "Yeeees, what is it baby, what is it?" she crooned back at them. It was not until Miss Aitken straightened up that she realised she'd had left the cats inside the house when she left to go to the doctor's. "How on earth had they got out? Oh don't say I forgot to shut that lavatory window again!"

The door to Miss Aitken's flat was slightly open but she knew she had shut it when she left: she remembered the click. She pushed the door fully open and Chloe and Viola ran in ahead of her, their tails in the air. "Come back!", she said, but they disappeared. "Is there anybody there?" she shouted, as rather tentatively she went in. She had a feeling that the flat was empty: people somehow make their presence felt, especially in the dark, and she had no feeling that there was anybody in the flat. As she moved forward to switch on the light her foot kicked a kit-e-kat tin. It startled her, but not as much as the sight that met her when she switched the light on in her living room.

That her flat had been untidy was an understatement. It now looked as though a whirlwind had passed through it. The piles of old newspapers had been kicked over and had slid like decks of playing cards all over the floor. Dozens of kit-e-kat tins had been swept off the sideboard and scattered over the floor. Drawers from the sideboard were hanging out, their contents strewn about. The cushions from the settee had been tossed onto the floor. "My God, I've been burgled!" Miss Aitken shouted in disbelief.

When the full realisation of what had happened dawned on her a feeling of panic, mingled with despair overwhelmed Miss Aitken. She reeled against the wall, sank her head into her chest, pressed her chin hard against her breast bone and sobbed. With her eyes tight shut, she muttered in a low, weary voice, "Oh no, this is too much!"

When she could bring herself to look again she could see that with the exception of one side-plate, her Coalport dinner service was missing. There was no sign of the Ormolu clock on the mantelpiece. An upturned silver serving dish was visible underneath the table. The drawers where she kept the canteens of cutlery were empty. "Oh no!" What am I going to do!" She had spent five of the twenty pounds Jeanette had given her in part payment for the things that were now missing. The table on which the television set had stood was on its side: there was no sign of the television. She righted the table and threw the cushions back onto the settee but she was too distressed at the loss of her things to carry on putting the place in order.

After closing the drawers Miss Aitken picked her way to the

bedroom. The light was on and the curtains drawn. The air was damp and there was a smell of cats but apart from the drawers hanging out of the dressing table, the wardrobe doors open and the bed mattress askew, where someone had pushed it to one side to feel under it, the bedroom looked almost normal. She closed the wardrobe door and pushed the dressing table drawers back in.

Most of the bits and pieces of cheap jewellery she possessed had gone from the dressing table top and to her grief and dismay she saw that her Mother's rings were missing. "Oh! No. Not mother's rings!" she cried. Despite her desperate need for money she'd not ever considered selling those rings. They had been a link with her mother too precious to ever part with. She began quietly weeping and then sobbing deeply as she pulled the mattress straight and wearily lay down, slantwise across the bed, her shoulder against the headboard.

When Miss Aitken had recovered a little she thought about asking one of her neighbours to call the police but she quickly realised she could not call the police: they would tell the Social Services people. But suppose whoever it was that did it came back? They must have the key. But how would they know where to come in the first place: there was nothing with an address on it in the purse? She dismissed the thought of anyone coming back. There was no reason for them to do so: they had taken everything there was to take. But then she thought of her handbag: they might come back for her handbag. No, there was only some loose change and a prescription in her handbag. But then she thought, would they know that. Her hand went involuntarily down to her thigh to touch, through her dress, the bulge in her stocking top where the fifteen pounds she had left from what Jeanette had given her was concealed. "If only Blackie would come back", she said, wearily, "Where can he have got to?"

Miss Aitken took one of the two Temazepam tablets she had left but fell asleep, from shock and exhaustion, before it had time to work. She must have slept for over three hours. It was almost nine o'clock when she woke up, in some considerable pain. Chloe and Viola were both on the bed, sniffing at her face and meowing pitifully: they had not been fed. She was aware from the damp warmth beneath her that again she'd had one of her accidents. She was feeling very low in spirits but when she remembered again that she had been burgled she just wanted to die.

She did however force herself to get out of bed to feed the cats. She gave them the smoked salmon she had bought for Blackie: she would have to get him some more when he came home. She took a milk dish from the clutter of pots in the sink, swilled it under the tap, and gave Viola and Chloe some milk.

Miss Aitken was too ill and demoralised to face tidying the place any more that night. She thought to see if there was anything on television to take her mind off things but then she realised that there was no television set to watch. The realisation brought on another bout of weeping. Miss Aitken was not an avid television viewer, indeed she disliked most of the programmes, but she did like to watch the wildlife documentaries and the occasional play. Blackie used to watch with her, though Chloe and Viola didn't care to. He would sit in front of the set his eyes following the movement. Once, when Nigel Kennedy was playing Vivaldi's Four Seasons, Blackie had started to sing at the sound of the violin. It had made her laugh uproariously.

She decided she would get into bed and try to read. As it was cold and damp in the bedroom she put the electric under-blanket, which she hoped would be dry by now, over the top of her, like an over-blanket, intending to turn it off before she went to sleep.

The pain in Miss Aitken's abdomen was worse than it had ever been and she found it impossible to concentrate on her library book. She now wished she had gone to the Chemist's shop for the stronger tablets she had been prescribed. She would have to make do with the last of her Temezapam and a drop of brandy. She still had left some *Courvoisier* Jeanette had given her when she had refused to take extra payment, for sitting later than usual one night: Jeanette had been out for a meal with her colleagues. That will get me off to sleep, she thought, but it was too much effort to get out of bed so she continued to try to read. It was no good, her mind kept returning to the burglary. She did eventually drowse off but before her sleep deepened she was awakened by a loud squawk from Chloe and a clatter of kit-e-kat tins. She thought she heard a voice and then a loud thud and again a most unnatural squawk from Chloe. "Oh! my God! I hope the burglars have not come back", she said, in a voice which barely escaped from her throat. She felt terrified but she did not panic. She hoped she had dreamt it. "Who's there!", she shouted. There was no answer but as she stared towards the door she saw a hand slowly creep round the lintel and switch out the light. She had time to see that the fingers were dirty and the nails edged with black. They wore silver rings and had tattooed letters that she could just make out.

When Miss Aitken didn't call at the Surgery the following Monday morning Dr. Furlow was concerned, and a little irritated with herself: perhaps she should have told Miss Aitken more honestly just how advanced her condition was. Miss Aitken needed immediate treatment and was to be admitted to Christie's hospital on Wednesday, the earliest she had been able to arrange; she needed to let her know. Miss Aitken was 'dead' but at least, with care, she might have a few extra months and they could do quite a lot these days to manage pain. She must see if she could get her into a Hospice. She decided to call on Miss Aitken that afternoon on her way back from her session at the drug addiction clinic where she was involved in a research project. Knowing Miss Aitken, she would have to seed the idea of a Hospice rather carefully.

Dr. Furlow got no reply on ringing Miss Aitken's door-bell. She took a notebook from her bag and wrote Miss Aitken a note confirming the date and time of admission. As she put the note through the letter-box a peculiar smell - a mixture of kit-e-kat and some other sort of cat food, she thought - made her shudder involuntarily. "What *do* people feed their cats on these days!", she said to herself. It was one of those smells that stay with you long after you have forgotten the original source and several times during the evening she secretly took a sniff at her clothing to see whether perhaps it was something on her coat she had picked up at the clinic.

Dr. Furlow had patients other than Miss Aitken to think about and other matters on her mind. She was particularly preoccupied with a paper she was to give at a conference on drug abuse which she was to attend for a week in the U.S.A.

As she was about to leave the surgery at lunchtime on the Wednesday, to catch her plane, she received a telephone call from the hospital informing her that Miss Aitken had failed to attend for admission. "Damn it!" she said out aloud. "I knew there was something I should have checked up on". At the risk of missing her bus to the airport she phoned the Social Services Department and asked them to send someone round, "urgently", to see if Miss Aitken was all right and to get her to "Admissions" at Christie's as soon as possible.

Dr. Furlow's phone call to Social Services created some debate in the office as to whose case list Miss Aitken should go on. They were short of staff: most of the Social Workers were overloaded. The manager was under pressure from the Director to keep within what was admittedly an under-funded budget. The new graduate trainee had only recently completed a CQSW and had been asked to work on her own far too soon. "If we put any more pressure on her she might 'crack up'," someone commented. "And Julie looks as though she is about to go down with 'flu'", someone added. "We can't anticipate that; Miss Aitken is in her area, give her to Julie" the Manager said.

On her return from the U.S.A. a week later, Dr. Furlow was dismayed to find in her 'in tray' a message from the Consultant at Christie's asking whether or not an appointment was still required for Miss Aitken. She telephoned Social Services immediately but nobody knew whether Miss Aitken had been visted. The hand was not properly over the mouthpiece of the phone whilst inquiries were made. Dr. Furlow heard someone say that Miss Aitken was on Julie's case load and that Julie had been off sick a week. "Oh! my God!", another voice said, "She asked me to call and I forgot clean about it!" It was the new member of staff..

"Hello, Dr. Furlow I think someone called round, but leave it with me, I'll check and get someone round there right away".

When Miss Aitken didn't turn up to baby sit. Jeanette was annoyed with herself. Miss Aitken had not looked well when she had last seen her and she had meant to call round to ask what the doctor had said about the pains in her abdomen. It was over a week now since she had last had contact. She should, at least, have put a note through her door to remind Miss Aitken that she was expected. She was so busy these days, what with school work and taxiing the children about. But she didn't want Miss Aitken to think she was over-eager to get her hands on her family heirlooms which she had, out of goodwill as a matter of fact, agreed to buy. She waited ten minutes or so before going down the road to Miss Aitken's flat to see if she had forgotten about the baby-sitting. Perhaps her condition had taken a turn for the worse!

Jeanette was surprised, and alarmed, to see a Social Services van standing outside the block of flats where Miss Aitken lived. As she got nearer she saw there was also a Contractor's van parked next to it, and a workman boarding up the window of Miss Aitken's flat. A thin looking stray black cat jumped off the wall as she approached and disappeared underneath the Contractor's van.

A fresh-faced, bored looking young policeman, his hands clasped behind his back, stood rocking on his toes and heels outside the entrance to the flat.

"I hope nothing's happened to Miss Aitken!" Jeanette said to him.

"Are you a relative?" he asked.

When Jeanette told him she was not a relative but a friend of Miss Aitken's the policeman said that all he could tell her was that Miss Aitken had been found dead, that afternoon, by the police: they had made an entry when a Social Worker got no reply earlier in the day. He told Jeanette that Miss Aitken had probably died of natural causes but because of certain features he was not at liberty to reveal, the police were, for the time being, treating the matter as a suspicious death. "Forensics are in there now. I'm afraid that's all I can tell you at the moment", he said.

Jeanette returned home in a state of distress. She had a soft spot for Miss Aitken, despite some of the reactionary political opinions Miss Aitken was rather too ready to express. Jeanette attributed these more to the background *Daily Telegraph* culture of her upbringing, and her social isolation, rather than any calculated nastiness of nature. She knew she was going to miss her.

It was several weeks later, after the Inquest, that Jeanette got to know, in detail, the unpleasant and upsetting circumstances surrounding Miss Aitken's death.

Dr. Furlow had gone round to Miss Aitken's flat immediately after having telephoned Social Services but could get no reply. There was a disgusting stench coming from the letter box. She immediately realised that something awful must have happened. She could see what looked like a dead cat on the hall floor. She went back to her Surgery and telephoned the police to ask them to force an entry. They in turn had contacted Social Services who had sent a Social Worker to acquire a key from the landlord: there had been no need to break down the door. The scene that met them when they entered the flat had been too appalling for words. Miss Aitken had lain dead in bed for eleven days.

.

The young social worker had fainted. When she came round she had become hysterical at the thought of what she might be responsible for but eventually calmed down sufficiently to accompany the policeman into the flat. She had required counselling later and had been off work ever since.

The police constable told the Inquiry the first thing that had struck him, on entering Miss Aitken's flat, was the noise. There was a steady hum of what sounded like bees but which in fact turned out to be, bluebottles: the flat was full of bluebottles. A desiccated dead cat lay in the hallway amongst a litter of stinking kit-e-kat tins. A cringing second cat screamed and spat at them before skidding on the linoleum and disappearing into the bedroom. He had picked his way across the squalor of the living room to the bedroom. The room stank of what he could only describe as the sweet sickly smell of partly boiled ham, mingled with the charred smell of burnt bedding. A half covered female body lay on the bed. One leg, partly clad in a stocking, was sticking stiffly out over the side of the bed. The woman was quite obviously dead. It had made him feel sick and he had rushed out of the flat and vomited. When he'd recovered sufficiently he radioed for assistance.

In his resumé of the circumstances of the unfortunate Miss Aitken's death, the Coroner said that dental records had proved conclusively that the deceased was indeed, Miss Aitken. It appeared that on the night of her death Miss Aitken had gone to bed with a book to read: the charred remains of a partly burnt book had been found on the bed. She had probably been smoking - she was a heavy smoker according to her landlord - but that was not the cause of the fire which had partly consumed the bed and inflicted burns to Miss Aitken's upper torso.

On what was a cold, damp night, it would appear that Miss Aitken had unwisely placed an electric under-blanket over her person in an endeavour to keep warm. She had suffered a heart attack and died: that was the cause of death the autopsy had revealed. It would appear the fire was a consequence of her demise and not the cause of it. In all probability, immediately after death, Miss Aitken's body fluids had come into contact with some part of the electric blanket overhanging the side of the bed and caused a short circuit and the subsequent fire: a fire which had eventually extinguished itself, as the bulk of the bedding had been wet. A fire safety officer examined the blanket and found evidence to that effect.

The autopsy also revealed that Miss Aitken had cancer of the bladder, liver and right lung which, though in an advanced stage in the case of the former two cancers, were not the cause of her death.

However, the Coroner said, there were a number of other, somewhat curious and disquieting features surrounding the death of Miss Aitken. There were slight, unexplained bruises at the side of what remained of Miss Aitken's neck but there was insufficient evidence to show how these had come about and they could have been acquired in a variety of perfectly innocent ways.

The top of her stocking had been torn off and there were lesions at the back of her leg as though force had been used to remove it. Why should Miss Aitken want to remove it, and why, one might ask, had Miss Aitken not used a pair of scissors or a knife: they were available close by in her kitchen? And where was the missing stocking top? It had probably been consumed by the fire but there was no forensic evidence to corroborate that this had been the case.

At this juncture the Coroner intimated that some members of the public might wish to withdraw as some of the detailed pathological evidence was of an extremely upsetting nature.

Miss Aitken's face, neck and upper shoulder had been partly eaten by her starving cat, Viola, which had subsequently been put down. How precisely her second cat, Chloe, sustained the injuries which lead to its death remain unclear. The veterinary report indicates that the cat had several broken ribs and died from internal bleeding from a ruptured spleen. These injuries could have been inflicted by a very hefty kick or, more likely, were sustained from impact with a car earlier in the day. Why Miss Aitken did nothing to alleviate the suffering of her cat, Chloe, remains a mystery, as she was known by the veterinary surgeon to be more than attentive to the needs of her cats.

Miss Aitken's flat was in a state of extreme squalor but when the police entered it appeared to be in an additional state of disarray. The living room looked as though someone, probably Miss Aitken, had been searching for something. There was no sign of a forced entry and as nobody knew what possessions Miss Aitken actually had it was difficult to tell whether anything was missing or not. The police initially believed that some of the features of Miss Aitken's flat were consistent with it having been burgled but they had not been able to conclusively establish that as a fact. If it were the case that the flat had been burgled how had the burglar gained an entry? All the doors and windows were securely locked from the inside and Miss Aitken's body was in her bed. It is highly unlikely that she had herself admitted anyone. Her landlord says he knew Miss Aitken had a television, and there was no television set in the flat, but Miss Aitken might easily have disposed of it herself. She had little money and she might well have sold it: we will never know.

Neighbours have said they heard nothing suspicious on the night in question, though why they did not report that she had not been seen for a week or more is a matter on which they might pause to reflect. The absence of the noise of her customary piano playing, which I am told was quite accomplished, was attributed to a recent complaint about noise by the gentleman living in the flat above Miss Aitken.

Having passed a verdict of 'Death from natural causes' the coroner expressed his concern over the apparent laxity of the Social Services Department: emphasising that had the request of Miss Aitken's G.P. for a visit by a Social Worker been fulfilled promptly, whilst it would not have saved Miss Aitkin's life, it would have made it considerably easier to investigate the matter of her death: her body would not have suffered the indignities that it had been subjected to. It was not good enough to say that the failure to visit Miss Aitken was the result of staff shortages and staff illness. Whilst this particular death had not, in any way, been contributed to by the failure of a Social Worker to fulfil the request of Miss Aitken's G.P.

for a visit, it did not take a great deal of imagination to envisage circumstances where failure to fulfil a G.P.'s request might have fatal consequences. He would not say more as he understood the matter was the subject of a Social Services Departmental Inquiry the outcome of which he hoped would be made public.

The day after the Inquest on the death of Miss Aitken, Jeanette woke up with a sore throat. It had been coming on for a couple of days but this morning it was so painful she thought she had better book an appointment at the doctor's and not go in to school. Her colleagues would not thank her for *not* 'spreading her germs': they would catch anything for a few days off, but she really did feel quite ill. She telephoned the School Secretary and left instructions about her classes. She telephoned the doctor but as usual the line was engaged: she had to dial over and over again. "I really must get one of those telephones that keeps on trying the number for you" she thought. When she eventually got through all the morning appointments had been taken and she had to be content with an afternoon one.

Jeanette would rather have gone back to bed but decided to go to the Chemist's to buy some throat pastilles - anything to get some relief! Jeanette asked the assistant for glycerene, lemon and honey pastilles but the pharmacist, who had come into the shop from behind the glass partitioned dispensary, suggested she "try this 'new' Merocaine".

Jeanette had known the pharmacist since childhood and though she didn't feel up to conversation couldn't refuse to respond when he brought up the topic of the Inquest on Miss Aitken. They both agreed that, despite the horrible after-events, Miss Aitken dying of a heart attack was probably 'a blessing in disguise'. She would not have survived an operation for cancer, considering the extent of its spread. They agreed that even had she been offered treatment she would most probably have refused it.

"She was on some quite hefty pain-killers though: 50 mg opioid analgesics if I remember correctly", the pharmacist said, wanting to impress Jeanette.

This was news to Jeanette: Miss Aitken had told her, the last time she had seen her, that she had been prescribed only Temazepam to help her get off to sleep. Jeanette knew those were sleeping tablets and quite mild ones at that. The pharmacist, however, was adamant that Miss Aitken had been prescribed morphine tablets in addition to Nitrazepam, as he called it, and Jeanette was in no position to argue.

"I hope I'm confined to bed for only three weeks when I go", the pharmacist said. "Three weeks?" said Jeanette, "She wasn't confined for three days. In fact, if the date of her death is correct, she called at my house the Friday she died".

"That's very strange, said the pharmacist, I'm sure the young lady who came in for her prescription said she'd been confined to bed for a fortnight and that was why she was collecting the tablets."Young lady, Oh! Really! When would that be?" Jeanette asked. The pharmacist went into the back room to check his records. He returned and told her the date. Jeanette realised it was the Monday. The Inquest had said the autopsy had established Miss Aitken's death as being on the previous Friday. "Why would anyone be collecting a prescription for Miss Aitken on the Monday when she was already dead?" thought Jeanette. When Jeanette explained this peculiarity to the pharmacist, his face took on a more serious, though distant look. He said, almost to himself, as if attempting to solve a perplexing problem, "Yeeees, how *did* she come to have a prescription made out to Miss Aitken?" and then out loud. "Come to think of it I was a bit suspicious of that young woman at the time. She didn't look the type of person Miss Aitken would trust".

"Not the type? What do you mean, not the type?" said Jeanette.

The pharmacist described the girl, as he now called her, as having a slightly 'punk' appearance. Punk was not a word Jeanette expected him to use but then she realised he was used to making up prescriptions for the addicts who attended the drug rehabilitation centre. The girl had, he remembered "dyed hair, a studded bomber jacket and Doc Marten boots. Oh!, and tight fitting trousers that finished half way down her legs. I remember now: I distinctly remember asking her why Miss Aitken was not collecting the prescription herself as she usually did. She said something about her mother doing cleaning for Miss Aitken and finding her ill in bed that morning".

"How very odd", said Jeanette, "I've not been in Miss Aitken's flat since last year but it was always most untidy and from what they said at the Inquest the place was in a terrible state of squalor. It had never been cleaned for months".

"I think I had better get onto the police about that prescription. There may be a perfectly innocent explanation but it looks very suspicious to me", the pharmacist said.

As she walked home Jeanette could not get her conversation with the pharmacist out of her mind: it intruded on whatever she thought about. A cleaning lady, that could never be!. Miss Aitken would never have been able to afford a cleaning lady. There must be a simple explanation as to why a girl like that was collecting Miss Aitken's prescription but what could it be? Perhaps Miss Aitken had been feeling too ill to go to the Chemist's herself, Jeanette conjectured. After all she did have a heart attack later on that evening. She might have asked the girl to take it in on the Friday and she had, somehow, forgotten. Young people are like that; so full of themselves and their own affairs. She'd been a bit like that herself as a teenager: constantly making herself up and mooning about after boys. "Ugh! Men!" she said out aloud, thinking of her ex-husband. Yes, the girl could easily have forgotten about the prescription until the Monday

But the thought came nagging back: why would she invent a story about her mother doing cleaning for Miss Aitken? That was a mystery, but, as the pharmacist had said, there was probably some perfectly innocent explanation.

Jeanette had not anticipated being off school and had nothing in the house for lunch: with the state of her throat was in she did't feel like anything much to eat. A little soup, she thought, would be all right, but as she was passing the fishmonger's her eye caught a special reduced price offer for smoked salmon and on a whim, to give herself a treat, being that she was not feeling well, she bought a quarter pound pack.

In the fishmonger's there was a conversation in progress about the Inquest on Miss Aitken. Though Jeanette didn't join in she learned that Miss Aitken had been in the shop on the Friday she died.

"I was only speaking to her that day!" the fishmonger said. "She called in twice. Once to buy some fish and then she came back later in the day to ask if she had left her purse". He had heard later that the purse had been found by someone and handed in at the newsagent's.

Jeanette reflected on what she had heard on the way home. Yes, perhaps that was the answer! If one of those addicts from the Centre had found Miss Aitken's purse and looked inside, and seen a prescription, he would, more than likely, have taken it. But then she rejected the idea: not because of a belief that addicts were honest but because an addict would have taken the prescription to the Chemist's to be made up before the loss had been reported. No, there just did not seem to be an explanation.

As Jeanette neared home the thin black cat she had seen, on the night Miss Aitken's death was discovered, darted out from underneath a parked car in front of her. She recognised it because most of its right ear was missing. The cat started to follow her but she paid no attention to it. She knew what cats were like and she did not want another one. When she arrived home the cat was still following. It ran into the garden when she opened the gate, its tail held straight up in the air, a slight curl at the end beckoning her.

The cat walked onto the lawn, yawned, stopped, extended its claws and plucked at the grass with each paw in turn. It then walked onto the newly hoed border and began digging with one paw, stopping occasionally to look round at her. It was just where Jeanette had, sentimentally, planted some anemones in memory of Miss Aitken. Before the cat could do much damage she picked up a small stone from the drive and threw it in the general direction of the cat. The cat leapt onto the wall and down onto the pavement out of sight. "Damned cats!", she said, mildly, "they never do it in their own gardens".

The Merocaine tablets did little to ease Jeanette's throat so she went to bed for a couple of hours, hoping to get some relief in sleep, but sleep would not come. She wished she had a Mogadon tablet but that thought only started her thinking again about Miss Aitken and the prescription. Her mind raced over fresh possibilities, each more fanciful than the last, but on the basis that the simplest explanation was probably the correct one, she concluded that Miss Aitken had most probably dropped her purse on her way home: one of the addicts from the Centre must have found it, taken the prescription, altered it, or added something to it, and asked a girlfriend to get it made up. With that matter settled she at last dropped off to sleep.

When Jeanette woke up her throat was worse than when she went to bed. She heated some lentil soup from a tin but it hurt too much to swallow and she left most of it. She didn't bother to take the smoked salmon out of the fridge.

Jeanette had an appointment the following day to see Dr. Furlow, her own doctor, but she had been called out to a birth at the Maternity Hospital. She was offered a revised appointment or she could wait and see Dr. Godfrey. She chose to wait.

In addition to being a G.P., Dr. Godfrey was an 'on call' police surgeon and as such he had been present at the Inquest on Miss Aitken. He had noticed Jeanette at the Inquest because she had arrived late and, much to her embarrasment, caused a minor disturbance in getting herself seated.

After prescribing a course of antibiotics for her throat he asked Jeanette had she been a friend of Miss Aitken. Jeanette told him that she had, in a way. She told him she'd got to know Miss Aitken when she answered an advertisement Jeanette had put in a local newsagent's, window for a baby sitter: she'd known Miss Aitken for years.

During the ensuing conversation Jeanette happened to say that Miss Aitken had no relatives and this led the doctor to wonder what had happened to that "rather fine piano" he'd seen amidst the squalor of Miss Aitken's flat. Jeanette told him that it was a Bechstein and had very nearly been hers. Miss Aitken had died before she had time to alter her Will, so presumably it had been sold and the proceeds sent to some 'Cats Shelter'. Jeanette also mentioned that Miss Aitken had arranged, on the very day of her death, as it turned out, to sell to her, her Coalport dinner service, an Ormolu clock and some silverware. "I gave her twenty pounds 'on account' as it were." When the doctor said how lucky she had been to get them Jeanette told him that far from being lucky she had lost her twenty pounds. She had nothing to prove the transaction, and had not wanted to seem mercenary, so she had not bothered to mention it to anyone. "So you never got them?" "No", she said, "I did not."

Dr. Godfrey put down his prescription pen and leaned back in his chair with his hands clasped behind his head. "That's very strange", he said. "I was one of the first people to visit the flat after her death. There was no Ormolu clock in the flat that I could see, nor was there any silverware, except, I believe, a silver serving dish which was found underneath a table. Surely Miss Aitken would not have tried to sell you things she did not possess! And I don't recollect any money being found. Perhaps there had been a burglary after all!"

The following day Jeanette's throat was much better but she didn't go in to school. It was a 'Baker day', as they were still called, after a former Minister of Education: she could not stand those contrived training sessions where half the staff confessed their sins and the other half promised to do even more work for even less pay.

At lunchtime she sat at her kitchen table, facing the open window, looking out into the garden. She'd finished her soup and was about to eat the smoked salmon she'd intended to have the day before. She cut some brown bread very thin and buttered it. She quartered a lemon, and was just about to squeeze it onto the salmon when the front door-bell rang. "Whoever can that be?" she said as she went to see who was there. It was the young police constable she had spoken to outside Miss Aitken's flat the night her body was discovered. He had come to ask her if she would be good enough to call at the police station later in the day, to make a statement. Some new information had come into their possession and the police were opening 'further inquiries' into the death of Miss Aitken. Jeanette was surprised and intrigued to hear this, and even more surprised that she was being asked to make a statement but she readily agreed to call at the Police Station as soon as she had finished her lunch.

When she returned to the kitchen, to her dismay the smoked salmon had gone: the plate was empty. She rushed to the window, but there was no sign of the black cat she expected to see.

BLACKIE

As Jeanette winked and turned the car into the drive of her house she was surprised to see the black stray tomcat, that had followed her home a few days previously, disappear round the corner of the garage. "That damned cat's still around", she thought. She was even more surprised to see her daughter's cat, Matilda, sitting on the drive: "That's very strange, Lynne should have been home by now. I bet she didn't do that washing up this morning either!" Jeanette drove forward expecting Matilda to move out of the way but the cat simply sat there. She tooted the horn but Matilda refused to move. "Oh! come on Matilda, I haven't got all day!"

Jeanette was a teacher and feeling very harassed by the pressures of her job, and bringing up two difficult teenage children on her own didn't help. There were problems, too, with Peter, her estranged husband, pestering for reconciliation. She'd asked her solicitor to send him another letter only that afternoon. She did not want cats adding to her difficulties. She tooted again and inched forward but still the cat refused to budge. "You stupid creature, Matilda", she said as she got out of the car to move the cat. As she bent to pick it up she noticed the cat's ear was torn and tufts of its fur were missing as though the cat had been fighting. "Goodness me Matilda, whatever have you been up to?" she said, as she moved her to one side.

When Jeanette looked up she saw the black stray tomcat that had been hanging around for days poke its battered looking head round the corner of the house and stare at Matilda with its evil yellow eyes. Jeanette shouted at the intruder and stamped her foot as though to chase it away but the head remained there, staring at Matilda. She had to throw a stone to get it to withdraw, but the cheeky animal peeped a second time and she had to run towards it, finally, to get it to go.

Jeanette went down the drive and closed the gates. Before she got back to the car her sixth-former son, Tom, arrived home. He left open the gate which she had just shut. Jeanette would have been most annoyed had she seen him do so. No sooner had Jeanette and Tom had gone into the house than the black cat's head reappeared round the corner of the wall again: it saw Matilda and ran towards her. Matilda squawked, ran under the car and out through the open gate into the road.

Lynne was late home from school. She'd gone to borrow a tape of the latest Cher recording from a friend and had stayed to watch a video of the Barry White concert which had been on television the night before.

As she approached the house Lynne could see her mother's car standing on the drive. "Matilda and Mum will be wondering where I've got to", she thought. "Matilda would be sitting on the bonnet where it was warm from the engine. Mum will be cross about the paw marks", she said to herself.

Matilda was Lynne's tortoise-shell cat. She was always waiting on the drive when Lynne arrived home from school. As soon as Lynne opened the gate Matilda would run towards her, her tail in the air, her back arched like a hairpin. Lynne would bend to stroke her rippling back and the tip of Matilda's tail would curl like a finger. Lynne would let the cat push her head forcefully through her lightly clenched fist. She liked to feel Matilda's small, cold nose and she loved the way her ears popped up from under her hand. Matilda would purr ecstatically. It was a daily ritual they each looked forward to.

The road was busy with tea-time traffic. Lynne noticed the driveway gate was open but she didn't see the stray black tomcat chase Matilda out through the gate: she thought Matilda must have seen her over the other side of the road. To Lynne's horror, Matilda ran into the road in front of a car and was squashed. The front wheel went straight over her middle. Through her fingers Lynne saw it happen as she gasped and clamped her hands over her face. Two more cars went over Matilda before she could get across the road. Lynne screamed, then collapsed, at the sight of the unrecognisable mess that had been her cat.

Jeanette came out of the house to see what the commotion was about and in her haste left the back door open. She was hurrying towards the gate but saw the stray black cat dash towards the house. She ran back to close the door. "Don't you dare!", she said, shaking her fist at it. When she reached the gate she stopped in shock at the sight of Lynne on the road. She raised her hand to her mouth and bit her clenched knuckle. She thought for one ghastly moment it was Lynne who'd been run over. In her relief that it was not Lynne, she made the mistake of saying "thank God it was only the cat". Lynne, her despair turning to anger at Matilda's death, screamed: *"Only the cat.! Only the cat!* I wish it *had* been me. You just don't care, do you?"

Jeanette put her arm round Lynne and took her into the house. "You're worse than Tom!", Lynne said, through her tears and sobs. Jeanette didn't say anything but the remark hurt her. She knew she gave in to Tom and that Lynne was aggrieved and jealous of the freedom she gave him to come and go. And Tom never did the washing up, it was true. Lynne threw herself onto her bed, covered her head with a pillow, and wept uncontrollably.

The driver of the car wanted to buy Lynne another cat but Lynne wanted Matilda back. She kept expecting her to walk into the living-room, even though she knew Jeanette had buried her remains at the bottom of the garden, next to Timmy, her previous cat.

Matilda had been a beautiful tortoise-shell cat: she'd been given to Lynne by her father, for her twelfth birthday, before he left them, two years previously. It was doubly tragic in that only a week before the accident Matilda had produced four kittens. Lynne was trying to keep them alive by feeding them with a pipette Jeanette had borrowed from school. "It was what Matilda would have wanted", Jeanette said. Tom made an effort to comfort Lynne, and even showed her how to use the pipette, despite his not getting on with her. "At least they're speaking to each other now", thought Jeanette, but deep down Lynne blamed Tom for leaving the gate open and causing Matilda's death. Tom suspected she would try, in some way, to get even with him, but he did now wish he had shut the gate.

Lynne kept the kittens at the side of her bed in a shoe box lined with soft rags. She woke up every three hours to feed and clean them and renew their hot water bottle. Unfortunately, one after the other, three of the kittens died. Just as it looked as though the remaining one, Boots, would live, the stray black cat again followed Jeanette home from the shops, got into the house and attacked the kitten.

Jeanette had only been gone from the kitchen a minute or so to answer the door bell but when she returned the fish she'd bought that morning, for lunch had gone. The plate was empty. She'd been about to put it in the fridge but left it on the kitchen table to answer the door. There were smudgy paw marks on the table and more paw prints on the sill beneath the open window.

"Damn that cat: it's done it again!", she said, as she went quickly to the window and leaned out expecting to see it,.

Jeanette did not like black cats: there was something malevolent and sinister about them and this particular one was especially evil looking with its wicked yellow eyes. "It's so wilful and persistent", she thought. "It's just like my husband: won't take no for an answer". She'd been trying to get rid of the cat all morning, with the odd pan of water, but it was clearly intent on adopting them.

The black cat was not in the garden and no hint it had gone that way. All she could see on the recently cut lawn was a small flock of starlings, jerking their heads, mechanically, up and down, as they moved in unison towards the border. The oily green sheen of the birds' muscular bodies reflected the sunshine as they gleaned their way across the short cropped grass. They looked like busy medieval peasants in a Breugel painting. One of the younger starlings made a quick run towards two or three squabbling sparrows to steal a piece of bread, causing even more commotion. There was no cat there.

In the side garden two or three sparrows were pecking at the bits of bread Jeanette had put on the rustic wooden bird stand that morning. Another was splashing water out of the birdbath. A Great Tit was clinging to the red netting of a bag of peanuts Lynne had hung from a branch of the Laburnum tree beyond the patio that separated the house from the garden. No cat had gone that way either. "Where can it be? Her hand flew to her mouth. Don't say it's gone upstairs to Lynne's room!" she said in alarm.

As Jeanette reached the foot of the stairs she heard a squawk and the black stray cat skidded round the landing banister and bounced down the stairs. An arm swung over the rail and a boot whizzed through the air and hit the cat on its back. It let out another squawk and dropped what it was carrying. Jeanette instinctively put out her hands to grab the cat but it was going too quickly for her. Its fur felt as smooth and as cold as water as it slipped through her fingers, but the strong sinuous body was what she remembered in the kinaesthetic corner of her memory. Tom's voice shouted: "Stop it! Stop it! It's got the kitten!"

Jeanette half expected to see the missing fish on the stairs but it was Boots the black cat had dropped.She carefully picked up the pitifully mewling kitten. The fur on its head was wet from saliva where the tomcat had gripped it and the kitten's head was swivelled round unnaturally to look over its back. Jeanette realised there was something seriously wrong with it. "Oh Tom!, you were supposed to be looking after this kitten for Lynne!", she shouted up the stairs. She knew as she shouted it was unfair to blame him but the words were out before she could check them.

Tom protested that he was looking after the kitten but he couldn't be expected to watch it every minute of the day. He'd been doing his homework and heard the kitten mewling and had gone into Lynne's room to see what was the matter. How could he be expected to anticipate a stray cat coming upstairs? He said he'd done his best to stop it. The cat had spat and clawed at him and snatched up the kitten before he knew what was happening. And with that he went into his bedroom and slammed the door in a teenage temper.

"I'm taking it to the vet", Jeanette shouted up to him.

While she was out her husband called and pushed yet another note through the front door.

The vet was intrigued to hear how Boots had come to have a fractured skull, though he did say such attacks by tomcats were not unheard of. "Stray cats are inclined to take up residence if they take a fancy to a place and they don't like rivals", he said. He was equally interested in Jeanette's description of the stray. "It sounds very like one of Miss Aitken's cats. She had a black cat which she used to bring to the surgery occasionally and that one had rather yellow eyes and a very chewed ear. I wouldn't mind betting it was one of hers", he said.

Jeanette had known Miss Aitken: she was an old lady who sometimes used to babysit for Jeanette, and Jeanette was somewhat shocked to hear the cat might have been one of Miss Aitken's. Miss Aitken had been found dead in bed, in her flat, and her body had lain undiscovered for nearly two weeks. Her cats had been in the flat with her and had eaten parts of her body to keep alive. It had all been very gruesome but she distinctly remembered that Miss Aitken's cats had been put down by the police vet. She had even promised Miss Aitken, at one time, that she would consider having the cats if anything happened to her but she'd been relieved that she had not been required to do so. It would be ironic if the stray black cat were Miss Aitken's, though how it came to still be alive was a mystery.

It had been a quiet day at the Oxfam shop where Lynne was completing her work experience project. She had been asked to do shoes but she preferred doing dresses. The brisk, bossy woman in charge had done the dresses herself. "It's so she can pick out the best before anyone else has a chance", Lynne thought, as she saw her take two expensive looking, practically new frocks into the 'staff only' room.

Lynne was bored with sorting shoes into pairs and that bossy woman had altered the prices Lynne had carefully stuck onto the soles. "Far too cheap", she said, without properly looking at them. "All a pound up dear: we're not a charity you know", she said, in a very loud voice, then laughed, "Ha! Ha! Ha!", and looked round at the two elderly women helpers for recognition of her feeble joke. Lynne disliked her, though she had let her buy a cat's sleeping basket at half-price. Lynne was hoping to use the basket for the stray black cat she had been feeding behind Jeanette's back.

Lynne made getting back to feed the orphaned kitten her excuse for leaving early. She arrived home out of breath and rode her bike into the open garage to deposit the cat basket. As she did so the black stray cat leapt out of a box in which it had been hiding and ran down the garden path. Lynne was surprised it made off so hastily. "You ungrateful cat!", she shouted after it.

Lynne went into the kitchen and gulped down a glass of Coke before taking off her coat and throwing it onto a chair. She ran noisily up the stairs and into her bedroom to see the kitten. When she discovered the box was empty she thought the kitten must have died. She rushed into Tom's room in a state of panic and distress. "Have you got the kitten in here?" she shouted.

When Tom told her the kitten had been attacked by the stray black cat and that Jeanette had taken it to the vet she rushed at her brother and began frantically hitting him on the chest with her fists, shouting: "if anything's happened to that kitten I'll never forgive you!", and having exhausted her anger she ran back to her bedroom, sobbing.

"I didn't let the bloody stray cat in did I!" Tom shouted after her.

The vet said if Boots survived a week she might just live but she was probably brain damaged and there was no telling what the long term effect might be. Jeanette desperately hoped the kitten would live, as much for her son's sake as for Lynne's. She didn't want the rift between the two of them to deepen. But try as she might Jeanette could not get Lynne to agree that her brother leaving the gate open was not the cause of Matilda's death any more than Boots' injuries were her fault for allowing the stray black cat to follow her home. It was quite uncalled-for for Lynne to say if her father been there he would have been on her side. Tom, it was true, had promised to look after the kitten whilst Lynne was helping out at the Oxfam Shop, but Jeanette felt herself to be partly responsible for what had happened. If she'd put the fish in the fridge before going to answer the door that damned black cat would probably never have come into the house. She blamed herself also for not having noticed the milk going down a lot faster than a kitten could possibly be drinking it. She was sure, now, Lynne had been secretly encouraging the stray with saucers of milk. If that were the case Lynne herself was partly to blame for what had happened, though she would never admit it. "Who knows, she might even have taken the cat up to her room on some previous occasion!" Lynne had been very upset when Matilda was run over and she obviously craved a cat, it was understandable, but Jeanette did not like, and did not want, the black tomcat around. Even if it had been Miss Aitken's cat, which she doubted, the thought that it might possibly have eaten some of Miss Aitken was extremely distasteful and she did not want a cat with that proclivity anywhere near the house let alone in it.

A week after the attack Boots was still alive and the black cat was still around. It visited the house daily. Jeanette had seen it slinking about amongst the shrubs at the bottom of the garden: sinuously winding its way along the border, pausing to lick the dew off the aubretia and raising its head high to sniff the stalk of a daffodil. She knew when it was about by the absence of birds on the lawn and the incessant scolding of the blackbird that was nesting in the ivy on the garage wall.

Matilda had shown little interest in birds but even so Jeanette had insisted she wear a bell: the black cat did not even have a collar: it was a different kind of animal. It moved with the stealth of a hunter. She had seen it pause, one foot frozen half way to the ground and she had seen it crouch, low, elongated, tail twitching, setting itself, its back-end swinging from side to side, its eye on a sparrow. That was good enough reason for not wanting it around, but the cat was clearly intent on adopting them. Jeanette had seen it squirting on the fence, making itself at home. It did not want rivals.

The cat had taken to depositing gifts of dead birds and mice on the doorstep. It did not eat or mutilate them: it seemed to have a technique of snapping their necks without it showing. It was most unpleasant for Jeanette, who was invariably first up, to open the back door and find a dead mouse or dead bird lying there. Jeanette would pick up a sparrow or a thrush and its head would loll limply over the edge of her hand. It was most distressing when she found a robin there. Jeanette was so appalled by it all she had taken to secretly throwing stones at the cat instead of saucepans of water. Water left signs and Lynne had created such a fuss when she saw her chasing it away. "Black cats are lucky, and besides it was not the cat's fault it attacked Boots. It was your fault for leaving the window open" Lynne said. Lynne was at a difficult age.

Jeanette argued with Lynne saying she did not want another cat at the moment, and especially a black one, but where cats were concerned she could not get Lynne to see reason. Jeanette most certainly did not want *that* cat, however remote the possibility might be it had dined off Miss Aitken and it would be very unfair to put Boots at risk of a similar fate.

Lynne said, irrelevantly, that the cat was only following its instinct. "Lions kill other lion's cubs when they take over a pride. I saw it on television". Jeanette countered that if it were instinct for cats to hunt birds Matilda would not have missed out. "The cat is either wild, vicious and evil, or badly brought up, and I do not want a debate about nature/nurture any more than I want a black cat, and that's final!"

It astounded Jeanette that Lynne should defend the black tomcat when it had almost killed Boots but Lynne clearly had a soft spot for the cat, despite its half eaten ear, neglected appearance and feral ways. She was probably hedging her bets, psychologically, in case Boots died. But Jeanette was rather tired of having her authority undermined by television. It was exactly the same at school. The children were so knowledgeable, despite what politicians said about television's harmful effects.

"Oh! well, it must be right if you saw it on television!", said Jeanette. She didn't wish to be too sarcastic. Lynne had, after all, been through quite a trying time, what with Matilda getting run over and her periods starting late. She was so hormonal at the moment, and her father lurking about, waiting to call and ingratiate himself the moment she went out, did not help, either

.

A few nights later Jeanette was sitting at the kitchen table marking a set of homework books. It was after midnight and she had been hard at it all evening but she just had to get them done before going to bed. The traffic had stopped, the children were asleep and the house had gone quiet. The central heating had switched itself off. She could hear the occasional creak of furniture contracting. Almost imperceptibly she developed an eerie feeling she was being watched. She had been very nervy since her husband had gone off with that floozie of a foreign language teacher: 'traded Jeanette in for a younger model' was how she had put it to her friends. Still, he'd got his comeuppance. She had heard it was not working out, but she was damned if she was having him back after he'd been with her, and to tell the truth she did not want him back. She glanced round: there was no one there. How silly of me she thought.

As Jeanette turned her attention back to the books her eye was distracted by a slight movement at the window and she caught a glimpse of a black shape. She thought, for an instant, it was her husband: it quite frightened her. It was the stray black cat, sitting on the window sill, outside, staring in. She fixed her eyes on it hoping to stare it out but the cat stared back at her, intently, its two enormous amber eyes, each with a slim black slit up the middle, unblinking, large as an owl's, glowing luminescently.

Jeanette had not previously noticed the cat had such big eyes. She wondered for a moment if the glass had a flaw and was magnifying them. Nor had she noticed the cat had such a handsome, intelligent face: she could see why her daughter might like it. The cat she had thought so evil looking, was, on closer inspection, quite attractive. She felt almost as though she had been hypnotised by it. She was amazed at herself.

The cat stood half upright at the window, its hind legs crouched like a grasshopper, its front feet barely touching the sill, stretching its neck, staring intently, dodging its head about from side to side as if wanting to see something beyond and behind her. She felt there must be somebody there but when she looked there was only the fridge on the one side and the old television set she had relegated from her husband's room to the kitchen, on the other. Surely it doesn't want to watch the telly, she said to herself, or is it something in the fridge it's after?

Jeanette went to the kitchen door and opened it. She knew she was making a mistake but her curiosity got the better of her. "Puss Puss Puss" she said, from the back of her throat, through her partly pursed lips.

She had expected some hesitation on the part of the cat but it ran in immediately, as if it were familiar with the place, its tail vertical, curled back an inch at the end. The cat stopped for a second or two, arched its back and wound itself between her legs, purring loudly, leaning against them to smooth its fur before running over to the fridge. Jeanette was astonished by the cat's engaging behaviour. It was either trying a new strategy to ingratiate itself or its character had undergone a miraculous change.

The cat pawed the bottom corner of the fridge door, as if trying to open it. "There's nothing in there for you", she said, but the cat persisted. She opened the fridge door, intrigued. To her amazement the cat grabbed a piece of cucumber from the salad rack and started to crunch it noisily, tossing its head back to get a purchase on each piece it bit off. Jeanette was so bemused that a cat would eat such a thing she let it finish it. When it was all gone the cat returned to the fridge to sniff for more. "What a strange cat you are!" Jeanette said, as she poured the cat a saucer of milk. "My husband, Peter, had a passion for cucumber".

She returned to her marking whilst the cat lapped the milk. It paused occasionally to look round at her from the crouch position it had taken up. When the milk was finished the cat raised its left paw, palm upward, licked it with its bright pink tongue and applied it to its face. After a few licks down the front of its chest the cat settled itself on its haunches in front of the television set and stared intently at the blank screen. "Don't tell me you *do* want to watch television!" Jeanette said in amazement.

Jeanette had difficulty getting the cat to go. She stood with the door open calling it. "Puss Puss Puss." But the cat ran under the table and would not come out. She finally got it to leave, with the aid of a broom. It skidded on the lino and ran rapidly past her out of the door to resume its place on the window sill. Its black form merged with the dark of the night. Its amber eyes stared intently into the room, following her closely as she cleared away the homework books.

When Jeanette saw Lynne giving the cat milk the following day she said nothing. Lynne glanced up guiltily and said: "Well? . . . How would you like to be without a drink all day? The poor thing's thirsty!"

"Don't blame me if it attacks Boots again", Jeanette said.

There was nothing Jeanette could do: the cat had weakened her resolve and it gradually insinuated itself into her household. Surprisingly it was Tom, who had never much cared for cats, whom the cat immediately took to, though Tom did encourage it more than Lynne did. Lynne seemed content, at first, merely to feed the cat whereas Tom gave it time and attention. Jeanette presumed Lynne didn't want to get too emotionally involved with the tomcat, probably for fear of being hurt in the way she had undoubtedly been by Matilda's death. Tom on the other hand seemed to want to atone for hitting it with his boot. He would rub his knuckles against the side of the cat's face and quietly talk to it: then smooth its ears down with firm strokes of his hand. If he stopped too soon the cat would force its head underneath his hand, asking for more. Or he would sit with the cat on his lap stroking its back. The cat revelled in the attention and would purr like a cricket. It was Tom who christened the cat Blackie. Jeanette secretly thought Peter would have been more appropriate.

Lynne soon became jealous of the way the cat had taken a liking to Tom. Tom had never much cared for cats in the past and it was unfair, Lynne thought, that the cat should constantly run to him rather than to her. After all it was she who had given it milk and bought it a basket and now he was enticing the cat away from her. "He's only doing it to get at me!", she complained to her mother.

Jeanette was not surprised by Lynne's outburst: she had noticed the cat's affection for Tom but was at a loss to know what to do about it. It had been the same with her husband, though the other way round. Lynne had always been her father's favourite and it had caused endless friction between the two of them. In the end Jeanette was forced to resort to the over-used formula: "Don't drag me into it: you must sort it out yourselves". But try as Lynne did the cat rejected her advances when Tom was about and would only come to her in his absence. She had even offered it a piece of cucumber Jeanette had left out of the fridge.

Jeanette had mixed feelings about the cat. There were certainly fewer birds about the garden these days and the wrens that used to flit about the bottom of the hedge had disappeared altogether. She had seen a sickening bloody goo on the path, the other morning, that looked as though a consumptive had spat there, and a cluster of tiny grey-brown feathers nearby. And she wished it wouldn't use the front garden border as a loo. She knew now what caterwauling meant: the black cat seemed to encourage, never mind attract, competition. Shortly after dark a she-cat and two or three of the local toms would space themselves out and yowl and whine interminably and walk endlessly round each other. On more than one occasion Jeanette had resorted to the saucepan of water to shut them up. Eventually there would be the most almighty racket as they fought and spat at one another. It was Blackie who invariably won: she didn't know why the other cats bothered.

But what concerned Jeanette most was the growing hostility Lynne was showing towards Tom because the cat so obviously preferred him to her. The more the cat and Tom got on together the further apart grew Tom and Lynne. Lynne had now begun using the cat to openly display her hostility to Tom. "Don't you go to that nasty Tom", she would say to the cat when Tom was out of the room but within earshot. "You're my pussy wussy cat aren't you? Yes you are". Tom now refused to speak to her.

The first time the cat jumped onto Tom's shoulder he thought he was being attacked and ducked out of the way in alarm but it soon became a regular performance.

When Tom came down to breakfast the cat would be waiting in the middle of the kitchen floor. As he came through the door it would gather itself for a leap. Tom would bend his knees slightly, incline himself forward, and the cat would spring onto his shoulder. With its four paws bunched neatly together, its back arched like a serpent and its tail twisting round Tom's head, it would brush its chin against his forehead and purr for applause.

The cat's passion for cucumber was no passing fad either: as soon as a cucumber entered the house the cat would know it. Even if the cat was out when the cucumber arrived the cat would sense it was there the moment it came in. It would run over to the fridge and wait in a state of agitation until given a piece and it never got sick of it. Tom once tried to glut the cat with a large cucumber but he did not succeed: the cat ate the lot. It could hardly walk after it had eaten it but it none the less went back to the fridge, pretending to sniff for more.

The cat was equally passionate about television. Jeanette had thought it strategic not to mention her late night lapse in letting the cat into the kitchen and was forced to feign surprise at its amazing proclivity for viewing. It would sit bolt upright watching the television for lengthy periods of time, its neat forefeet in front of it, its head following the movements on the telly as if intent on understanding what was going on. One night, shortly after its admission to the kitchen on a regular basis, a Vivaldi violin piece was being played by Nigel Kennedy. The cat meowed and yowelled melodiously throughout. It was astonishing!.

Boots got bigger and stronger as Blackie got cleaner and fitter and

Lynne eventually took the cat upstairs to her bedroom to see the kitten. She even asked Tom to go with her in case of trouble and Jeanette was quite pleased at this apparent truce. Surprisingly Blackie showed not the slightest hostility towards the kitten. On the contrary, after sniffing it for some seconds he began to lick it all over, but then ignored it and scratched at the door to go downstairs.

When Boots was house-trained she was given the run of the kitchen and to Jeanette's surprise Blackie displayed great patience with the kitten: he allowed it to plague him, even when he was watching television. Apart from the occasional tail twitch he didn't seem to mind even the mock runs the kitten made at him or the clumsy attempts to stand on two feet to box with him which the kitten never tired of practising.

The kitten turned out to be slightly spastic and did everything rather clumsily. As it got older it flipped its left foot when it walked and found it difficult to run. If it tried to follow Blackie along the top of the garden railings it would fall off, and miss the jumps, but apart from that it was a perfectly normal cat.

Each night, well before Jeanette went to bed, Blackie would ask to go out. He would sit by the kitchen door meowing and scratching at the draught mat until the door was opened for him. He never came back until morning. No one knew where he went to or where he slept, or even if he did sleep at night. "He's just like my ex-husband", Jeanette thought. Tom suspected he spent the night under the lorries parked in the street. On several occasions, looking out of his bedroom window in the early morning, he had seen the cat crawling out from under one or another of them. "He will get himself killed if he's not careful", Tom thought. Sometimes the cat would go 'on the tiles' for two or three days but he had never stayed away longer, except on the last occasion.

When Blackie had been absent for three days Jeanette began to get worried, at four days Tom did, and after a week Lynne was convinced he must have been run over. "It's not fair having a cat, living so near a main road", she said. Tom was convinced he'd been killed by a reversing lorry but they had not heard news of a cat being killed. An advertisement in the local paper produced three telephone calls but none of the cats Lynne and Tom went to see turned out to be Blackie.

Both Lynne and Tom were equally upset over the cat's disappearance but it seemed to be bringing them closer together: they were talking to each other now. It was ironic, Jeanette thought: that the affection for the cat which split them apart should now be bringing them together. It had been the same at first when Peter had left.

As there was no dead body they couldn't properly mourn the cat's presumed death but there was a certain depressing sense of loss about the house. Blackie had been a character and they all missed him, perhaps more than each of them was prepared to admit.

Jeanette was pleased that Tom and Lynne still remained friendly when, as time went by, inevitably, reminiscences about the absent cat's habits and exploits became less frequent and Blackie joined the pantheon of ghosts of pets past. Jeanette knew the cat's love of cucumber would, over the years, grow and be mythologised and there was no questioning that he would become a legendary fan of breakfast TV.

Some three months after Blackie had gone missing Jeanette was in the kitchen finishing defrosting the fridge. She had put most of the contents in the freezer in the garage but the salad basket she had left on the kitchen floor. It was nearly midnight and she was ready for bed. The back door was open slightly to let Boots in after her trip to the loo.

Imperceptibly Jeanette developed the same eerie feeling she was being watched that had come over her the night she had first seen Blackie at the kitchen window. She glanced round but there was no one there. "I must get something for my nerves", she thought.

As Jeanette rose from the fridge and turned to wring out the cloth she had used to mop up the last of the melted ice her gaze passed across the window. She started and let out an audible gasp. She could have sworn she had seen her ex-husband, or was it Blackie crouched there, his front feet barely touching the sill, stretching his neck, staring in at her, but when she looked again she realised that what she had seen was the movement of her own reflection. "I really *must* get something for my nerves!", she said. A few minutes later the door creaked open another inch or two as something brushed against it. She looked round, wide eyed. It was Boots.

Jeanette slept badly that night and got up early, just as 'Farming

Today' was coming on the radio. She went downstairs to make herself a cup of tea and stood in her dressing gown in the kitchen waiting for the kettle to boil. She regretted not having put her glasses on. She couldn't see at all clearly without them and she liked to look out on the garden. She might take a walk in the garden, later, and drink her tea. She loved the early summer mornings when the sun was up and the shadows were long and the dew gave the flowers that special cool freshness.

She heard a blackbird give its warning cry as is skimmed low across the lawn to glide up into the tall pear tree next door. It sounded like a stonemason bouncing his hammer on a gravestone, she thought. And as she did so she felt a draught and shuddered and noticed she had left the window near the fridge wide open all night. "That was very careless of me", she thought. She went across to close it and as she did so her foot caught the salad basket and she bent down to straighten it. There before her, beyond the chair, in front of the television, she saw the prostrate body of her husband. She fainted.

When Jeanette insisted it was her husband and not the cat she had seen, the doctor said she had been overworking and needed a few days rest. It was not unusual for people under stress to transform what they saw into what subconsciously was in their minds, he said, but Jeanette remained unconvinced. She had definitely seen her husband.

The vet said that from the state of the cat it had clearly walked a great distance, possibly the length of several counties. He recognised it as having belonged to Miss Aitken. The only explanation for its condition was that it had been carried off on the back of a lorry, or even underneath one. He had heard of similar cases. The cat was thin and emaciated and its fur displayed all the classic signs of undernourishment and malnutrition. Parts of its body were ulcerated and its pads were worn out and bleeding. It was just possible, with some careful nursing, that it might recover but he would be surprised if it did. "Don't give it solids for a while: keep it on milk and sloppy foods until I've seen it again", he said.

Jeanette wanted the cat destroyed but she kept this to herself as she feared the effect on the children. Lynne kept Blackie in the box in her bedroom that she had used for Boots and Tom fed the cat with the pipette they had used to feed the kitten. Boots came up the stairs to see what was going on. She had grown a little older and less playful whilst Blackie had been away and merely sniffed at him. When she did eventually pat at Blackie, playfully with a paw, he did not respond. After a few days, as Blackie got a little stronger, Tom gave him a little bread and milk on a spoon and he ate it. He attempted to walk but his feet were still too sore.

The following evening Tom and Jeanette were going to a Careers Convention. Before leaving, Jeanette said, "Now remember, Lynne, if anyone calls, and especially your father, you are not to let them into the house. You must pretend there's no one in. Do you hear me?"

Shortly after Jeanette and Tom had gone the doorbell rang: it was probably her father, and though Lynne wanted to answer the door she ignored it.

After doing the washing up Lynne carried Blackie downstairs to the kitchen to let him watch television. She took a knife from the cutlery draw, went to the fridge and rummaged in the salad basket for a cucumber. Lynne wasn't sure the cat would be able to eat solids but she thought she would try him with his favourite food. "Just look what I've got for you", she said as she brought the cucumber over to the cat. Blackie meowed and feebly tried to take a bite off the end of it as she bent down close to him. Just as Lynne was about to cut him a small piece the doorbell rang again. As it was after eight, and it might be Tom; Lynne thought she had better see who it was this time. She put the cucumber and the knife on the rug next to the cat's box and went into the hall to answer the door, saying to herself as she did so: "I hope that is Tom, and not daddy again: I hate not being able to let him in".

It was Tom. He had forgotten his key and wanted to be let in but Lynne couldn't open the door for him: it had a safety lock and had been locked on the outside. "You'll have to go round to the back: my key's upstairs", she shouted. "Well go and get it!" Tom said, "I can't go round there with all these books". Tom had brought a pile of books from the car for Jeanette who had just dropped him off as she was going on to visit a colleague and did not want to risk leaving them in the car. Tom knew it was really one of the 'Dates'

BLACKIE

she'd been having recently: he'd heard her on the phone.

Lynne pushed her key through the letter box to Tom and he let himself in and in doing so his knee, which had been propped against the door supporting the books, collapsed as the door opened and the books fell into the hallway. Lynne helped him pick them up and as they walked through to the kitchen Lynne told him she was just trying the cat with a bit of cucumber. Tom dropped the books onto the floor again. "Oh! for God's sake Lynne!", he shouted, as he hurriedly pushed open the kitchen door.

Blackie was lying in a contorted posture, half out of the box in front of the television.

"You stupid girl, Tom shouted, as he ran forward. "If that cat's dead Lynne, I'll never forgive you!"

There was no sign of life in the cat. Despite Tom's prolonged attempts to revive it, the cat remained very dead. A large lump of cucumber was lodged in its throat.

Tom ran up the stairs shouting: "I'll get you for this Lynne", but the bedroom door was securely locked.

It was the following day that they heard their father had committed suicide.

MOVING

The heavy door swung shut. The bang bounced off the wall and boomed down the stairwell ahead of her. She stopped, teetering on the top step, then recovered and steadied herself. "Damn it, I've forgotten my stick again". She would have to go back. Life, these days was full of false starts for Margaret Gabison. Much as she loved Italy she would be glad to move back to England. She just couldn't cope any more: her wobbly legs, the dizzy spells. No matter how much she racked her brain before she set out she always remembered she had forgotten something the instant the door slammed shut. And then there was the problem of remembering what it was, "I hope I picked up my keys" she mumbled, as she rummaged in her super-market bag for her purse. She felt safer with her purse in a throw-away plastic bag despite her friend Pamela having told her repeatedly that the thieves were onto it. "Oh no! Don't say I didn't put my purse in!" She felt in her coat pocket for her spare key. "Good", she said out aloud. "Thank goodness that's there". The key fitted badly. The lock was a complex Italian one with three barrels which mated into holes, like dowels. It was difficult for her arthritic fingers to turn. but she had somehow learnt the knack. She pushed the key in sideways, jiggled it about and then pulled it out slightly and turned. "Oh come on, come on. Please open!" There was an audible click as the lock finally obliged.

André's hat and coat hung on their peg on the facing wall of the hallway where he had put them ten years previously. "I forgot my stick", she shouted as she turned into the hallway. She stood for a moment in front of the long mirror looking intently at the stranger staring back at her. "My god, I can't believe that's me". The figure she was looking at seemed shorter; she was quite tall. The person in the mirror seemed narrow, stooped, lopsided and scraggy; she was straight, smart and quite full-figured. The faded brown raincoat with the reinforced cape on the shoulders looked like hers and the scarf - she would know that fawn scarf anywhere - she'd had it for years. But that creased and crumpled, lined skin! That was never hers. No wonder that artist, Gormley was it, Anthony Gormley, had asked to photograph her when she'd met him in the Royal Academy whilst visiting England. "The Angel of the South, I don't think!" She could still poke fun at herself. "But he did send me a copy. And just look at my hair!" The dyed, chestnut brown hair that fringed from underneath her black, pudding-basin, knitted hat looked thin and frizzy. "I wonder if I should buy a wig?" She pushed past the ancient exercise bike draped with umbrellas and festooned with assorted rainwear. "I must get rid of that bike", she mumbled. It was years since she had ridden it. The state her knee was in she would not even be able to get on the blessed thing. The sixty watt bulb struggled to illuminate the tall hallway made dingy by the dusty brown raffia wall-covering which André had insisted on keeping. The Leonardo *Madonna* sketches and the sepia Raphael *Cartoons*, despite their beauty, did nothing to relieve the gloom. The angle-iron shelves, crowded with André's books and rows of carefully labelled video cassettes took up a quarter of the width and made it impossible for two people to pass without embarrassingly intimate contact. "I must phone up and see if one of the language schools will take André's Greek and Russian books", she thought, as she pushed open the living room door. Her purse was on the table. The stick on the back of a chair.

The lock catch clicked again and the heavy door once more swung shut. Again the bang bounced off the wall and boomed and echoed down the stairwell ahead of her. "I'll miss this old building", she said out loud. The 18th century apartment block was an impressive one; four stories high with a flat stucco front and tall windows graced with wooden shutters. It was located on one of the seven hills of Rome in the *Centro Storico*, on the edge of the *Esquilino*, "the Quarter of the future" according to some. Not far from Santa Maria Maggiore, one of the four great Basilicas of Rome which, along with St. Peter's had dominated the city since mediaeval times: but the stairs were murderous. Again she stopped, teetering above the top step. "Living on the second floor without a lift at eighty-six is no joke" she mouthed to herself. She was all right with the hand rail. She could place her stick on the step below and grip the rail with her left hand. It was that damned turning at the bottom of the stairs that defeated her. She changed hands for her stick and relied on the wall. She must mind the first floor flat doormat, then step down that extra deep step into *the atrium* as she grandiloquently called it, without falling. People told her that she had a habit of emitting a continuous low whistle like a bat to comfort herself as she carried out these life threatening manoeuvres. "I don't think I whistle", she said indignantly.

There was no mail in her post box, just a few circulars and a note from the Administrator, nothing from Lily. Lily was André's daughter by his first marriage. She lived in Winston, Salem, USA and was far from well at the moment. "Perhaps tomorrow", she said out aloud. She would collect Signor Rubeo's note on the way back. "I hope it's to say a price and a date for the sale of the apartment has been agreed". She would have to contact Mr. Zumstein to arrange the removal of her furniture to England. Four thousand pounds was a lot of money. Perhaps she should get another quotation. "Oh dear, so many things to see to!"

The step down to the heavy, wooden, brass-studded street door was an easy matter after the stairs but holding onto the wall whilst pulling the door open was tricky and took all her strength. She waited outside the door until it shut itself; until she had heard the click. She didn't want one of those illegal Albanian immigrants getting in. How stupid of Pamela to actually invite *two* of them into her apartment just because they had made a fuss of Simba. "What was she thinking of!" The dog walker had been ill and Pamela had been out exercising her Alsatian, Simba. The dog looked extremely fierce but was really 'a big softy' and craved affection which the two passing Albanian immigrants had been only too willing to give it when it failed to growl and bark at them. Pamela got talking to them and when one asked to use the toilet and the other asked for a drink of water she invited them in. One kept her distracted whilst the other supposedly went to the loo. After they had gone she discovered her purse and 250 Euros was missing from her handbag. "After all the lectures Pamela's given me about being more careful in this city of thieves and vagabonds!", Margaret said out loud.

Quattro Cantoni was a steep street made narrow by the assortment of cars and motor cycles parked permanently either side. The few useful shops there had been closed during the Esquilino's "downhill era", though one, as part of the long awaited renaissance, had recently opened again as a studio-gallery displaying a few ultra modern garishly coloured paintings and one or two pieces of contorted pottery pretentiously displayed on isolated pedestals. She glanced wistfully towards the steep terraced steps leading down to the Via Cavour. Last year she could have managed to get up and down those steps if she held onto the wall. She could not do that now. If she had one of her dizzy spells she'd be finished. She turned to walk up the hill towards Via Paulina and her daily destination, the café down the other side of the hill and round the corner on the Via San Martino ai Monti.

Quattro Cantoni was 'tarmacked' for a short distance and easy on the feet but when it reached the intersection of the Via Paulina it still had the original Roman-style cobblestones. They had become irregular over the centuries and though smooth were quite slippery. Pietrocini the Italians called them to commemorate Saint Peter, the 'rock'. The city council wanted to replace them but the conservationists had organised successful protest marches. "They're a damned nuisance!" she said, when people marvelled at the antiquity of the cobblestones.

Much to the annoyance of Margaret and her neighbours a seedy, disreputable club called *The Blue Moon* was premised in Quattro Cantoni; a hangover from the days when the district had been even more down-market. It advertised pornographic movies showing in the early evening and strip shows later on featuring Dolores, Marina and Gina, so the billboard said. As she passed, one of the girls came out looking as though she had recently risen from bed. She was young, perhaps nineteen or twenty, with a good figure accentuated by tight back jeans and a clinging sweater. The high-heeled shoes were inappropriate. She proceeded to beat the carpet she had brought out with her. A cigarette hung from her faded lipsticked lips. It reminded her when André had arrived home late one evening saying he had been to the pictures. When Margaret asked him where, he'd said *The Blue Moon*. Been there "out of curiosity". She had been horrified in case one of the neighbours had seen him going in.

When she got to the Via Paulina she rested, leaning on the wall at the corner. She looked down the street at the side view of Santa Maria Maggiore silhouetted against the blue of the cloudless morning sky. "I'll miss that view", she thought, "but I won't miss that damned bike". The bike which was now nothing more than a bent skeletal frame, the wheels having long since been stolen, had been chained to a post for the last five years or so. It blocked the narrow pavement of the Via Paulina forcing people to walk on the road, on the outside of the parked cars. It was a one way street and though there were not many cars using it those that did usually drove fast and gave little time to get out of their way. If she didn't leave Rome while still in one piece it would soon be too late!

She continued her slow hobble along Quattro Cantoni. There were no pavements here, as was the case with most streets in the historic quarter. The cars were parked bumper to bumper both sides of the narrow road and so near the walls of the buildings there was no refuge or support. They were a damned nuisance but she never ceased to marvel at the way the Italians were able to manoeuvre their cars into the most minute looking gaps and get them an inch from the wall. "You have to take your hats off to them", she was for ever telling complaining visitors. "And at least it's one-way". Her knee, which was becoming increasingly painful and bent, was so stiff these days she could hardly walk the length of the street. "When I get to England, with its wonderful wide pavements, I'll be able to use one of those walking frames with wheels".

A pair of middle-aged, grey clad, wimpled, lay order nuns, engrossed in conversation almost knocked her over and would have done so had she not expostulated loudly in English. As she passed the super-market she remembered she was out of milk. "Must get some on the way back", she said, to reinforce her increasingly unreliable memory. Only three months previously she had fallen in the super-market and broken a bone in her wrist. She had been reaching up to get a tin of Campbell's soup from a high shelf and must have had one of her dizzy spells. She didn't even remember falling but when she came to she was in a hospital bed with her wrist in plaster. Her friends thought she had died and was lying undiscovered somewhere when they failed to raise her on the telephone. Alison and Rachelle contacted the Administrator to search her apartment - not there. "Did you look under the beds?", yelled a slightly hysterical Joyce. Susan 'phoned the British Embassy twice a day for three days. Pamela phoned the police and the hospitals but there was no record of her being admitted. Everyone was frantic with worry. They even phoned Wendy, her goddaughter, in England to report her missing. It was Margaret herself who solved the mystery. She phoned Pamela from Salvatore Mundi, a large public hospital, to ask her to bring some clean underwear. It transpired that contrary to official practice Margaret's name had not been put on the hospital computer, so for three days no one knew what had happened to her or where she was. "And do you know, Pamela never came to the hospital", she told everyone. It was quite unreasonable because Pamela lived outside Rome and had Parkinson's disease. Pamela would not, however, admit it, despite a badly shaking arm which she held with her other hand to mask the fact. Pamela could just about manage to drive her car to her local shops but was daunted by the busy inner-city traffic of Rome. When this was pointed out to her Margaret had to admit that perhaps she had been a little hasty in condemning Pamela. "But she could have rung!", she said, vehemently.

There were red, white and green flags bedecking the Government building which stood half-way down the hill and just beyond the ancient Convent which in former days had housed several hundred *Little Sisters of the Poor.* Now only a dozen or so nuns remained and those either elderly, Indonesian or black. In contrast to the plain facade of the Convent the Ministry was a much more impressive building, again of considerable antiquity. It was built in the Classical Italian style with a large solid base which accentuated its height. Two flights of steps either side rose to a balcony with balusters and an ornamental parapet giving access to the front door. The first floor rooms were high with tall windows and decorated columns either side. The upper windows were smaller and balconied and the roof corniced in typical Italian style. The building was open to the public on one day each year but somehow she always managed to miss it or had got the day wrong. She would never get to see inside now that she had decided to go back to England. "Thirty opportunities and I've never taken one of them", she mused. She looked at her watch and realised that it had taken her nearly twenty minutes to get to where she used to walk in five.

Just beyond the Ministry the road widened and the traffic flow became two-way. There was a turning off on her left which created a dangerous bend. The traffic sped up the hill and turned across her path. There was no 'crossing' and she walked so slowly that even when the road in front of her was empty by the time she had got half way across a stream of cars might come. She leaned against a parked car, praying it had no alarm, until someone overtook her. "*Signor, Signor. Per favore.* May I take hold of your arm". The man obliged and the pair of them slowly crossed the road, the man with his arm up to warn the traffic. Despite this precaution there was one car which didn't stop: it veered perilously close in the driver's rush to get round them. "Damned cheek" she shouted.

She thanked the man. *"Grazie Signor. Grazie tanto"*. Ahead of her down the steeply sloping gradient several roads met and skirted a plain, ancient *Torri dei Capocci* - a Roman square tower of impressive height - one of several dotted about the city. They were built by 'Capocci' in the early medieval period as refuge towers for the citizens of Rome fearful of attack by the Visigoths. This particular tower had been refurbished inside and there were people living there now "could you believe!". Margaret turned left into the Via Martino ai Monti. Two chairs were standing as usual a little way into the road to prevent cars from parking and blocking the doorway of Mario's bar. As there was no pavement the bar was not allowed to have tables and chairs outside but Italian laws are flexible and policemen are fond of coffee. When the weather was sunny, which was most of the time, she could sit outside on one of the chairs and eat her brioche or ciaccolata and drink her espresso or a café lungo. It was a little too cool for outdoors today, she thought.

Mario's would have been a strong contender, had there been a prize, for the smallest bar in Rome. It was barely three metres wide by five metres deep: open from six o'clock in the morning until ten at night. A door to the left allowed access to a public space, barely a metre wide, but running the length of the room. Against the wall as you walked in was a tall drinks refrigerator dispensing Coca Cola and a variety of other soft drinks; then a small square table with two stacks of free local newspapers; a deck of four white plastic chairs; a half round table and another stack of two plastic chairs. The back wall was tiled with large square mirror tiles which doubled the depth of the bar and made it look busier and more crowded than it was, rather than more spacious as was probably intended. The narrow counter to the right finished a metre short of the back wall and allowed for a small, square toilet cabin. An end lift-up-section of the counter allowed access to behind the bar where Mario and his plump wife squeezed past each other to get to the coffee machines attached to the outer-side of the toilet wall. The wall behind the counter was likewise mirror-tiled but only to half way up. Above the tiles were shelves containing a few well spaced bottles of herbal liqueurs and spirits. There was room on the wall for two or three small advertisements and a large, dominating poster advertising *Birra*

Moretti, Dal 1895. It showed a seated, squat, elderly Italian peasant with a paunch, wearing the trousers and jacket of a creased, blue, pinstriped suit and a nondescript shirt with a slack-knotted, patterned, blue-grey tie. A wide, dark-brown, trilby hat shaded his round lugubrious grey face, accentuating his bushy, walrus moustache and yellowed teeth. He was holding forward a raised litre glass jug of lightly frothed, golden-brown beer. A beer *Pressione* stand was fixed to the counter and at the end, near the door, stood a curved glass case containing a variety of brioches, some plain, some with custard or chocolate inside: never jam or marmalade thought Margaret, crossly. A square, silver serviette dispenser stood next to the glass case. There was little room to rest a coffee cup on the counter. A haze of cigarette smoke hung high above the bar: surprisingly the bar didn't smell of smoke.

"Buon giorno Mario. Buon giorno signora", Margaret said as she entered. *"Café lungo, per favore. Caldo. Molto caldo"*. She was renowned for complaining that she could never get a hot coffee in Italy. She took a plate off the counter and ignoring the tongs opened the glass cabinet and took a brioche. She walked on to the back of the bar and placed the plate on the half-table. She struggled to dislodge one of the two interlocked plastic chairs only to drop her stick on the floor with a loud clatter. "Damn, Damn, Damn", she muttered. "Here, let me help you Signora ", Mario's wife said as she came out from behind the bar. *Grazie. Grazie tanto"*. As she sat down she almost missed the chair. Mario had banged the heavy metal cup against the base of the coffee machine to dislodge the old grounds. That noise always made her jump. She flinched visibly too at the loud hiss of steam as the milk frothed into someone else's coffee. The two smartly dressed men in suits standing at the counter engaged in some jocular banter with Mario, threw their heads back to drain the last of their coffee and left shouting *"Arrive'derci Mario" "Arrive'derci Signora"*.

Margaret opened one of the two free newspapers she had picked up before sitting down. She glanced at the headline announcing the shortly to be introduced law prohibiting smoking in cafes and bars. "I can't see the Italians obeying that. They're terrible at obeying laws", she said to herself. As she stuffed the newspapers into her plastic shopping bag her eye caught the headlines on the second newspaper: 'Immigration Protest March'.

"Un cafe lungo. Molto caldo", Mario said, with his usual broad smile as he brought the coffee out to her. *"Grazie, Mario, Grazie"*. Mario was a short, stocky Alpine, barrel-chested type of northern Italian in his late fifties. He wore a short-sleeved, navy-blue shirt and an off-white apron. He had thick muscular arms and a tuft of chest-hair showing at his throat but he was balding, grey-faced and had an early morning stubble. He looked far from well. It was his first day back in the bar since his heart attack. His wife and daughter had been coping, doing single-handed shifts for the past six weeks. They needed the money but the strain was beginning to show in the wife's face, Margaret thought.

Mario's wife, Gabriella was a buxom woman and a little bit tartish in appearance: a scaled down version of those big busted women on naughty postcards people bought at popular seaside resorts. Dark wavy hair down to her shoulders—a little too long, and too much red lipstick on over-large lips. And she certainly had the bulging bust and the big bottom. Her face was typically Latinate and could have been Spanish but for the pleasant openness missing from her Andalucian counterparts, Margaret thought. She didn't much like the looks of those heavy-faced, middle-aged, matronly Spanish women with their disagreeable scowls who sat chattering like machine-guns, in foursomes, and smoking their smelly cigarettes in the café-bars of Madrid or Málaga but she liked the look of Gabriella. "How are you feeling now, Mario", Margaret asked. "So so" he said, rocking his right hand in the air. "He shouldn't be back at work yet but I can't keep him away", Gabriella interjected. "You mustn't do too much Mario", Margaret said.

The bar was getting quite busy so there was no scope for further conversation. She sat, holding her coffee cup in both hands, pensively staring into space, reflecting on the time it was taking to sell her apartment and the row she had had with Dr. Sposi and his daughter Christina, over its sale. If only she had sorted the matter of the 'extensions' out sooner, she reproached herself.

When she and André bought the apartment some thirty years previously they had noticed the bathroom and kitchen extension did not appear on the plans. They were not particularly concerned at the time. The rooms were well-established parts of the apartment, built-on in the pre-war era of Mussolini, and besides, all the other flats in the building had similar alterations and additions. It was true, however, that because the building dated from the early eighteenth-century it was classed as historic and had protected status. The 'extension' was thus illegal but they were assured by the vendor that an amnesty was given every ten years or so on payment of a small fee. Because the alterations and additions were at the back, and not visible from the front, they would be condoned and registered and all would be well. This was, after all Italy, and nobody took much notice of that kind of thing. And sure enough, over the years, several amnesties had been offered but for one reason or another - they had been on holiday at the time or André had been ill - they had not taken advantage of them. It was only now that she wished to sell the apartment that the matter had been noticed and drawn to Margaret's attention by the Administrator and had become important. Margaret had mentioned the irregularity to her solicitor, Christina, whom she knew well and who had acted on her behalf previously in several minor matters. Christina was the daughter of a former work-colleague at the Food and Agricultural Organisation of the United Nations (FAO): Dr. Sposi. Margaret had taught Christina English as a child. Christina assured Margaret that the matter of the 'extension' could be cleared up on payment of the small fee, but it might take some time. Margaret had her doubts and was kept awake at night by the fear that she would be prosecuted over the 'extension', fined and told to remove it.

Signor Rubeo, the Administrator of the apartment block, mentioned to Dr. André Santovelli, a high official in the Bank of Italy, and a good friend of his, that Margaret wished to sell her apartment. Dr. Santovelli was not without ready money. He lived in the apartment block. Margaret knew him to say *Buon giorno* to. He was very interested in buying the apartment and made Margaret an offer of 480,000 Euro through Signor Rubeo. On the advice of Signor Rubeo Margaret accepted this offer but without consulting Christina and in due course against Christina's advice. Christina thought the offer far too little but Margaret insisted it was acceptable. With some reluctance Christina arranged a *Compo-Vendetti* meeting where a formal agreement to buy and sell would take place and a deposit lodged. Dr. Santovelli was keen to buy but raised objections at the meeting over the irregularity of the 'extension'. He tried to have inserted an obsolete clause, which the Italian Goverment had long ago barred, to the effect that Margaret would be liable for the cost of any repairs to the building for a period of seven years. Margaret was not present at the meeting and Christina rejected this out of hand as outrageous. Dr. Santovelli withdrew his offer. Margaret subsequently paid Christina's firm 1,000 Euros for the work done on the *Campo-Vendetti,* despite no agreement to buy and sell. Christina advised Margaret to put the apartment in the hands of an Estate Agent and to ask 600,000 Euro for it.

Margaret was annoyed with Christina and blamed her for the sale having fallen through. Had she been at the meeting herself she would have been prepared to accept a lower offer. And she was not satisfied with the dilatory way Christina had been progressing the matter of regularising the 'extension', nor with the price at which she recommended the apartment be sold. It was too much Margaret thought. It would never sell at that price with the matter of the 'extension' unresolved. She would be stuck in Rome for ever. Her dizzy spells were more frequent now and she wanted to be rid of the apartment and move to the flat she had bought in England where help and support were on hand. Eventually her patience, which was notoriously short, though she would never admit it, had run out. She rowed with Christina and told her she was going to let the Administrator and his solicitor-son handle the sale. Christina was astonished and very annoyed with her. She warned that in her opinion the Administrator and his son were not disinterested parties and that she was in danger of being swindled. Margaret would not hear of it. "Signor Rubeo is a nice man. His son is a nice boy". She trusted him. He would look after her interests she was sure. Despite pleas from Christina's father, Dr. Sposi, himself a lawyer, whom she had known for more than thirty years, she rejected their advice and fell out with the pair of them. Christina sent her "a huge bill" for 4,000 Euros for the work she had done and when Margaret complained that Christina's father had intimated that the work would be done cheaply Christina simply referred her to the list of Solicitor's Standard Charges. It was the same charge that would have been made had a sale been completed. Margaret maintained she had been robbed by Christina but she nonetheless paid up. "I never would have thought Christina would do such a thing", she told everyone. She refused to countenance that there might be another side to the story.

Margaret confided in Signor Rubeo that she was depressed and fed up with the delays in selling her apartment. She wanted a quick sale: she would be dead before she ever got to England. Signor Rubeo said he would see what he could do: his son would deal with the legal side of things. "As you are an old friend I'll ask him to do the paper work free of charge", he told her. He promptly informed Dr. Santovelli about the turn of events. Dr. Santovelli was overjoyed that the 'difficult' Christina was off the scene. He wanted the flat to house his estranged wife as part of a divorce settlement. They were still good friends and she wanted to live in the centre of Rome. A flat so near her erstwhile husband would not have been Signora Santovelli's first choice but her husband was underwriting the purchase and she could always sell it and move if things didn't work out. On her husband's advice she made an offer of 400,000 Euros with an agreement to make no fuss over the fact that there was an irregularity over the bathroom and kitchen.

As she came out of her reverie Margaret shouted out aloud: "I really must sell. I just want to be rid of it. I can't cope any longer. I know everyone will be cross with me for "giving it away" but I just want to be rid of it!". It was quite irrational. A couple of Mario's customers turned and stared at her.

The bar was getting increasingly busy. People came in, ordered espressos, downed them in one, left a few coins, and went, hurrying off to work. *"Ancora café Signora Gabison"*, Mario shouted to her. *"Non Grazie Mario*, I must be getting along", she said, as she fumbled behind her chair for her stick.

Margaret stood for a moment outside Mario's bar debating whether to attempt one of the circular walks she used to do when her legs were stronger or to go back home. It was months since she had done anything more adventurous unaided than go for her morning coffee. "If I stop walking I'm finished", she said, to nobody in particular, but she couldn't make up her mind. There were so many important buildings and churches just round the corner from where she lived and she wanted to see them one last time. She could be down the Via Cavour to the Forum or the Coliseum in fifteen minutes - well not any more. She quickly ruled out going right to San Pietro in Vincoli: too far, and not worth it now that they had cordoned off Michelangelo's *Moses*. You could no longer get near enough to see the detail nor the fine quality of the marble. And those chains in the glass case they claimed had bound St. Peter were pretty obviously fakes. "Better to retain earlier memories than give yourself disappointments", she said. "Perhaps I could manage the hill up to San Martino ai Monti".

The hill was indeed quite steep. The road skirted past the refuge tower and went up past the side of a former Monastery, which had been built using the stones of the old Roman wall, and past a very old building housing the present-day Italian Secret Service. The church of St. Martino ai Monti was a very important one, rebuilt in the 18th Century, and housing an impressive slab of ancient Roman stone retained from an earlier 4th Century church on the site. The slab contained an inscription in square capitals commemorating Constantine's reunification of the Roman Empire in 324 AD. and the Nicene Council of 325 AD. which Constantine had held to enforce orthodox Christian belief. Margaret had read somewhere that Constantine had to bang the heads of the Bishops together in order to get them to agree on only four, true gospels, to be included in the Christian Bible out of the twenty-one contenders. A ceremony had been held in San Martino ai Monti the year after the Council to ratify the Nicene Creed.

Margaret turned left up the Via di Santa Prassede intending to have one last look in the church of Santa Prassede. It was built in the 5th Century, but rebuilt many times. She wanted to see the famous stake that Jesus was supposed to have been bound to and flogged by the Roman soldiers. The church probably wouldn't be open. It never was. "I can carry on round to Santa Maria Maggiore and have a look at the mosaics", she decided. As predicted Santa Prassede was closed and Via di Santa Pressede was longer than she thought. She had to rest several times. She had forgotten about the stretch with the Irish pub and the pavement tables. "How can people drink beer at this time of the morning", she marvelled as she rested yet again.

The roads sweeping round the front of Santa Maria Maggiore were wide, busy and daunting. She turned left to go down to the pedestrian-crossing near the top entrance to Via Paulina. "Plenty of taxis this morning", she observed. It was not always the case. There was space at the side of the Basilica for twenty or thirty taxis but there were never any there when she wanted one and as she could not stand for more than a few minutes these days she seldom took one. "I hate crossing that road", she would shout when people told her: "You should take a taxi". People, Margaret mused were more than fond of giving her 'helpful advice', despite the fact that she rarely heeded it. The traffic ignored the 'crossing' and there were so many fast motor scooters nowadays. Even doctors and solicitors had them - they were the worst offenders - whizzing over 'crossings' and jumping the traffic lights. There had been a period, not long ago, when the traffic had behaved itself but it was almost back to its former chaos. Everyone was so selfish. It was Silvio Berlusconi's doing, she was sure.

The circular, green kiosk, on the pavement in front and to her left, was open with the shutters off the sides. It was thickly decked with international newspapers, colourful magazines and racks of postcards. "I must send a card to my cousin in Beaumaris telling her I'm coming back to England: we might be able to meet up. I've so little family left", she reflected. She looked across the Piazza Santa Maria Maggiore at the monumental column Pope Paul V had erected in the seventh century and beyond to the street leading to the Stazione Termini which in the evening was the parade of mini-skirted prostitutes and exotically attired transvestites. She let her eyes pan towards the terrace of steps leading up to the entrance of the great Liberian Basilica of Santa Maria Maggiore. There were the usual beggars in their usual positions by the door of the church with their hands held out as usual. They had such pitiful expressions but such whining voices she was always torn about giving them anything. Already there were numerous people sitting on the steps amongst the pigeons, and small knots of tourists with cameras, and guides standing about on the spacious pavement in front of the church. "Probably Japanese", she said aloud, causing a passing couple to turn their heads and stare at her. "My god, they probably think I'm the mad woman who lives in that box!" she said, this time to herself.

The cardboard box, housing the notorious German woman street-sleeper, on the corner of the Viale del Monte Oppio had the flap flung back to reveal a seedy dark interior with a mattress and disreputable looking bedding. The woman was not simply eccentric she was mentally ill but not sufficient so as to warrant being 'sectioned'. She had lived on the same spot in the street for what must be getting on for twenty years - she was now in her early fifties. Despite several attempts by the authorities over the years to remove her she was always back the next day. And she had her supporters. The cardboard dwelling she had constructed was just under three meters long by one and a half metres wide and about the same in height. She had covered the structure with bits and pieces of different coloured plastic sheeting which had weathered and faded and was held together by sticky tape and string. She spent her days either sitting in the doorway of her home hugging her knees and chunnering or roaming around the immediate vicinity shouting abuse in either German or Italian at passers-by. She was almost certainly suffering from Tourette's syndrome because much of her ranting was scatological and her arm and head movements involuntarily erratic though at times she appeared calm. Occasionally she emerged from her box well turned-out in Levi's and a sweater, her shingled, greying fair-hair washed and neatly groomed. At other times she was unkempt and quite aggressive and threatening to people. The locals who were used to her took no notice, they knew she was harmless, but strangers fended her away shouting back at her, or stood and stared, alarmed. Margaret had been told her relatives in Germany sent her money and this must have been true as she never begged and appeared well fed and clothed. Her presence on the street had become such a feature of the district the newspapers had done articles about her.

Margaret considered the 'crossing', looked at the hoards of cars racing up the hill when the lights at the bottom turned green, and thought better of it. She wouldn't be able to get up all those steps to the Basilica anyway and she had been there many times before. The high mosaics on the ceiling of the recessed balcony above the

door she would have liked to have seen again but they were only viewable on one day during the week and though she thought today was the day she couldn't remember if there was a lift. "Probably not". "Well at least I've had a bit of exercise", she said, as she turned left into the Via Paulina and walked along the raised, railed duck-boards that served as a pavement beside the high wall of the building which held the army finance offices and back towards home.

As she once again fiddled with the key in the lock of her apartment door Margaret remembered she'd forgotten the milk. "How could I forget the milk. I walked right past the place", she said to herself. "I'll have to get Anandra to go for it, or get some later when I take my prescription to the Chemist. How could I forget it!". As she entered the apartment she heard the sound of running water and at first thought she had left the tap on in the kitchen but it turned out that Anandra had arrived early.

Anandra, her Sri Lankan domestic help had worked for her for two years, ever since Secondina had developed Altzheimer's disease and become too old and forgetful to work any more. Secondina had lived alone but her cousin, who was a Bishop, had arranged for her to be looked after in a Convent. She had given the nuns and the police no end of trouble, wandering off and not being able to find her way back. Margaret had come across her in the street on more than one occasion, miles from where she lived. It was a blessing when, a couple of months ago, she finally died. Secondina had come every other day but Anandra came only two mornings a week. He did the washing up, dusted, Ewbanked, and put the washing in the washing machine. He was not particularly thorough and never cleaned the mirrors despite repeated requests and she was sure, irrespective of his protestations to the contrary, that the washing machine was only doing a cold wash. Still, he was better than no help at all and he was always willing to go to the shops for her or lend her his arm when accompanying her on longer trips to the Chemist.

"Buon giorno Anandra: How are you today?" "A Mr. Zumstein phoned to say he will call round at two o'clock today to explain his quotation and do a proper inventory of the things you want to take to England", Anandra replied. "He can't do that. I haven't sold the place yet!", she shouted. "Anyway I'm meeting Alison at the FAO at one o'clock. I shall have to ring him". She rummaged in her handbag for the Administrator's note, which she had remembered to collect on the way in, but she couldn't find it. "Now where did I put that damned note!", she said, as she retrieved her plastic shopping bag from the handle of the exercise bike, took out the newspapers, and tipped the rest of the contents onto the dining-room table. "Not there. Oh damn, where did I put it?" "Is this what you are looking for? You left it on the kitchen table", Anandra said, handing her Mr Rubeo's note. "Oh good. I knew I'd put it somewhere where I could

easily find it".

She opened Signor Rubeo's note with some trepidation, fished out her glasses from her handbag and struggled to simultaneously translate the Italian and to read Signor Rubeo's spidery handwriting.

Dear Mrs. Gabison,

Signora Santovelli is not prepared to increase her offer to 420,000 Euros. She says 400,000 Euros is the maximum she can offer because of the uncertainty regarding the kitchen and bathroom and the fact that she will have to completely refurbish the apartment. This may be a disappointment to you but I strongly urge you to accept the offer as it might be a long time before another buyer comes along and another buyer might not be as accommodating about the kitchen and bathroom as Signora Santovelli. Please phone me as a matter of urgency as to whether or not you agree to 400,000 Euros. If you do agree my son will draw up the necessary legal documents for signature and we can meet with Dr. Santovelli and his wife and my son next Thursday evening in his apartment for everyone to sign and agree the sale with a view to a completion date of 21st January, 2005.

Best wishes, *carissima Signora,*

Luciano Rubeo.

Margaret read Signor Rubeo's note with a sinking feeling of apprehension bordering on panic. She sensed she should hold out for 420,000 Euro but what could she do? She had to move to England. She dreaded falling down and being left lying, unable to contact anyone. When she broke her wrist she had arranged for a girl, one of her language students, to live-in with her for a few days until June, her friend, kindly came over for a month from Madrid, but there was no one near she could reliably call on. Most of her friends had died or lived outside Rome. Anyway she didn't want anyone living-in. Her health was getting worse by the day. And those injections Professor Bruno, her Neurologist had prescribed didn't seem to be doing her much good. "He's the Pope's Neurologist, so he must be good", she told her friends. The tablets Dr. Falconi, her G.P., had recommended were not doing her much good either and they were very expensive! "I must book to see Professor Bruno again before I leave Rome and get him to write a note for me to show someone in England", she thought. And I must see Doctor Schultz again about my wrist: he might be able to do something about my knee. Doctor Schultz was the orthopaedic surgeon who had set the bone in her broken wrist. He was not easy to get hold of. He lived in Munich and flew to Rome for clinics only twice a week. "No, I really must drop the price and get rid of the apartment quickly. I just want to be rid of it! I can't enjoy Rome anymore so what's the point of living here!"

Having decided, Margaret phoned Signor Rubeo and left a message on his answer machine to say she accepted Signora Santovelli's offer and that a meeting the following Thursday would be all right. She then telephoned Mr. Zumstein to arrange for him to come at two o'clock tomorrow rather than today. "I've a prior engagement I'm afraid", she explained. She looked at her watch and exclaimed "Good lord, is that the time!" She had to be at the FAO at one o'clock and there was her prescription to get made up at a Chemist's. She couldn't believe the morning had nearly gone. "I'll have to get Anandra to walk with me to the Chemist's shop at the Railway station. It's a long way but I can at least be sure of a taxi there".

The visit to the Chemist was not a success. She had picked up the old prescription in mistake for the new one. It had the name of the new tablets and the name of her injections written on the back but the Chemist wouldn't accept it without a doctor's signature. Anandra offered to go back for the new one but whether he would be able to find it was another matter. He helped her into her Taxi before heading off back to the apartment. No sooner had the Taxi left the station than she remembered she had forgotten to ask Anandra to get the milk. "Oh well, I'll just have to drink my tea black. It won't be the first time".

The Taxi unexpectedly swung right out of the station rank, then left, and headed down towards the Via Cavour. "There's a demonstration", the driver told her when she asked why he wasn't taking the more direct route. "The Italians are always demonstrating about something or other", she said. "It was Iraq last week and Animal Rights the week before that. They're always demonstrating". Then she remembered reading in the paper there was to be a demonstration protesting against immigration policy. "It will be immigration", she told the driver. Silvio Berlusconi proposed sending illegal immigrants back to their home countries but many had become established and had been living in Rome up to ten years. They had married Italians, owned homes and had families. Margaret was ambivalent on the issue. She didn't like the idea of families being deported or split up. Some of the children had been born in Italy and spoke only Italian, but she was not sympathetic to the Albanians who were into prostitution, begging on the streets and a great deal of thieving. The Taxi came to a halt as a contingent of protesters was allowed by the police to cross the Via Cavour. She could hear the chanting and whistles through the glass of the taxi window. Numerous floats went by, packed with people. There were dozens of colourful banners flapping between poles declaring Communists, Anarchists, Socialists, Christians, Albanians, Iranians, Iraqi's, Blacks, Gays, this or that trade union, etc., to be against the legislation and a sea of individual black and white placards saying "Berlusconi Out" in big bold type. Young people were handing out leaflets or selling various partisan newspapers. The police were in no hurry to get the demonstrators across the road and Margaret noticed that the Taxi meter was ticking on at an alarming rate. "Immigration is costing me a small fortune", she said to the driver when they finally resumed their journey.

As they turned left out of Via Cavour and headed down the broad Via Dei Fori Imperiali, which Mussolini had built to accommodate his grand, mass parades of black-shirted, uniformed, strutting *fascista*, Margaret glanced right towards Trajan's column, Capitol Hill and the Imperial Forums where the archaeologists were still hard at work. "I don't suppose I shall ever again see that disappointing sculpture of Romulus and Remus, being suckled by the she-wolf. Nor that giant, gold-plated, bronze statue of Marcus Aurelius astride his golden horse, or the Roman Forum's magnificent, sculpturally decorated Arc of Septimus Severus", she reflected, wistfully. "This might even be my last ever look at the Coliseum", she thought, as she looked out of the Taxi window at the fake Roman centurions with their red plumed helmets, plastic gunmetal breastplates, swords, short leather skirts and thong-wrapped legs, posing with the tourists for expensive, memento photographs. She bent forwards and looked upwards. Despite the ravages of the twenty centuries since it was built in 80 A.D., the so called Flavian Amphitheatre was still for her the most impressive monument of ancient Rome. The Taxi sped on, trying to make up lost time, round the back of the Coliseum and on past the vast *Circo Massimo,* where for hundreds of years the ancient Romans held their chariot races. Then past the high banked ruins of the ancient city wall with the ruined Baths of Caracalla in the distance beyond. How many times had she been there with André to the open-air opera. Her mind flipped back to the spectacular Aida she had witnessed where live elephants had come out of the ruins and on to the stage, and the horses had reared up in fright, and Maria Callas had sung so magnificently. Well, all that was gone now. There was more traffic here and the Taxi slowed and crawled towards the lights. She looked at her watch. By the time they reached the FAO she was ten minutes late.

The armed security guard in the glass kiosk at the gate refused to let the Taxi through. It seemed security had been stepped up for all UN buildings since the UN offices in Baghdad had been blown up by a suicide bomber and Manuel de Carrera and a dozen or more UN staff killed. Margaret had to alight on the cobblestones outside the gates, then struggle with her stick through the kiosk, and walk up the drive to the glass-fronted entrance. The security man in the foyer recognised her and waved her past the small queue of people at the scanner and through to the desk where she showed her pass and picked up a visitors tag to clip on to the lapel of her coat. She asked the woman at the desk to phone Hilary to tell her she was on her way up and would see her in the restaurant on the sixth floor.

The FAO was very good to retired ex-employees. In addition to a generous pension it allowed them access to the building and the use of its shopping, banking, restaurant and recreational facilities. It meant that Margaret could meet her friends, both retired and still working, for coffee or lunch and talk over old times. Today she was meeting just Hilary and Alison. They were both much younger than Margaret. Hilary still had a year to go to retirement, Alison had been retired two years or more. She had known them both since she came to the FAO from the UN in America, thirty years ago. Hilary was now secretary to a very senior person as Margaret herself had once been. Alison had likewise held a top job as a Conference Organiser and had arranged conferences in practically every country in the developing world. She had also been the FAO's union organiser for the staff and had been a very forceful negotiator. She was good at languages too. She had met and married an Italian General, older than herself, who had managed to evade imprisonment after the war and had got himself a top job at the FAO. His family owned land and property in south Tuscany and were well known in that region. His grandfather was the man who discovered the famous Etruscan tombs at Tarquinia. "Just imagine digging in your garden and finding one of those marvellous tombs. The thrill of being the first person since the sixth century B.C. to see those delightful painted frescos with their varied themes of domestic life, banquets, hunting, wrestling, juggling or ritual games where groups of boys pursue seaside sports. Or perhaps he discovered first the 'tomb of the dancers' with their graceful movements and flying draperies. Imagine the impact of the painted colours when he first held his torch to them: black, yellow, red, white, blue and green preserved by the darkness for two and a half thousand years!" Margaret had seen the plaque commemorating him and his discovery on the front of the museum. The museum housed the famous Etrurian terra-cotta, life-size, winged horses; an important collection of stone sarcophagi with reclining figures and some, as yet, indecipherable inscriptions and a collection of both black and red-figure Etruscan buccero ware with those elegant line-figures depicting scenes of hunting, war and everyday life, and some impressive plaster wall frescos removed from the more vulnerable tombs. Margaret loved to visit Tarquinia.

The General had died the year Alison retired which left Alison free to indulge her passion for the game of golf which she played at every opportunity. She was on various local and national golf committees and was in Rome for a Golf Presentation dinner of some sort so it was a good opportunity for Margaret to meet up with her.

When she reached the shopping area, despite being late, Margaret went in to the bank and drew out some money before taking the lift up to the restaurant. The restaurant was busy. There were people of all nationalities milling around the food counters, many wearing traditional dress. Africans in long, flowing, colourful print robes and fez-style or soft, pill-box hats. Arabs with beautifully laundered white garments, traditional head gear and neatly trimmed, well-groomed beards. Grey-clad Indonesian girls wearing the Muslim hijab and one or two sinister-looking Islamic women with startlingly bright eyes dressed in the jilbab or the jet-black burka.

Alison had secured a table on the terrace and had left Hilary to guard it. She waved as Margaret came into the restaurant. "We thought you had got lost", she said. "I was just coming to look for you. We're on the terrace. It's such a nice day. We thought we'd avoid the crowd". "Oh good: I like it on the terrace", Margaret said. Alison carried her tray out for her.

After exchanging greetings with Hilary, Margaret propped up her stick against the fourth chair and sat down. The stick promptly fell to ground. "Oh leave it ", she said, when Hilary stooped to pick it up. "We got you a glass of red wine and a jug of water", Alison said. "Oh thank you". After bringing each other up to date with their lives Margaret had to give a detailed account of the death of their former colleague and friend, Grace. Whenever they met these days there was always someone they all knew who'd died. "One day it will be me", Margaret thought.

A few weeks previously Grace, who had moved to New York, had stopped off in Rome on the way back from Japan, where she had been to see her daughter. "I'm just here for a couple of days" she had announced when unexpectedly she had phoned. With so little time she had not been able to see everyone but with Margaret being such a close friend, and more or less contemporary in age, she had made a special effort. She had stayed in an hotel rather than with Margaret, as she usually did, and Margaret was a little put out about this, but no matter, she had met up with Margaret and Rachelle for lunch at Trestivi. Afterwards Rachelle had driven Grace to the airport. She had seemed perfectly OK when they had bid her goodbye, despite her eighty-odd years. Indeed Margaret had thought how well she looked and how active compared to herself. It came as quite a shock to her when the following day she heard Grace had been taken ill on the plane and had died. She didn't know the full circumstances but rumour had it that she had died not long after take-off from Rome. Rather than have the plane turn back the cabin crew had moved some of the passengers to other seats saying the lady was ill. They sat a steward with Grace until they had passed the half-way mark to New York and then screened her off.

The story seemed far fetched, even apocryphal, but she did die and she did end up in New York. "Knowing Grace she would have wanted a discount on the fare had she been taken back to Rome", said Hilary. The remark lightened the topic but it was not in good taste and Hilary looked embarrassed with herself at having made it. Shortly afterwards she excused herself, saying she had to get back to the office. Alison too had to leave, if she was not to be late for her presentation meeting. Margaret though, was in no hurry. It was probably the last time she would visit the FAO and now that she was going back to England it was probably the last time she would see Hilary. Alison too, though Alison did have brother who lived England: in Hale, Cheshire, which was quite near Northenden where Margaret had bought a flat. So she might see Alison again. By an almost Hardyesque coincidence Alison's brother was the architect who had designed and built Boat Lane Court, the semi-sheltered accommodation Margaret was moving into. She would of course phone both her friends, frequently. She got up to retrieve her stick but lingered on the terrace. The panorama before her was probably the best view of Rome there was, and the sky was so clear today. She could easily pick out the familiar landmarks: the Coliseum, the great dome of St. Peter's, The Basilica of St. John in Lateran, the first Christian church to be built in Rome, and the world for that matter, and most of the other major churches and Basilicas, all of them clearly identifiable. "Ah well!", she said, as she finally left the terrace and headed for the lift. She asked the desk to call a Taxi for her.

Margaret was exhausted when she finally got back home. She would have loved a cup of tea but there was no milk. On the table was a note from Anandra saying sorry he had not been able to find the prescription. "It must be here somewhere", she said. "I'll look for it when I've had a lie down".

Margaret still felt exhausted the following day. She tried to sort out some drawers but they were full of things she didn't know she had: things that triggered off memories. She made very little progress. The pile of things to take with her had grown enormously whilst the pile of items to throw away was still minisculely small. There were dozens of necklaces, chains and assorted broaches and bangles, things she would never wear, she'd never worn most of them when she'd bought them, and sets of commemorative coins, old wrist watches, and all sorts of gadgets and junk. And all the books, pictures, and ornaments she and André had accumulated over a lifetime. She couldn't take them all. And there were those drawers in the bottom of the wardrobe with thirty-years of unwanted Christmas and birthday presents Lily and other people had sent to André: key-rings, cuff-links, wallets, propelling pencils, diaries, pens in elaborate gift boxes, bottles of deodorant, after-shave, shaving sets for travellers, wash-bags, sponge-bags, and dozens of wrong size gloves, socks, shirts and jumpers - everyone knew André never wore jumpers. She could open a gift shop there was so much stuff. And how was she going to get rid of that enormous wardrobe and the built-in cupboards in the bedroom and what about the shelves. Her head was spinning. "Oh god", she said, "I wish I wasn't going", but she knew she had no choice. It would be easier with the clothes.

Most of her clothes were out of fashion, too big or had been attacked by moths. All André's remaining clothes would have to be disposed of. "Anandra can get rid of them, and I shall give him that coloured blanket: he'll appreciate that". She felt sorry for Anandra. He'd been sending money back to Sri Lanka to support his wife and family for the past three years and had instructed his brother-in-law to buy materials month by month to enable him to build a substantial extension to his house when he returned to Sri Lanka, which he planned to do soon. He had recently received a letter from his wife saying that the building materials had all been stolen. What with that and the Tsunami devastating his country he was very despondent. Margaret had given him two-hundred and fifty Euros to cheer him up but that hardly made up for the stolen bricks.

Mr. Zumstein was due at two o' clock. He rang the street bell promptly and she pressed the buzzer to let him into the building. For some reason she walked away from the door and went down the hallway to the kitchen but she couldn't remember why she had gone there. She hadn't taken her stick with her and when Mr. Zumstein rang the bell to the apartment it took her so long to get back to the door Mr. Zumstein was on his way back down the stairs by the time she opened it. Mr. Zumstein came back up when he heard the door open. "Pleased to see you again Mrs. Gabison. I wanted to call to explain the quotation I sent you".

Margaret was impressed by Mr. Zumstein. He was immaculately turned out. Today she noted he seemed to have on some kind of uniform. Matching trousers and waistcoat in smart grey twill material and a brand new dark blue body warmer with a badge or crest or some sort of colourful personal monogram on the left breast. "You're looking very smart today", Margaret said . "Not really, I'm on my motor scooter, so I've had to dress accordingly. It's much easier for getting about the City. I've put a chain on the machine so I hope it will be safe outside. You don't think I could put it in the hallway downstairs do you?". "I don't see why not", Margaret said. "But will you be able to get it up the step?" "Well, perhaps not", he said.

Mr. Zumstein smelt of after-shave. On his previous visit he was sporting gold cuff-links: on this occasion he had a plain gold earring in his left ear. Margaret found it difficult to stop her eyes wandering to it. "Must be a new fashion", she thought. His complexion was fresh and his hair fair and brushed back without a parting. It looked full and healthy. Despite the earring he was by no means effeminate and certainly not homosexual. She knew he was married and had two small children. He was a cultivated man. He spoke several languages and impeccable English with only the very slightest hint of an accent. He had told her on his previous visit that he was actually Swiss, his father being a German-speaking Swiss national who had married a Scottish woman. He had been brought up bilingual but used Italian in school. His parents had moved to Rome for business reasons some twenty years previously. The family business was now well established and flourishing. They did removals world-wide, shipping furniture and belongings by sea and by road. They could even send items by air he informed her. Mr. Zumstein asked how the sale was progressing and she told him the apartment was as good as sold and that she wanted to get the details of the removal settled quickly. "There's no reason why we can't do that today", said Mr. Zumstein.

Mr. Zumstein had been recommended to Margaret by friends at the FAO who had used his services. They all spoke very highly of the reliability and efficiency of his firm. Mr. Zumstein for his part was keen to keep up the connection with the FAO. It had given him access to other UN agencies and to the wider diplomatic corps. These agencies frequently moved staff abroad and gave generous removal allowances to their staff. They paid promptly and well for the security and reliability his firm guaranteed. "We are currently removing the entire contents of a foreign embassy", he proudly informed Margaret. When Margaret suggested that her modest furniture and possessions might be too small a job for his firm Mr. Zumstein replied, rather pompously: "No job is too large or too small. We have frequent road haulage to England and containers going by sea every two weeks or so. Provided you give me one month's notice I can guarantee a delivery date. When were you thinking of moving?" Margaret told him completion of the sale would almost certainly be 21st January. "In that case we would need to collect the items on 21st December if sending them by sea, to avoid the Christmas period, or early January if we were taking them by road. I could probably reduce the price if we take them by sea. The quotation I have given you is for road transport". Margaret was getting confused. How could he give her a quotation when he didn't yet know what she wanted to take with her, when indeed, she didn't herself know what she wanted to take. "Don't worry about that", Mr. Zumstein said, "It won't make much difference how much you take". "Why won't it make much difference? It must make a difference", she said somewhat heatedly. "No it won't make any difference". But Margaret insisted it would.

Try as he might Mr. Zumstein could not get her to grasp that the sea container had a finite capacity and it was up to him to fill it. Her possessions would only take up a small amount of space in the container which was often only three-quarters full anyway so it wouldn't make much difference, a few items more or less. If he used the land route he could vary the size of the van. The fuel costs were only very marginally different for small or large vans. The major costs were the drivers' wages and accommodation and they were the same irrespective of the size of the van. This was all too much for her. "It must make a difference if I take more", she kept insisting. Mr. Zumstein gave up. "Why don't we make a list of what you want to take and I will send you a revised quotation showing what it will cost by sea and what it will cost by road. At this stage I would like to keep both options open", he said. "Why can't you decide now. I need to know now. If my furniture goes how am I going to live?", she shouted. Mr. Zumstein was somewhat startled by her anger but he remained calm. "You said last time I was here that you were only taking one of the beds and one bed-settee and that you were not taking many of the chairs, or the television and that you would have enough things you were not taking to enable you to live here for weeks if necessary". "That's true", she said, suddenly deflating, "I did say that." Mr. Zumstein took a pad from his briefcase. "Why don't we make the inventory. If you are in doubt about any items take them with you and get rid of them when you get to England".

"But I don't want to take them with me. It will cost me money!", she screamed. "But I've explained. It won't cost you any more to take them or leave them", Mr. Zumstein said, with incredible calm.

Making the inventory was the worst experience of Mr. Zumstein's professional career. He had never before come across such a difficult, volatile, indecisive client. He was used to people getting emotional about leaving their homes and familiar possessions; that was understandable, but this lady was so irrational and obsessed with irrelevant, trivial cost considerations she made his head spin. Her friends from England had spent days with her putting red stickers on the items of furniture she was going to take and green stickers on the ones for disposal. The inventory should have been a simple matter but she couldn't seem to understand the system now that her friends were no longer in Rome. "That one should have had a red sticker. This one should have a green one. Why has this one got a white sticker. I can't take that it will cost too much. Why hasn't this got a sticker on it? I want that chair. No I don't want that one I want this other one. I'm sure I was going to take that other bed-settee". At one point Mr. Zumstein was convinced she was totally red-green colour blind. And she was frantic with worry about the difficulty of getting rid of the things she didn't wish to take. "What if nobody wants them and I can't get rid of them? The place has to be clear on the day of the sale. The sale will be called off. How am I going to pack everything up? It will take me weeks". Mr. Zumstein could not seem to get through to her that he would arrange for his men to come round two days before the main removal date to wrap and pack all items she was taking to ensure that nothing got damaged or broken in transit. He explained time and again: "I will send a van and some men round on the 20th January to clear any items you are not taking. They will either take them to a rubbish tip if they are worthless or put them into a store for eventual disposal to second-hand dealers if there is any value in them. There will be a small charge to defray the labour costs but it will not be much and I will get my men to leave the place clean", he emphasised.

"I don't want to leave the place dirty. It must be clean: I have my pride!" Margaret shouted. "It will be clean, I promise you", said Mr. Zumstein. She was still fretting about it when he left.

Shortly after Mr. Zumstein had gone Margaret telephoned Anandra to get the details of a fellow countryman he knew who did removals to Sri Lanka. "I must get another quotation", she told him.

Wendy, her god-daughter, spoke to Margaret on the phone that evening to get an update on the sale and removal. She was dismayed as Margaret recounted the turn of events. What on earth was Margaret doing rowing with Christina and agreeing to drop the price by such a colossal amount. It made her feel weak in the stomach. And how could anyone find Mr. Zumstein, whom she had met and found charming, difficult to deal with. She was furious with Margaret. But she had to 'bite her tongue' over the price of the flat. It had gone too far and Margaret had not listened to reason. So be it. Perversely Margaret would accept the most inimical advice from comparative strangers, or self interested people such as the Administrator, but she wouldn't listen to the most obviously sound advice or caution from her friends. "You really must accept Mr. Zumstein's quotation. It's not dear and you don't know what Anandra's friend is like. Even if he can do the removal cheaper I wouldn't trust him. Anything could go wrong. He's only used to sending small items to Sri Lanka", Wendy counselled. "Well, we shall see", said Margaret with a somewhat crestfallen note in her voice. She thought she was being very prudent getting another quotation. "Money doesn't grow on trees you know". Wendy was flabbergasted.

Mr. Zumstein's quotation arrived in Margaret's pigeon hole two days after his visit. She replied promptly by letter accepting it. The decision had been taken out of her hands. Anandra's friend didn't think he could manage a removal to England. He had never done one and he was doubtful his van could contain all she might or might not take.

Thursday came round slowly for Margaret but when it did she felt most apprehensive. She wanted everything settled but she felt out of her depth with the complexity of it all. "If only André were here", she thought. But then recollected that André had not been the most practical of men. He'd been all right with intellectual matters and very good at languages. But practical things? No, she had to admit he'd not been very good at practical things.

Signor Rubeo and his son were due to arrive at six-thirty, half an hour prior to the meeting with Dr. Santovelli and his wife, but they came ten minutes early. It was just as well because Margaret was beginning to get butterflies in her stomach bordering on panic. She had placed a whisky bottle and glasses on the table to offer them a drink. She knew Signor Rubeo liked whisky. She jumped when the knock on the door finally came, jogging the table and making the glasses clink. After exchanging greetings Signor Rubeo said: "I don't think you have met my son, Angelo, have you Mrs. Gabison?". "Of course I have. You used to bring him with you when you called on André but it must be at least ten years since I last saw him. You remember me don't you Angelo?". "Not really Signora, but I've heard a lot about you from my father". After one or two reminiscent exchanges Signor Rubeo and Angelo both accepted her offer of whisky with enthusiasm. Margaret poured herself a small amount which hardly covered the bottom of the glass and added a good measure of water. "To a successful transaction", Angelo said raising his glass. "To a successful transaction", said Signor Rubeo.

Signor Rubeo's son explained the details of the document of sale to Margaret: the timing of the exchange of deeds; the contract and the guaranteed bank bond that would be made out in her maiden name. "Why does it have to be in my maiden name?", she asked. "It's to do with women's rights to own property. The transaction has to be in your maiden name as required by Italian law", Signor Rubeo's son 'explained'. "It's ridiculous", Margaret said. "I've almost forgotten what my maiden name is!" When at last they went upstairs to Dr. Santovelli's apartment to meet his ex-wife and her lawyer she was very little the wiser.

Margaret thought everything to do with the sale of the apartment was more or less settled. She was quite shocked when Signor Rubeo's son and Signora Santovelli's lawyer started again discussing the price and the 'extension' but she sat in silence, listening, and let them get on with it. It seemed that despite her previous compliant stance Signora Santovelli was not happy about the 'extension' and was attempting to reinsert the obsolete clause giving her rights to reclaim the cost of repairs if anything was found wrong with the apartment for a period of seven years after the date of sale. Margaret remembered the warning Christina had given, prior to the row with her, about agreeing to such a clause. "I can't agree to that", she suddenly interjected. "Well in that case I'm not sure I want to continue", said Signora Santovelli. "Can you excuse us a moment", Signor Rubeo's son said. "I need to discuss the matter in private with Mrs. Gabison". Sensibly for once Margaret resisted the thinly veiled pressure and insisted that the clause be not included. But as a concession, and with Signor Rubeo's encouragement, she agreed to drop the price still further to 380,000 Euros. When they finally left Dr. Santovelli's apartment the deal had been done. Margaret felt bewildered. She still had considerable misgivings but she thanked Signor Rubeo and his son, nonetheless, for their help. As they were about to leave she took Signor Rubeo on one side and pressed 2,000 Euros into his hand. "I can't let your son do all that work for nothing", she said, choosing not to think about the 'back-hander' he had undoubtedly received from Dr. Santovelli for getting the apartment at such a pleasingly low price.

"I just wanted to get it over and done with", she told a dumbfounded Pamela next day.

The following morning Margaret phoned Mr. Zumstein and told him she accepted his 'overland' quotation and the arrangements for the removal. Next she phoned the FAO and asked the booking assistant to try to get her a cheap flight to Manchester on 23rd January. Unfortunately there were no cheap flights available on that date. "The single fare is 758 Euros - you would be better getting a return - the cheapest is 332 Euros". Yet another mystery Margaret was unable to begin to fathom but she felt too defeated to tax her mind any further.

The period between agreeing the sale and her departure from Italy was the most miserable of Margaret's life. She was feeling increasingly depressed and disconsolate. She longed to go out for a walk in the City again. "If only I could go out, just once more", she kept saying to herself, but she knew she just couldn't do it. She had dizzy spells almost every time she stood up now and she was fearful of another fall. The prospect of cold, rainy Manchester with its leaden skies and chill winds did nothing to lighten her spirits. And there was a limit to how much time she could demand of her friends on the phone. Embarrassingly she sometimes forgot who she had rung and rang them again an hour later. She had even phoned Lily in America twice in twenty minutes. "It's no fun being old", she said to herself, ever more frequently.

She gladly accepted Rachelle's offer to spend Christmas with her but returning to the bleak apartment afterwards was not a pleasant experience. As she left Rachelle suggested she stay with her on the nights of 21st January and the 22nd January: she would drive her to the airport on the 23rd. Margaret accepted Rachelle's offer enthusiastically though she was embarrassed to tell Signor Rubeo and his wife that she would not be taking up their offer of accommodation and transport. She knew Signor Rubeo fairly well but she didn't know Signora Rubeo at all, and anyway, she much preferred to stay with Rachelle.

As arranged Mr. Zumstein's men arrived early in January and packed up her belongings and furniture, "Ninety-five boxes, can you believe", she 'phoned round telling everyone. They had to be transported in a truck in small numbers to Mr. Zumstein's warehouse as Quattro Cantoni was too narrow for a full-sized removal van. After her things had gone her surroundings were bleak and austere. The apartment seemed strangely hollow and echoed eerily. It was no longer her home. Despite the exceptionally mild weather she hardly dare venture out. She sat musing on her past life in Rome, the people she had met and worked with, or reflecting on how many had moved away or died, or spent her time reading or watching the television. All her videos had gone in the boxes.

Anandra arranged for various people to come to the apartment and take away anything they wanted. The nuns came from the Convent and took clothes in black plastic bags for distribution to the poor and needy but no one wanted her wardrobes, they were much too big. When she looked for the coloured blanket to give to Anandra she couldn't find it. "Oh damn", she said. "It must have gone in one of the boxes".

There was nothing much for her to do on the day of the final transactions which concluded the sale of the apartment. Mr. Zumstein's men came bright and early, packed things up and carted them away. Then set to cleaning the place. Margaret was picked up by Signor Rubeo, the Administrator, as arranged, and whisked off to a government office where the exchange of deeds and bond and cheques took place and the keys to the apartment were handed over. Signor Rubeo then drove her to Rachelle's house. Two days later she was on the plane, winging her way to Manchester.

Being on an aeroplane brought Grace to mind. For much of the flight she had read a book to avoid thinking about her friend's recent death but when she stopped reading her thoughts turned back to it. Grace had been so much looking forward to getting back to New York and her family. But she had at least seen her daughter and to die suddenly like that on a plane was far preferable she supposed to a drawn-out painful illness. Not like André. He never got to see his daughter. Lily had become diabetic and was having problems with her general health. Her eyesight too was failing. They had been planning to visit her in the States but André had collapsed and been admitted to a hospital emergency ward with a recurrent heart problem and put on life-support. He recovered enough to be moved to a general ward but complications set in: he too had diabetes, kidney and eye problems, and sadly he died. How much better for André if he too had collapsed and died on a return flight after seeing his daughter, she mused. He would not be happy to see Lily now though, the state she was in.

Margaret had visited Lily almost every year since André died. She stopped going two years ago when the journey became too much for her. Margaret felt sorry for Lily. Her mother, like André, was Jewish, though in André's case being Jewish hadn't meant very much. The mother took Lily to Israel as a child to live on a kibbutz but got fed up with it, went to America, and left Lily there. From all accounts the kibbutz was not a happy experience and left its mark on Lily. By a sad irony Lily trained as a dietician. When finally she escaped from the kibbutz and followed her mother to America, like many young American men and women with problems, she comfort ate and became seriously over weight. She was a small person, barely five feet tall, which accentuated her bulk and did nothing for her appearance. She developed diabetes and subsequently glaucoma and retinal problems. She never married. As the years went by her problems got worse and by the time she reached fifty she weighed fourteen stone, was a registered blind person and unable to drive a car. These problems in turn curtailed her employment opportunities. Now, approaching sixty, she was fifteen stone, diabetic, blind and unemployed and living on meagre social security. Margaret frequently sent her money, which helped, but could not, of course, cure her problems.

Despite these morbid thoughts, or perhaps because of them, she finally let her head sink onto her chest, slumped slightly sideways and dropped off to sleep dreaming of Mr. Zumstein, his van and her furniture.

Mr. Zumstein's van was due in Northenden on Monday 24th January but the drivers had made good speed through Italy and France. They had made quick deliveries in Milan and Paris en route to England and arrived at Calais sooner than originally planned. Much to the annoyance of the two drivers there was quite a delay at Calais. The van was stopped at the entrance to the docks, their papers checked and the van searched by the police for illegal immigrants. Despite the closure of the detention camp at Sandgate illegal immigrants were still a problem: attempting to bribe drivers or concealing themselves in or under vehicles. They were stopped inside the dockyard area too by Customs and a couple of sample boxes chosen at random, opened and searched for illegal drugs, tobacco and alcohol. Margaret's underwear and nighties did not count as contraband so they were allowed to proceed. They just managed to catch the overnight ferry and still saw a chance of saving a day on the trip and earning a bonus from Zumstein and Sons. Instead of a leisurely drive, with breaks, through England and a night in a motel, they had made an early start, sped up the M1 and M6 and arrived in Northenden at about eight a.m. on Sunday morning. They had phoned Wendy on the contact number to let her know of their early arrival. Fortunately for them she was free to go to Boat Lane Court to meet them. Later, Margaret had 'phoned from Rome airport to confirm that she would be arriving in Manchester at three o'clock, terminal two.

Zumstein's van was a big, white, container-carrying pantechnicon with Zumstein s.p.l., Translochi Internationali, Roma, Italia, emblazoned across the front and sides in large red lettering, with bands of green running above and below. There was no mistaking where it had come from. Had it arrived later in the day it would have caused quite a stir at Boat Lane Court. Life for many of the residents was routinised and dull. The arrival of a new tenant was quite an event and one from abroad especially so: "Is she English? She doesn't look English. How old do you think she is? I wonder if she has a husband. Is that her son who takes her out? Who's that woman that comes round?" Speculation and gossip would be rife for weeks. They would be frustrated with the 95 boxes. Nothing would have interested them more than to peep from behind their curtains at Margaret's furniture and belongings and to speculate on its quality and value.

The driver had difficulty manoeuvring the van into the car park at Boat Lane Court. Wendy attempted to guide them in with hand signals but it was too dangerous so she left them to manage on their own. Naturally the driver wanted to park the van with the back close to the doorway giving access to Margaret's flat but this was impossible to do without blocking-in a number of parked cars. "It will be all right to block them in. Nobody gets up this early", the duty Warden shouted.

The driver had just completed the final manoeuvre when they heard a loud, reverberating banging on the side of the van. "I didn't hit anything did I?" the driver said to his mate. A voice shouted: "You can't park that bloody thing there. I'll be wanting to get my car out later". The voice belonged to a small, portly man in his seventies with a round, red face and a shock of pure white hair. He was pushing a wheelchair occupied by a sagging woman of similar age who, by her mouthing and gestures, had clearly had a stroke. "Bloody foreigners: I wouldn't mind betting they've a couple of dozen illegal 'wops' in there. The whole bloody country's overrun by bloody immigrants. Going to the bloody dogs it is!" The Warden looked embarrassed. "It's all right Jeff. It won't be there long and they'll move it if you want to get out". Fortunately the Italians spoke very little English though they could sense the hostility. "Take no notice. Old man", said Wendy, with emphasis, in her best Italian. Jeff glowered. He couldn't understand Italian but suspected it was something derogatory about himself. When he was out of earshot the Warden said to Wendy: "He's never happy unless he's got something to grouse about. He's always going on about immigrants. I wouldn't mind but I don't think he's ever seen one in the flesh".

When the men finally opened the van Margaret's 95 boxes looked quite lost in a corner even though some of them were fairly large. They quickly set about the task of unloading, handing the smaller boxes to each other off the back of the van as though they were empty and manhandling the heavier ones onto the trolley with little show of exertion: they were clearly strong and used to the job.

The lift at Boat Lane Court was quite spacious but some of Margaret's furniture was big and cumbersome and had to be carefully manoeuvred up the stairs to the second-floor flat. It was heavy work but you never would have guessed. Even the iron-framed bed-settee gave them no trouble. They had the skilled man's knack of making difficult work look easy. They unpacked the larger items of furniture and placed them in pre-arranged positions in accordance with the plan Margaret had made on a previous visit. The bulk of the smaller boxes were stacked in the second bedroom or in the corridor of the flat, to be dealt with later.

The two men finished unloading and unpacking by one o'clock and were anxious to be on their way South. They had a 'pick-up' in Antwerp and another in Brussels before heading back to Rome and were anxious to cross the channel that evening. They had been told by Mr. Zumstein to collect the balance of the bill for the removal on completion of the job. They were dismayed to be told no cheque was available. "Mrs. Gabison didn't send one because she expected to be here to pay you on Monday as arranged", Wendy explained. "You will have to wait until she arrives, which will be four-thirty at the earliest, I should think". The men were very unhappy. Wendy offered to give them a cheque in Sterling but they said they would have to speak to Mr. Zumstein to authorise this.

Several attempts were made to contact Mr. Zumstein but he was not answering his mobile. They sent text messages but got no reply. After almost an hour of trying they finally made contact with Mr. Zumstein's brother. He rejected the offer of a Sterling cheque and told the men to await the arrival of Mrs.Gabison and obtain a Euro cheque. Wendy consoled the men with sandwiches and a few cans of beer and sat them in front of the television on the bed-settee they had just delivered. Fortunately there was a football match on - from the Italian premier league as luck would have it.

The plane from Rome was on time. But Margaret was late. Having ordered a wheelchair she was last off. She then had to wait for the man assigned to collect her luggage to meet up with the man assigned to push her wheelchair. "Can't you get someone to hurry him up. My friends will think I missed the plane", she said impatiently to the man with the wheelchair. "Don't worry love: he'll be here in a minute". "It's all very well saying don't worry. What will I do if they've gone!"

When the stream of passengers and luggage-trolleys coming through Customs had dried up and the groups of relatives and friends meeting them had ceased laughing, hugging and kissing and throwing their grandchildren in the air, the waiting area became silent, bleak and deserted. Ten minutes elapsed and the Captain and cabin-crew emerged with their tiny black cases trailing behind them like tails. Bob and Wendy, the friends meeting her, exchanged meaningful glances and began to have doubts as to whether or not she had in fact caught the plane.

There was great relief when at last the wheelchair, with Margaret in it, emerged, pursued by a man with a trolley supporting two very large suit cases. Margaret looked hunched, drawn and only a quarter alive. She was looking straight ahead with a bleak, far-away expression on her face: the journey had clearly taken it out of her. But her face changed and her looks cheered when she saw familiar figures.

Despite discouragement the two helpers refused Bob and Wendy's offer to take over the trolleys. They insisted on accompanying Margaret to the car park, unloading the luggage, stowing it in the boot of the car and manoeuvring her into the front passenger seat, for which they received, as they clearly expected, a ridiculously large tip.

"Not too bad", Margaret replied, to Wendy and Bob's enquiries about the flight. "But the meal was te—rrible", she said, drawing out the 'e' and accentuating the 'r's' in her characteristic way, "And do you know, they added fifteen Euros to the fare for the meal. The last time I flew the meal was free. All they gave us was a sandwich and a drink and it was a pretty awful sandwich: a hard, dense, tasteless roll with some cheese and ham in it that gave me indigestion". I need my Alka Zeltzer: I wonder where it is!

The road to Northenden was clear but it was nonetheless after four-thirty when they reached Boat Lane Court. The two Italian removal-men were greatly relieved by Margaret's appearance on the scene but their expressions turned to frowns and irritation as Margaret rummaged about in her handbag for her cheque-book. She kept repeatedly zipping and unzipping the numerous pouches inside and outside the bag. "Not there", she said calmly. The second, bigger bag, inside the plastic bag she had been carrying likewise failed to produce the cheque-book by which time she was starting to panic. "But I had it in my hand", she insisted. "I was looking at it in the car when Rachelle drove me to the airport. It must be here!", she shouted.

First Wendy and then Bob searched the two bags but without success. Neither was it amongst the bundle of documents together with the three cheques, drawn on three different banks, which comprised the 380,000 Euros for the price of the apartment. She could not find her NatWest cheque-book either. "Oh Margaret, you are a nuisance. Just sit down and think", Wendy said. Bob was getting anxious too, and looking at his watch. "I'm afraid I'm going to have to go soon. I said I would be at Lynda's at seven o'clock and I haven't packed yet". Bob was going to Gran Canaria the following day. He had asked Lynda to alter her original holiday date so as to be available to help Margaret unpack and settle in only to find that Margaret had given him the wrong date. It was by luck rather than good fortune that his holiday booking was the day it was and he had at least been available to meet Margaret and drive her from the airport.

After more searching and a fraught debate Wendy phoned Rachelle in Rome. Rachelle searched her car but neither of the cheque-books was there. "Rachelle says they are not in the car so just sit down and think. Did you take them out on the plane?". Margaret sat down and the two Italians stood up. "Signora, we have to go. We will miss the boat". "It's not my fault!" she shouted at them. "I didn't ask you to come today!". "Now calm down Margaret and just think. When did you last have your cheque-book". Bob said. Margaret quietened down. After a minute or so she said: "I left my Euro cheque-book with Signor Rubeo. There was only one cheque left in it and I signed it and left it blank so that he could pay the telephone and the electricity bills and after paying them add two hundred Euros for all the trouble he has gone to with the sale of the apartment and fill in the total amount. Wendy and Bob looked at each other, appalled that the Administrator should be holding a signed blank cheque of Margaret's after all that had happened. The drivers were getting increasingly agitated.

Wendy phoned Signor Rubeo. Margaret took the phone from her and spoke to him. The conversation was in rapid Italian and neither Bob nor Wendy could understand what was being said. Margaret seemed to be going through the full range of human emotions, switching from violent anger, disbelief, silence, mirth, laughter, agitation, calm. It went on and on and on. The two Italians who could understand at least Margaret's half of the exchange gave each other frantic looks as they mirrored her mood changes and repeatedly tapped their watches. When the call finally ended Margaret quite calmly said that Signor Rubeo had her Euro cheque-book and the NatWest one as well. She must have given him both by mistake. "He's going to put the NatWest one in the post to me. And he's going to try to contact Mr. Zumstein and phone me back", she announced. "When?" asked Bob. "He didn't say", Margaret replied. Everyone was getting very annoyed and irritated with her. The two Italians were beside themselves. They were frantically punching away at their mobile phones like a couple of Pitman's gold medal typists. Margaret was quite relaxed now that her cheque-books had been located.

"Ringing", shouted one of the Italians. He had finally got through to Mr. Zumstein senior. When told that Margaret had arrived minus Euros and Euro cheque-book and the that only options were to accept payment in Sterling or for the men to wait in Northenden until the banks opened on Monday, Mr. Zumstein said he would contact his son and phone back.

Margaret's phone rang again and the two Italians leapt to their feet. It was Signor Rubeo to say that Mr. Zumstein's wife didn't know where he was or when he would be home. The two Italians threw their hands in the air in despair and jabbered animatedly to each other, then sank back dejectedly onto the settee. When Bob asked Margaret for a translation she wouldn't give one. Wendy whispered: "they think he's with his girlfriend". It was another fifteen minutes before Mr. Zumstein senior phoned one of the Italians on the 'mobile' to say they could accept a cheque from Wendy in £'s Sterling for the equivalent of 2,400 Euros. The two Italians hugged and kissed and ruffled each other's hair. One of them even ruffled Wendy's hair and would have given the same treatment to Bob's if he'd had a bit more. "You would have thought Italy had just won the World Cup", Margaret said.

The two Italians were given an excessively generous tip by Margaret in £20 notes which was the lowest denomination she had. "To compensate you for doing such a good job and being so patient", she said. They thanked her effusively, *"Grazie, Grazie Tanto Signora"*, and left saying they might just catch the overnight boat to Calais if they drove non-stop to Dover.

The stress and panic was not a good start for Margaret's arrival in England. Wendy was glad she had agreed to have her stay with her at Spath Road for a few days rather than move into Boat Lane Court immediately. Bob was relieved to be heading for Gran Canaria.

Margaret was anxious not to lose or misplace the cheques handed over to her by Signora Santovelli. They were protected by the Bond but she would not feel happy until they were in her account: and besides, they were losing interest. Wendy had agreed to take her to the Northenden branch of NatWest first thing Monday morning to transfer her account and deposit the cheques.

Margaret's bank in England had always been the NatWest branch in Tavistock Square, London, and she had kept the account open out of loyalty and for sentimental reasons throughout her years in Italy. As a matter of fact her first job on leaving school had been as a clerk in that very branch of NatWest. The war had come along and she had been conscripted into the War Office as a Secretary which in turn had taken her to Italy, seconded to the Ministry of Transport with responsibility to the Merchant Navy. Just after the war she had met and married André and had lived first in America for a few years and then Italy ever since. She had changed the name of her NatWest account to Gabison on marriage. "Now here I am living back in England and the first thing I do is go to the NatWest bank", she mused.

On Monday morning Wendy drove Margaret to the bank and accompanied her inside. There was a small queue which they joined at the counter. "Why does there always have to be a queue when I go to a bank. It was the same in Italy". "Oh it's the same everywhere. They've cut down on counter staff to save money", Wendy said. "Well they damn well ought not to. I can't stand for long. I'll have to sit down !" No sooner had she sat down than it was her turn to be served.

When she presented Signora Santovelli's cheques to pay in the clerk immediately noticed that they were made out to her in the name of Margaret Mitchell, her maiden name. The manager confirmed that to be paid in the cheques would have to be made out in her married name, the name on her account. "I have a marriage certificate and a

Passport, why can't you accept them as proof of identity", Margaret said getting somewhat agitated. The queue behind her was lengthening and getting restless. "I'm afraid that is not acceptable. The easiest way out is to obtain new cheques made out in your married name and get the others stopped", the bank manager told her. "But I can't do that. The law in Italy says property transactions by women have to be done in their maiden name". "Well, I'm sorry Mrs. Gabison I'd like to accept them but I'm just not able to do so. I'm sure you will be able to have the cheques made out in your married name. Why don't you contact the person in Italy who issued them and ask her to discuss it with her bank". Margaret did not want to do this. The matter of the sale was over and done with as far as she was concerned. "I want to speak to the manager of my bank in London", she said in a very imperious tone. "Certainly you can, but I think you will find that his advice will be the same as mine", the manager said, agreeably.

When the clerk looked on the computer for the phone number there was no Tavistock Square branch, it had been incorporated into another branch as a cost cutting measure. After considerable delay the account was located at a nearby branch and the manager summoned to the phone. As predicted she received the same advice as she had just been given in Northenden. She was very put out by the matter and became increasingly agitated. Wendy tried to reassure her. "It's only a little interest you'll lose. It's not the end of the world Margaret!".

As soon as they returned to Wendy's flat Margaret phoned Signor Rubeo and asked him to contact Signora Santovelli as a matter of urgency and ask her to make out new cheques. He phoned later in the day to say that Signora. Santovelli would only make out new cheques on condition the old cheques were first sent back to her. Margaret wrote 'cancelled' across the three cheques and put them in an envelope addressed to Signora Santovelli. She toyed with the idea of registering the letter but rejected it. She knew the Italian postal system. Getting the signatures of recipients who might be out could delay matters up to a week or more.

Margaret phoned Signor Rubeo daily and he contacted Signora Santovelli but the envelope with the cancelled cheques in it never arrived. "Are you sure you put the correct address on?", Wendy asked. Margaret could not remember. "Perhaps I didn't put Italy on it. I think I might have put England. I'm not used to sending letters addressed to Italy, or maybe it's been received and Signora Santovelli is not letting on". Wendy very much regretted not checking the address and reproached herself for not advising the letter be registered. Matters were at an impasse. Signora Santovelli was adamant she would not issue new cheques until she had received the cancelled old ones but the old ones refused to turn up.

Margaret became increasingly concerned that she was not going to get any money for the sale of her apartment. It was bad enough having sold it for well under the market price but to be left with nothing was almost too much to bear. "I should have registered them", she said ruefully.

Days went by and there seemed to be no solution. Eventually Signor Rubeo consulted his son and at last a solution was suggested. Margaret would have to return to Rome, visit the police and report the cheques lost. After a period of time, possibly three months, or even as long as a year, the loss would be regarded as confirmed and new cheques could be issued. Margaret thought this a most unreasonable idea: "I can't go back to Rome. I don't feel up to going back to Rome". A three-month wait for her money was unacceptable also: a twelve-month wait outrageously so. Signor Rubeo's son offered another solution. Margaret should report the disappearance of the cheques to the British police, obtain a certificate of loss and send it to him. He would consult with Signora Santovelli's solicitor and, hopefully, Signora Santovelli would agree to issue new cheques. Surprisingly this 'solution' worked. There was no problem in getting the kindly constable in south Manchester to put the 'loss' in the station's Lost Property Book and give her something that could be called a 'certificate'. "You are too kind ", said Margaret. "It's been a pleasure serving you", said the gentle P.C. "He must have been on the 'Customer Course'", thought Margaret.

The manageress of Boat Lane Court willingly faxed a copy of the certificate of loss to Signor Rubeo's son. Signora Santovelli at last agreed to make out new cheques and to send them direct to Margaret's bank. On 15th March, 2005, Margaret received a letter from the NatWest Bank confirming that the sum of 380,000 Euros had been paid into her account. It had taken almost two months to get her money. She had lost the interest but "Oh the relief!" "Yes", said Wendy.

Margaret manoeuvred her walking frame out of her flat and into the spacious, warm, carpeted, second-floor landing of Boat Lane Court and pulled the door to behind her. "Damn it. I've forgotten my umbrella, again". She would have to go back. Life in England was just as full of false starts and problems as in Italy, but here, much to her relief, and despite the weather, they were easier to cope with. The key fitted easily into the lock. There were no difficult stairs to negotiate. The lift came promptly, and there was a seat inside, and she was whisked quickly to the ground floor. Her wheeled walking frame enabled her to feel safe on her own in the street and she could walk at twice the speed she used to walk. There was a basket for her handbag and a flap over it which she could use as a seat if she got tired or had to wait for a taxi. There were plenty of shops nearby and one or two cafés: the staff at 'Boat Lane Court' were pleasant, attentive and not intrusive. There was someone constantly on call. The cooked, lunch-time meals were varied, of good quality and reasonably priced. She had a cleaner in twice a week. There were alarm cords, telephones and panic buttons. She had registered with a nearby G.P. and had seen Professor Raymond Tallis, a leading Neurologist working at Hope hospital, quickly and free on the National Health. After thorough tests he said yes, she had some brain deterioration but it was a result of ageing and there was nothing anyone could do about that. He had advised her to stop taking the pills and injections the Italian Medical Mafia, as he called them, had prescribed for her. They were not doing her any harm but they were not doing her much good either and they were ridiculously expensive. She had to admit she felt no worse for stopping the Italian medication. She still had dizziness when she stood up but she felt less worried about it since seeing the famous Professor Tallis. Physiotherapy might help her mobility he advised: "that can be arranged".

She could keep in touch by phone with people in Italy. She had friends to take her out occasionally, to parks and stately homes. She still had her independence. England was not Italy and Northenden was certainly not Rome - sadly she could no longer live in Rome – wherever she lived, Rome would forever live in her. She was optimistic. Eighty-seven she might be but life in general was still very much worth living.

About the Author

Boris (Bob) Wild was born in Prestwich, Manchester and grew up on a Council Estate. Aged 16 years he took up an apprenticeship in the Printing industry. His national Service was spent in the Royal Army Medical Corps. He secured a lectureship in Printing at Manchester College of Science and Technology and later an MSc.(Tech.) at UMIST, an M.A. (Econ) and a PhD. in Sociology at Manchester University. He taught Printing at Manchester Polytechnic, (later MMU) and Social Science for the Open University.